# RAT & DEMON

SHATTERED GODS
BOOK 6

CHRIS FOX

CHRIS FOX WRITES LLC

# PREVIOUSLY ON SHATTERED GODS

We are six books into this series. Over a million words. Since *Rat & Demon* is the shortest book, I decided to include all of the Previously On chapters this time around.

Trust that book 7, *The Price of Godhood*, will be closer to the length of the others. This book, however, needed to be the length that it is to tell the story as it needs to be told.

You'll see why by the time you get to the end. Hopefully it's worth it! In case you feel it isn't, I dropped the price of the book below the others to reflect that it's less of a fantasy doorstopper. It's still one of my longer books, but *Fomori Invasion* sort of raised the bar.

If you want to know more about the *Shattered Gods* setting, there's a whole bunch of lore, artwork, and other goodies at magitechchronicles.com (including a mailing list where you can beta read the next book).

If you want to start *Rat & Demon,* feel free to skip the next five chapters. For everyone else, let's get to it!

**In an announcer's voice:** *Last time on* **Shattered Gods...**

Our story begins with Princess Li in a prologue, because if Sanderson and Jordan can have prologues, then so can I!

Li is an *air* mage from totally-not-China flying on an airship toward the capital city of Hasra where she's about to begin the next term at their royal academy.

We can't have a scene with just one person, so Li is talking to her attendant Bumut, a shaggy troll who likes knitting because he can use his own fur to do it and also likes murdering things that threaten Li.

Li notes that there is a small mountain range below them, even though she doesn't remember it from the last time they flew this way. And it isn't on any maps. That's odd. I'm sure that won't be important later.

A trio of drake riders assaults the ship, basically small flying dragons with the intelligence of a dog. Li and Bumut fight them off, but one of them makes it below decks and damages the airship's reactor.

They crash upon the mysterious mountain range, but survive and find shelter in a strange pair of caves that are totally not the nostrils of a behemoth.

The mountain range, a spider-mountain, wakes up, and Li finds herself trapped atop it with Bumut. She can fly, but Bumut cannot. The chapter ends with Li fleeing toward a city called Hasra to warn the Imperator, while Bumut tries to escape on foot. Spoilers, he makes it. You see him again in this book.

We flip to our main character, aka the author stand-in, aka 17-year-old Chris. Xal, an angry teen, is emptying a bucket of piss into an abyss, so basically the equivalent of the day job most of us work. Xal lives in the dims with his mother and sisters, a walled prison on a rock island surrounded by a moat that seems to have no bottom.

Xal's people have the blood of demons and served the Hasran Imperium before the Imperator turned on them and slaughtered their people. They were incredibly powerful battle mages called eradicators and won wars for centuries.

Were. The survivors are given just enough food to survive, and every decade or so, they are conscripted into the trash legion and hurled against the Hasran's enemies, the Fomori.

In order to survive, Xal and his "friends" Nef and Tissa delve down into the warrens, the corridors and tunnels that snake down through the rock below their hovels.

Nef is clearly a bully and in charge, while Tissa only looks out for herself. If you've played *The Magitech Chronicles RPG*, Tissa is a Stalker, and Nef is a Larcenist, while Xal is an Eradicator with no *fire* magic.

Our trio heads up into one of five spires that just so happen to resemble the grasping hand of a titanic god and are in no way attached to an arm that extends deep down into the earth where it has leaked a lake of blood and grown an army of demons.

Xal has found a journal that allows them to bypass the wards and enter the quarters of a famous eradicator named Ark Elias, Xal's grandfather and a hero from the last war.

Inside, we find a bunch of loot that doesn't matter and an eradicator uniform, which matters a LOT. Almost as much as the tiny shard of voidglass he finds on the floor, Xal's first tiny knife.

There's also a magic mirror, which Xal uses to establish a portal into a dark cavern near a demon-infested lake. What's the worst that could happen?

They open the mirror, sneak through, and find a lake of

demon blood...pure *void* magic. Tissa vanishes, but Nef and Xal both drink, gaining magic, or more magic in Xal's case.

Nef partially mutates into a demon and gains a mouthful of fangs. This pisses him off, so Nef stabs Xal in the back and slits his throat, then leaves him for dead.

Xal is discovered by a big, scary demon, who we learn is not at all scary. His name is Kazon, and he is polite and friendly. He explains that Xal will heal because he just drank divinity. He gives Xal some demon bread and lets him gather a bunch of salt from the shore, then sends Xal on his way with what urchins in the dims consider a small fortune.

Xal chases down Nef just as he's turning in the day's loot to the Hasran garrison, who buys all books and magic items that urchins find. Because Nef is a demon, they seize his loot and rough him up.

Despite Nef's betrayal, Xal feels guilty and gives Nef some bread and salt, then gives an old woman named Panya the rest. He promises that he'll tell Panya a story, and pay attention to that because it's subtle, but important. Panya is no mere rando NPC. >=)

Xal heads home and tells his mother what happened, and we get a chance to know his three sisters a little. All four are important, and it's very clear that these are the bedrock of Xal's life. Loyalty and family are what he is all about.

He plays a game of Kem with his mother, and we get the sense that he's never won before, but now wins easily. Something changed down at the lake of blood, but we don't know what it is. Nor are we given any time to think about it, because UH OH, it's time for Xal to begin *The Road of Trials* for you story structure buffs.

Up to this point, we've heard THE CALL (dun dun dun) mentioned a bunch of times. It's even in the book's description. We know it's going to happen. And it does. Three deafening peels signal that each family must cough up a sacrifice.

Xal's mother wants to go, but he's like, did you not read the back cover? I got this. So he marches off to war, and he's very angry because 17-year-old Chris was very angry. I had a mullet though. Xal does not, because no one should have a mullet at that age. Sorry, people with mullets. The 1990s were a dark time.

Anyway, the Hasrans send a commander to collect recruits, a tengu named Caw, basically a walking, talking raven who would kick your ass for looking at him.

Nef, Xal, and a bunch of people who don't matter to the story are herded over a drawbridge and off to the Temple of Dalanthar, where they train knights.

Xal meets his best friend for the entire series...a foot-and-a-half-tall rat *fire* mage named Saghir (see the short story *Saghir* for details). Saghir and Xal hit it off right away, and we like Saghir because he's awesome.

We get a training montage under Caw (mon-tage...*Team America*. Go watch it). Then Xal and friends are marched out of the city. They are the least important quint, in the least important century, all the way at the back of the trash legion.

High above them fly the nobility, including our princess Li. By this point, we've had another chapter from her perspective and met the Imperator, who we don't like because she's a slaver and kind of a bitch on top of that. We also meet her son Prince Erik, Xal's future nemesis, but we're on the fence about him. He seems cool, but he's pretty arrogant.

They're all watching an arena match, and most of the people fighting die. Li is horrified, but the Imperator explains that the survivors are magically empowered by the arena itself.

Anyway, back to Xal. The nobles are flying in their airships while the trash legion marches on foot. People quickly begin to fall, and one kid, Seth, who we pity because the author leaned hard on that, gets executed by Caw. Ruthlessly.

Yeah, it's that kind of book.

Up until then, people weren't sure if I was going to do it. Maybe the trash legion would be safe. Nope. There is no safety for anyone. I mean, it's not full *Game of Thrones*, but I wanted to make it clear no one was safe.

Xal quickly bonds with the survivors, and several become important to the plot. Ena, a butcher's daughter with *void* magic in her blood. Morog, an orokh (neanderthal + orc), Saghir, and a deaf healer by the name of Jun, also from totally-not-China.

Jun heals Xal's feet, which inspires him to lead the quint. He takes care of his little group of misfits and keeps them alive when others die along the trail. Xal really steps up, and we're impressed and feel bad that he's going to die.

Before they march past Hasra's massive outer wall, Tissa shows up, proving that she escaped the dims somehow. She gives Xal the cold shoulder and goes and hangs with her brother.

The reader is like...I feel like I'm supposed to like her, but I don't. In fact...I *really* don't like her. Tissa sucks. So much so that my very first bad review is a two-star spending like three paragraphs complaining (justifiably) about Tissa.

To those people, I would ask...please watch Tissa's small but important role in this book. She may not be who you think she is, and if you don't like her...well, perhaps there's a reason. ;)

Anyway, they've almost made it to Chonair Pass, where they will be sacrificed to the Fomori, when Saghir remarks that hey, that mountain range right over there isn't on the map.

Readers are smart. Cunning. Y'all puzzle out details I never thought you would from little scraps and tidbits I dole out. So of course, you knew exactly what was about to happen.

The spider-mountain wakes up and wrecks a large part of the trash legion. Since Xal is at the very back, he and his quint live. But a lot of other people do not.

We flash to Li again. The armada pursues the mountain, driving it before them with powerful spells from a trio of ancient Elentian airships. *PEW PEW PEW.* They drive it directly toward Li's homeland, to her growing horror. You know, in case it wasn't already obvious the Hasrans are bastards.

The remains of the trash legion get one more night to camp and worry about their survival, and Xal uses it to train with Morog and Caw. During this training, Caw tells Xal to flee when the battle starts and again mentions the cliff. We've now had it from like four places.

Go up the cliff.

I've also mentioned by this point that the cliff looks like it could crush an entire army if the army stood directly under it....

...So the Fomori army obligingly marches out of the jungle. They crush the trash legion, and Xal runs. Wasps, bears, and druids, oh my. People are getting offed all over the place, and Xal desperately guides his quint up the cliff, even though he knows they're going to die anyway.

A bear rushes them, and they manage to kill it, but not before it rips out Smithy's innards. We feel pretty bad even though Smithy was a jerk because we're not jerks. Tissa stops to have a snack on him, and most readers are like... yeah, this chick is ruthless. #Vampirelife

They reach the edge of the cliff. More bears are coming. Did I mention there's a giant walking wasp hive and that wasps have carried away a red-shirt character, Isis? Things look bad.

But Xal won't give up.

He guides his quint over the side of the cliff since the wind keeps the wasps away and bears can't climb. They work their way down the cliff...right above the enemy army.

Xal sees that the entire cliff could be knocked loose from the rest of the mountain with a couple of void bolts. He just happens to have a couple of void bolts. So Xal brings down the cliff and crushes the army.

He knows he's falling to his death. We know he's falling to his death. Smart readers see that there's like...52% of the book left on their Kindle. So he can't die. But how are we going to save them?

Enter Princess Li! Li, Erik, Darius, and Crispus are all flying when Xal's quint falls. They save Tissa, Xal, Ena, Jun, and Morog.

But not Nef.

He falls into the wasp hive right before millions of tons of granite crush him and the hive both. Splat. I'm sure that's the last we'll see of him.

The rest of the survivors are flown back to Prince Erik's airship, the super fancy one that fans of *The Magitech Chronicles* recognize instantly. For the first time in his life, Xal sees magical luxury, warm baths, and excess food.

Everything looks great. Erik and Darius are pretty cool. Crispus is kind of a dick, but not enough to ruin things. Up until this point, it looks like happily ever after. We had our march of death, and now things will get better for Xal, right?

Nah.

We get an interlude from Erik's perspective, and his mother, the Imperator, places a geas on Erik. A magical command that forces the prince to hate Xal and basically makes them enemies for life.

The next day Erik is a complete ass to Xal, and Xal has no idea what he's done to deserve it. He chalks it up to nobles being nobles, though he has started to get to know Princess Li, who is genuine, and mega-hot, and totally not based on my wife.

We arrive at definitely-not-Hogwarts and find that there are four temples, each competing against one another. These temples are divided by the Steward they worship. Dalanthar, Zaro, Celeste, and Aelianna.

Xal and Saghir end up in Celeste, along with Princess Li, a tall fighter named Ashianna, and the overweight kid at your high school that everyone picked on, Ephram.

They take some classes you don't care about, but most of their activities are focused on three things.

First, at the end of the semester, they'll be making a run at the Reactor, a divine *fire* Catalyst. One where they will die without the right magical protection.

Second, each temple fields a five-man team for a sport called arena, which is exactly what it sounds like. In *Shattered Gods*, the arenas are divine, which means the terrain, and/or monsters people fight are determined by the arena itself. The more powerful the arena, the cooler things it can do.

Xal's arena team is a huge underdog, with Erik's quint of awesomeness being favored to win and Crispus's quint being right behind them.

All of Xal's other friends, including Tissa, Ena, and Morog, end up in Zaro under Crispus.

The last house only has two people, not enough to even field a team. Jun, the deaf girl who survived the trash legion, and a tall red-headed warrior named Macha.

Macha is a Fomori spy, and not a very good one, but since the Hasrans think all the Fomori are giants, it never even occurs to them that a spy is possible. Clearly, they have never seen *Robotech*.

To survive the Reactor, Xal quickly realizes he and Saghir will need a metric-ass-ton of gold to afford *fire* resistance gear. But they have no money. They can't even afford basic gear for school.

Princess Li suggests they hire a tutor, and since they only know one, Xal chooses Caw, the trainer from the trash legion. They don't realize that Caw is an arena champion from Gateway, one of the largest arenas in the world, and a blademaster of legendary skill.

Caw agrees to train them, and we get another montage. Montage! They're getting stronger, but they still need money, so Caw enrolls Xal and Saghir in death-match fighting called the pit. There's even an illegal pit fighting joke, which is aimed squarely at the guy this book is dedicated to. Miss gaming with you, Max.

Anyway, Xal and Saghir win in the pit. They win big. They're getting stronger. Xal abandons his staff, and the reader realizes him being some asthmatic mage might have been a red herring. He's getting stronger and faster and learning to use his shortsword, the little shard he picked up at the beginning that we didn't think was important.

Remember that little shard as you read *Fomori Invasion*. There was a scene in *Shattered Gods* where Xal gets it magically forged into a shortsword, and we're told about magical limit. This little shortsword can gain power from the Reactor and from up to two other Catalysts afterward.

So now Xal is a better fighter. He's got drakehide armor and a sword and is ready for the Reactor. Only two things are standing in his way.

First, the arena tournament. Xal's been getting wrecked all term. He's never come close to winning. They're up against Erik. It's a no-win situation, like using clubs against a modern tank.

So Xal gets smart. That's kind of his thing.

The arena configures into a game of capture the flag, except with pillars over a field of lava. If you fall, then you die.

Xal acts like he has his team's flag and runs off to the corner. The rest of his quint goes and retrieves Erik's flag. Meanwhile, Erik, Darius, and a well-named character called Brutus use Xal's face as stress relief, then toss him in the lava. He wins but ends up in the medicus.

Enter the mentor character.

Xal's aunt Lucretia survived the purge of the eradicators and the fall of Xal's house. She serves the Imperator as an advisor, always doing advisor-y things behind the throne. She smuggles Xal some more gold and gets him access to an eradicator's manual so he can begin learning their battle magic.

Xal has also gotten to know Kazon, the big scary demon, who is more like a very large uncle. For the first time, Xal has support and friends and is able to bring food home to his family, who badly needs it.

The finale of the book is two-fold. The first part is the Kem tourney. Kem'Hedj is based on real-world Go, but with 3 independent boards. Xal is a prodigy, but with an added benefit.

He has the memories of one of the most ancient war gods that has ever lived. These abilities mean that if he does not focus on the game directly and lets his subconscious steer, then he's almost guaranteed to win.

Xal beats Erik, and he beats Li, the best Kem player, by focusing down her blouse instead of on the game board. Hey, he's based on 17-year-old me, and at 17, I was eight parts hormones and two parts angry.

By winning the Kem tourney, Xal and Saghir have enough coin to buy everything they need for the Reactor. Things are looking up! He's won both the arena tourney and the Kem tourney. He even gets a date.

While Xal is recovering in the medicus, Jun expresses her feelings and begins teaching him ESL (Elentian Sign Language). He shares his first kiss and brings Saghir home to meet his family and Kazon.

In storytelling terms, this is the calm before the storm. All the little subplots have been resolved, and now all that exists is the run on the Reactor. The finale.

To compound matters, we get a scene with the Imperator demanding that Erik execute Xal within the Reactor, since they will not be scryed there. Erik is conflicted, but ultimately agrees and convinces Darius and Brutus to help him.

Since Lucretia is in the room when Desidria gives the order, she's able to quietly slip away and warn Xal through a dream. Xal knows that he's going to have to fight for his life, not just against lava salamanders and magma elementals, but also against the royal heir, armed and equipped to kill dreadlords.

It gets worse. Ephram, Xal's closest Hasran friend outside of Saghir, worships Prince Erik and has been spying for him the entire book. Ephram warns Erik that Xal has somehow learned that he's going to be ambushed.

Erik's mother sabotages things so that the prince and his quint go into the Reactor with a big lead. Crispus and his quint are allowed in next. Then finally, Xal and his quint.

Ephram slows them down intentionally and ensures that they're the last to reach the Catalyst. They trek across fields of lava, dodging magma elementals hundreds of meters tall (a cubit is about half a meter).

Finally, Xal is forced to leave Ephram behind. Even knowing he's probably a traitor, Xal feels bad and uses some blink spells to catch up to Ashianna and Li, who've long since abandoned Ephram.

Xal and Saghir are swallowed by a lava salamander, and it looks bad, but Xal blinks them back out. They land and realize they're close to the Catalyst! A giant ruby is right in front of them.

But Erik is standing between them.

Xal blinks them past (he does that a lot) and touches the Catalyst. We see inside the mind of a god. Specifically, the Heart of Fire, which is part of an ancient war between the elements. When Hasra sliced off 10% of the Heart of Fire and flew it back to create the Reactor, they permanently upset the balance in that war. Oops.

Everyone who Catalyzes sees this and learns the truth. Xal experiences his vision, and then he and Saghir pop back into reality. Erik is waiting. He and his quint are going to kill Xal, but Li, Ashianna, and Saghir all stand with him.

We flash to Tissa. Now up until this point, we've really disliked Tissa. She's mean. She's judge-y. She's dismissive. But she does care about Xal. Tissa convinces Crispus to intervene, in exchange for her becoming a companion (think *Firefly*).

We still dislike Tissa (a lot, and again, that's not acciden-tal), but at least Crispus intervenes and prevents Erik's quint from killing him. Crispus demands that Erik fight a duel with Xal.

Erik sees no way out and we get our duel. To our shock (we're not shocked), Xal turns the table and wins the duel.

We see a final chapter from Macha's perspective where the Fomori are doing villain things and planning a massive invasion of Hasra. One Hasra neither suspects nor can prevent.

Xal graduates from school. He's survived. But he's made an enemy of the crown prince and the ruler of the entire Imperium. Yikes. And that brings us to Fomori Invasion....

# PREVIOUSLY ON FOMORI INVASION

**In an announcer's voice:** *Last time on* **Shattered Gods...**

Fomori Invasion was a beast of a book. It clocked in at 1,100 pages, so big that we had to reduce the font for the paperback and still hit the max page count. Despite that, it is somehow a rushed book.

Xal flies all over the world, and we see Calmora, Enestius, and Valys before finally returning back to the name of the book...the Fomori Invasion. I admit it. I covered too much ground and probably should have taken multiple books to tell that part of the story.

I did it because I wanted to get to *God of the Sands*. I have wanted to write this part of Xal's story for a decade.

The TL;DR of Fomori Invasion is Xal and Saghir fly around to a bunch of Catalysts to get power-ups. Every time, Xal gets the best ability, and every time, Saghir gets magic.

The Fomori trash Hasra, utterly wrecking them as they set up for a final invasion. They are waiting for their hero, the Morrigan, Macha, to return from forging a weapon for the Prince of Demons, with her sidekick Ephram.

Macha and Ephram forge the sword, which turns out to be called Nef Arius. If you've read *The Magitech Chronicles,* this sent up huge red flags. Xal's friend Nef is somehow connected to Nefarius. Perhaps even its origin.

Macha assumes that "for the prince" is meant to kill the prince, but in reality, she just made a sword for Xal and reunites him at the end. Xal and Macha fight, and Hasra wrecks the Fomori, who are broken and flee into the forest.

Behind it all lurks Lucretia, and every time one of her chapters start, you hear ominous music for some reason.

The book ends with Xal's mother selling him into slavery in exchange for releasing all the residents of the dims. Xal frees his family and his people, but is shipping off to the Blasted Lands to die as a sacrifice in the Arena.

## The Long Version

The book picks up with Balora, queen of the Fomori, plotting the invasion. We learn that the Hasrans have been carefully blinded, and when they strike, they hit several locations at once.

First, we pick up with Xal and Saghir, who have spent the summer breaking up rocks in Chonair Pass, cleaning up the mess Xal created when he collapsed it on the Fomori.

They're attacked by a Dullahan, which most people will recognize as a headless horseman. Xal manages to destroy it, but it's one of those rare fights where it takes more than one chapter for something to die.

Xal and Saghir flee before an army of wights led by the Morrigan, a crow goddess and binder, the most feared of the Fomori. They run back to their commander, who happens to be Erik aboard one of mommy's airships.

Erik is already under assault, surrounded by wights. In

addition, giant spiders are flinging eggs filled with tiny burrowing spiders. It's a kill-it-with-fire situation, so Erik does, using the crown his mommy has told him never to use. Ever.

Flash back to mommy. Desidria is chilling on her balcony, monologuing, as villains do, when the Kraken pops out of the bay and starts whooping her fleet and her port.

Desidria draws on the Reactor's enormous power and sears the behemoth until it flees. Then she scries for the druidic circle that bound the creature in the first place. She finds them and turns 24 of the most powerful Fomori druids into a smudge on the shoreline.

She's all happy with herself...until the real invasion starts.

The Fomori come flooding through Hasra's outer wall. They've been creeping up through the forest for weeks, carefully blocking Hasran flame readers and making sure if their fire dreamers detect anything, it was the Kraken attack.

The Fomori take all the territory between the outer wall and the river, forcing the Hasrans to fall back to the inner wall.

At this point, any sane and logical commander would counterattack. Hasra has a fleet of airships that can kill things safely from a distance...but they don't attack. We see from Caw's perspective, and he's pissed they get no help.

But Desidria does nothing. She won't let the airships leave the city itself, lest they be destroyed by Fomori mages. She's panicked, because when she tries to attack the Fomori, she finds that Erik took the power she needed. The Reactor is dry...unless she wants to permanently damage it.

Desidria goes into full shutdown mode, which we see from Lucretia's perspective. Lucretia uses the opportunity to overtax Calmora, Enestius, and Valys in an attempt to foster civil war. Totarius Enestius, Crispus and Darius's father, shows up and demands Desidria pay back the Guild.

They argue and flex at each other, but end up making an agreement that is very relevant to the book you are holding. Desidria agrees to give the city of Gateway to the Guild at a rate of 10% a year until they own it outright. This is a huge concession and buys her peace and Guild support.

Flash back to Xal. He and Saghir are aboard Erik's airship. It gets shot down, and they crash a couple miles outside Hasra. The survivors flee for the walls, and Caw leads a legion out to cover them. Brutus, Erik's well-named sidekick from the last book, was killed by the spiders, and after Erik and Xal safely reach the wall, Erik sends Xal back to retrieve the body.

He succeeds, but we see the Fomori steal the airship. That won't be relevant later in the series or anything.

Xal makes it back to town, which is justifiably panicked by the invasion. So if you were a monarch whose city was just invaded, needed powerful mages, and just happened to have an eradicator at your disposal, what would you do?

You'd put them on an airship and ship them away from the war, of course. Desidria sends Erik, Xal, Li, and the rest off to a standard school year where they travel from province to province, picking up Catalyzations.

For the rest of the book, we get Caw's perspective and see the legions forced to camp outside the city walls. They receive reinforcements as people are unwillingly expelled and conscripted, basically any citizens deemed useless.

On the other side, we see Xal living in the lap of luxury and basically dealing with normal high school pressures. The war is a distant thing for Xal, whose primary focus is on survival.

One wrinkle I haven't yet mentioned...the demotech

shirt from the previous book has grown into his flesh, and he isn't sure why. Kazon tells him that it is growing and needs magic, but will eventually mature to adulthood. You get to see what that looks like in this book.

Xal and company arrive in Calmora, aka not-China, and stay at the royal mountain where Li's mother maintains a tenuous rule. Calmora is in a quiet war with the dream wyrm Khonsu, one of the missing flights from *The Magitech Chronicles*.

Xal is still technically dating Jun, but you can tell he's attracted to Li. Some people gave me grief about how quickly Xal's romance with Jun imploded, but I'd argue you may not remember the two-week cycle that is high school. Depths, that was 1994. It's probably like an eight-minute cycle now.

Xal gains the Grace of Shu, a powerful *air* ability that makes him all dodgy, and Saghir gets *air* magic. Xal's sword also reveals itself as the first blade...Narlifex. *The Magitech Chronicles* fans have big questions.

We get a martial arts training montage, and once Xal has some basic skills, he's pitted against Niu, the girl who broke him and Jun up. And Li's archnemesis. It turns out Niu is a dragon. Xal and Li go toe-to-toe with her and drive her off before she can wake the lightning people, which she claims will wipe out Li's people and the seraphim living above them, her dad's people.

Before we have time to digest what happened, we're in the air once more, this time taking an airship to Enestius, where Crispus and Darius are royalty. Xal learns how to use his new sword and gains the Fortune of Lakshmi, which is basically super-luck. Saghir gets *dream* magic, which unlocks both illusion and divination. Super rat!

There's some drama between Crispus and Erik, and Erik

comes out on top as a complete bad-ass, while Xal tries to avoid attention and focus on the war. He just wants to get through the term without anyone figuring out that his shirt is demotech.

Before we can process, we're in the air again, this time on griffins flying to Valys. The class arrives at the Hammer of Reevanthara, where we meet Lukas, a jovial instructor with a large nose, a great smile, and a very powerful wife.

Xal gains Immovable Mountain, which means he can no longer be moved, and it blunts all damage he takes. If you search for the phrase Immovable Mountain, you'll find it like 200 times in this book. It's so powerful.

Saghir gets *earth* magic.

Li and Xal finally kiss and have a brief, awkward romance.

Then we're in the air once more! It's back to the war. Xal and his classmates are added to the military under Erik's command, with Ashianna as second. The griffins fly to Teophilus, an island belonging to the elfen, but before we can get to know them, we're in the air again!

The last part of the book is all battle battle battle. Xal proves his skills as a general and connects with Praetor Etrian Valys, Ashianna and Gavius's dad and a good friend of Xal's grandfather. He takes Xal under his wing, and we're instantly alarmed because every time Xal gets anything, it's taken away.

Erik asks Xal to lead a group to the lake of blood, and he does. More *void* magic! Everyone has a vision of Xal as a powerful demon lord, saving the world from an even more powerful demon lord. They emerge able to learn to be eradicators, and Xal teaches them the basics.

Hasra takes it to the Fomori with a daring night strike,

and they fly over their ranks on griffins, backed up by Calmoran *air* mages. It's Xal's plan, and it works!

Unfortunately, Macha has also become a bad-ass and shoots Xal's griffin out of the air, killing it. Saghir saves Xal with his *air* magic, but they're cut off as the rest of the Hasran military heads back to the city.

Macha and Xal do the 1-v-1 thing, and Nefarius defects, becoming Xal's weapon. They brawl for a while, and Xal holds his own! Before we can see who the stronger one is, the Hasran military finally sallies out, along with the armada, and the Fomori retreat. Ephram says hey and keeps Xal and Macha from killing each other, fulfilling his role as the peacemaker.

The Fomori are largely beaten, and Hasra stands triumphant. It was anti-climatic, and some readers were left wondering how Desidria let things get so bad. Bad enough that she agrees to let Lucretia use the dims kids as new eradicators...that Lucretia controls. What's the worst that could happen?

Xal comes back after being rescued, victorious, and is presented to Desidria. His mom is there. Uh oh. Because Xal is underage, his mother still legally controls his fate and has chosen to sell him to Desidria.

Desidria, we learn, is going to send Xal to Gateway. Apparently, the despot there, Sabinia, needs five god-souled for a sacrifice that will evolve the arena. Xal will be the fifth. In exchange, all dims residents are freed.

Xal considers it a bargain and is proud of his mother. He goes gladly to his fate, knowing that he saved his family...all he ever wanted.

Erik sees the injustice and breaks the enchantment his mother placed on him through sheer will. He decides to help Xal, and the book ends with Erik giving Saghir money and helping him free Caw, who was imprisoned for killing his commander for being a dumb-ass.

Caw and Saghir set off after Xal, who is stripped of everything and sent to his death.

And that brings us to the next book, *God of the Sands*.

# PREVIOUSLY ON GOD OF THE SANDS

**In an announcer's voice:** *Last time on* **Shattered Gods...**

*God of the Sands* is much shorter (thank god) than *Fomori Invasion*. It's a tighter story, probably because the bones of it came from someone else's imagination.

Back in 2015, I joined a *Shattered Gods* campaign my long-time friend Aaron was running called *The Return of the Prophetess*. Aaron is a fantastic GM, and it was possibly my favorite game, doubly so because it took place in my own world.

Aaron fleshed out the Blasted Lands, the shaldeen, and the impossible city of Mandala. I got to play through the arena in the very first incarnation of Xal in a world I had run campaigns in for decades.

If you hate Sabinia or Magnus, thank Aaron Jordan.

Anyway, the short version of the story is this.

Five god-souled are to be sacrificed to the Gateway Arena to increase its size, a holy ritual. Xal is one of these five. But they refuse to die. They keep winning fight after fight.

Eventually, they escape in the middle of a fight and follow a prophecy out into the desert. Xal becomes a god. Literally. They come back and curb-stomp the Hasran garrison.

Caw gets killed by Magnus, and Xal gets revenge. Magnus is such a crazy foe that it takes more than one chapter to kill him.

Saghir just keeps getting stronger and now has the first staff. Xal has the first armor. The end.

## The Long Version

At the end of *Fomori Invasion,* the Imperator made a deal with Xal's mother Nix. She sold him into slavery, and in exchange, Desidria freed all the dims urchins.

Xal was 100% on board with this deal, and the two were doing the secret demon-fist-bump, even though it was going to cost Xal his life. I mean his mom was broken up, but Xal was super on board.

Anyway, *God of the Sands* picks up with Xal arriving in the desert city of Gateway. He's been collared, stripped of weapons, and can't cast magic. He's tossed into the slave pens for one night, and while there, saves an old woman from some hyenakin thugs so the reader will think Xal is a good guy.

The next day he's brought to the arena. He makes a new friend along the way, but I can't remember his name, because he dies like 14 seconds after Xal meets him.

We're introduced to our villains Sabinia and Magnus, who are presiding over the games. Their goal is to sacrifice five god-souled and 95 chumps to force the Arena to evolve. This happens whenever an arena has seen enough combat, spilled enough blood, and acquired enough worship.

Magnus is wearing Xal's sword Narlifex in the sheath that Li made, so we know what happened to the first blade.

They have a grand melee where Xal is supposed to die, and things look bad. They have no real weapons or armor. Then Saghir creeps up to Magnus and breaks the binding holding Narlifex.

This allows Xal to summon his weapon, and armed with the first blade, he lays waste to his opponents. He and the other god-souled win. They're supposed to be over-whelmed, but instead kill all opponents.

As their victory occurs, Mother Elaheh, a catkin and spiritual leader of the shaldeen animal races, rises into the air and gives prophecy. She names Xal and the others the hand of fate and goes on and on about all the cool things they're going to do.

Magnus flexes on the PCs, and we see right away that he's the big bad we're going to have to overcome at the end. He takes a particular liking to Xal because of the sword thing and spends a lot of the book making Xal's life hell.

Meanwhile, Saghir and his lost love Alsara (from the short story *Saghir*) are reunited! He meets Alsara's brother, and the three of them quietly build alliances for Xal.

They link up with Caw, who arranges to become Xal's trainer at the new ludus that has been tasked with preparing the hand of fate for the Arena.

It turns out that Caw was also trained at this ludus, and we meet Nomaus, the catkin who forged Caw into a champion of the Arena. We also meet Xal's new master, leader of the House of Battiatus.

Fans of *Spartacus: Blood and Sand* should instantly recognize that name. That was the house where Spartacus trained. What they may not realize is that Crixus and Spartacus were real people, who really led a slave rebellion, the third servile war.

The House of Battiatus was also real. Given that I was arranging a slave revolt, I figured I'd sneak it in, and I also meant it as an homage to the show, which is excellent and worth your time. Every time you hear apologies in my work, it came from that series!

Xal and the hand of fate train during the day and are turned loose into the slave pens at night. The pens are a lawless place, and we quickly meet two important people.

The first is Zelek, the Steward. He appears as a crippled old man, then as an elfen, and once as a kodachine. He shadows Xal the entire book, but doesn't reveal himself till the end.

The other is Mina, a cute little catkin child. Mina happens to be blind, which astute readers realize is a hallmark of divination. The eyeless, servants of Zelek, remove their own eyes to better perceive the future. They literally offer their eyes to the flame. Eww.

Anyway, Mina carries around a doll named Sir Bitey, who is her best friend and mentioned often. Sir Bitey is the First Lion, not just a rag doll. The soul of the First Lion, an ancient and powerful ancestor spirit, which shamans like Mina commune with.

Mina is destined to become the next prophetess, to dethrone Sabinia, and free the people in her city. But to the reader, she is the kid Xal keeps saving until the clues began to pile up.

Meanwhile, Xal begins his side quest to become a dedicate of Celeste. He begins working at her temple and meets the love interest, Sabri. Sabri is a sultry, fiery, intelligent scribe and ultimately helps Xal escape the Arena. There's also a fade to black moment, and then Xal feeling guilty the next morning because he feels like he's betrayed Li.

Li is based on my wife, so this is unsurprising. I feel guilty even writing about being with another woman. But Li is having a fling of her own at the same time, which you'll learn about in the short story *Princess Li*, so Xal shouldn't feel too bad.

Xal goes through several montages. He gets stronger and faster and becomes a true blademaster under the careful tutelage of Caw and Nomaus. By the time they escape during the last arena fight, Xal is the equal of the other four members of the hand of fate, Gronde, Brim, Gakk, and Isharah.

Each of these characters is based on a character played in the pen and paper campaign run by Aaron Jordan, the guy who *God of the Sands* is dedicated to.

Gronde = Aaron
Brim = Max
Gakk = Luke (Also Professor Lukas)
Isharah = Jeff (Also Kit from *The Dark Lord Bert*)
The White Necromancer = Travis (Also the Dark Lord White from *Bert*)
Loxclyn = (Kathy Gregg, a druid she has been playing for 20+ years)

There is so much history in this world. So many people have left their mark in the dozens of campaigns we ran, from the Ashlands to the Blasted Lands to the Maw.

Anyway, our hand of fate escapes from the arena by being washed over the cliff / escarpment, and is saved by Saghir, who whisks them down to their goblin allies. The goblins help the heroes reach the underground sea beneath the city, where the marid rule the Heart of Water.

Magnus and Sabinia are pissed. Magnus takes a legion and pursues the hand of fate out into the desert. As he's leaving, he pays Caw a visit, and the two duel.

Caw dies. =(

It was hard to write. But Caw gets to have the last laugh. He comes back as a force ghost / ancestor spirit, and Xal reconnects with him in the desert. He also meets Caw's biological son Hadi, and the two become allies. But I'm getting ahead of myself.

Xal is armed with Nefarius and Narlifex. He's strong and skilled. A true badass now. He's a champion of the Gateway arena.

They stop by the Heart of Water, and he gains the Grace of Marid, to match his Grace of Shu. He can no longer be bound, mind-controlled, or poisoned. Remember that little detail as you read *I, Demon*. It's relevant.

The hand of fate escapes through underground caverns, and when they finally reach the surface again, they emerge in the verdant triangle, an oasis belonging to the druid Loxclyn, a sylvan, or plant person.

Loxclyn agrees to help the hand of fate, but puts Brim to work in her bedchamber and everyone else to work in other ways. Before they leave, she tells them of the White Necromancer, part of the prophecy, and we learn that the two worked together and have no love for each other.

The party heads to the pyramid, and inside, meet the White Necromancer. The WN has an army that could crush everyone in the cycle at the same time. He shows them this army and smacks Xal and friends around easily when they try to fight him.

WN explains that this is his own pocket reality, which is

why he's so strong, but if he comes back to the cycle, he'll be just a normal lich. It's why he stays here. WN will be relevant later in the series, but is also an inside joke, because our buddy Travis really did this. He really made an invincible army and conquered the world. Happened in an Exalted 1st edition game.

The party moves on into a sand storm, which carries them to the impossible city, which is run by sphinxes who served the gods who used to run the cycle. Readers of *The Magitech Chronicles* saw these gods exit the cycle in the novel *Godswar*. These are their servants, the ones they left behind to keep it all running.

Xal reached his second tomb in the impossible city. Inside, he witnesses a vision of his former incarnation meeting with Neith, the First Diviner, and a major character in *The Magitech Chronicles.*

When Xal emerges, he is a true god, complete with a religion. He can receive worship and grant miracles. He is the god of the sands.

He and the hand of fate unify the kodachine raiders in the desert. Doing so requires Xal to go into the lair of Apep, the dragon, to face the flame. Xal does so and receives the starsword Asi.

He finds the strength to cast Nefarius aside and leaves the blade in a pool of lava. He's learned that Nefarius is a reincarnation too, and that the blade is responsible for plagues that have ended civilizations. He doesn't ever want Nef finding Tissa.

Remember Magnus? He's having a tough go of it. He shows up at the verdant triangle, and Loxclyn eats his entire legion. He rides a magitech griffin out into the desert, but can't find Xal, because Xal is in the impossible city.

Finally, Magnus happens across Nefarius and takes up

the blade. He knows Nefarius is god-forged, and while he'd rather have Narlifex to compliment his own dark sword, Maladrieve, he'll settle for Nefarius.

Xal and the kodachine march on Gateway. They retake the city, at great cost, and Xal has to fight Magnus 1 v 1. For the very first time, it takes Xal more than one chapter to kill an opponent. He gets kicked through walls, and there's a dance off at one point, but finally Xal triumphs...and eats Magnus.

Xal gains power every time he consumes an enemy. Enemies strong in magic effectively become snack-sized Catalysts for him. Killing Magnus also dramatically increases Xal's worship, as Gateway knows he is one of the heroes that freed him.

Sabinia is still alive at this point. She's holding Mina hostage, and our other heroes are trying to free her. Things look bad...until Sir Bitey descends from the stars and eats Sabinia's soul. And then everyone claps.

Mina, the new prophetess, is left in charge of Gateway. The slaves are freed. The shaldeen are once more in charge of their own city. Isharah stays to guide the new prophetess. Brim and Gronde head off into the desert to unify the rest of the kodachine, since that will be kind of important in the second half.

Saghir goes and hides Nefarius somewhere no one can find him.

At the very end of the book, the Stewards meet to discuss what happened. Zaro is wearing Nefarius. He trailed Saghir, so Nefarius is still a threat.

We don't see what happens, but it's pretty obvious that Xal is going to be enemy #1 in this book. Hasra knows exactly who toppled their government, who killed Magnus. And there will be consequences.

Welcome to *I, Demon*....

# PREVIOUSLY ON I DEMON

**In an announcer's voice:** *Last time on* **Shattered Gods...**

*I, Demon* kicked off with the Night of Black Blood, one of the pivotal moments in Shattered Gods history, about 20 years before Xal was born. The Knights of the Dawn and the Stewards helped the people of Olivantia rise up and slaughter Olivanticus and his dread council.

It set the stage for a lot of the first part of the book, where Xal and Ducius do the buddy-cop thing. They head to the capital where Ducius wanted to recover the artifacts of Olivanticus. These immensely powerful objects would also allow Xal access to his second tomb, located under the Skull of Xalegos, which Ducius now controls.

Before he starts the quest, however, we see Xal and Saghir leaving Hasra by boat. A strange god shows up on board with hair and beard of living flame and introduces himself as Jet. He gives Xal a powerful magical talisman, but we aren't sure who he is or why.

Spoilers—he's the dragon who was protecting the Heart of Fire when Elentia tore off a hunk to make the Reactor. We saw a vision from his perspective when Xal touched the Reactor in book I. Sedjet is awake and wants revenge on the Elentians / Hasrans.

Back to Olivantia, where Saghir is waiting at the Skull and Xal and Saghir embark on the aforementioned buddy-cop trip. Along the way, we see just how cunning Ducius is as he converts more people to his cause. He uses Xal as muscle, and Xal kills several demigod knights, absorbing their power in the process. These were some of my best written fights IMO.

Xal and Ducius reach the capital, and Xal beats down Dalanthar in front of his followers, breaking the Steward's religion, which turns out to have been Ducius's goal all along. Ducius finds a powerful airship, and together with Olivanticus's grandson Temis they recover three artifacts. Each of them keeps one, which brings Ducius's total to two, while also putting Temis on the map with his one.

Xal gets the Ring of Olivanticus, which he needs for his tomb. Afterward, he gives it to Saghir, which gives our favorite rat a near infinite supply of magical pool.

Only after the battle with Dalanthar does Xal realize what he's done. He helped dreadlords overcome the Steward of Justice, and of course, Valys knows about it. He's a demon, allied with dreadlords, who fights Stewards. In short...he's the bad guy as far as Praetor Etrian is concerned.

Xal slinks back into Hasra and gets his third tomb. He gets his tomb and learns what his aunt is after. The void titan Gortha is trapped in the Umbral Depths, and the only way out is destroying the cycle. That's what Lucretia is after.

Xal confronts her, but the problem is that she has a game-breaking artifact called the Flame of Obeisance. All demons must obey. She orders Xal not to harm her and to kill Saghir if she dies. Yikes.

Xal uses an ability he got at the Skull called Word of Xalegos, which paralyzes Lucretia. Saghir evacs them, and they flee the city.

He and Saghir learn that Erik is leading the Hasran forces in invading the city of Lakeshore. Xal shows up to stop it.

Desidria has other plans. She fires the Reactor to wipe out Lakeshore and both armies, but Xal shocks everyone by taking the blast...he absorbs the magic using the pendant that Sedjet gave him earlier, just as Sedjet planned, and it powers Xal up instead of hurting him.

Then he wrecks the Hasran forces, embarrasses Erik, and kicks Crispus into the Endless Lake. He basically presses pause on the war. Unfortunately, when he returns to Valys after having saving them, Dalanthar is already there, and the Praetor is forced to banish him.

Our last cool scene is Sedjet, who invades the Reactor. Desidria's defenses are down. The Reactor is dry. He turns into a massive fire dragon, tears apart the upper levels of the Reactor, and eats the Imperator and her crown. Gulp. Spicy!

**The Long Version**

The book opens from Karl's perspective, a simple blacksmith in Olivantia. He and the Knights of the Dawn kill the local dreadlord, which is happening all over the country in different cities. By dawn, nearly all the dreadlords are dead, and the people of Olivantia are free for the first time in centuries.

Yay! For like five minutes.

Magic is immediately outlawed. Any magic. The Temple of Dalanthar grows in strength, and we see this over the next three interludes. Each time, it jumps forward in time, and we see the nation developing into the oppressive state it has become.

Meanwhile, Xal and Saghir are picking their way across the continent, so that by the time they arrive in Olivantia, the reader knows what kind of threats they'll face. They won't be able to use magic openly, and if they are discovered, they'll be killed.

They meet Darius in Hasra before leaving, and he tells them that Xal is known far and wide as the traitor who led the slave revolt in Gateway. We also learn that Jun is pregnant and that Darius really doesn't like Xal very much.

Xal takes the warning to heart and decides to leave right after he sees his family. He heads to the dims and is ambushed by Ena. We get a quick fight, then some overdue hugs. The last we saw of Ena, she drank too much from the lake and went feral.

Ena helps Xal use the tunnels under the city to escape via a pirate port called Southpoint, where they are able to book a ship crossing the Endless Lake. Just before they leave, a strange man named Jet jumps aboard with a flaming beard and hair. Obviously some sort of god. He's really important later. For now, he gives Xal a pendant of fire protection, just 'cause.

That night Xal and Saghir sneak off the ship and fly directly toward Olivantia since it's way faster than taking a boat, and they were only booking passage to throw people tracking them off the scent. They fly over a new *spirit* Catalyst where the Fomori druid circle was wiped out, but decide to stick to the main quest for now.

Xal does take the opportunity to finally missive Li and is overjoyed when she missives back and the pair begin to reconnect. They invent sexting.

We jump to Ephram, who has met up with a tribe of

horselords who adopt him as a mascot since they can see he's a shaman. They ride across the plains but see a massive tribe of orokh plainsrunners and flee. They end up at the *spirit* Catalyst Xal and Saghir flew over, and Ephram is able to take over.

He becomes the guardian of a weak *spirit* and *earth* Catalyst and takes care of the wights and ghosts there. He also learns that the orokh tribe is led by none other than Morog. Morog is taking over all the tribes and appears to be their prophesied chosen one.

I'm writing a separate book entitled Morog, which covers his rise to power. He's one of my favorite characters. Anyway, we'll get to see more of him, but his role in this book is pretty small.

Flash back to Dalanthar, who has arrived in Olivantia and is now meeting with Karl. We see them put the belt, dagger, and ring of Olivanticus in a vault to protect them since they suspect dreadlords are coming for them. And they're right.

We flash to Xal, who is being led from Lakeshore by Gavius across the river to the Skull of Xalegos. Gavius takes them to his master, the guardian of the mountain... Ducius, Erik's brother, a character we met back in *Fomori Invasion*.

Ducius is happy to work with Xal, but shows him that Olivanticus created a seal over Xal's tomb. He can't get in without the Ring of Olivanticus, and Ducius just happens to know where it is. He ropes Xal into going with him to the capital and leaving Saghir behind.

Saghir isn't cool with that, but Ducius has na'elfen servants, and their leader Liloth agrees to teach Saghir to be a summoner. Once he gains *spirit* magic, he will be invited to join the dread council, which will make him equal to

Ducius. Saghir reluctantly agrees. He doesn't like it, but they have no other way into the tomb.

Ducius and Xal join a caravan heading east, and this is where things get fun. They are traveling in a caged wagon to protect them from consumed attacks and are locked in with a priest and three acolytes, all of whom will kill Xal and Ducius should they learn the truth.

Instead, Ducius manipulates the acolytes into hating the priest, which isn't hard since the dude is an arrogant prick. A "mysterious consumed attack" takes the priest's life, and now Ducius is in control of the acolytes. He admits who he is.

If the acolytes want to, they can turn him in. They have the chance when they reach the next town, but none of them do, even though they know he's a dreadlord. His rise has begun.

Unfortunately, there's a powerful knight in town, and Xal sees Mikhail—basically the Juggernaut from *X-Men*—hassling a mousey scribe named Levi. Xal intervenes, knocks the knight into a hole, and then flees the town with Levi and Ducius.

Levi is terrified because he knows that Xal is a demon and Ducius a dreadlord but gradually learns that they aren't as evil as he feared. Ducius masterfully converts him as he did the others.

Flash back to Hasra. Ashianna is minding her own business when Crispus, Bha, and Tissa show up to arrest her with about a dozen guards. Ashianna leaps out her window, and we get an awesome escape scene.

Erik intervenes and gives Ashianna his magitech griffin, so she escapes. The war between Hasra and Valys has begun, so suddenly the reader was like—did I miss a chapter?

Ducius and Xal reach the capital, and Ducius stops at a midden heap, which turns out to be the scene of an ancient battle. He raises the wights there and creates an army of unliving to serve him. This gets parked for the moment, but comes in handy later.

They enter the city and meet with Temis, the grandson of Olivanticus and a sexy vampire with sexy vampire hair. Temis seems cool, and we like him, even though he leaks angst everywhere. Temis agrees to help them break into the spire where Dalanthar is holding the artifacts they need. There are three, so each of them gets one. Everybody wins.

We flash to Saghir to see him mastering summoning. Montage! He's befriended Liloth and she's agreed to take a pact, so that Saghir can summon na'elfen to defend him. He's really starting to get OP.

Xal and Temis start their part of the plan but are unexpectedly ambushed by, like, fifty knights. Xal is super OP by this point and cuts them all down easily. You know when you're playing an RPG, and you wander back to a zone way lower level? These chumps are grey.

But then their boss shows up! Mikhail is here. Jugg's gotcha!

Xal and the heavily armored knight brawl, and Mikhail breaks Narlifex. The upper third of the blade shatters. People who've read *The Magitech Chronicles* were all HOLY SHEEET, because they recognize this moment, which appears to occur with every incarnation of the sword.

Narlifex animates the shards of the blade, and Xal uses them like a swarm of piranha. They get in through the helmet's eye sockets and shred Mikhail. Then Xal eats him and gains power. His demon-sheep transformation continues.

Unfortunately, Xal loses Asi in the process. He can't use

it anymore. His arm goes completely numb, thanks to the curse. It's left in the street, and they have to flee, leaving it for anyone to find.

Ducius invades the city with his army of unliving, which makes an excellent distraction. Dalanthar heads directly there, so he isn't in the tower to protect the artifacts. He leaves behind Nadya Quickblade, the most skilled blade-master currently living, for anyone keeping score. She has a 9 skill. Xal has a 6, but higher agility. She's still better in a straight fight. Better than Magnus or Mikhail.

Anyway, Ducius invades the manor of Reverian, an important dreadlord and Temis's dad. Ducius slaughters the nobles inside who are having a party, but spares Karl and his daughter, who is important in *The Ashlands*.

He heads below and finds the dreadlord Reverian's airship, which is on par with the best of the Hasran armada, though it is smaller. Ducius is moving up in the world. We're still not sure if we like him. He seems cool, but we all know he's a dick and are waiting for the inevitable betrayal.

Xal and Temis make it to the tower's vault room, but Nadya is there and ambushes them. She's seen the *Star Wars* prequels and remembers the Dooku fight, so she takes Temis out right away by kicking him out a window.

Now it's 1v1, and she knows that she's older and better than Xal.

To make matters worse, she draws Asi...she recovered the starsword. She goes hard for Xal, but Xal perfected running like a little *&^%$ way back in book 1 when Erik was chasing him. He leads her around for a long time, knowing she can't hold Asi forever.

The duel goes on for a while, and Xal holds his own. Eventually, Nadya drops Asi, and Xal eats her. His power grows again, and his demon form completes the sheep upgrade. Full ram horns.

They get the artifacts and flee. Xal finds out Temis survived the fall, and they link up with Ducius on his new airship. Xal is about to land on the deck when a beam of sunlight breaks through the storm clouds at about 2 am and spears him, knocking him to the ground far below.

This beam is incredibly powerful and summoned by Dalanthar's shield, one of the artifacts of creation, which house the magic of one of the most powerful gods to ever live, Rei. A god famous for smiting demons.

Yet somehow Xal shrugs the beam off like it's nothing. Curious that.

He then kicks Dalanthar's ass all over the courtyard. Ducius uses illusion magic to project the battle into the sky so that the whole capital watches as Xal just wrecks the Steward of Justice in a fair fight.

Dalanthar has no choice but to flee, which breaks his religion in the region, while netting Xal many new followers.

They board Ducius's airship, then head to the blood wood to drop off Temis at his manor. Along the way, Xal sees the Tree of Blood for the first time. It is terrifyingly powerful, and he senses an unexpected kinship with it.

I'm sure that's not important and won't come up later. Nothing to see here.

We flash back to Erik who has gathered his army. He is sailing on Lakeshore with the full Hasran armada and a legion of troops. The invasion has begun.

We flash to Tissa, who along with Bha, has been attached to the Ghost Fleet under Totarius's command. They absolutely destroy a powerful Valysian city, and they make it look easy. It's clear the author is building up the bad guys so Xal looks cooler when he finally fights them.

Xal returns to the Skull and is now able to remove the barrier to his tomb. He descends into the Forges of Xa, where god avatars are constructed. There's even a demonic clawed hand in one of the stalls, which shows how large the avatars were. The hand is like 125 feet long.

The shade of Xalegos reveals himself. He's been the caretaker of the forges for thousands of years. He has all the memories of Xal's former incarnation. He explains that he is the seventh and that Xal is the eighth. Each time, they grow more powerful, and more souls are added.

Xal touches a sigil which drags him down to the center of the world, which is hollow. There Xal sees the Eternium, the source of all life within the realm. This is where primals come from, and he sees them being released as wispy balls of light, floating up into the world.

He also finds his tomb, of course, and sees a vision of the First Diviner, Neith, who *Magitech Chronicles* fans know intimately. She's a giant arachnidrake. A spider-dragon.

Xal returns to the Skull, where Saghir has just gained *spirit*. Xal touches the Catalyst too, but gains the top-tier ability as usual. This one is stupidly overpowered. It's called the Word of Xalegos and paralyzes anyone who hears it. Just say "despair," and you have at least four rounds to beat on your opponent without them fighting back.

We flip to Lucretia, who is attending Desidria. The Imperator is growing less and less stable, and Lucretia is trying to capitalize on it. She wants Desidria to fire the Reactor and wipe out the Valysian fleet. Possibly all of Lakeshore. Desidria is reluctant, but we already know it's going to happen.

Xal and Saghir fly toward Hasra to collect the third

tomb, but this time they stop at the Fomori Catalyst, which Ephram now controls. We get a fun reunion, then Xal gains *spirit* magic.

They make it back to Hasra, where they are ambushed by demons. Xal destroys them easily. They link up with Ena, who takes them to Kazon and Xal's mother Nix in a super secret meeting. Not so secret, as Lucretia finds them during the meeting.

Xal treats her like family. The others don't trust her, but she's never done anything but help him, so he's reluctant to make her an enemy.

She helps him get his third tomb, and Xal has a vision of Gortha. She reveals all sorts of things. For one thing, this vision is in the extreme past, and the Umbral Depths aren't dark yet. Gortha calls the realm where she dwells Kem'Hedj, the universe that the titans created before the Great Cycle, which will one day become the Umbral Depths.

She also mentions something even earlier, a place called Kemet, the black land. This was the very first place the titans made and apparently can still be reached by tricking time even though it's been destroyed. That won't be relevent in about two books. Not at all.

Gortha also has black skin and white hair. She's very attractive. Readers of *The Magitech Chronicles* instantly recognized Nebiat's appearance (one of the villains from that series), and it raised some big questions.

Meanwhile, Erik invades Lakeshore and wins. He kills Lukas, their old instructor from *Fomori Invasion*. Lady Shulk is going to be pissed.

We flash to Ashianna and the Praetor, who are in a war council, planning their response. The council is derailed when Dalanthar shows up and explains what Xal did in

Olivantia. It ends in a fight, and the Praetor kicks Dalanthar out. Things are tense.

Back to Xal.

Xal confronts his aunt. He now knows that in order for Gortha to be free, the cycle must be destroyed. That is what Lucretia is after. She admits it. He tells her it's over and he won't serve her. She whips out a super OP artifact, one of many she's gathered, and proves Xal wrong.

The Flame of Obeisance can control any demon. She orders Xal not to harm her and to kill Saghir if she dies. It looks bad, but Xal uses that paralyze ability he got, and they are able to escape and flee the city.

They beeline for Lakeshore and arrive just in time to stop Erik from killing Praetor Etrian. Xal wrecks Erik and his army.

Desidria finally agrees to fire the Reactor and is going to wipe out Lakeshore, but Xal leaps up and takes the blast. It powers him up, thanks to the artifact our buddy Jet gave him in the beginning. Xal is even stronger now.

We flip back to Sedjet, our dragon bro. Sedjet goes full wyrm and attacks the now weakened Reactor. He wrecks the upper third and eats Desidria and her crown, BURP. An ignoble end, but one that leaves Lucretia alive and in power.

The book ends with Lucretia implanting another demon prince. She puts the soul in Bha, who merges with Xakava, the second prince. It's a cool development, but Bha is a ten-year-old girl who hasn't been to nearly as many Catalysts as Xal.

How is she going to be a threat?

She's not the one Xal needs to be worried about just yet.

Trust me, he's about to have all sorts of bigger problems. Welcome to *The Ashlands*....

# PREVIOUSLY ON THE ASHLANDS

**In an announcer's voice:** *Last time on* **Shattered Gods....**

Totarius got implanted with Xa's soul and became the chief bad guy. He allied with Khonsu, whose children have taken control of Calmora. Li's people are screwed.

Erik is ambushed and killed, then replaced by Crispus as the new Imperator. We're pretty sad, even though he was the season one villain.

Xal rolls out into the Ashlands and gets his final soul, but there's a plot twist. The tomb is for Rei, a god of light inserted directly into the cycle by Om, the creator. Reeva joined that soul to Xal and plans to use Xal to win his war against Gortha, the titan of void.

Xal beats up some Stewards and kills Dalanthar, which creates a job opening. They fetch Erik's soul, resurrect him, and make him do it. Erik becomes the new Steward of Justice.

Meanwhile, Totarius wins the civil war and captures Ashianna and the Praetor by using Gavius against them. Now Totarius is ready to focus on raising titanic avatars.

Xal ends the book retreating to join Ducius and Temis since Olivantia is the only place they're not considered enemies. When he arrives, Ducius asks a very strange question. How are Jun and her baby? What an odd question.

I wonder why he's interested.

### ...How about the long version?

*The Ashlands* kicks off with Totarius and Khonsu making an alliance in the dream realm. The dragon is big and scary, and Totarius is a fly in a spider's web. We don't know what they are up to, but Xal's enemies getting together is never good.

Flip to Lucretia, who is surveying her ocean of *void* magic. She asks Kazon if it's enough to raise a titanic avatar, a kaiju-god basically, a behemoth larger than the spider mountain, and he's all...yeah, I guess you could do that.

Now we know the stakes. Lucretia wants to implant Xa, the oldest demon prince, and get Bha into an avatar so she can conquer the world. Not a bad plan, especially when you have a flame that controls demons.

Xal and Saghir are blissfully unaware. They're hanging out in the Forges of Xa, where they use a scavenged reactor to make their first airship, *The Fist*. It's a giant floating hand since that was the only spare part available within the forges to house their reactor.

Flip to Li who is investigating a slaughtered village at the very edge of Calmora. Niu ambushes her and her charges, but the battle ends in a stalemate, and Li retreats to the mountain. When she arrives, she finds that Professor Ting has been dream-bound. Dragons control him and many of her people.

In the process, we also learn that Ting was the man that

Li slept with during *God of the Sands*. Yes, there will be a short story about that. Hopefully not long after you finish *Rat & Demon*.

We flip back to Xal who is being introduced to the dread council. Saghir is officially welcomed, and Xal gets to play the sidekick for the first time. He leans into the strong silent bodyguard.

The dread council gather their airships, *The Fist*, and Ducius's ship the *Return*, and they roll out to kill a vithi, which will make the tree vulnerable. It does not go well. Xal goes toe-to-toe with a na'elfen named Yeva, but the fight is interrupted by the vithi smashing them both.

Xal has the chance to kill the vithi using a blast of *fire* magic from the Reactor but spares it for a reason he can't really explain. That foreshadows what he learns in the Ashlands, or it was supposed to anyway.

I'm never sure if you're picking up what I'm laying down. The obvious stuff flies right by sometimes, but the obscure hint connecting characters from *Deathless*, *The Magitech Chronicles*, and this series, which won't even be published for three more years?

You've already successfully guessed it. How? How!?!?!

Anyway, back to the recap.

Kazon escorts Tissa to the forges, a popular location on the world map now that we can fast travel to it. She fixes the first bow. There's, like, a cost or something, but I can't remember what it is, so it probably isn't very high.

The Dread Council returns to Temis's manor, and Xal can feel the enmity from the Tree. It seems kind of pissed that they jacked up a vithi. Saghir and Xal tell the dread council thanks for the tea, but they're going to roll out, and they do, aboard *The Fist*.

See ya! Good luck with the Tree. Hope it works out.

They leave Ena behind, mostly so that she can spend time with Liloth, while keeping an eye on Xal's interests.

Li has dinner with her mother, who reveals that Khonsu's elder children are awake and have come to the mountain. She thinks the elder wyrm has gradually weakened their culture over many generations and talks about how many more guards there were three generations ago, during her childhood.

She also reveals that the people of the heavens have cut contact. They stand alone. Li's dad and his people fear that the mountain is compromised. Yikes.

In the next chapter, Li is at a Kem tourney, but instead of fun, it's terrifying. She can see many people around her dream-bound, but one kid, Haitao, also seems aware of them. He totally won't be important later.

Xal and Saghir reach the Ashwall and try to find an ashrunner that will take them to the capital. It isn't very effective. No one is impressed by them, and all these unliving pirates laugh when they try to act tough.

Eventually, Xal and Saghir find an old couple with a small ashrunner, Tap and Ann, who will take them to the first city in the Ashlands. From there, they might be able to hire passage further. Before they leave, the Steward Celeste tracks them down and warns them that they're going to get ambushed by the Stewards Dalanthar, Amarigen, and Zaro while out there.

She knows Xal is vital to the cycle's survival and says that others feel the same.

Celeste takes a covenant to Xal, so now they can pray to each other, sort of like walkie-talkies, but with worship.

We get a scene showing Dalanthar's super-cool ashrunner, which is way higher in magitech level than anything in this era. Amarigen carries the ashstaff which—wait for it—lets you control the ash.

Flash back to Totarius, who dutifully makes an alliance with Lucretia, even though he doesn't know why Khonsu asked him to do it. You knew though. By this point, you realized that Totarius was going to be the candidate for the final demon soul and that Khonsu was maneuvering him into position.

Damn, you're smart.

And attractive.

Anyway, Totarius plans Erik's assassination, which they successfully pull off several chapters later. It requires them to distract Vhala and complete several other small side-quests before we get a cut scene with Erik dying. He kills a lot of the guards they bring, but eventually even Erik goes down.

We're sad. Sad-ish? Eh, I didn't really feel much when he died. I know who Erik one day becomes in *The Magitech Chronicles* and will always have a soft spot for that person.

Back to Xal. They get ambushed by unliving pirates, and Xal predictably wrecks them since he's a literal god of combat. We don't give him very many encounters he can actually win easily, so he knows that something bad is coming.

They make it to Agora, the unliving city closest to the edge of the Ashlands, which suggests some sort of linguistic link with Agora for the geeks among you.

Predictably, Xal and Saghir can't find passage and have to give up. Tap and Ann agree to take them back to Agora, where they can board *The Fist* and try to come up with a new plan. They start sailing back, but an ash storm rises out of nowhere, and they are forced to seek shelter in an abandoned city.

The Stewards spring their ambush, and Amarigen uses the ashstaff to fling Saghir to the bottom of the ash sea. That's a big game over right there. Most readers were confused. I don't kill main characters like that, and Erik just died.

Was I going through a divorce? Had I been replaced with an AI ghostwriter? Or, far more likely, did Saghir have some way to save himself? Search your feelings. You already know the truth.

Not only did Saghir get out, but he did it by using a divine binding spell stored in Ikadra, which I've been mentioning *at least* once a book since he got the staff in *God of the Sands*, along with constantly mentioning the spider mountain's location so we could put it in the right place.

I have been waiting, and waiting, and waiting for this moment.

So now Saghir has a spider mountain as a mount, and it digs him out of the ash. He gets revenge on Amarigen and Zaro and steals the ashstaff, so now he has that too.

Meanwhile, Xal makes it to the capital. He's kind of pissed because he thinks Saghir is dead, so he executes Dalanthar and takes the shield. Along the way, we meet an unliving noble from the Elentian Empire. Sanur is one of the shamed and serves as our tour guide.

He takes Xal to the Imperator, who is wearing the Crown of Command. He also claims to be the best sorcerer in the entire cycle, but his clothing is literally moldy. How good of a sorcerer can you be if you don't have spells to clean and preserve clothes? Dude hasn't showered in four centuries.

Xal heads downstairs to his final tomb and finds that it is a tomb of Rei. Rei is the god who created the Stewards, which means Xal created the Stewards. In addition to being a super powerful *void* god, he's also a super powerful *life* god. Coolness ++.

It seems kind of power-gamey, like the sort of backstory that would make your GM roll his eyes and then hand it back and tell you to do it over again. But Reeva, our resident titan of Mary Sue-ness, shows up and tells Xal it was his doing.

He merged the souls so that Xal will help him win the war against Gortha. Xal sees a vision of Rei and Reeva and just how much they hated each other. Rei was inserted into the cycle by the creator, Om, and Reeva is still butt-hurt millions of years later.

Xal is left with a big powerup and Dalanthar's shield. He rolls out with Tap and Ann, and they run into Saghir. Oh, they're also fabulously wealthy because the Imperator let them take his entire treasure trove. They can afford cheese on their burger every time now.

They roll out of the Ashlands, and Saghir wisely uses the ashstaff to gather huge amounts of ash all over the spider mountain, which they use offensively against the blood wood. They march back to find the capital under siege, but they break it easily because the Tree is really not prepared for a storm of ash or a spider mountain.

I mean who is?

Meanwhile, Crispus sends Tissa to Calmora to assassinate Li. When Tissa arrives, she's paired with Niu, who badly wants Li dead. The trouble is that Li's father evacced her to the Halo, where she can't be reached.

Li gains *life* magic and comes back down to the mountain, where Tissa ambushes her. They brawl and argue about Xal, then Niu intervenes. Tissa gets annoyed and kills Niu, then offers fealty to Li, who accepts. The two are suddenly on the same side.

Xal rolls out on *The Fist* to pick up his girlfriend, but when he gets there, a dragon crotch-kicks him, so he never gets that heroic I-saved-you moment. Before reaching Calmora, almost casually, Xal destroys most of the Ghost Fleet.

This terrifies Totarius, who is aboard the Ghost Fleet, and he flees to join Lucretia. He begs her for power, and she merges him with Xa, the last demon soul, the oldest and most powerful. The merging is good.

Villain side just got a whole lot stronger.

Xal counters by getting the band back together. They bring Ephram and Macha to the spirit world, fetch Erik's soul, and bring it back.

They still need someone who can resurrect him, so they bring Li to Gateway where she briefly meets Xal's ex and acquires *water* magic. Once she has it, she's able to bring Erik back, and then Xal promotes him to Steward of Justice.

Our crew heads to the last place where they are safe, Olivantia, where they take shelter with Ducius and the dread council.

The book closes with Totarius capturing Ashianna and the Praetor, which he is only able to do because Ducius gave him a ring that controls Gavius. Gavius sets the trap, and Ashianna walks right into it.

Flash to Erik joining the Stewards in a pantheon meeting and realizing they're chumps, and he's going to need to whip them into shape.

The epilogue has Lakshmi enter Khonsu's court and warn the dragon that the godswar has heated up. Elder gods are being dispatched to slay him. Tuat and Volos, the brother assassins, are coming....

# PROLOGUE

Celeste gripped her golden staff in one hand, the power thrumming within the sentient eldimagus, then stepped from her fluttering pavilion, once white but now stained grey by soot, torn in many places, some hastily repaired while more recent damage had been ignored.

At first, the mages had spared time and attention to repairing their tents, but the invasions into the Swamps of Orlon were ceaseless. There were no breaks, and the longer a mage, even she, fought, the more of themselves they gave to the cause.

She strode up the well-worn footpath to the top of the adjacent hill, dominated by a mighty cypress tree, picking past scorched and blackened bits of the trail as she reached where the morning sun already stretched. It warmed her, even as the sight below chilled her soul.

Normally the shell protecting the Great Cycle was completely invisible to all save the most powerful of scrying fields, yet here it was obvious to the naked eye, simply from its lack in the area known as the Rent.

A towering crack split the swamp before her, a crack in reality, a fissure not unlike those used by *void* mages whenever they wished to skirt the rules of travel. Through that crack lay unbroken darkness, impenetrable but far from empty.

Row upon row of demonic soldiers, bonecrushers mostly, pushed through the gap, attempting to invade reality at the behest of their dark masters. Hundreds poured through, only to be met by a withering storm of fire, void, earth, and wind.

Demon after demon died, but for each one that fell, another strode through the Rent. And while the demons were endless, the mages were not. The demons pressed out and gained ground, fanning out past the gap to seize a bit of the swamp.

It proved to be a ruse, which made Celeste smile. A male voice bellowed orders, and the sky darkened under the weight of arrows. Enfilade volleys converged on the demons, slaughtering them from the safety of several nearby hilltops, all flanking the path the demons were forced to take.

Yet arrows, too, had limits. Every archer began the day with forty. Most ended with none, then had to return to camp to fletch as many as they could for the next day. It was sustainable, if barely.

But what if something drew her away from this place? What if the looming godswar began in earnest? She would be needed in many places at once, yet nowhere else was as important as this. What did the war matter if the demons gained a beachhead here? They would link up with the princes, and reality would fall.

The Rent must be held.

To her great surprise, the flow of demons slackened. Cries sounded from the Rent, horrible demonic cries, thick with fear. Something was slaughtering them from the rear. What could possibly challenge demons at the heart of their strength?

A chill worked down her spine despite the morning sun as the chaos around the Rent died away. Mages ceased their casting, and archers lowered their bows. Blessed silence fell for the first time in months as the defenders watched the Rent in horrible expectation.

Long moments passed as streamers of smoke rose from the demonic corpses littering the passage through the Rent. Finally, an eternity later, a pair of human-sized figures strode from the blackness, a precise three paces from each other, each holding a blade in one hand.

The man on the right had white hair and a grey blade like a hole in reality. It burned to look upon, and Celeste sensed the blade's kinship with *spirit* even as she made out the screaming faces along the blade. Delicate wings flared behind the white-haired man's back, and she realized he was a dragon in hybrid form, a thing spoken of often in the histories but rarely witnessed in her lifetime. Most of the dragons old enough to master such a feat had departed the cycle, and those remaining were slumbering, save for Khonsu and his oldest children.

The figure on the left matched in most ways, his scales the same mottled white, but his blade a shard of jagged ice, one that exuded hunger like heat shimmers around a fire, ready to devour anything and everything it touched.

Both elder wyrms were covered in blood and gore, the result of slaughtering so many demons as they entered the cycle. They walked alone, the demons clearly deciding that discretion might be the better part of valor.

The power rising from both dragons was immense, and in their shadows, she observed the size of their draconic bodies. Should either one assume their true form, they would be large enough to grapple Khonsu, a true avatar such as had not been seen in the cycle since the Exodus.

Celeste gathered her courage, then summoned her magic, pure will in this instance, and levitated from her hilltop to place herself directly in the path of the approaching elder wyrms.

The pair altered neither their path nor pace, slowly approaching Celeste, then stopping a dozen cubits away. The white-haired one stepped forward and delivered a bow that spoke of a reverence for tradition and custom.

"Greetings, human," the dragon rumbled, the voice far too deep to emanate from such a throat. "I am called Tuat, wyrm father of *spirit*. This is my brother, Volos. My brethren have appointed us to dispense justice. We have come to hunt our brother, Khonsu, wyrm father of *dream*. We seek permission to enter the cycle for this purpose."

Tuat delivered another bow, then stepped back and sheathed his sword. Celeste relaxed as the painful weapon was hidden from view, but that only highlighted the dangers of its wielder and his strange brother.

Her staff thrummed in her hand, and Celeste instinctively sought the words it offered. "On behalf of the cycle, on behalf of the anointed, you are granted entry to pursue your quest, until its completion, and for no longer."

"At that time," the other brother spoke, "my brother and I will depart the cycle in peace, as per the accord struck during the Exodus. We seek only to redress this wrong and will abide by the ancient dictates while within the cycle."

"Then we have an accord," Celeste spoke, the words pulled again from the staff. "On behalf of the cycle, on behalf of the anointed, I grant you permission to enter the cycle with your full power for the duration of your quest, but for no other purpose nor personal gain."

A sudden pulse pushed outward from the staff, the magic and will far beyond what she herself or even the staff was capable of. For an instant, it touched something greater, the same Catalyst the crown commanded, and used that reality-defining power to create the exception that would grant these gods entrance.

The pulse shot up into the sky, covering the land in all directions. Celeste stared in awe as she realized that it would touch the entire cycle, not just the life realm. Every god and every mage of strength and discernment would have felt the act. They would all know that elder gods had entered the cycle...the game had changed.

Guttural screams sounded in the distance, and a new army of chitinous demons burst from the Rent and began their assault. Celeste's battlemages renewed their rain of death, groaning under their burdens once more as they defended the gap in the cycle that would allow their enemies entrance.

"My thanks." Tuat nodded, then he and his brother leapt into the sky, pulled aloft by powerful wingbeats.

At roughly a hundred cubits, Tuat wrenched his painful blade from its scabbard and slashed at the sky, parting it like silk and exposing a pathway into the spirit realm. He and his brother dove through, and the slash in the veil vanished, sealing the two gods within the spirit realm and away from her magical senses.

Could they truly remove Khonsu?

The other Stewards must be warned, but she already knew forcing them to action would be all but impossible. They were too divided, too bitter, and too ossified. They would not stir to action in the needed way...all save Erik, their newest member. He still thought like a mortal. If she could recruit the young Steward of Justice, then she might galvanize the others into action.

He could be found in Olivantia, near Xal, whom it appeared she might have to seek out once more. Prophecy or coincidence? The elder gods were arriving. The first pair had been benevolent, but what if something more sinister arrived? What if the titan of the void or one of her monstrous children forced their way inside?

Only one thing could defend them. Only one thing could preserve the cycle. A champion needed to don the Crown of Command and tame the Catalyst it controlled. Celeste had some idea of what was required to do that, but only an idea. Jhordil had worn the crown but never mastered it, and thus she had never witnessed such a thing.

The ancient histories listed many rituals and spoke of anointment, but she had no idea yet what that entailed. Xal must be made anointed, or another found, and placed where they could push back the forces arrayed against them.

Would that it were Conclave, but Celeste sighed and leapt into the sky. She morphed into wind, vanishing from sight as she merged with the weather, rising into the sky and accelerating toward Olivantia.

Time. They needed more time.

Yet there was no more to be found.

The godswar had arrived, and they were not prepared.

# 1

## NO MORE TIME

I stepped past my writing desk and the heavy tome I was using for a journal, out onto the balcony of the quarters Saghir had fashioned for Li and me near the top of the spider mountain's central peak. We were above the clouds and flights of birds, and below them our army, if it could be called that.

In the distance, to the east and north, sprawled the blood wood, teaming with hostile life. Countless eyes loomed under the foliage or amidst the branches, every squirrel, owl, bear, and na'elfen consumed and focused on spreading their contagion.

That was why we had come. What we were building to oppose at the moment.

More followers arrived at our growing encampment daily, and even from there I spied Erik's blazing blue sword and golden shield as he bellowed orders. A full legion of cadets stood before him, the very first of their people to learn to fight in the ancient Elentian way, the same way Caw had trained me.

"You've got that pensive look again." Warmth pressed

against my back, and Li's arms encircled my waist. "You need to enjoy yourself, or at least relax a hair. Even when we're playing Kem, you're a thousand leagues away."

"Nothing has tried to kill me in over a week." I turned to slip an arm around Li's waist and lent her my attention. "The longer we stay in one place, the less likely that is to remain true." I knelt and kissed her briefly, then released her and stroked her hair. "We aren't safe here. And if we stay, then I cede all of Hasra to Totarius."

Li gave an understanding nod, then released me and moved to the small stone table where she prepared her daily tea. Fire and water flowed from her hands in equal measure around the cup she'd left out the night before, and the familiar scent of herbs filled the chamber.

I took up my part of the morning ritual and crossed to kneel at the baking stone I'd erected, where I began to prepare the morning's sweet cakes, the more edible cousin to what I'd grown up with. The fire I'd summoned crackled in the hearth, a lump of smoldering magma that offered a rocky scent I rather enjoyed.

"I have to tend to my home as well," Li murmured as she picked up the kettle and filled two stone mugs. "I know I should be more focused on that, but some days the best I can manage is focusing on the next step."

"I should be less focused on the horizon." I cupped the cake in my hand and flipped it, the heat pleasantly warming my palm as my resistance bled off most of it. "We need to win Ducius's war before we can tend to Calmora. If I thought we had a prayer, I'd ask Saghir to—"

"Now that you've mentioned me," my furry friend interrupted as the ratkin rippled through the window, his sketchbook under one arm, a fantastical rendition of Alsara poking out from one side, "I can pretend as if I were not eavesdropping. Are there enough to share? I've grown rather accustomed to them."

"Of course." I smiled covertly at Li, who returned her own quickening my blood. I broke eye contact as my cheeks flushed, then slapped the first cake down on the end of the stone stable. "First portion is yours, my friend. The farmers in Olivantia have fields of wheat a dozen leagues across, and that's just one farm. Once that's harvested, we'll be able to eat for months, and that's being conservative. Those that planted it are no longer alive to protest."

"I suppose that is the problem with having so few remaining mouths to feed." Saghir landed next to the cake and used a bit of air to slice off a piece, then levitated the sizzling cake up to his snout. "Our army will grow once we depart these lands, and I cannot be away soon enough. If not for the obligation of having joined the council of dreadlords, I'd already have said my polite goodbyes. I loathe this dreary land."

"We have nowhere else to go." I snatched off the second cake and tossed it to Li, who caught it midair with her magic, creating a plate of air beneath the pastry so that it hovered near where her tea rested in the air. "And we still have the Tree to deal with. That's not an evil I want spreading at our back, and we owe Macha a sapling."

Shouts came from outside, and Saghir's ear cocked. My tattoos and Li's both cooled as our sensed activated and we, too, picked up the sounds.

"Ducius is arriving." Li spoke first. Her expression soured, and she rose to her feet with a sigh, her breakfast obediently following. "I'd rather not be here when he arrives. The more I spend time with him, the less I wish to tolerate more. I'm going to gather my students and begin the day's lessons."

"Of course." I leaned in for a brief embrace as she passed.

"How many students have you accumulated?" Saghir's expression brightened, and he removed Ikadra from a void pocket. "I would be happy to demonstrate greater paths or handle any other magical classes you wish taught."

"I'm dividing them by aspect," Li explained as she wound a leather tie into her hair, then tucked her ponytail behind her head. "Right now basic history, literacy, and logic are most important. That and self-defense. Once I have the new dedicates at that level, they'll be ready for you. Right now I'm just building you up in their minds. They're terrified. They know you control the mountain."

I nodded along at her words, agreeing with her explanation. These people needed to understand who they were and how to take care of themselves. After that, they could determine their own destinies.

"There he is." I nodded out the window as Ducius and Temis floated down from his airship, the *Return*, which was so sleek and polished compared to *The Fist*, which currently hovered over Erik's encampment under Ena's watchful command. "If you want to avoid him, I'd get—"

My girlfriend vanished from sight, only a hint of her laughter and perfume left as she her presence retreated. By the time she'd made it away, knocking sounded at the door below.

I vaulted the railing and landed in a crouch in the entryway, then rose to open the door and admit the pair of dreadlords. By the time I'd done so, both men had removed their cloaks.

"You came directly?" I raised an eyebrow at Ducius, his golden hair freshly shorn along half his scalp, the new fashion that had caught on in the Olivantian capital. "I thought you left Temis to tend to the war."

"I did." The smug dreadlord extended a hand, then withdrew a dark wooden staff from a void pocket. "But circumstances have changed enough that an impromptu council meeting is required. Nothing formal, but if we can add Master Saghir? Ah, there he is."

Ducius turned to glance upward as the ratkin floated down to join us and then landed upon my shoulder, Ikadra still clutched in his hand, the sapphire muted and dark at the moment.

"Now that you are here," Ducius continued, shifting to take both myself and Temis into the conversation, "we have enough to form a rough quorum that the others will respect. I've come with dire news. Valys has truly fallen. Totarius rules in all but name, yet his son is free to rampage and ruin. And Crispus is coming to Valys, which puts him directly upon our border. That move is meant to be a threat, one I take seriously."

"They're risking war to get to Xal?" Temis cocked his head, then pursed his lips as he struggled for understanding. "I don't understand the logic. They have to be depleted from their own civil war. What purpose does attacking another nation so swiftly serve? Do you really believe they'd attack us? This has to be defensive in nature. Perhaps he is pacifying Valys."

"That's part of it." I turned to the blood wood with a sigh, staring out the window at the ruined land the consumed had left. This nation needed us if it were to have any prayer of dealing with the Tree, but doing so meant I couldn't deal with Totarius. Clearly he'd taken advantage of that. I turned back to the impromptu council. "Hasra needs a target. They need a villain, one to blame all problems upon. They need to focus the people's anger, and few things will do that as neatly as a nation of dreadlords."

"It is not us they come for." Ducius gave me a deprecating smile, as if to say I should have already seen this. "They come for you. You are their bogey. Their demon in the night. They fear you. You slew a Steward. Now they place every ill at your feet. From Valys to Enestius to Hasra, all know you are the worst sort of villain—disloyal and you eat children. I'm told the same is true in Calmora, though I lack adequate spies there. The few I had have gone quiet."

"What of Ashianna?" I asked, my mind turning to the Praetor and his family.

"Ashianna is still in custody, as is her father. It isn't clear what the Imperator will do with them." Ducius cocked his head. "My spies also tell me that Jun is heavy with child. It's quite possible that when she gives birth, she and Darius will be summoned."

That caught my attention, and I eyed him sharply. That was the second time he'd mentioned Jun, and so far as I knew, he had no connection to her. I disliked his interest and wondered again at the motivation. Unfortunately the smooth-talking dreadlord had already moved on.

"Crispus and his father have consolidated power, while mine rots in a cell." Ducius rolled his eyes in a way that suggested he blamed his father for the fate. "If you do not take action swiftly, they will ensure everyone under their control reviles you and worships them. Even your pet Steward will not change that."

I considered that briefly. My journals could be used to persuade people if I could get the truth out, but too few would read them. I needed another way.

I was about to reply when a force quite unlike other magics I'd seen rippled over me. A towering wave of power and will, gold and brilliant like the sun, shone past us. It was so tall it reached the very shell protecting the cycle—I was certain of it.

As it passed, I was left with an understanding. Two elder gods had been granted entry to the cycle, using divine authority woven into its very center, the place I'd recently visited. The place where I'd learned that I was both a god of light and darkness.

But I hadn't made the cycle. I hadn't made this. I had no idea what was meant by anointed, but I suspected that I knew who could tell me—Reevanthara, assuming the titan would listen.

"What just happened?" Temis whispered as we joined the army below in staring upward.

"The godswar has officially begun," I provided, my hand falling to Narlifex's hilt, the blade's eagerness clear in the way it thrummed in the dragonscale scabbard. "Elder gods have arrived. More will be coming. We are out of time."

"Then you had better resolve this war swiftly." Ducius nodded through the window at the blood wood. "I have detached Liloth to aid you and Temis while I return to the Valysian border and see what can be done there. Contact me when you have news?"

"I will." I nodded back, my gaze briefly touching Saghir's. I found my frustration mirrored there. We had no swift way to resolve this war, and we needed to. I couldn't just linger there while elder gods entered the cycle doing who knew what.

## 2

## MOBILIZATION

Ducius departed, thankfully, but Temis remained. Liloth was nowhere to be seen, but I suspected she'd already headed to *The Fist* to seek out Ena as the pair had been denied any time together since the war had begun in earnest.

We threaded out the front door and down the walk, which led us to Li's squat stone kamiza atop the first large hill. About a dozen students had gathered outside in neat lines and were drilling the same morning exercises I'd seen Li perform all the way back in Hasra in House Celeste. So odd that we were now the adults.

"You look tired if you don't mind my saying so." Temis eyed me sidelong as the cultured dreadlord fell into step next to me.

Saghir sat on my shoulder, but I assumed the comment was directed at me, so I answered it. "I was up the better part of the night writing."

"Oh?" Temis raised a delicate eyebrow, his handsome face the very image of Olivanticus, his grandfather.

"I'm penning my memoirs." I hated how pompous that

sounded and quickened my step as we headed up toward the kamiza. "I want to recount everything for my next incarnation. Now that I know these memories and this story will be useful, I want to make sure I give my replacement the kind of support I was denied."

"A noble goal," Saghir broke in. "I've been reading over your shoulder in the evenings, and I am quite impressed. Your rhetoric and storytelling are...deceptive? They draw you in and refuse to let go."

Our conversation trailed off as the students bowed to Li as one, then came streaming back down the hill, laughing as they separated into groups of excited friends. I recognized their expressions...the excitement of being dismissed from class early with unexpected free time.

Li came after, still panting from exertion but smiling after her charges. "They've come a long way. I hate to dismiss them, but they're unmanageable after whatever happened to the cycle. Did you feel that pulse? Any idea what caused it?"

It hadn't occurred to me that other mages would feel it differently than I had. I'd seen the crown and had been to the Catalyst that powered it. Was that why I could detect the specific words? Or was it the fact that I housed Rei's soul?

"Two elder gods entered," I explained, earning shocked glances from all three friends, and I was glad to include Temis in that number. "I don't know who or why, but I heard a voice when the pulse passed."

"The connection makes sense." Li nodded as she fell into step on the opposite side of me from Temis. "The question is what do we do about it?"

"It's ignited a sense of urgency." I sighed under my breath as I led my growing group down the hill toward Erik, then below him toward Macha's encampment, where the

Fomori largely kept to herself. I would need both for what was to come. "We need to draft and execute a plan to push the forest back even further. We need to deliver the kind of blow that will make this nation safe for a generation, and do it swiftly. Then I want to be away from this place. Calmora needs liberation. Lukantria has mercenaries, and we just happen to have an ocean of wealth to shower them with. Being shackled here may cause us the war."

"So you're leaving us." Temis's stilted speech told me the dreadlord's feelings had been hurt. "I had hoped you considered yourselves a part of this nation. Saghir especially, as he joined the council. Our fates are one. This is your home now, or it could be if you would let it."

"I can't." I glanced up toward the central peak, but Ducius's ship had already departed. "I think you know why."

"I don't trust him either." Temis gave a frustrated snarl under his breath, a curse I couldn't quite make out. "I don't precisely regret allying with Ducius, but I can see it costing us, and that cost will only rise. I'm told it was the same in my grandfather's day. A great man, undoubtedly, but one whose ego and lack of moral character forever poisoned his legacy."

"You already know how I feel about him." I'd never heard quite that shade of venom in Li's voice before.

Only Saghir kept his opinion to himself, though I did catch him watching Temis. We were allies, but the lack of trust was impossible to miss. I'd wager Temis was well aware of it, even if he wasn't reacting. Was Saghir considering leaving the council? Was that even possible?

The tension thickened as we approached the drilling legion before us, led by Erik's fierce cries. I was impressed by how far they'd come. They weren't so different from the trash legion in that they lacked armor, but Erik had provided every soldier with a long spear and a stout shield, each designed to lock together in the Elentian way, though their owners seemed completely ignorant of that fact.

They stood alone, each warrior fighting by himself, unconcerned about his neighbors. I recognized the lack of experience and knew Erik would cure it soon enough. Elentia had not been built in a day, it was said.

"Vhala, lead them until I return. Drill the phalanx until they can finally do it right," Erik boomed, then stepped aside as the dark-skinned companion rose from where she'd been watching along the wall and moved to assume the position Erik had vacated.

Erik trotted over to us, then rested his shield in the snow and lowered his voice to a comfortable level. "I figured that pulse would get you down off the mountain. Any idea what it was?"

"Gods entering the elder cycle." I shivered, and not from the cold. "Two so far. More could come. That makes finishing the war here a priority, and I wanted your estimates on time for your troops."

"Two weeks?" Erik glanced slowly back at his men, then turned back to me before speaking again so they could not see his face. "I could shorten that to a week if I had to. At this point most of it is self-sustaining. They'll train each other. What concerns me more is equipment. We don't have enough steel, and none of it is enchanted. The consumed will cut them down like wheat, even if they hold a line. Spears are a start, and we do have mages, but we're well short of being Knights of the Dawn."

"I'll see what Ducius can secure." I resisted glancing in the direction the dreadlord had vanished. "He's been claiming for a while now smiths are working day and night in the capital, but I haven't seen anything come from it yet. For what I have planned, we may not need the weaponry. I'm thinking about a raid."

"Oh?" Erik raised an eyebrow. I knew I had his interest.

"Before I give you the details...I have news." I wanted his mind on the task, but he needed to know. "Ashianna and her father have been taken. Crispus has taken the throne, and your father has been arrested."

"I see why you didn't lead with that." Erik gave a weary sigh, but the new weight did not bend his posture in the slightest. "I'll need to think on how to handle that. For now, I can plan a raid, but I need to understand the objective and how you plan to get it out. Or are we strictly focused on casualties?"

"We're after a tangible target." I glanced further down the hill at the cluster of pine trees where Macha had taken shelter. "I want to retrieve the sapling we promised her. I figure that should kick the hive, so to speak, and that's where you come in. They have to respond and could well attack the mountain en masse. When they do, your troops need to be able to hold their own."

"I make no promises." Erik looked back at his legion once more. "I'm proud of them, but we need equipment, and there's no substitute for experience."

"That we can remedy soon enough." I nodded at Erik and he fell into step with us as we continued down the hill. "Let's go get Macha and plan this thing properly."

# INTERLUDE I - TOTARIUS

Totarius—he thought of himself as that name, a fitting personality for this incarnation—entered the realm of dreams and waited. Here he was less than. His powers weak and muted. The very suggestion would have sent him into a towering rage a year ago, when the dream was the sum of his powers.

He'd used the gifts Lakshmi's Hoard bestowed upon him, but those powers were not his. Not truly. Nor could he use them against Khonsu. The wyrm was the dream titan's champion in this realm. Every titan would have one. A proxy to wage this war without risk to themselves.

Those memories lurked within him, yet when he reached for them, they vanished like smoke. He could sense the shape of them but not experience them properly.

The maelstrom of chaos around him did not shift to reflect his thoughts, of course. Even he possessed such basic mastery here. That meant when the dream began to shift, he knew he was being pulled by the wyrm.

Totarius gave himself over to that pull and tumbled across an imaginary map of the world, up and up into the sky, like an airship making for the shell itself. He stopped rising near a bank of clouds so large it could conceal an adult wyrm, and within that bank stirred a pair of enormous lantern eyes, slitted as only a dragon's could be.

"Hello, demon prince. I see you have fully realized your destiny," Khonsu rumbled, thunder in the clouds, his tone more respectful than it had been when Totarius had been a mortal. Perhaps even a touch worried about his reaction, that he might carry a grudge.

Totarius allowed the moment to stretch before finally speaking. Here he had no power, but at the same time... he had all of it. "Indeed I have, mighty wyrm. I have come because of the force we both detected. Elder gods have come and have been accepted by the cycle. Those gods are not here to end me. Their mandate, as I understand such things, only allows them to fulfill a chosen mission. Have you any thoughts as to what that might be?"

"Tuat," the cloud rumbled, the eyes flashing purple-pink. "And Volos. My cousins from the spirit flight. Both are ancient, and unlike me, neither has ever truly created a brood. They cannot be bothered with offspring. They are too busy killing. They hunt gods. Elder gods. Especially elder gods who disparage dragons."

And there it was. Totarius raised a trembling hand to his breast, and it came away wet with blood. Hot pain wrenched through him as a blade punched through his chest, the blade forged from a terrible grey metal, its surface full of screaming souls. Souls he knew were imprisoned in the blade.

The blade and wound vanished as if they'd never been, but the message was clear, even if Totarius could not remember. At some point, one of his incarnations had been struck down by either Tuat or Volos or both. Khonsu was trying to put him off guard, to regain the initiative.

"I lack those memories." Totarius did not disguise the frustration in his voice. "You do not need to convince me they are mutual enemies. You are an ally, and they have come to eliminate you. Do you require aid? What can we do to stymie this threat so that we can focus on conquest of the cycle? I believe we're both aware of how limited our remaining time is before more and more gods flock to our location. We must end this war swiftly."

"Let us clarify our alliance." Khonsu blinked from inside the cloud, thunder rumbling once more. "I seek magic, and to escape the cycle. I am not often transparent in my motivations, but in this instance it is important you know I do not seek to preserve the cycle, merely pillage what I can."

"Then you suspect what I seek to do." Totarius hated being so direct and sensed the wyrm felt the same. "Both of us understand the urgency. If you are telling me that you can handle these assassins, then I will focus on the raising of avatars and the destruction of the cycle."

"We have an accord, then." Lightning flashed, blinding and total, the thunder deafening. "You will not see me again within the cycle, but I have a feeling we will be drawn together once more before the end."

Once it faded, the wyrm was gone, and Totarius was left hovering in the sky. Would Khonsu truly depart the cycle of his own accord?

He could not help but smile. Their positions had reversed in less than a year, and now the wyrm faced greater threats than he did. Meanwhile Totarius could safely raise an avatar from the southern ocean, while his puppet son solidified control over the Hasran Imperium. Enestius, Hasra, and tiny Ildonis were all firmly in his pocket.

Now Valys had fallen as well, in name at least. It would need to be actively pacified, but that could be accomplished swiftly, so long as Totarius ensured his son was aware of the strategy. The boy was cunning enough, but laziness and self-confidence had ruined the boy.

Once Valys was dealt with, they could finally converge on Gateway, without worrying about threats at their back. That was the real key, as its conquest would remove the Heart of Water from any potential enemies, while also fracturing the kodachine horde back into competing tribes. A victory he would enjoy, but one to be considered after other problems had been dealt with.

Totarius closed his eyes in the dream and awoke in his own bed, in the Hasran palace, his quarters one level below his son's. A glance out the window at the sky ensured he had not wasted too much time. It was not yet eleventh bell, which meant his son would still be awake and either drinking or whoring, or both.

He rose from bed, freshened himself in the wall mirror, grabbed a flagon of wine, and departed his quarters. Laughter echoed through the corridors as the party spilled out into smaller gatherings, only those of true standing allowed anywhere near the throne room itself, where the real players met.

Totarius delivered a few nods to random lords, all people he did not know and had no association with. Three were wise enough to coyly return that nod and gave away nothing. Those would go far and make much of what he had given them. The others eyed him in confusion, long after he passed them.

It did not take long to make the source of the music and the bulk of the laughter. He entered to find his son atop the throne, a wench on his lap, his hands encircling the woman's tiny waist. That did not prevent Crispus from drinking. The dark-skinned beauty poured rivulets of wine down her chest, and the Imperator greedily drank while onlookers laughed.

Yet there was a nervous edge to the laughter, a manic need to be having more fun than your neighbors, to not be spotted as the one ruining the party. Totarius glanced at the ceiling and found what he sought. A half-dozen new heads had been added to the old, all magically preserved so they did not rot, and each would forever carry the victim's terrified expression the moment before their head was separated from their body.

"My son!" Totarius boomed as he strode in the center of the room. Dancers and sycophants scattered, leaving him a wide vantage. Near silence fell, as all watched to see how the Imperator would react. "I see you are celebrating. Would that I possessed your youth. You make an old wolf proud." He raised his flagon and drank deeply, the wine staining his tunic in a way his old self would have enjoyed, but that he now found wasteful.

There was no need to demonstrate wealth by destroying your own possessions. That spoke of a desperate need to prove oneself to others.

"Father!" Crispus shot to his feet, and the woman atop him tumbled off, thankfully caught by courtiers standing next to the throne, who helped her back to her feet, apparently unharmed. "It is a true pleasure to see you, old wolf or no. I received a letter two days ago. Do you truly think I should relocate the court to Valys? Take the Praetor's palace for my own?"

How could the boy ask such a question in front of so many eyes? Was he truly absent cunning and self-preservation? Or was he shaping public opinion and rumor, getting them to think he was? Totarius came to neither conclusion but acted as if the slip were intentional.

"I do." Totarius enjoyed another long pull from his wine before continuing, which bought him the time to formulate a proper answer. "Going to Valys sends two important messages. First, it tells the nobles who supported you there that they were wise to do so. You may punish those who conspire against you and reward those who helped present the city."

"Wise counsel." Crispus crooked a finger, and his courtesan brought the wine flagon once more. No tester. No caution. The boy simply drank, then grinned down at Totarius. "And the second reason?"

"The future." Totarius folded his arms, letting his body language show his son they'd shifted to a serious topic, without shaming the boy as his old self would have done. "The necromancers are rising once more. Olivanticus and his dreadlords will come again, and when they do, Valys must be ready to oppose them. Your arrival there allows you to garrison the old border forts and begin preparing for war. It will also make your final move a surprise."

"What—? Ahh! Final move. As we've discussed. I see what you mean." Crispus gave a wink, but the emotion never reached the eye that stayed open. It was an act then. A masterful one. "Can I interest you in some meat? Or a wench?"

Totarius shook his head, then waved absently, still smiling wistfully. "I'm too old for such things. I long for my bed. Good night, my son. Enjoy all the rewards you have earned."

Totarius left to the sound of his son's booming laughter, a bit heartened that Crispus appeared to be playing the game of rumors absent skill. Did the court suspect the truth of the "final move" they had been discussing?

The hammer would need to fall upon Gateway soon. The treasury was empty, and even Enestius's vaunted wealth would be stretched thin in the coming days. They needed coin. They needed fire dust. They needed slaves.

In addition to the Heart of Water, Gateway possessed all three, and if his son was as skilled as he hoped, not a person in the west would see the hammer coming until it fell.

# 3

# DIVINE AID

Full twilight fell as I approached Macha's solitary position in a ravine between two of the spider mountain's craggy legs. Her temporary structure would vanish the moment the mountain stood, which was likely why she chose it. No one else had joined her, and since Ephram's departure the previous week, the Fomori had been completely alone.

It suited her. Or I thought it did.

Shouts came from a small copse of pine trees on one side of the ravine that had somehow managed to survive the mountain's frequent lumbering. A trio of figures exchanged blows, each combatant flowing between each other with grace and skill.

Ena launched a roundhouse kick that Macha dodged, then Ena flapped her wings to leap over the return back-hand Macha attempted. Tissa came in swinging Nefarius, the blade humming past Macha's nose as the taller Fomori hopped back.

Seeing them work wasn't just a thing of deadly beauty, but also showed that my forces—it was still weird calling them that—were growing. My allies had become friends in a way I'd not seen since we were all students back at the Hasran academy. They might all have looked different, Macha taller than a normal human, Tissa wreathed in darkness, her ghoul nature exposing itself, while Ena's demonic nature screamed itself in every attack. She didn't even carry a weapon anymore, just used claws, wings, tail, and fangs.

"Cease!" Macha bellowed then stepped back, lowering her guard in a way either Ena or Tissa could easily have taken advantage of.

Neither did, and both Ena and Tissa landed, panting as they pivoted to see us. Only then did I notice Liloth sitting under the trees, dark eyes glittering in the darkness as the na'elfen watched Ena hungrily.

"What brings you down out of your pretty fortress?" Macha boomed, though she wore a jovial smile. Her freckled cheeks were flushed from exertion and the cold.

"News and orders," I gave back as I stepped out ahead of my party and approached Macha.

Behind me, I noticed Li moving to stand with Tissa, Saghir on her shoulder, and Ena heading over to the trees to sit with Liloth. Only Erik stood with me as we approached Macha and found her much taller than either of us.

"You're growing by the day." Erik raised a blond eyebrow, still the arrogant prince, even while holding the artifact shield that proved he'd matured into a confident and fair leader. "Is there a limit? Eventually, we'll have to cart in wagons of sheep to keep you fed."

"I'd be worth the investment." Macha extended a hand, and Erik clasped it, the two of them vying for dominance for several moments before releasing each other and stepping back. "I can still scarcely believe we are allies. Strange times indeed." She turned to face me, her scarlet hair fluttering behind her as the frigid breeze increased. "What news? Can you explain that pulse earlier?"

"Gods entering the cycle." I shivered at the thought. "More are likely to come. That means we're out of time, and I need to start making brash, unpredictable moves. I hate that style of play, but if we want to win this match, I need to adapt."

"What mission do you have in mind?" The Fomori folded her arms and eyed me sternly. "You promised me a sapling."

"And that's exactly what we're going to deliver." I nodded over at Saghir atop Li's shoulder where he was laughing at some quip. "Saghir has located it. We know where it is. The consumed have fortified the wood but have done so in a way that clearly expects us to assault the Tree directly. If we instead go for the sapling, we'll likely have it before they realize what we're after. We plant the tree on this mountain, then retreat back to safety until we can find a way to get you home."

"They'll respond immediately," Erik countered as he planted the shield in the snow and leaned against it. "We can expect a—oh, that's why you want my legion to be ready. You're baiting them into an assault."

"Precisely." I peered off into the dense foliage, innocent enough from this vantage, just a simple redwood forest with trees that were entirely too large. They were studying me even as I studied them. "Now that we've discussed the plan, it's best to assume the Tree has spies and has learned of it. We'll be moving out in less than a bell, and I'd like both of you to accompany us for a the direct assault on the sapling. We'll use *The Fist* to get it back to the mountain."

"I am pleased to see you are a demon of your word." Macha nodded gratefully, then strode over to her pack, picked up an enormous bow, and began stringing it. "I will stand ready, and we will provide ample reason for them to seek vengeance."

A high wind began above, and I cocked an ear. It wasn't natural. I shifted into demon form, then leapt into the sky for a better look as I eased Narlifex from his sheath. I was aware of Ena rising behind me, close enough to support me should there be a threat.

Brilliance not unlike sunlight came from the west, all the brighter since true night had fallen, and then a glittering star fell in their direction. The magic filled me with familiarity. It had originated from me. From Rei. I relaxed, then drifted back to the ground as the blazing ball of light crashed into the snow.

When the light faded, Celeste stood there, golden hair flowing behind her white and blue parka, her staff of office cradled in her hand. The playful expression I'd hoped for was entirely lacking, and in its place, I found worry and...fear?

"Did I miss some sort of group missive?" Erik called as the Steward of Justice strode over to join his sister. "Or are you here for some other reason?"

"We'll have words, brother, but for now, I have come to speak to him." She nodded in my direction, so I stepped up to join them. Celeste's heavy gaze fell upon me. "You are aware of the elder gods entering? How much do you know?"

"Names." I gave a shrug. "Tuat. Volos. I know they are here to fulfill some quest, but not much else. It's all...feelings and vague impressions."

"I suspect I know why." Celeste gave a deep sigh. "Clarify will come once you are anointed, which involves some sort of ceremony or possibly a series of deeds, or both. We understand very little about the workings of the cycle, the actual magitech behind its construction. The closest I've come is a tome from Gateway that speaks of the process from the perspective of a god who became anointed."

"In the meantime, we have a war to prosecute. Do you need something specific from us? Who are these gods? And should we be concerned about them?" I tightened my grip around Narlifex.

"They are dragons and have come to police their own." Celeste's expression softened, which I took as a good sign. "I believe they may be able to kill Khonsu, or possibly drive him from the cycle at the very least."

"Truly?" Li blinked at that, hurrying over to join us and making it apparent she'd been eavesdropping. She ran over the snow, her feet not quite touching it as she sprinted over. "If Khonsu is gone, then all we have to deal with are his children. We could free my homeland. Bumut and the rebels are just waiting for some hope and a bit of support."

"Khonsu's children are formidable," I murmured, the wheels already turning in my mind. "Even as strong as these new gods are, I don't know what they can achieve unaided. We should help them. Our work here won't take more than a few bells. Maybe a day. Afterwards we should missive Tuat and Volos and request a meeting. We help them get what they want, Khonsu's head, and they help us free Calmora."

Li's smile quickened my heart, but then it fell just as suddenly when her expression tightened. "It may mean I have to leave. We might be parted again...unless there's a way we could all go?"

The hope killed me, but I forced cold calculations.

"Not yet." I turned toward the malevolent forest before us. "Not until we've dealt with matters here. We need Ducius and the council as strong allies at our backs. Then we can move on and start scooping up mercenaries in

Lukantria." I rested a hand on Li's shoulder. "We can send you and Celeste ahead to meet with Bumut and pave the way. Ready the rebellion, and when the time is right, together we'll drive the wyrms from your land. If we're lucky, they'll depart on their own once Khonsu is dead of fled."

She smiled at me, but I could tell she didn't quite believe it.

"I'm willing to help," Celeste added belatedly, and it occurred to me I'd assigned her a task without even asking. "The princess and I can accomplish much. I will missive the draconic brothers. In the meantime, I will aid you against the forest, if you will have me. The sooner we finish your work here, the sooner we can move on."

The last piece clicked into place. I had clarity now. The time had come for action, and I was more than ready.

# 4

## SKIRMISH

The time for war had come at last, and I welcomed it. I nodded to Saghir, who raised Ikadra, which prompted the spider mountain into motion. A rousing cheer rose first from Erik's legion, arrayed inside the courtyard of the lower keep Saghir had raised from the stone.

Answering cries came from divisions of archers, each split into groups of one hundred, all safely ensconced in towers lined with murder holes. There was simply no way to reach them short of magic or tearing down thick granite walls.

Those towers lined every approach. If someone were somehow able to climb one of the spider mountain's precarious limbs, they'd be met by an onslaught of death, both magical and mundane.

My senses also picked up the spectral haze shimmering along snowfields all up and down many slopes. Every last one contained dozens of wights under Temis's tight control. The sheer number awed me, a testament both to the Dagger of Olivanticus he'd recovered during our assault on the capital what felt a lifetime ago and to his own strength.

On top of that, we had *The Fist*, but I held that in reserve, as I planned to use it to carry the sapling once we'd uprooted it from the forest floor.

First, we had to get there.

I peered out at the forest, conscious of all the eyes upon me. Li stood to my right and Temis to my left, with Saghir atop my shoulder. Erik had declined and instead stayed below with his legion. Macha waited in the courtyard below, currently fletching more arrows.

Ena, Tissa, and Liloth were all close—of that, I had no doubt—but none were anywhere I could see them. I, on the other hand, stood out in the open and carried the weight of all those gazes.

I raised a hand, then lowered it. Saghir waggled his staff, and just like that, the mountain lurched forward, the land quaking beneath us. The tallest of the massive redwoods barely scraped the mountain's belly as we advanced into the forest.

The malevolence tightened around us as the forest woke, and in that moment, I began to suspect something. I'd been viewing the trees as separate entities, but more and more I wondered. Was this all one tree? All one organism? Is that how the tree knew everything so swiftly and why I experienced the same oppressive will no matter what part of the forest I interacted with?

I flared my wings above me and stood tall, a visible symbol. To my pleasant surprise, fresh worship trickled in. Three people took covenant in that moment, newcomers who'd arrived recently, likely seeking food and shelter, but were now beginning to believe, as the bulk of our followers did. I didn't demand it, yet my religion had spread among them.

If only I could find a way to spread that influence beyond my line of sight.

We marched deeper into the forest, the spider mountain's limbs crushing and splintering trees as it scuttled forward. That scuttling eventually slowed as the trees grew larger and more numerous, the way between them clogged by a new problem.

Vast twisted vines encircled many trees and spiraled through the forest, their length dotted with thorns sharp enough to skewer the unwary. We marched above it all, our followers safe as the mountain stepped gingerly over a particularly dense portion.

In the distance, I spied the tallest of the trees, the one I'd always assumed was some sort of leader. There was power there, certainly, but the will was no more oppressive than it had been.

The mountain abruptly shifted north, away from the tree.

"We approach the sapling," Saghir squeaked, his reedy voice almost lost even to my senses, drowned out by the endless quaking and felling of timber all around us. "Do you believe the Tree will suspect our true motives?"

"Undoubtedly." I leaned on the railing and scanned the forest to the east, the heart of the wood. "We've spent a lot of time planning for this. Let's hope our defenses are sufficient."

"They would be," Tissa whispered from behind me, in the shadows, "if you would allow us to use all the tools at our disposal."

"This is the opening gambit," I muttered, still watching the forest as I addressed her concerns. "If we show everything we can do simply because it's the most expedient way to address a threat, then the Tree, and anyone else watching, will be able to anticipate and plan for it later."

"This is why you lead war, and I focus on sorcery." Saghir gave a chittering laugh, beady eyes glittering as he peered down at the forest. "I will refrain from using the ash or any high-magnitude spells. We'll allow our conventional forces to shoulder the labor."

As he trailed off, the entire forest began to quiver, particularly the vines with their enormous thorns...they were retracting. The vines became smooth spiraling paths as they wound around all eight of the mountain's legs, and even the behemoth struggled as the multiplying vines wound ever upward.

A tide of black figures, small enough to rival ants initially, flowed up the vines. My senses gave me clarity, and I could see the expressions on individual consumed faces. Most of the scarlet-eyed monsters had once been human, though other wildlife, including bears and here and there a wolf pack, were still present.

"Ready yourselves!" Erik's voice boomed over the entire mountain, which was so large the words themselves dislodged snow from the highest peaks. "We hold the line, and we do not break. Nothing reaches the citadel!"

"For justice!" rang from a thousand throats, all eager to please their new Steward.

The consumed charged up the vines, then onto the rocky slopes. They howled their hunger as they sprinted through the snow. At first, the defenders did nothing. The horde grew closer and thicker and had nearly reached the base of the lower fortress where Erik was defending.

Volleys of black arrows arced from every tower, along with a smattering of spells from the witches, hedge doctors, and rare mages that had joined our cause. The combined effect was devastating. First dozens, then hundreds of consumed fell, their bodies piling in the snow.

Yet they forced progress. Each wave made it a bit further, and while hundreds eventually became thousands of dead, there appeared to be no end to the consumed army.

"Liloth," I boomed. "Ena. Macha. We have work to do."

I leapt from the fortress wall, my wings flaring as I flew low down the mountain, my gaze focused on the tide of consumed about to reach Erik's citadel. His pikemen held the walls, but if they were allowed to come unhindered, eventually the very mortal defenders would be over-whelmed.

I landed before the tide, alone, and began my work. I flowed faster than they could move, slicing off every limb or head that came within range. My companions landed behind me, then stepped up and joined the line.

Together we formed a bulwark, and the consumed screamed their rage as they tried to end us. Some flowed around us toward Erik's walls, but at a reduced flow, enough that his pikemen and mages were holding them at bay.

I leapt into the air and breathed. Not flame, but light. I don't know how I did it. Like many things since my final tomb, it was half instinct tied to the soul I'd inherited. Motes clung to the skin of hundreds of consumed, and every last one shrieked as their bodies burned to ash.

"Effective!" Ena roared up at me. "I thought we weren't revealing new powers, though. How come you get to show off?"

She stabbed a consumed through the skull with her barbed tail, then used it to hurl a dozen more back with enough force that their bodies shattered upon the granite hillside.

Liloth flowed through consumed with a pair of void-stone daggers a few cubits away, while Tissa wielded Nefarius. All three were far beyond anything we faced, and I realized this was...easy?

"My mistake." I landed and spun Narlifex, slashing the throats of a pair of consumed, then kicking one of their corpses into the next one. "I was just experimenting, but I showed more than I'd like to."

Then there was only concentration as my friends and I kept the consumed at bay. I don't know how long it went on, but an eternity later, horns sounded from the wood below. The remaining consumed wheeled as one, then retreated down the vines, which retracted of their own accord.

The spider mountain lurched into motion once more, and then we were past the ambush and moving into the northern forest where our target lay.

I scanned the human ranks, the mortal legion under Erik's command, and found them panting, but alive. They sprang into action, quickly clearing the walls of consumed, while the mages came out to burn the corpses with either fire or acid.

"Liloth," I called, spinning to find the na'elfen chatting quietly with Ena as they rested together on a boulder. "What do you think the na'elfen's next move is?"

"They opposed our passage without knowing our destination," she called, rising but coming no closer. "Now they will study our passage until they have divined it. When they do, I do not know what Yeva will do. She may attack. She may allow us to take the tree and see what we do with it. I am not privy to the sacred lore she has access to, and without it, I don't know why she does what she does. Not fully."

"Very well. We'll send a team to get the tree. You and Ena

will shadow me. If Yeva comes for the sapling, then we'll stand ready to drive them away." I glanced up at Li's kamiza, where she and Celeste still waited. Both stood ready to intervene, but neither had taken a single action as of yet. "I'll dispatch Li and her team. Let's get down into the forest and start scouting."

# INTERLUDE II - LI

Li waved her hand, directing the wind about them as she carried herself, Tissa, and Macha down toward the clearing below. It ruffled her wings, teasing their use, but she left them flattened against her back, invisible under her cloak. They were still new. Alien. All of her combat instincts and abilities had been honed without them.

Sooner or later she'd have to master their use, but for now...her command of air would be enough. She turned her attention to the ground below, studying the scene of the impending conflict.

The forest was thinner here, with large gaps between the redwoods, including the largest tree in the area, with smaller groups radiating out from it.

They landed swiftly, and she spun in place seeking threats. Nothing.

"We are alone, for now." Saghir landed on her shoulder, and Li flinched, unused to the contact. She forced herself to relax and listen to the rat. "We should work swiftly. Erik and Temis are guarding the mountain, but I do not like being unable to go to their aid. How do we extract such a tree without harming it? It is utterly massive. *Air* magic will not be able to lift it. Perhaps *earth* to carry it along the surface?"

"The tree will resist," Macha warned as the hulking Fomori, their largest member, stepped to the fore of their little group. "You'd need to rip it free first, then transport it. So long as the roots remain in contact with the earth, the tree can both draw power from the land and influence it."

"We came prepared for just such an event." Saghir drifted off Li's shoulder and raised Ikadra, the sapphire aimed skyward.

*The Fist* descended rapidly into view, as the strangest airship in creation approached the redwood sapling, itself taller than any mortal tree could hope to reach. Nothing impeded the vessel as it wrapped around the tree's upper half, at the point just barely thin enough for it to reach all the way around, then tugged upward.

Nothing. The tree did not groan, nor did it move.

"There was no way it could have been that easy." Tissa snorted and rolled her eyes. She turned to their last member, Celeste's clothing muted grays and dark blues now, and her staff now hidden away. "You're supposed to be powerful right? Can you use your magic to move the tree?"

"Not unaided." Celeste gave a sigh under her breath. "It's a pity few of you had time to receive a proper education in magic. Moving that tree will require greater magnitude than I can generate. My artifact cannot be used to aid us, only personal and considerable magic. Master Saghir and Mistress Li are both quite powerful as well, as is Macha, I believe. Between us, we can devise a spell to do what we need. We merely need to decide on a way to do it safely."

Li couldn't help but glance over her shoulder at the forest around them. The malevolence was growing, the whispering of leaves and the creaking of the great trees. The whole forest was waking. Something is coming, it said, something to punish and devour you.

"Can we shrink it?" Li wondered aloud as she nodded toward Saghir. "If we could change the tree's relative size, it would be easier to transport."

"We possess great magic between us," Celeste gave back in that patronizing way of hers. Xal never saw it, perhaps because the Steward had a soft spot for him, but that courtesy had never been extended to her. "But not even our collective power can move that tree. It undergirds the cycle. I fear we will have to find some great avatar to pull it from the earth. We could try to shrink it, but in all likelihood, the magic would fail, while also drawing the immediate ire of the forest."

"Would that Macha were older," Saghir offered, his voice conciliatory, showing he'd also heard the tone Celeste had used. "If shrinking the tree will not work, then perhaps one of us could grow? I remember the Fomori. They reached a great size. If we had their leader here, she could likely wrench that tree free. She vaulted the Hasran wall, and that tree is a span shorter."

"Macha would be sympathetic to such magic." Celeste tapped her lip with a finger, then turned to Li. "We can link our spell to increase the magnitude, though I believe Master Saghir lacks *life*."

"He still has a role to play." Li tried not to revel in adding part of the plan. She wasn't going to just be ordered about. Not even by a Steward. "If we succeed, perhaps Saghir can remove the earth around the roots as much as possible to make it easier for our giantess to—"

An arrow flashed into the clearing, black fletched, but

Tissa bisected it with her humming blade, scarlet and ugly, then vanished into the shadows.

Darkness descended all around the clearing, total, but the wall stopped well short of them. At first, Li tensed, but then she recognized it. That was Xal, not the na'elfen. He'd added another layer of protection.

"We must work swiftly." Li turned back to them, ignoring the darkness, even though enemies might burst out at any moment. "Let's try our ritual. Enemies are upon us, and we have no idea if Xal can keep them at bay."

"Of course." Celeste's hands came up, both of them, and began to sketch a dizzying latticework of *life*, *water*, and *spirit* sigils. "I'm laying the groundwork. I don't mean to slight you, but I have more experience."

"What must I do?" Li swallowed her pride. The Steward was faster and more precise, though not by much in Li's estimation.

"Create a conduit of *life* and *water*," Celeste instructed, her gaze focused on her work, which now sprawled for several cubits around them, the collective light bathing everything up to Xal's wall of darkness. "Once it's created, you'll simply need to wait until I complete the spell. When it fuses, it will draw strength from both of us, and feed that to Macha."

Li nodded then raised one hand and began to sketch. She considered adding a second, but that would have just been showing off. There was no place for vanity here. She quickly and efficiently added her own sigils, until she had joined the spell and could feel it tugging lightly upon the reservoir in her chest.

"Well done, child," Celeste muttered absently as she continued to sketch with both hands. This spell was well advanced of what Li had done in the past. The question was why? And how? There were so many more sigils than she expected. "There...ready yourself."

Li had no idea how to do that and gasped as icy water doused her entire soul, somehow. Enormous power was drawn out of her and fed to the spell, while a similar amount flowed from Celeste, with one notable difference.

A clear energy, a magic Li had never wielded, infused the spell. Divinity, she was certain of it. This was the first time she'd actively participated in such a spell, but given her proximity to Xal, not the first time she'd seen one.

Wave after wave of protection and evolution magic flowed into Macha, the sum of the spell, itself likely scribed in the early days of the Elentian Empire. As Li studied the effects, she realized why the spell had been so potent.

Celeste had not merely used a simple growth spell. She had also increased Macha's age, capitalizing on the Fomori's limitless capacity for growth. Macha surged upward, her clothing bursting at the seams as the suddenly naked giantess grew and grew in size.

She towered over them, a dozen cubits, twenty, then more, fifty, a hundred, and still more. On and on she grew, until Macha was very nearly the equal of the tree.

As the spell died away, Li blinked and realized that the ground wasn't spinning. It was actually moving. Rivulets of mud flowed away from the roots beneath the tree, first upward, propelled by gravity magic, then down again into a small pond. Saghir directed the spell with his golden staff, large ropes of *water*, *spirit*, and *earth* flowing from him.

Macha took a lumbering step, and Li instinctively shot up into the air, flying away from the tree-trunk leg. The Fomori's hand slowly rose, then seized the trunk of the tree. Her other hand settled further down the base, and a deep groan, like an elephant but far larger, rolled out of the fiery-haired giantess as she tore the tree free of the ground, wrenching it away from the area Saghir had weakened.

The tree's thick roots extended for hundreds of cubits, and they wiggled like vicious snakes as they tore free from the soil. Macha held the tree at arm's length, narrowly avoiding the writhing mass, which seemed to sense her, and leaned in her direction.

Li risked a glance at the wall of darkness Xal had created and realized it extended as high as the forest. She cocked her head and in the distance heard combat. Sword on sword. The ringing came so swiftly that it could only be one person fighting.

Who opposed him? Who was good enough to keep him at bay? Even Dalanthar had fallen before Xal, and it was only through the flame of obeisance that his aunt had bested him.

A chill fell over her. That wasn't her fight right now. She needed to trust Xal and tend to her part of the mission. They needed to get the tree back to the spider mountain now before the forest summoned more aid.

Xal would be fine.

She shoved the disquiet voices down and focused on her duty.

# 5

## PRICES

I waited in the shadows outside the clearing where Li worked, the darkness no barrier to my vision. Somewhere nearby, both Ena and Liloth lurked too, but they wouldn't be able to see me any more than I could see them. We were all of us ready for our ambush, and it came before I expected.

A tide of consumed sprinted at the darkness, hundreds of humanoids screaming at the top of their lungs as a binder forced them all to the same jerky movements. They would reach Li's position before I liked it unless I intervened.

"Let's get the preliminaries started then." Power thrummed within me, and I dropped from the redwood limb I stood atop, falling dozens of cubits to the forest floor.

I slammed Narlifex into the ground all the way to the hilt. The ground was infused with *void*. The trees were infused with *void*. Everything, every living thing, all shared that same nature.

"YaaaaaAAAAAAAAA!" I roared as I willed the first blade to drain the power from the forest floor, in the same way I had drunk Magnus and so many others.

I pulled power into myself, and it came. First from the dirt and roots, and then from the consumed atop it. Wave after wave of dark power surged down into the ground, through Narlifex and into me. I pulled more and more, and the consumed began to drop to their knees.

One by one, they slowed until not a one moved. They collapsed to the forest floor, writhing as I ate the Tree's influence. I couldn't remove the seed, but perhaps I could kill it. I tightened my grip, gritted my teeth, and *drank*.

I had no illusions about my vulnerability. That was the point, after all. The best way to prevent the na'elfen from reaching Li was to offer them a more tempting target. Now they had it.

The last consumed fell, followed by relative silence. We could still make out the battle raging on the slopes above, where Erik and Temis were keeping the consumed from taking the mountain, but they were distant things.

Only natural sounds emanated from the forest around me. Yet I knew we were no longer alone.

I rose and slid into Shu stance, scanning the darkness and waiting. I did not have to wait long.

I did not know many na'elfen, but one I could recognize was Yeva, the pale-haired dark-skinned woman who had battled me to a standstill and who might have bested me if Liloth hadn't intervened.

"I have brought playmates for you." Yeva flicked her wrist, a subtle gesture, but four na'elfen warriors shimmered into view. "My business is with Liloth. What you do here, this desecration...it is evil. Evil beyond reckoning. This tree is sacred, and you seek to uproot it? One of the pillars of the cycle? There are many times I have dreaded my duty. Today I relish it."

I did what any smart combatant did when they feared

they were outmatched. The unexpected. I charged, blurring across the forest floor in a storm that kicked up needles in my wake. I conjured a void blade in my off-hand and shifted into Xakava stance as I launched a whirlwind of strikes, all aimed at different vital targets.

Not a one hit.

A sword somehow materialized in Yeva's hand, and she calmly parried every one of my attacks, though the effort was clear in the tightening of her expression. At least I was making her work for it.

I kept enough presence to keep all four na'elfen in my peripheral vision and noted that they all simply stood there, confused. Honor seemed to keep them at bay, or perhaps it was the simple knowledge that their leader would inevitably kill me.

It left them completely unprepared when Liloth and Ena materialized behind the same target and slashed throat, wrists, and belly. Ena finished the poor woman with a tail spike through the eye.

The three remaining na'elfen instantly shifted to support each other, and that was the last I saw of the other melee. It was all I could to do keep Yeva's weapon from my throat, the blade glistening with what I assumed must be poison. Thanks to the Heart of Water, I didn't need to fear that, but cuts would slow me.

Eventually, she pivoted a bit too fast, and I ducked to the side to avoid her foot scything into my jaw. Her blade came at my leg, the one supporting my weight, and it took too long to hop out of the way. The strange wooden blade sliced through the first armor, which seemed to recoil from the attack, leaving me to take the blow.

*Am not immune to poison, like you,* the first armor

rumbled. *Will be fine. Cuts let you know you are alive. They are punishment. Don't let blades land.*

"I see your armor knows." Yeva gave a laugh, then twisted and thrust her blade low, nearly catching my ankle.

If not for my wings furiously pumping, it would have caught me, and that was not an injury I could afford.

"The poison is insidious and final." The na'elfen bared her fangs, and her eyes flared with *void*, black and purple. Powerful beyond knowing. "It is intended for my sister. Not you. Yet if I need to remove you, then—"

I slashed high, then low, then round-housed her in the face. My foot connected, and she staggered back several cubits, her feet sliding in the dirt. A single line of black blood leaked down her lip, and her eyes narrowed.

"Then you'll have to do less talking and more fighting." I glared hard at her, but in the corner of my eye, I spied something that caused elation.

One of the other na'elfen had gone down. Now it was two against two. If I could keep Yeva at bay for a little longer, I'd have help, and we could end this.

The forest floor surged up, and earth grabbed both of my legs, yanking me down in an attempt to immobilize me while Yeva's blade descended toward my throat. Again the first armor flowed aside, and sharp wood punctured my artery, then buried itself deep in my chest.

My cloak acted of its own accord, flipping down to seize Yeva's ankle, then yanking backward suddenly, knocking her off balance. I swept my leg around in a scissor kick and caught her other ankle, spilling her atop me.

A dagger rammed up at my gut but clanged off the first armor, and the blade shattered. I could scarcely breathe, and agony had narrowed my vision but not enough that I couldn't focus on the target before me. I head-butted Yeva with my full strength, then again, my horns goring her face both times.

She staggered back and away, her blade emerging from my chest with a disgusting pop.

I staggered too, my void blade vanishing as I collapsed to the forest floor, one hand bracing me against a root, the other using Narlifex to haul myself back to my feet like a cane.

"I am impressed." She cocked her head and studied me with an unreadable expression. "Were you not desecrating this wood, I would allow you to leave. I have no wish to kill you, yet you are a threat to all of creation. Flee. Or I will kill you."

*This fight is beyond us*, Narlifex hissed. *Her mastery is greater than ours.*

I recalled the fight with Magnus, which made the principle clear. In that moment, I had become a god, but the lowest rung of god. Stronger and older gods had greater mastery. Reality bent more to her will than my own. It was no longer about how swiftly I could swing a blade.

Back then I'd used worship to increase my mastery and had never felt its lack so keenly. I couldn't best her with a blade. I could only delay and hope that proved to be enough.

Time elongated. I dodged blow after blow, but several more found their mark, and blood now flowed from my shoulder, gut, and leg. Had I been susceptible to poison, I'd have been long dead, but because of her specific form of attack, I was doing far better than I had any right to.

Behind Yeva I caught sight of the other melee and winced when a blade caught Ena, disabling her left wing and sending blood spraying all over the tree behind her. Ena recovered but was on the defensive, and Liloth was in no position to help her.

I ducked another swipe, then hopped backward over a root and held my ground. The redwood at my back gave me a defended flank, and cracking me like a nut wouldn't be easy.

My increased perceptions continued to work as time stretched, and thoughts flitted through my mind, connections forming. They seemed random, until they weren't. There was a solution here. I knew it to the depths of my soul.

She was faster than I was.

*You are distracted*, Narlifex growled.

I leapt over her blade, then flipped backward out of the little hollow where I'd been sheltering, which positioned the tree between us and forced her to advance in a predictable way.

Was there a stance I could use? Xakava wasn't serving me. I was taking too many hits.

Why was the stance named after Xakava? My sister was a mage, not a warrior. Why name an aggressive stance after a mage who relied on staves, range, and stealth?

It made no sense unless Xakava's previous incarnation had been far more martially inclined. If that was true of Xakava, then why not me?

Yeva lunged around the tree, but I rolled backward around it, keeping it between us.

When I had first arrived at the academy, I'd seen myself as a mage. That had changed when I'd learned that Xalegos, my demon soul, had been a blademaster. I'd assumed I'd been meant to swing a sword.

I ducked as Yeva's sword punched through the redwood's

trunk and barely escaped with my life, rolling away from the tree as I awaited her next approach.

Perhaps there was a magical solution. I was no archmage, but I had summoning, destruction, and divination. I had *life* magic.

What would catch Yeva—

Her blade came unexpectedly from the side...I don't know how...through a fissure, maybe? I couldn't dodge, and my cloak lashed out defensively, encircling the blade. Yeva wrenched the weapon free, and the cloak gave a subsonic scream of pain.

Rage boiled in me. If the first armor feared that poison, what would it do to my nameless cloak, a companion that had saved my life countless times?

I reached inside of myself, half instinct and half raw need, and found *life* magic waiting. I commanded it to manifest as light. Brilliant light that blazed as the sun, as no light had ever blazed. The sudden brilliance did nothing to hinder my gaze, but Yeva's skin began to sizzle, and she fell back around the redwood in a hiss of pain.

The sudden light upset the balance in the other melee as well. Both na'elfen and Liloth shielded their eyes. But Ena had seen me use *life* before and seemed to recover more swiftly. She punched one of the na'elfen in the chest, and her fist emerged out the woman's back, heart clutched in her fist.

The surviving opponent twisted to face her...and received a dagger to the kidney from Liloth.

In that instant, a lessening occurred...the great source of power I'd been battling was gone. Yeva had vanished somehow. A teleport? Burrowing through the ground? I supposed it didn't matter. She'd been forced from the field, but the cost had been high.

I held my cloak in my hands and watched as the material softened from black to a dull grey as if the ink were draining from the fabric. I couldn't use *life* to heal it, but if such a way existed, I would find it.

For now, I didn't even have the luxury of tending to a fallen companion. We needed to flee before the Tree's forces returned with more aid.

# INTERLUDE III - DARIUS

Darius could not help but pace the corridor, the floorboards creaking in precisely the same place each time he passed. There were cries from within and the stern words of the midwives, but as of yet still no wail from a new infant seeing the world for the first time.

Was it a boy? Or girl?

Would he be a decent father or...more like his own father? More like Totarius.

No, he'd never be that. He might make his own mistakes, but his son, if he had one, would make his own choices and carve his own path without fearing that he'd be ostracized for it.

Or that child would if he could get Jun away from all this. Darius glanced at the guards flanking her birthing chamber. They barred his entry because they did not answer to him. This wasn't his manor. It was his father's. At least in their eyes.

"Waaaaaaahhhhhh!" A tiny, beautiful, perfect wail

warbled through the door, followed by Jun's exhausted panting.

Darius raised a finger and sketched an illusion, then left it standing where he'd been and rippled through the door, passing into the birthing room with the guards being none the wiser.

He'd expected to enter a room of joy, with his wife being presented with her new babe, but nothing could be further away. All four guards had their hands on weapons, their faces twisted in disgust. Was the child disfigured? Could it be so horrible?

Darius darted around the midwives, who were avoiding looking at Jun, all save the one swaddling the babe. He leaned over her shoulder to smile down at the little fellow and found...alabaster skin and a shock of blond hair. The very image of Erik.

Numbness stole over Darius and he dropped to his knees, the occupants of the room still unaware of his presence. How? *How?*

He forced himself to his feet, propelled by righteous anger...until he spied Jun's expression. She was smiling until the babe was presented, and then...utter confusion stole over her features, then horror as the implications became clear.

*No,* she signed desperately, even as she cradled the babe with her other hand. *I am faithful. I would never.*

None of the guards could sign. They had no idea what she was saying, but their anger and wrath seemed clear. Darius shimmered into view, drawing their eyes and those of the midwives.

"You will send word to my father immediately." Darius stabbed a finger at the lead guard, or the oldest at least.

"Ensure he knows what has transpired here. The babe and my wife are to be kept under guard at all hours. She is not to leave, but she will be treated with all honors and courtesy. If you vary even a word of this, neither my father nor my brother will be able to save you. Are we of one mind, Captain?"

"We are, my lord." He bowed, then waved at the other guards, who sprang into motion to carry out his orders.

"None of you will speak of this," Darius boomed, using the same authority his father had, a whip these people had heard crack many times before. "Not a word leaves this manor. If I hear that anyone has learned of it, then everyone here dies, as do all your families to the third cousin. Everyone. Now, see to my wife's needs and the babe's comfort."

Once everyone was in motion, Darius finally turned to his wife. Meeting her gaze took more courage than facing Erik's mother ever had. Tears streamed down her beautiful cheeks, and her eyes were all confusion and pain.

Darius rushed to her and wrapped an arm around her, then the other around the babe in her arm. He positioned his face so she could read his lips. "We will discover the truth. I do not believe you have betrayed me, but I see no easy explanation. My father will leap to conclusions. We are in great danger. I will do all I can to protect you and the babe, but you must recover swiftly if you are able."

He did not say that they must be ready to travel. He did not dare even sign it. But she took the meaning from his gaze. She knew that they might have to run or face the wrath of a family far more concerned about honor and appearances than they were about the truth.

*Father will discover the truth of this*, Darius signed, knowing it was easier to lie to her that way. *We will find the true villain and see they are brought to justice. Clearly, we are meant to think Erik is at fault, to separate me from him and from you. It will not work. Rest, my love. We will make this right.*

# 6

## DEPARTURES

I magine my shock when I banished the darkness around the great sapling and witnessed what our companions had achieved. They'd already uprooted the thick-trunked tree, and a version of Macha that rivaled the cyclops queen herself sprinted through the forest with great quaking steps, the sapling held before her like a bushy spear.

Unfortunately, the longer Macha ran, the shorter she became. Fortunately, she'd reached the base of the spider mountain's leg and was already tugging the tree up the rocky slope.

I flapped into the sky, winging between thinner and thinner trees as we neared the tree line. Ena flitted behind me, kicking off a redwood trunk to draw even as she flapped her wings, the damaged one out of tune but still enough to carry her airborne with Liloth cradled in her arms. It was enough, but it left us vulnerable.

If we were attacked now....

I banked suddenly, gaining altitude, then scanned the malevolent forest behind me. No new threats emerged. The consumed armies, what remained of them, still assailed Erik's keep, but they were falling to wights as Temis's unliving army devoured them from the rear. That fight had already been decided in our favor.

Moments after I reached the spider mountain's limb and landed upon the first joint, the mountain stood up as if it had been waiting. I dropped down and landed on a ridge above Macha's position, then held on to a thick pine trunk as the spider mountain lumbered south and west, retracing our steps back to the origin of our path, well beyond the refuge of the trees.

The slide down to where Macha had finally collapsed with the tree was grueling, but I pressed on, despite the pain of my wounds and the rocks and snow bouncing off me. I pulsed *life* through me, but the magic did little to combat the pain or damage. The blade Yeva had used had been... awful. I might have resisted the poison but not the spiritual damage it had inflicted.

I landed in the snow, dropping to one knee from exhaustion, and panted as I took in the sight before me. The immense sapling lay propped between a narrow ravine, its roots sprawled across the ground, where they had already begun wriggling into the soil. As I stared...the tree pulled itself erect, its roots reaching deep into the spider mountain.

An enormous bellow shook snow from every peak as the behemoth bellowed its pain. Hundreds of eardrums popped, maybe more, and I knew the healers would be dealing with the fallout from that one cry for days. I knew it well from my time in the legion and wept for my followers, who were suffering because they'd followed me.

Liloth and Ena landed behind me, but I was more focused on Macha. The Fomori's eyes fluttered open, and the naked giantess came to her knees, blinking around. She was easily three times my height, if not more.

"Our spell has faded," Celeste's clear voice called, the playfulness from Gateway still long absent. She glanced at the giantess. "This is unexpected. It appears that we have permanently aged the Morrigan."

"That may be to your benefit," Macha boomed in a much deeper voice as her shadow fell upon us, "provided you can find me clothing and a weapon. Are we likely to be under attack soon?"

"Doubtful," Liloth called as she limped into the clearing, staring suspiciously up at the tree. "Yeva and her na'elfen suffered losses, and every life is precious. They will be taken back for funerals and grieving. Those cannot be replaced as they do with their endless armies of consumed. She will come for us but in a manner we do not expect, one fitting her motives. I cannot predict what that might be but doubt we will see her again this day."

"Xal?" Celeste's clear voice came from the side of the clearing, and I shifted to face her.

The Steward of Magic wasn't focused on the tree or on Macha any longer. She stared up at the fortress on the high peaks, where Saghir had already disappeared with *The Fist*.

"What is it?" I followed her gaze but couldn't judge her concern.

"I just felt a tear in the veil. Someone entered from the spirit world." She frowned warily up at the fortress. "They are immensely powerful. I believe that one or both of the dragons have accepted our offer for a meeting and likely await our return."

"Let's not keep them waiting then. Li and Saghir are already up there." I began flapping into the sky, each powerful beat carrying me higher, the wings as natural as the rest of my limbs now. I could scarcely recall a time when they'd felt odd now.

By the time I gained enough elevation to reach the battlement, our guest had already made his presence known. A humanoid with dragon wings and tiny scales dotting alabaster skin stood atop the corner tower, hand resting upon the hilt of a long straight saber.

Narlifex gave a low wordless growl of recognition, but as the blade said nothing, I didn't press. Instead, I flapped down to land a few dozen paces away, Celeste's cloud of wind resolving into the Steward just a step or two from me.

Li came rushing up a stairwell to meet us. The tension stretched as all parties assessed each other, but I broke it by stepping forward and bowing to the wyrm.

"Greetings, Tuat." I gave him a bow and hoped I had the right brother. "Thank you for answering Celeste's missive."

"I care not which of your servants called for me, demon prince and sun-god." Tuat waved dismissively at Celeste and never once glanced in her direction as he sized me up in the way one sword master sizes another. "I would settle this business quickly so that I might enjoy a brief respite before Mother sends me off on yet another hunt. My brother lacks my patience and lurks in the spirit realm. I...."

Tuat trailed off when he spied Li, and his eyes widened like saucers. He recovered himself swiftly and turned back to face me, but his eyes continued to flick toward Li.

"Why have you called for me, titan-to-be? You will have to wed the flame yourself. I cannot aid you. Even if it is merely instruction you seek, I cannot grant it." He gave a deep sigh. "Much as I would enjoy relieving you of your ignorance, my vow upon entering the cycle prevents it. I cannot tarry, only pursue my quarry. You know where my cousin Khonsu roosts in this realm. You know of his schemes. Tell me, and I will see him driven from the cycle."

I was aware of Erik and Temis bursting from the same stairwell that Li had emerged from and Ena landing upon the wall, with Liloth slipping immediately into the shadows. Tuat responded to none of them. His gaze was fixed upon me now, unwavering. All business. He didn't seem at all concerned that we'd surrounded him with our most powerful people. Saghir was likely here, too, since Li had come, and while I couldn't see him, I wagered that Tuat probably could.

Still no concern.

"I will tell you what I know," I offered when I realized the moment for my response had lengthened more than I'd have liked. "Khonsu has conquered the land we call Calmora, which belongs to her people. She can tell you more." I nodded reluctantly at Li.

"Truly?" Tuat raised a scaled ridge where an eyebrow should have been. He turned slowly back to Li and spent his time sizing her up...hungrily. I didn't know if it was attraction or something less definable, but I couldn't deny the connection and hated how small it made me feel. "If the daughter of the sky and stars is involved, I would hear this tale from her lips. She who will preside over the end of creation has not appeared since...well, it doesn't really matter, does it? Let us pray your mother's soul has not also returned. I cannot aid you, Nunut, nor your people. I hunt Khonsu and Khonsu alone. His children—he gathers them like shiny baubles—will nest like snakes and need to be hunted and slain as such."

To hear one dragon designate another as a serpent signaled the deepest of insults. There was real hatred there, enough to distract me briefly from all the things he'd just called Li. I watched her reaction carefully and noted the flush in her cheeks. She stared at Tuat with unwavering conviction, and I knew her well enough to gauge that reaction.

Nothing he'd said had rung false. She had learned a great deal in the Heart of Water, it seemed, but shared little. I didn't begrudge her that, but at the same time, I had so many questions. She ended the moment by clearing her throat and stepping forward.

"Removing Khonsu is enough. His children are formidable, but perhaps we can time our assault with yours?" Li gave him a shallow bow. "I do not ask you to break your vow, but if we can travel together, then perhaps the knowledge we share will aid you in hunting your quarry. Khonsu has manipulated my people for generations. My mother could aid you too."

"And if a few of his elder children should die as we seek him, more's the better." Tuat gave a short, dry laugh. "Very well. How are you called in this life?"

"Li." She delivered another bow with none of the titles she had a right to. Then she turned to Celeste. "I realize you likely have other business to be about, but...we could use your help. My people I mean. I know worship of the Stewards is decreasing. If you help me free my people, then they will aid you in turn. We still venerate knowledge."

The Steward's face was torn, and her gaze flicked between Li and me. Finally, she nodded, her blond ponytail bobbing. "Very well. I will accompany you and mighty Tuat, for a time. Worship will be needed in the days to come. Your people have long aided us in holding the Rent, and we need your support. Yet I fear for Xal. He must become anointed, and we have not aided him in finding even a starting point."

"Don't worry about me." I forced the words out, even as they broke me inside. Sending Li away and into danger was the very last thing I wanted. Yet I wasn't a boy any longer. I had become a man and needed to make a man's choices. A leader's choices. "We are tied to Olivantia for the time being, but eventually we'll leave for Lukantria. After that, we'll have the forces to aid Calmora. If you've already freed them, wonderful. If not, then we have an army to help you break the dragons."

Li's eyes were wet with emotion as she met my gaze and smiled. "I'm sorry. It isn't what I want."

"We each do what we must." I swept forward and gathered her in a hug, then raised my wings to shield us as I kissed her. Her own wings rose to touch mine. "We will be together again."

"I won't tell you to be careful," she whispered, a single tear sliding down that perfect cheek, "if you don't ask me. We each do what we must."

Our wings came down, and we parted with a painful finality, one that I feared might be permanent, even though I had no logical reason to suggest it.

"Come." Tuat whipped his saber from its sheath, then slashed at the air next to him, exposing the spirit world, which I now recognized well. "Step through and I will close it behind us. Do not fear my brother. He will not harm you, though he is...fearsome. He does not enjoy hybrid form as I do."

Celeste leapt through the slash with her staff held high, and Li followed, giving one last glance my way as Tuat stepped through and closed the slash behind him.

She was gone. Again.

"It will be all right, my friend." Saghir landed on my shoulder, shimmering into existence as he dropped whatever spell had been hiding him. "You will be together again, and I will see Alsara."

"Xal?" Erik's voice came from behind me, and I didn't at all enjoy the hesitation in his tone. "We need to talk."

"What about?" I steeled myself as I turned to address the once-prince.

"I need to leave...for a time." Erik heaved a heavy sigh. "I've asked Vhala to stay until I return, so she can continue the men's training."

"So you are coming back." I didn't try to hide the relief. I let him see how much it meant that he was coming back, or at least I tried to.

I also didn't say I knew why he'd asked Vhala to remain behind. He feared she could be used against him. Which told me where he must have been going. His words confirmed it.

"I have to help Ash." Erik shook his head slowly. "What's happening to her and her father, and depths, my father too...I have to see what can be done. Valys is not someplace I want Crispus ruling unopposed. I need to see her set free and see if I can set things right."

"The temples are torn down," I pointed out. "How are you going to deal with the Imperator? What if they imprison you?"

"That's the best possible scenario." Erik gave a wicked grin, which only made the bastard more handsome. "It will force all the other Stewards to respond, and collectively, I believe that ends badly for Crispus. If not? I can be a counter-influence. Many refuse to give up the old ways, and I think I can rally them to my cause. They followed justice, not Dalanthar, and while I might look a little different—"

"You made war on them," Saghir pointed out dryly from

my shoulder. "They will not forget Lakeshore. So far as they are concerned, you are on the same side as Crispus."

"I'm not saying it will be easy." Erik heaved a sigh. "I have to try. I'm heading out as soon as the mountain settles for the night."

"How are you getting there?" So far as I knew, he lacked the magic to fly, and Ashianna had his griffin.

"On a horse, of all things." He perked up at that, smiling. "I think it will be good for me. It will take some time to reach Valys, but maybe I can renew the faith wherever I pass and show people I'm fighting for them."

I considered offering him transport, but his mind seemed made up, so I extended a hand in friendship. "Luck to you, Steward."

Erik accepted it, his grip firm as he smiled back. "Luck to you, demon prince. We're all the world has."

# 7

## IMPOSSIBLE CHOICES

I returned to my quarters after patrolling the entire fortress. I wanted to be certain no na'elfen had stowed aboard the mountain, though even after a thorough search and a liberal amount of scrying, I couldn't be certain we were safe.

Saghir had taken up residence in my quarters now that Li was gone and was presently using his tail to dab paint onto a canvas, which was angled away from me. He blinked up at me over his spectacles, smiling as I landed on the ledge and climbed inside.

"Welcome, friend Xal." Saghir waved a hand, and *air* magic pulled the paint from his tail and returned it to his easel. "I had hoped we could dine together. I thought you might relish the company as your, ah, more desirable choice has departed. I know that absence well. We could play Kem if you wish."

I dropped down into a comfortable chair one of the carpenters had generously crafted from the fallen redwoods on the south slope and eyed Saghir's work.

He'd sketched himself being sucked under a tide of

incredibly realistic ash, magic making the canvas flow as if alive. I could even hear the ever-present wind, its low whistle taking me back to the time upon the dunes. It expressed all the bleakness of that situation, with no words needed. It didn't matter what language the viewer spoke— they would take away the emotions Saghir sought to convey.

"This magic is.... I don't have the right words." I gawked at the painting, which continued to shift and change. "How did you make it?"

"Magical inks." He gave me a rodent grin. "I've been collecting magical materials, most from this very wood, then I mixed it with ash for the darker hues. I infuse my will into canvas as I paint. The results are...remarkable."

"Yes, and more." The wheels were already turning in my head. So much more effective than any tome. "Would that we had hundreds of these. If we could set up a temple and funnel people through, by the time they left, they'd know the truth about every one of our struggles."

*We are not alone*, Narlifex hissed. *I sense a powerful foe.*

I leapt to my feet and eased my weapon from its sheath as I scanned the shadows around the hearth where a magical flame smoldered. I detected nothing but trusted Narlifex's instincts. He'd clearly caught something I'd missed.

"Apologies," a familiar feminine voice spoke from the corner, and I spun to face Yeva as the na'elfen sat down at my writing desk, then scooted the chair to face us with a thigh-high leather boot. "I have come alone, in peace. I seek a parlay. If you refuse, then I will depart in peace, as I came."

Saghir had already raised a paw to sketch a spell, and a nimbus of water had appeared around him, but he was merely glaring at the na'elfen, waiting for my reaction, I supposed.

"What is your objective in coming alone?" I glanced briefly at Saghir. "Can you get down to the sapling and make sure it's protected and this isn't some sort of ruse?"

"Of course." Saghir flitted over to the window, which burst open at his approach to allow his passage. It meant the world that he hadn't wasted time asking about my safety but had just done as I'd asked.

"I seek peace." Yeva extended a slender fist, and when her hand opened, it displayed a tiny black seed with wiggling tendrils extending from the top and bottom. "Given what I saw today, that will not be achieved unless I can show you what it is we truly seek. If you take the seed, then you will understand the Tree. You will know its mind and understand its agony and what it seeks. The Tree is mad with pain, which grows less as it grows larger. Increasing its size decreases the pain and thus our own pain. As the madness fades, the Tree's voice has become much clearer."

"You want me to implant that thing in my own body?" I raised an eyebrow and made no move to accept the seed. "Wouldn't taking it give the Tree the chance to control my mind?" My thoughts strayed uncomfortably to the flame my aunt had used.

A rush of wind interrupted our conversation, and when it passed, Liloth stood upon the same window sill Saghir had vacated through. That explained why he'd gone without question and why he'd left the window open. Clever.

"Give him the truth, Yeva." Liloth leapt into the room, then stepped to the side to allow Ena to enter.

Ena's eyes glittered with rage, and the demon flexed her claws as she eyed the na'elfen. This was personal, it seemed.

Yeva drew my attention again with her words. "The Tree will seek to control you through the seed, and through the seed, it will be eternally connected. It will know your mind. However, it cannot control the strong-willed. It cannot control me. My choices are my own."

Liloth scoffed at that, a snort of pure derision. "You are a puppet. If he takes the seed, he risks becoming the same. One in three are lost. He should know that."

"Why is the tree in pain?" I asked, changing the tactic suddenly.

Yeva eyed me for long moments before answering, as if to determine whether or not I was mocking her faith. "A great corruption lingers within it, the source of the pain. The Tree was grown to contain this evil, but this lore is recorded nowhere. What I know I know from its mind, from placing a hand on its bark and communing with it. You could do the same and learn what it needs. What it fears. I cannot deal with this corruption, but perhaps you can."

"Or perhaps I'll be consumed by it." I folded my arms and eyed her back with the same appraising glance. "What would I benefit from this arrangement? I take tremendous risk. For peace? The Tree will not stop coming."

"It might if you were able to heal it," Yeva pointed out, then glared at Liloth. "Even she will tell you of our earliest prophecies. The day will arrive when the Tree's fate is decided, light or dark, and the cycle will pay the price. If nothing else, the seed will grant you tremendous power. Strength. Speed."

"Hunger," Liloth spat.

My mind flitted back to Lucretia's flame. I couldn't afford to become the largest weapon in the Tree's arsenal. At the same time, Olivanticus had made the same choice and had taken the seed. So had Liloth. Both were their own masters.

"The seed is a great gift," Yeva continued. "Before the

corruption, such seeds were rare. Now the Tree awards them en masse, in desperation, as it seeks to escape its pain."

"She speaks the truth, but the cost is great." Liloth's eyes narrowed further.

"The pact with Olivanticus," I began, trying another angle. "You clearly had a truce. Is it possible to establish another? If I take this seed, are you claiming you will keep the consumed from this nation?"

"I can make no such promise," Yeva admitted with a helpless shrug. "The Tree bartered directly with Olivanticus, and they came to their own arrangement. You would have to take the seed and trust that you are able to negotiate as well as he did. At the time of the agreement, there were other lands for us to expand into. Now we have conquered much, and there is no fresh border to exploit, only the Ashwall to the east and the sea to the south. The Tree ever seeks fresh blood, yet if you can cleanse the corruption, then it will no longer possess such vile hunger."

"I will need time to decide. How long will you give me?" I sheathed Narlifex, slowly, and did not break eye contact.

"A full moon if you wish." Yeva blinked at me. "I cannot stay the Tree's wrath, but we will not assail this mountain until that time has passed. If you wish to accept my offer, come into the forest and approach a redwood. A seed will be presented."

"Thank you." I nodded cordially, and just like that, she was gone.

Liloth and Ena were left scanning the shadows in vain. There was nothing.

Silence fell, save for the crackling flames in the hearth. It was Saghir who finally broke it, and I didn't know when he had returned. "The sapling is fine and well guarded by Macha. I heard the offer. What will you do, friend Xal?"

"I don't know," I admitted, slowly shaking my head. "I can't afford to be controlled. Not by my aunt nor the Tree. But she dangled tempting fruit. If we could cleanse the Tree somehow...what would that do? Perhaps we could remove all the consumed. It sounds impossible, but if we achieved it...."

I trailed off and awaited their response. I'd rarely been so genuinely confused on the correct course of action.

No one spoke. The decision was on me, and I knew it. I hated it.

## INTERLUDE IV - ERIK

Erik had nearly finished assembling his belongings when he first noticed the strange bundle resting upon the table in the entryway. The package was wrapped in a sky-blue silk, with little stars emblazoned on it. Circular, about the size of a large round shield, just big enough to stand upon, but not big enough to protect the entire body. Useless in his estimation.

"She left it," Vhala murmured from the corner where she sat upon a cushion, eyes closed. "Celeste. She said that it belonged to Dalanthar, and now it belongs to you. She also said that his estates are yours, though they are buried under the ash."

"That's fitting somehow." Erik snorted a self-deprecating laugh. He was rich again...with a fortune he could never touch. "Let's see what object survived?"

He removed the wrapping, which revealed a golden disk. At first, he thought the disk a shield as he'd suspected, but there was no handle nor other means of holding it. A single ring of runes ran along the outer edge, so he bent to read them.

"It's a...flying disk?" Erik leaned back and peered down at the device. The instructions appeared fairly simple.

"Perhaps you will not need to walk to Valys after all." Vhala's eyes opened, and she rose, lithe like a cat, then padded behind him and wrapped her arms around his waist. "It was a foolish idea. You were putting off seeing Crispus, I think."

"It would be helpful to arrive at the head of a large army." Erik considered the legion or legions he could assemble if he walked.

He absently wrapped an arm around Vhala, enjoying the way she nestled there. It hadn't gone farther than simple affection, but he was pleased they were both finally expressing the attraction they'd felt for so long.

"Of foreign troops?" Vhala gave a snort and an eye roll. "You know they'd never follow invaders. They'd unify, and Crispus would use it against you."

"I know." Erik sighed as he gazed down at the disk. It simplified things. He could be in Valys by nightfall tomorrow if it moved as fast as a griffin. "Why didn't Dalanthar use it, I wonder? He's never shown with it in paintings or statues, only a griffin."

He checked the disk and noted that the age and maker's mark had been appended to the end. The year was...125? On the Elentian Calendar? That made this bit of magitech nearly a thousand years old. Perhaps it predated the domestication of griffins. Or maybe it was faster or conveyed some other advantage.

"For Justice," Erik intoned as he placed his hand atop the disk. The gold began to vibrate, then the bottom emitted a soft white light, and the disk rose into the air.

Erik willed the disk to move, and it shifted far enough to fall off the desk, then landed just above the floor, levitating.

He stepped atop it and willed the disk to rise. It warbled a bit further into the air.

"You look ridiculous on that thing." Vhala gave a rare laugh, her cheeks dimpling.

"Now I can see why Dalanthar didn't use it." Erik gave back a sheepish grin. "Well, at least I'll never be able to take myself seriously. They're going to laugh from Olivantia to Valys."

"At least you will arrive safely." Vhala folded her arms and eyed him sternly, her good humor evaporating. "I do not like being asked to remain behind, but I will ensure your troops are ready when you return. Ready for war."

"I have no doubt." Erik rested a hand on her shoulder. "I will be back. I promise I will find a way."

"Go." She turned from him and settled back down atop her cushion. "Do what you must and worry not for your vassals. We will manage until your return."

Erik gracefully guided the disk into the air and wobbled out the window and into the sky. As he rose, he realized the base of the disk blazed like a sun, and all below were able to see him. Sudden laughter echoed up from below. Not kind laughter either.

He was going to miss Vhala so much. She'd never stop holding up a mirror, one he occasionally needed. Even he could admit that.

He gained altitude swiftly and noted the many people below pointing upward. Erik willed the disk to greater speed, but to his horror, found it to be much slower than a griffin. Still faster than a horse, particularly while flying, but it would take longer to reach Valys than he'd expected.

The disk made good time as he winged north, over the foothills to the range bordering the highlands of Arlen, then west over the abandoned farmland that had once belonged to dreadlord serfs. Their country was in rough shape, which was easy for him to ascertain long after dark since the disk kept the surrounding countryside well lit.

Thankfully, he never seemed to grow tired, so if he could avoid inhabited areas, he might be able to reach Valys without trumpeting his arrival days in advance.

*I have extended my strength*, a warm elderly voice rumbled in his head, a grandfather Erik had never possessed. *You will possess it so long as you work to enforce the ideal of justice. Your purpose is noble, and thus you are a god so long as you are about my business.*

Erik didn't answer but rather mulled what he'd just learned. The shield let him forgo sleep. What else would being a god convey? He'd puzzle it out, likely, but it was a pity Celeste had included nothing like a welcome tome to introduce him to his role.

Would the shield serve in an advisory capacity?

Nothing. The voice was silent.

On and on they flew, night deepening as he flew for many bells, then lightening again as the sun returned. They were passing over a small hamlet that still had life in it. A boy of not more than ten sat atop a hill, a flock of sheep all about him enjoying their pasture. What must Erik have looked like? He raised his gauntlet and waved.

The boy waved back.

Erik stood a little taller as the sun rose, and he pressed on through northern Olivantia. There in the distance loomed the three citadels he'd been raised to fear, which had been the bulwark for the dreadlords across many wars. He kept his distance, though he didn't rightly need to, but there was something about the imposing edifices that bothered him.

The mist to the south cleared, and out of it rose something larger and even more imposing. The Skull of Xalegos, a sobering look at just how large the avatars were. Was that what was coming? Would Totarius be able to raise one? Or someone else? If they did, what could they possibly do against something like that? Whatever had been attached to that head was large enough to impress even the spider mountain.

He turned back to the horizon, toward what he knew. There ahead raged the mighty river separating Olivantia from Valys, flowing out to the Endless Lake. North of those imposing rapids lay six fortresses, the mighty Valysian settlements the subject of most of their childhood war fantasies. It had been those battlements they'd manned as they'd repelled the binders and their armies.

Erik flew closer and closer, and as expected, the griffin patrols finally detected him. A pair winged above, then turned around and flew back to the closest border fort. He kept on, not bothering to look at them as he flew over their fort.

Most gazed up in confusion, some in wonder, a few in derision. He ignored them all and kept north, a griffin line to the Hammer itself, where his fate lay for good or ill. By the time he reached the caldera, a cloud of griffins and an airship trailed in his wake. They kept their distance, but many kept crisscrossing him with their shadows, showing they were there, watching.

Erik kept a dignified posture, aware of just how slowly the disk moved, how long it took him to pass over the fertile farms lining the valley inside the crater where the mighty hammer gleamed. The place had never been home to him at the best of times, but he had lived here for much of his early life.

He descended toward the royal quarter, the Praetor's

familiar manor unchanged at the top, and Erik's father directly below it. That was his destination, and he landed in the spacious courtyard outside the eyrie.

It felt like there should have been some sort of mechanism to shrink the disk, but since there wasn't, he opened a void pocket attached to his belt and hauled the awkward thing inside. By the time he'd closed the pocket, a quartet of alarmed guards in Hasran scarlet and gold sprinted into view, each leveling a pike in his direction.

"Are those really necessary?" Erik rolled his neck, then his shoulders, and then began the rest of his warm-up exercises. He hadn't drawn his sword yet, but the shield was lethal enough, should it come to that. "This is my estate. You cannot bar me from it."

"Ah...." One of the guards turned back to the others, but they all avoided eye contact, forcing the speaker to advocate for them. "The manor was seized by the crown. Your father has been imprisoned, my lord. This place belongs to the crown now."

"Who is in residence?" Erik's fist tightened around the hilt of his sword. There were too many guards for a garrison. A glance inside showed a dozen more. There was a lord present here.

"I will escort you, my lord. This way. Please." He bowed to Erik and made no mention of Erik being armed, which was a breach of protocol, but a wise one if the man wanted to live.

The guards led him through his own home, through the entryway, and into his own dining hall, which had been completely redone in Enestian finery, all purple and black.

"As I dwell and till, it's true." Totarius gave a delighted laugh as he rose from the table, where he sat eating alone, dressed in comfortable silks with no visible weapon save a slender rapier at his side. "You are alive somehow. My little brother put you back into play. Amazing. So much effort, and for what? An arrogant little boy? Why have you come, Steward? You will find no succor here. Your temples have been burned and salted. The people no longer follow your small-minded ideals. They are free now."

"It's a rather sad state for the Stewards, I agree." Erik sat heavily at the table and helped himself to a bowl full of the spicy noodles in the closest dish, which was more at home at Calmora than Valys. His mouth began to water immediately. He wasn't precisely hungry, but at the same time, he was starving. "You don't mind, do you?"

*I can sustain you,* the elderly voice murmured, *but you are still mortal, with mortal needs.*

"Not at all. Eat your fill." Totarius leaned back in his chair and dabbed at his lips with a napkin. "When you are done, you are welcome to stay the night if you wish. It's late. You might not be able to find an inn. What if something untoward happened to you? Unthinkable. My sons would never forgive me."

"I'll make my own accommodations," Erik supplied between bites as the bowl rapidly disappeared. "If either Darius or Crispus wants me, they can missive, and I will come."

He rose absent his dignity, but with a full belly and more knowledge than he'd had when he arrived. Small victories. No one had said this was going to be easy.

# 8

# FREE TIME

I leaned on the balcony railing just outside my quarters and surveyed the mountain below me, proud of all we had achieved but also troubled by growing apprehension. I should have been doing more.

I didn't know how to use the time I'd been given. I could maneuver, briefly, without anyone trying to kill me or a pressing destination to reach. No more tombs. No nation to rescue. Our immediate problems were being handled by Li and Erik, which left me cooling my heels, as they had both had to do at different times.

I hated it.

The camp ran itself with incredible efficiency, as did the legion. Everyone had urgent business to be about, save me. Even Ena found tasks, tending to the growing sapling and watching for invaders and spies.

All I had to do was consider the offer to implant a seed into my chest that would join with my body and possibly my soul...a decision I badly wanted to avoid. The stakes were too large, and I knew too little to make an informed decision.

So I focused on my writing, adding hundreds of pages and very nearly catching the story up to the Battle of Lakeshore. I didn't know if I was doing it justice, but the story poured out of me.

Saghir spent the time in my quarters but largely in a comfortable silence as he painted and I wrote. I loved the company and the raw creation. It healed my soul in a way I hadn't realized I needed, just the space to not be hunted.

The morning of the third day after Li had departed, Saghir rushed through the window in a blast of frigid air, his arms wrapped around a slab of redwood about the size of a tome, which had been painted in his style. It...was me.

"Come, friend Xal. Witness a miracle." Saghir arranged the slab, which was roughly the same size as his easel, about the size of a standard tome, and showed me the painting he'd made. "This is the moment we fell from the cliff."

I gaped at the image, which showed us tumbling amid rocks. Beneath us, I could see the giant wasp hive and some of the bears slaughtering our friends far below. It was a horrific moment that would stay with me forever, and this captured it perfectly.

"Watch." Saghir brought me back to the moment as he ignited his finger with a blue flame, then plunged it into the painting.

He yanked his finger out a moment later, and the art was ruined in that location. I opened my mouth to protest, but as I did so, the image...healed itself. It was repaired as if the damage had never been, the grain of the wood once more unbroken and the magical ink restored.

"How?" was all I could manage.

"Some property of the wood?" Saghir's excitement was contagious. "I do not know, but the implications are wondrous, are they not?"

"They are." The wheels were turning again. "How thin could you make the canvas?" This one was about half the width of a finger, wider than I'd have liked.

"Hmm." Saghir lifted himself into the air and drifted up to inspect the edge of the redwood slab. "Very thin. Not paper thin, but nearly so. I will have to experiment. I do not know how thick it must be to retain the magical ink."

"What if you make, say, a dozen of these sheets, each one with its own image and small script at the bottom with a paragraph or so?" I scratched at my beard, which was thickening and thus useful in the cold environment at this altitude.

"Hmm." Saghir zoomed back around to inspect the painting itself. "I could do that and well. I begin to see what you have in mind. If we presented the right scenes...you could share our story with a handful of pages instead of the massive tomes accumulating upon your desk."

"Precisely." I couldn't help but smile. Our intellects were so similar. "I need a way to influence people, but tomes are not going to do it. What if our new—I don't know, story-tomes? What if the storytomes could share it more effectively?"

"Brilliant." Saghir's eyes glittered with a fever I recognized...the urge to create. "I can conceive of the scenes but not the words. If you were to arrange them into some coherent order and add words to bind them into a story, then someone could read it in a comfortable afternoon before the fire, instead of weeks."

"They might even read together," I realized, nodding at the canvas. "Given the size, more than one person could view at the same time. Whole families could gather around a tome."

"I could modify the sound as well." Saghir's paws began

to tremble and his smile widened. "We could say the words aloud, in my voice. I could be the narrator, like in a mummer's play. The only question is...where do we begin? Can you perhaps describe a series of scenes to accompany those I have already painted? I am wishing to capture the horrors of the trash legion and our first meeting. Your memoirs capture it perfectly, but I do not know how to distill that down to so few images."

"Hmm. I think I can do that." I was still grinning at the original image, the idea of what we could create dancing through my thoughts. Could we really do this?

"I'll get to work on thinner pages." Saghir plucked up the canvas with a tendril of air. "I will return, and then we can begin our work in earnest!"

He zoomed out the window, leaving me with the work of choosing which scenes to include. It was a daunting task, but I settled on those with the most emotional impact. Moments like Caw executing Seth along the trail before we'd even left the Hasran walls.

Time disappeared. I found myself loving the task, sketching notes as I picked key moments from our journeys. There were so many. Whittling them down would be the most challenging part.

*This is dangerous*, Narlifex warned in a low whisper. *Such things are not meant for you.*

I expected Bronya to add something, but the first armor remained silent, as she had ever since my cloak had...died. I'd been trying not to think about it. In a fight that had been so pointless.

*Dangerous*, Narlifex hissed, *because anything you build will become a target. It can be torn down, and your enemies WILL destroy it. You waste time creating and then need to protect what you create. It makes you vulnerable.*

I sensed there was more behind the words, something to do with prophecy or curse or whatever I wanted to call it. Whatever the blade's concerns, I tried to ignore them but was only able to finish one more scene before rising and moving to the window.

The world was moving, even if I was not. I couldn't ignore that.

There were enough scenes for Saghir to work with. I gazed out at the darkening twilight and wondered about the seed. Should I take it? Was there someone or something I could consult before making such a decision? Or should I leave it to intuition?

I didn't have answers.

I returned to the writing table and got back to work. Action was better than no action.

# 9

## RAT & DEMON, VOLUME 1

I managed to avoid the seed for three more days and in the end, decided against implanting it. I didn't missive Yeva or make a formal declaration, but in my heart, I knew I wasn't going to take the seed unless a compelling reason caused me to reassess.

Those three days were lonely. Saghir was gone, working in his own quarters on the new thinner redwood sheets, and that left me with far more time than I'd have liked. I spent it studying spells I'd meant to learn but had never found the proper time to study.

That proved a wondrous distraction and got me through all three days. I managed to learn seven new spells in that time too, which I won't bore you with.

My lore binge finally ended when the window swept open and Saghir swept through, this time a larger bundle of redwood slabs in his arms, all cut to incredibly thin widths. He likely had dozens in that little stack.

"You will not believe what I have created, and all this without the greater path of artificing." Saghir laid the stack on the table...and then opened it. It was a tome, bound so cleverly on one side that I could not even see the binding. "Behold!"

He opened the book, and the first page showed Saghir arriving in Hasra aboard an airship. The whole city stretched before him, and he had somehow managed to infuse the Reactor and the surrounding city with foreboding. The soft hum of airships and the yells of hawkers that emanated from the tome added to the effect.

"Rat arrives in Hasra." Saghir's reedy voice came from the tome, reading aloud the words scrawled along the bottom of the page in a delicate script. "He is a slave. Tribute from the city of Gateway, to be added to the trash legion, an army of misfits sacrificed in battle."

I could scarcely believe it. No words came to mind. Instead, I leaned forward and turned the page, exposing two more, both in a single larger scene spanning the pages. I began to weep, even before the tome read the words aloud.

Seth's pudgy form knelt in the mud, and Caw's spear burst through his chest, ending his life in a single strike, the rain pelting streaking both pages so they appeared wet and slick. Behind it all loomed the Hasran wall.

"The costs began to mount," the tome said. "Our first victim fell before we left the outer wall. The trail claimed many lives. We were ill-prepared, given no boots nor real weapons."

I flipped page by page, watching our march up to the pass and the appearance of the spider mountain. It showed our battle in detail across multiple pages and ended with our slow climb to the cliff, then us falling in a shower of rock, the first image he'd shown me ending the storytome.

"Look at the cover," Saghir prompted from my shoulder, raising his reedy voice.

I flipped the tome gently over and blinked down at the title...*Rat & Demon, Volume 1.*

"If I had a few hundred of these, the world would finally know the truth about us." I ran my hand along the cover. "This is beyond incredible. I don't know what I envisioned, but this is so much better."

"Then you will love the final revelation." Saghir rose into the air and waved me away with a tiny paw. "Clear the area around the book, please."

I backed away from my writing table. Saghir lowered his paw in a chopping motion, and a blade comprised of pure air materialized directly over the tome. It sliced downward, cutting the book cleanly in two even as my mouth fell open to offer protest.

"Fear not. All is well." Saghir darted down and fetched his copy of the book. "Watch. Remember how the ink healed itself? You will scarcely believe this."

I picked up the remaining half of the book and eyed the torn edge. It was already growing back, the cover and the pages underneath.

"It will take a bell or two," Saghir explained as he stowed his half in a void pocket. "Once the process is complete, you will possess a copy and I an identical copy."

I froze, then did the math in my head. "So, if I understand this correctly, two becomes four becomes sixteen, and so on? We could truly make thousands of copies...if this is true. Is there no limitation?"

"A minor one." Saghir sighed. "These books are flush with blood, but creating a new copy will use it up. If you seek to keep the tome alive and to create more, it must be offered the blood of the living. Livestock will suffice, or a person's own blood if they are not squeamish. I thought the limitation fitting, given our nature, I a dreadlord and you a demon."

"These tomes are alive, yes?" I held mine up and noted that the growth continued. It healed so swiftly.

"Indeed." Saghir nodded.

"Then they are an extension of the Tree." I shuddered as I considered what we were doing. "We'll be spreading the Tree, just in a much less violent way than the consumed."

"Interesting. I had not considered that." Saghir removed his spectacles and cleaned them with a whoosh of air. "I do not know if that is a good thing to do. I will leave it to you to decide if the cost is worth it."

"It might be." I scratched at my beard again. It itched. Perhaps I'd shave it. Li wasn't here to appreciate it anyway. "I could take a seed and offer the tomes as my part of a peace bargain. It might be possible to end the war somehow, or at least declare a truce that will allow the Olivantian people to recover."

"I have not asked, but...are you going to take a seed?" Saghir replaced his spectacles and fixed me with his unblinking stare.

"I don't know." I sighed and replaced the tome on my writing desk, then lent Saghir my full attention. "If I take it, there's a risk I'll lose control, but...that's not the real fear if I'm being honest. I don't want to link with that thing. I don't want it to always be a part of me, seeing what I see. That gives it so much influence, even if I retain control. Is this thing really a force I want to strengthen just to strengthen my own cause?"

"I don't know," my friend admitted. He landed on my shoulder and rested a hand gently on my neck. "I am glad it is not me making such a decision."

"Would you mind bringing the first complete copy to

Vhala and explaining to her how it works?" I knew I was changing the subject but did it anyway.

"Of course, friend Xal." He rose into the air. "I will be about it at once, and I will explain to her its use. Then I will bring copies to other groups. Li's followers could benefit, I think. They are still training in her kamiza, for they know she can scry them and fear she watches them all daily. It's quite amusing to see. No sorcerer has that much time nor *fire* magic to spare."

"That warms me." I laughed, and part of the burden I'd been carrying since she left had eased. We hadn't made plans to missive each other. In a way, not knowing was easier. I didn't want to be a distraction. She likely felt the same. "I'll get started on the story for the second volume."

"Truly." Saghir perked up, his smile becoming a full grin. "I had not dared hope you could spare the time, but I would dearly love to begin work on the next set of pages."

"I don't know how much longer I'll have time, but for now...I am happy to be your muse, master artist." I found myself laughing as I seated myself at my table once more. This was far more fulfilling than being the dark hero in a darker tale.

Maybe in another life my fate would be different.

## INTERLUDE V - ERIK

Erik chose to take a coach to the palace, an indignity that would have incensed his younger self, the noble child accustomed to being the central star in the heavens. Were Vhala here, she'd have chided him and told him that he could do with some humility, and she'd likely have been right.

The brashness of his youth had been burned away and replaced with confidence. He knew he was among the very best at what he did...war. He also knew that he couldn't live with the political machinations his mother had used to control her realm. He craved Justice, even if he wouldn't have called it that at the time.

The coach rumbled to a halt outside the Praetor's palace, and Erik waited patiently as the footman opened the door, then added a step for him, as if he were some dainty matron.

Perhaps not all the brashness was gone.

Erik leapt from the coach, a good thirty cubits into the air, then descended to crash to the stone directly outside the double doors leading into the manor, new cracks radiating outward. He planted a boot against the door and kicked as hard as he could, cracking the frame and knocking the door to the marble just inside the entryway.

A pair of flustered guards blinked at him, both holding pikes straight up, neither making an attempt to threaten him. He glared first at one, then slowly turned to glare at the other. Neither met his gaze. Both straightened.

That told him something important, though he couldn't articulate what. Xal likely could have. He was much better at subtext and nuance, which is why he'd frequently won when he should have lost. Erik, on the other hand, had relied on brute strength.

It had been a mistake then. It would be a mistake now.

*Then why use it?* the elderly voice prompted, startling him. He'd nearly forgotten about it.

*Because,* he thought back, rather proud of himself, *if I act like they expect me to act, then they will see what they expect to see. I want to be mistaken for a boy given too much power. Like Crispus.*

Erik stepped through the shattered oak doorframe and onto the polished marble walk. More guards waited inside, also in Hasran finery. They came from a variety of provinces, but none were native to Valys.

"Where is your master?" Erik speared the lead soldier with his gaze, who was a captain in his middle years with a puckered scar just under the left eye. "Take me to him. Now."

"At once, your, ah, eminence." The man bowed, and then the rest of the guards awkwardly followed suit.

Erik strode past them without a second glance, his golden shield held low at his side and his sword hand well away from the hilt. He knew the house well and followed the path to the dining hall, where he could hear boisterous and familiar laughter.

Erik reached a final set of double doors, with a pair of Enestian guards in purple and black guarding this door. Their eyes narrowed as he approached, and he knew the Steward bluff wasn't going to work with this pair.

"You *will* announce me." Erik glared at the closest one.

"The Imperator has given orders not to be disturbed," the woman growled back, shifting into a combat stance, though not one he recognized. Likely some exotic Enestian martial art.

"I didn't say it would be voluntary." Erik hurled his shield like a discus, and it caught the woman in her breast-plate, launching her through the double doors, which burst open but did not break.

The force of the blow carried her all the way through the room, where she slammed into the opposite wall and slid down into a crumpled heap.

"She will require healing," growled the man seated at the head of the table. A familiar dark-skinned man with an ostentatious crown and a contemptuous sneer. "Healing is expensive. How will you pay for it, pauper Steward?"

"Your hospitality leaves something to be desired, Crispus." Erik extended a hand and the shield flew back into it. "The rest of these toadies might polish your ego, but I've been Imperator. It doesn't much impress me. I have a feeling you'll meet the same fate I did. I wonder if anyone will care enough about you to hunt down your soul and bring you back?" Erik looked around and noted Totarius and...Darius? He ignored his friend, for now at least, and turned to Crispus. "Where is Tissa?"

Crispus paled and shifted in his chair to glance behind him. When he turned back, his features were twisted by rage. The blow had landed. It seemed the new Imperator feared the same assassin who'd been used to kill his predecessor.

Erik badly wanted to look at Darius, to smile and greet his friend, but that would only bring unwanted attention. In his peripheral vision, he spied a seated woman...Jun. She was nursing a babe swaddled closely to her breast, though Erik couldn't directly see the baby. Joy for his friend's happiness flowed through him.

But why would Darius be here? It couldn't be voluntary.

"I have already outlived you, Steward." Crispus smiled savagely as he raised his goblet, wine sloshing over the side. "To my eternal health, and to the downfall of false gods. I have torn down your temples—did you know that, Erik? You have no idea how happy it makes me to know you are the new Steward of Justice. Steward of a broken religion. A broken man. My father warned me you'd come. What is it you think you can find here? The people will not follow you. They have long memories. I am the hero who supplanted you. You? You're the villain who tried to conquer them. I saved them."

The feverish glint in Crispus's eyes told Erik how badly the new monarch needed his words to be true, but Erik didn't need to speak with the common folk to know they were a beautiful lie his sycophants were telling him. These people hated Crispus as much as they hated Erik, and the longer he dwelt here, the more their hatred would grow.

"To your eternal health." Erik strode over to the table and picked up a full goblet sitting before a man who had not touched it. He downed the contents and slammed the goblet down. "I won't drink to the downfall of the Stewards. Like it or not, they'll be around long after you and I are dust."

"I have a question, if I may be permitted, Your Highness." Totarius ventured from his chair at Crispus's right hand where he sat languidly, like a cat gloating over a kill.

"Of course, Father." Crispus waved absently at his father, but his gaze never left Erik.

"Were you involved in a dalliance my daughter-in-law?" Totarius rose to his feet and stabbed an accusing finger at Jun, who was thankfully looking away and could not hear the slander. "Are you the reason my grandson is clearly the issue of another man?"

That rocked Erik to the core, and all he could do was blink in confusion. He had expected possible arrest. He had expected political maneuvering.

But this?

Erik's gaze went to his friend and found Darius staring right back. There was so much pain in Darius's shining eyes, a hair away from tears. There was no accusation there, but there was a question. Did you do it, that glance asked.

"No," Erik snapped, never looking away from Darius. "This despicable act is no fault of mine. I had no knowledge of it, though my mother certainly could have conceived of it as a way to destroy your family, and set the plan in motion even after she knew the hour of her death. To get you to blame the wrong man and then do something...rash. What does Jun have to say about it? Or the Temple of Zelek? You must have paid for scrying."

"They know nothing," Darius rasped, his voice barely recognizable. What must he have been through? "Every scrying showed Jun has been faithful to me. Only I ever came to her bed. An illusion was employed, but we have no idea who did it or how."

"There are literally hundreds of nobles who have blond hair and my complexion," Erik pointed out, looking from Crispus to Totarius, and then back to Darius. "You know me well. Is this act something you could see me implementing? What would I possibly gain from it? I don't possess illusion magic, and if I required company for the evening, I have never had a problem securing it. Darius has been my friend since we were children. You are being used, though I don't know by who. You have many enemies. My brother perhaps? He's certainly capable of such a despicable act, and would relish the division he has caused among his enemies."

"No." Totarius slowly shook his head, expression unreadable. "I have an alliance with your brother. He'd have no reason to jeopardize that, certainly not for something so trivial. I am not fully convinced of your innocence, nor are the people of this city. Rumors are already flying. They say my son has been supplanted by the child Imperator."

Erik glanced at Jun, who was watching him now. She raised a hand and signed, *I have been true. I would never betray my husband.*

The shield thrummed at his side, and he knew to his core she spoke the truth. He nodded to her and offered an empathetic smile.

"For whatever it's worth," Erik began as he looked to Crispus, the real power here it seemed. "I can tell you in my capacity as Steward of Justice that Jun speaks the truth. She had no knowledge of the betrayal. Someone certainly has, and you've already stated illusion was likely involved. That means we can't know what happened, but we do know she is innocent and should be treated as such."

"I make the laws," Crispus snapped, eyes wild. "Not you, Steward. You enforce the laws *I* make. If I say she dies for bearing this insult, then she dies, and there is *nothing* you can do to stay my blade."

"Of course, Your Highness," Erik quickly agreed, then sank to one knee. Humility was the only course left.

"Brother, please," Darius pleaded, then also sank to his knees. "Erik didn't do this. Jun didn't do this. Someone has used my family to insult you and Father. Your wrath is righteous, but it should be reserved for the fool who targets our family. It falls upon me to find the culprit, and Erik can help me do that. Please, Your Highness, allow us to find the person who did this and present them to you for punishment. Then your terrible wrath will have a proper target."

"Very well." Crispus waved magnanimously with his free hand, every finger decked with rings. "Know that my patience is not infinite, however. Find the culprit soon, and she lives. I may even allow you to determine the babe's fate, depending on my mood. Be swift."

Erik rose to his feet. "Thank you, Your Highness. We will not fail you."

## 10

---

## REVELATIONS

I awoke out of a daze, sitting at my writing desk with the stylus hovering over the parchment. I hadn't fallen asleep precisely, but my mind had been wandering for some time. A fiery phoenix burst through the window and spoke in Erik's voice, which returned me to reality.

"I have the worst news imaginable." Erik's voice was tinged with an emotion I'd never heard from him. Fear. "Jun and Darius are in the capital, and her life is in danger. She gave birth to a child who greatly resembles me or another Valysian family. I don't know who. I can make guesses, but I have no proof. I thought you should know. I do not require aid."

I dropped my stylus and rose to my feet. I didn't have to think about it. I didn't have to mull Erik's words. I knew immediately who would both be devious enough to pull off something so awful and have the resources to make the terrible crime reality.

Saghir had already returned to his own quarters, but it was best I did this alone anyway. Saghir hated Ducius and might take rash action before I determined the truth of things.

I raised a hand and sketched a reply, the phoenix winging out the same window. *I'll have a chat with your brother.*

Then I shifted to demon form and leapt out the window. I missived Saghir to tell him I was leaving and Ena to summon her. By the time I'd climbed into the sky, Ena was winging up to join me, her wings fully healed.

"What's going on?" she called over the wind as she drew even at the same altitude, our powerful wing beats keeping us more or less stationary.

"We're going to go have a chat with Ducius, or I am rather," I called back to her. "I need you to ensure no one interferes, that's it."

"Done. Do I want to know why?" A sudden gust carried her higher, but she quickly returned to the same elevation.

"Trust me...you don't. This could come to blows, so be ready." I winged toward the lights in the distance, which I knew corresponded to the capital, the city of Olivantia. Ducius rarely left it these days, the spider at the center of his web.

I flew unerringly toward the palace, the land darkening as true night fell. By the time Ena and I reached the city's outer walls, the stars twinkled above, and the spirit moon hung ominously above, lighting our way.

The palace loomed before us at the center of the city, perched upon the highest hill. There at the very top, the same level where I'd fought for my life and seized the very artifacts that had empowered Ducius, burned a roaring fire. A solitary figure stood upon the balcony, and even without my senses, I knew exactly who it was.

I landed on the rain-slicked stones opposite Ducius, who

had his hands clasped behind his back. The handsome noble appeared unarmed, not a surprise, but what did surprise me was his expression. Sadness. Grief. He had been crying.

"Is it true?" I didn't bother with a greeting, instead stalking toward him, my hand resting on Narlifex's hilt. In demon form, I must have been intimidating, but he appeared more sad than anything.

"Are your suspicions true?" he replied, blinking as a light misting rain began, beading his hair with water. The moment stretched. "Yes, more or less. The crux of them, anyway. The child is mine, but I did not crawl into her bed and do the deed myself if that's what you're asking."

"Xal?" Ena demanded from behind me. "What is he talking about?"

"In a moment. Let me get to the truth of things first," I reassured her, then slowly eased Narlifex from my sheath and glared at Ducius. "How did you do it?"

"A spell from the waning days of the Elentian Empire. A powerful noblewoman wished to bear her lover's son, without her husband being the wiser. Her solution was brilliant." Ducius slowly unfolded his arms from behind his back, his hands wrapped in stitched leather gloves rich with embroidered runes. "The spell requires a special set of artifacts and reagents to work. I needed Jun's hair for one, and one from Darius. A surmountable challenge, thankfully. During their lovemaking, for a single evening, the first time, it was me, not him. My body. He was merely a surrogate for me and delivered my seed, not his own. Darius did the deed. His wife has never touched another, save you, so far as I know. Yet I can see from your expression and know from my scrying that you view this as the worst sort of betrayal. I don't understand."

"You violated her," I growled, the need to kill growing within me, barely containable. "You violated him. I am not close with Darius, but what you did would be wrong no matter who you did it to."

"Let's agree to disagree on that point." Ducius slowly folded his arms, every motion made to allay my fears. "What will it take for you to get past this? That possibility exists. I know you see it too. What could we still accomplish together? You are gambling the fate of the cycle in alienating me. It makes no sense to throw away such a fruitful alliance because of a—well, an out-of-hand prank, from my perspective."

"Why?" My eyes narrowed. I knew, and the blade knew, Ducius's life hung in the balance.

"Eternal life." Ducius tensed but made no move to retreat. "The boy is tethered to my own soul. In the event that I die, he is one potential vessel I might flee to. My soul and consciousness would override the boy's own, and I would continue on. Dark, perhaps, but a necessary precaution. We are battling for the cycle itself, Xal. If you grow squeamish over tactics, we are all of us doomed. Please. See reason. You can be as angry as you wish. You can deal only with Temis if you wish. But please don't do anything rash. We will both regret it."

"Why her?" Narlifex thrummed in my hand, his life balanced on the edge.

"She's powerful." Ducius shrugged, his expression clinical. "So is Darius. The child will be well cared for. I know Darius far better than you do and have always hated him. He will be violently angry, at first, but he will see that Jun loves the child, so he will accept and raise it as his own. That child will be protected, loved, sheltered, and wealthy. And if I do not die, then he will age and die without ever knowing we were linked. I apologize for endangering our alliance and for harming those you care about. Is there a way we can move past this?"

"I don't think so." There was no hesitation. I followed my instincts. At least I had control again. I slammed my sword home in its sheath and enjoyed the way Ducius flinched. "I will tell Saghir, and I expect he'll wish to leave the council. If he does, then we'll take the spider mountain north, away from your nation. We don't seek war with you, but you won't have our aid any longer. Call it a truce if you like."

"You're letting him live?" Ena stepped into my field of view, her expression tight with anger. "Make it make sense."

"His life isn't ours to take," I snarled, though the anger wasn't at her. "That belongs to Jun and Darius. Erik asked me to find the truth, and I have. If Jun asks my help? There isn't a rock you can hide under, Ducius. I will find you. And I will still find a way to triumph. I'm not compromising my principles to secure an easy win. And I'm not spending even one more moment in your presence."

I leapt into the sky and began flapping away.

At first, I worried that Ena wasn't following, but after several tense heartbeats, she leapt into the sky and followed me. I didn't know how Saghir would react. I didn't know what the consequences would be. I didn't care. I couldn't let this stand.

"You did the right thing," Ena roared over the wind as she pulled up alongside me. "I'm sorry I questioned you."

"Don't be," I called back, genuinely grateful. "You're my conscience. I hate that I have to let him live. For now, at least. But he's right. I have to be pragmatic. We're playing for all the stones, in all the worlds that have or ever will exist."

"Then why did you break the alliance?" she called. "I don't understand."

"I don't know." I hated the admission. It sounded so irrational. "I can't live with it. I can't. Maybe it's the wrong choice, but it's the only choice I feel I can make and still look Jun in the eye. And Li. And myself."

"I hope it doesn't hurt us, but I'd have killed him outright, so you're ahead of me, at least." Ena gave a harsh laugh. "At least you've learned the truth. Let's hope Saghir sees reason. I'd just as soon be away from here."

"What about Liloth?" I eyed her sidelong, the spirit moon painting the right half of her face an eerie grey.

"We both know she and I can't stay together." Ena gave a huge sigh, audible even over the wind as we sailed over the sleeping nation. "We'll see each other again, but we are fighting different wars. I will miss her, but knowing who she serves? She'll stay with him after this. She might already know. I'm attracted to her, but this.... It tells me just how ruthless she really is. How different we are."

I didn't reply. How could I? I agreed with everything she was saying. Was there a way to salvage this? I certainly hoped so, because if not, I'd just gone from a bad situation to a worse one.

## 11

---

## PRICES

By the time Ena and I landed on my balcony and strode into my quarters, Saghir and Temis were already there. Saghir sat in midair, a tiny mug of steaming tea between his paws. Temis sat in one of the wooden chairs next to my writing desk, his hands folded in his lap and his long dark hair tucked under a woolen cap.

A copy of *Rat & Demon* sat on the desk before Temis, and his eyes were locked on the pages as he slowly turned them, devouring the story. He didn't even appear to realize I'd arrived. Completely mesmerized.

I couldn't feel any of the joy I would have that morning, in light of what I'd just learned.

Saghir glanced up to meet my gaze, his smile melting as he caught my mood. He asked nothing, which I realized must have been due to Temis's presence. "Welcome back, friend Xal."

Temis still didn't look up but was nearing the end of the tome. He completed the last page, then glanced up with a start, blinking at my presence. "I didn't realize you'd returned. Apologies." Temis's excited expression crumbled to ruin. "I already know. Some of it at least. Ducius messaged me the moment you departed."

"Then you won't be surprised by my reaction." I contained my anger and sat in the chair opposite him, shifting back to human form by the time my rear reached the seat. "I cannot work with Ducius. Not after this. What he did to Jun is indicative of his character. It's only a matter of time before he betrays you, and the council, and me, and anyone and everyone else. You have to know that."

"Of course I do." Temis's handsome features shifted into a frown, not an expression I was used to seeing. He picked up a mug of tea, savored a sip, then set it back down. "It was the same with my grandfather, I am told. They needed him, but every one of his dreadlords knew they were expendable. Merely pieces on a Kem board, with him the player. That's what he seeks a return to. I have to stop him. The question is...will you help me do that or abandon me to fight him alone?"

"A clever tack," Saghir interjected. His expression was neutral. "Before we proceed...you both know of his crime. I would hear the truth."

"He impersonated Darius and sired Jun's child," I gave bluntly. "He did it to enact a spell to tie his soul to the boy. It makes him immortal, in a way. He can obey the dictates of the cycle, without ever really dying. The power is undeniable, but the cost is monstrous."

"I see." Saghir's expression darkened to almost feral. "We deal harshly with rapists in Gateway. Generally they are staked to the ground atop a scorpant hive, and honey is smeared on their nether regions. A few survive, but they serve as a warning to the rest. Now that I am a summoner, I could bring my culture directly to Ducius. I have always hated him but never knew why. Now I do."

Temis heaved a significant sigh.

"All I can do is offer my apologies." The cultured dread-lord rose awkwardly but made no move to leave. "The question remains...where do we go from here?"

"Xal?" Saghir turned toward me. "Have you given that course thought? If we are no longer attached to the council, we can simply leave and deal with more pressing problems. We have acquired the sapling and have no reason to remain here."

"So you have no loyalty to the council then?" Temis's voice had taken on a hard edge, and his eyes glittered. There was the predator I'd expected.

"None." Saghir rose into the air and stopped at Temis's eye level. "Nor do I have animosity. I have friends. You are one such. Liloth is another. Yet there are but a few more. I do not care for this dreary land, nor for the war with the Tree, that badly seeks to corrupt my friend. Xal is in danger here. Our mission is to save the cycle, not to win your squabble."

"You could give me the ring and go," Temis suggested, a weariness in his tone implying he didn't really believe it would happen. "That would put me on even footing with Ducius. I could counter his influence, and perhaps out—"

"You are impressive in many ways," I interrupted, "but if you think you can outwit Ducius, you are already bound and simply don't know it. You exist as controlled opposition. If you become real opposition, then expect Ducius to escalate and it to end with you having no artifacts, and him possessing all of them."

I expected a harsh rebuttal, and Temis's mouth did open, while his eyes flashed rage. Yet that fanged mouth clicked shut again soon after, no words escaping. Temis nodded and refused to meet my gaze. "I realize that. Almost I think it better I present Saghir with my artifact, but that would rob me of any influence I do hold. I am out of my depths. I cannot both win this war and contain Ducius. Today is a dire one. A pity. On any other, I'd have called your new storytomes a marvel. Now? They scarcely matter. Their existence will not aid me nor stop that monster from swallowing my nation. Ilsa is just as bad, his paramour. Not a shred of empathy nor compassion between them."

"I am sorry, friend Temis." Saghir's tone held genuine regret, but his defensive stance never slackened. He was still ready for battle. "Would that it could be otherwise, but it cannot. Please take the storytome and return to your lands. I will missive Vhala and have her break the news to the legion. Every soldier can decide to stay or go, but we are likely taking much of your new military with us when we depart."

For the first time, I became aware of a conversation taking place behind me. Ena hadn't said a word since we returned until Liloth materialized from the shadows. The pair were whispering together in fierce tones, and it was growing more heated. I tried not to overhear their very private conversation, but that was impossible.

"—not betray him. Cannot betray him," Liloth pleaded. "My people's survival depends upon him."

Temis cleared his throat awkwardly. "Well, then...I will be off. Liloth, I trust you can make your own arrangements to return to the capital?"

"I—" Liloth turned a plaintive look at Ena, who averted her gaze. "I will return with you if you will permit me. It will save me days of running the shadows to the capital."

Ena tensed but said nothing. I stayed out of it.

"We'll be on our way." Temis strode to the door and plucked a soft-furred cloak from the peg on the wall, then wrapped it around his shoulders. "I am so sorry it came to this. Such a promising day ruined by such a stain of a man. One day all of us will find a way to be free of him. It may take an eternity, but his sins *will* catch up with him."

"Sooner rather than later," I growled, power flaring within me. Will manifested in a glow around me, a palpable need to end Ducius's life for what he had done. I should have taken it when I'd had the chance, and honor be damned. "We will meet again, and so far as I am concerned, we are not enemies."

"Xal," Liloth began haltingly, my name awkward on her lips. "Perhaps there is a way to avert some of this fate. If you were to take a seed, a terrible risk I know, you will become an intermediary to the Tree, as Olivanticus was. You might not be confident in your ability to survive the bonding, but having seen you, I certainly am. It is a burden, to be sure, but if you take it up, you might be able to win my people away from him. We would make powerful allies."

"I will consider it," I offered but shook my head slowly. "Probably not right now. Embroiling myself further in this war is a risk. Celeste tells me I have to find a way to become anointed. And I need to help Li free her homeland. I need to help Erik free Ashianna and her father. I need to bring Macha and her sapling back home. There are many vital causes to deal with. Choosing this fight leaves my friends alone in all the others."

"Xal." Ena's voice was an open wound, all emotion. "If we leave this undone, who knows when we will come back? I'm speaking as a hound, not as a lover about to be parted. If the Tree can be an ally, if the na'elfen can be allies, we will never have a better chance. Let's do what needs doing and quit this place. But let's not leave prematurely."

"She speaks wisely, I think," Saghir murmured, bowing to Ena. "If we leave...who knows when the fates will allow us to return? If the decision is not to take such a seed, then let us go. If it is undecided? Or if you may take one? Now would be the time."

"If her people need a savior," Ena added, "let it be you instead of that soulless bastard."

"We only offered fealty," Liloth added in a rush, "because Olivanticus could achieve what the Tree needed."

I reached into my pack and withdrew the copy of *Rat & Demon*, which had been half a book when I'd added it. The copy was whole and undamaged now, and every page was living redwood. I had a bargaining chip.

Could I shape the Tree's behavior? Could I prevent it from waging war on Olivantia? Countless lives would be saved...and I would also be taking immense pressure off a man I'd just converted into an enemy.

It was still the right thing to do. I felt a fool doing it, tactically speaking, but some part of me sensed this was the proper path. I didn't want to regret it later.

"Very well. We'll salvage something from this fiasco." I rose and shifted back to demon form, flaring my wings behind me. "I will take a seed, treat with the Tree, and see what accord can be reached. If I can free Liloth's people, I will. I do not know what to expect, but that question cannot answer itself. Wait here. I will return."

I strode to the balcony and leapt into the night, gliding down the mountains toward the malevolent forest below. It watched me even as I studied it, each of us aware of the other as I approached. I didn't stop at the fringes of the forest. I flew deep within it, slowing only when I approached the great Tree itself, which towered over its neighbors.

The floor beneath was littered with pine cones. Seeds. I didn't know exactly how it worked, but I glided to the ground and landed outside the shimmering barrier created by the vithi, as close to the Tree as I could get without attempting to breach it.

I reached down and plucked up a small cone, smaller than the pine cones near Hasra, tiny in my massive demon fist. I opened my hand and peered at it. It lay there innocently...until tendrils burst out and began worming into my flesh. There was pain, but far more discomfort, especially at the idea of that thing tunneling into my body. The tendrils flowed in for long moments, then abruptly ceased, the cone nothing but a withered husk now.

Discomfort surged up my arm, then flowed into my chest. I gritted my teeth against the pain as the tendrils flowed from my chest down to my stomach and up my back along my spine. I could feel them violating my flesh, remaking as they went, bonding to me in a way that could not be easily undone.

*Demotech is always so*, Narlifex hissed. *Pay the price and embrace the power.*

I didn't have time to respond. The tendrils reached the back of my neck, and blinding pain assailed me. It was indescribable, really. Pain is the closest analogy, but it was more the remaking of my mind, my memories and consciousness being torn apart, a visceral tide of will deciding what my new form would be.

*No!*

I clenched my hands into fists and held on to the present. To my senses. To the forest around me, to the trees swaying above, the mighty redwoods creaking as they screamed their adulation, the growth of their collective.

The invasion pushed, but I pushed back. My will against its will. I allowed some of the remaking but drew boundaries as I wished, hemming in the Tree's influence within me. It was a game of Kem, racing through my body and my mind, desperately claiming territory while the Tree did the same.

An instant or an eternity...it was the same. When it ended, I blinked up at the Tree, which was now a part of me, its mind lurking in the corner, watching. It was massive and primal and completely unlike a human. It could not think. It could not reason with speech. Yet it had imperatives. It must survive, at any cost. It must spread. That was the only way to contain the contagion within it.

If it failed, the world died. I saw within it what the Great Trees were. The Columns of the Cycle. They anchored dream and spirit and life together and existed in all realms simultaneously. I could see it now, see it from the Tree's memories. Impressions mostly, but it could see and hear through every part of itself, and many consumed had eyes and ears, and those too were contained within it.

In theory, I could find anyone in the collective using the seed. We were all connected. Yeva. Liloth. And every mindless consumed within this forest. Suddenly I was a part of it and no longer a direct enemy.

The Tree no longer saw me as a threat, though I imagined that could change in an instant if my actions warranted it. Then the whole of the forest would come for me.

Sadly, there was no immediate relief. No answers. The link existed now, but I saw no way to reason with the Tree, to offer it a deal. You do something, and in return I do something else. There was simply no way to communicate that.

I gave a sigh and leapt into the sky, flapping back toward the spider mountain. Perhaps in time, I could deepen the connection, but thus far it had been nothing but a disappointment.

I couldn't save this country.

I couldn't even save myself.

# INTERLUDE VI - CELESTE

Celeste had never been comfortable within the spirit realm. Zelek, the stewards's most solitary member, sometimes dwelt here. He'd warned her millennia ago that many divine beings had gone to ground within its misty depths, hiding from the rest of the gods, and many still retained most of their power.

In short...the godswar had never ended here, and losing a skirmish with such a being could send her spinning into the maw and leave her artifact trapped outside the realm of creation, forever diminishing the remaining Stewards.

They strode along a path flanked by a thicket of skeletal trees, their grasping branches straining for her and occasionally catching a strand of hair, which lost its color the instant it was pulled from her and then tumbled to the mist shrouding the ground.

"Steward, a word?" Li fell into step behind her, the princess's eyes cast down to the trail, respectful but not so dutiful as they had once been. Girl no longer. She had truly become a woman. A fine one.

"I'll provide counsel if I can." Celeste used her staff as a walking stick, the color bleeding into the ground briefly each time she took a step.

"You are able to aid me," Li ventured hesitantly as her feet all but floated over the trail. "What are the limits? What will the staff permit? Can you battle dragons? And if not, what kind of sorcery do you bring to bear? That sounds so crass, but I have to understand the situation. I do not wish to expect something you cannot provide."

Despite the question, the princess's attention was reserved for the shadow high above darkening an already dreary sky. Volos, the mighty wyrm who watched over them and ensured that no one and nothing took an interest in their passage.

"My artifact will not permit me to intervene directly." Celeste struggled to keep the irritation from her voice. The constraints chafed more than they ever had. "I can offer guidance, miracles, and very little else. I cannot rain destruction spells on them, or rather I could, but I am a very mortal battlemage, with very real limits. Your friend Saghir, with his ring, possesses as deep a pool as I do and would likely be nearly as useful in my stead."

A dozen paces ahead of them stalked Tuat, but the white-haired wyrm stooped and turned to face them, expression grim. "My cousin's children will possess similar spells and more. Many are old even as I measure such things and remember the cycle's glory, before the first war that tore it asunder. Your plan seems...foolish. Why not simply anoint the demon prince and allow him to tend to the problem?"

"I—" Celeste didn't want to admit they hadn't the slightest idea how, but her pride was the least of her concerns. "Such knowledge has long been lost to us. I have tomes referencing the anointing, but only vaguely, and none explain the precise trials involved."

"I don't understand." Tuat cocked his head, peering at Celeste with those slitted inhuman eyes. "You yourself are anointed. How did this occur without your knowledge? And do you not possess access to Mount Shyar?"

"My artifact is...anointed." She was making assumptions there, but they seemed reasonable enough. "It is a shard of power gifted to me by the god Rei. All my brethren bear one."

"Ahh." Tuat's expression shifted to discomfort. "Then I have overstepped my bounds. I must take greater care. If you are not truly anointed, then telling you how to become so would break my oath. I could, however, ask a question like why do you not simply ask Mount Shyar to show you the knowledge you seek?"

Celeste froze. Her eyes widened. Everything, absolutely everything, was re-contextualized by that comment. What else could Mount Shyar show her? How did she communicate with it? She was the Steward of Magic. It was her duty to find out, and she'd have wagered all the coin she'd ever amassed that her staff would allow her to issue orders.

"Are you all right?" Li asked, peering at Celeste. Oddly Tuat was peering at Li, studying the princess sidelong. Hungrily. It wasn't physical attraction. She'd seen the way Xal eyed the girl, and this was a different kind of hunger.

"Just thinking." Celeste brought herself back to the situation at hand and forced away the other lines of thought. "It seems I can return to Mount Shyar and learn precisely what Xal will require to become anointed. If that's the case...I do not believe I can stay with you in Calmora. Once you are situated, I must go."

"I see." Li's expression hardened, and the princess started up the trail once more.

Tuat fell into step beside her, leaving Celeste trailing after.

"I do not like him," came an unexpected voice from beside her, and Celeste gave a start as she turned to face Tissa. She'd all but forgotten the girl was with them. The brooding assassin glared after Tuat, but then she gazed skyward. "At least the one in the sky isn't hiding what he is. Without your help, or theirs, are you sending Li and me to our deaths in Calmora? We came because we expected divine aid. If you abandon us, what chance do we have?"

"Greater than you know," Celeste countered, then started up the trail after Li and Tuat. "Tuat recognizes your mistress. I do not know of Nunut or her lineage, but she is close to the titans or a titan herself, like Xal. She carries the first bow, though I note that wisely she keeps it out of sight in a way you did not. You are hound to a demon prince and have murdered an Imperator in his own palace. You bear the blade of rage, Nefarius, borne by a Steward and a demon prince and forged by a goddess. I would not discount the pair of you just yet. Li has also mentioned a resistance led by her friend Bumut. You will not be entirely alone."

"All that eases your guilt," Tissa countered, glaring at the Steward. "It does nothing to aid our victory."

Then the assassin was gone once more, flitting through the spirit realm where she seemed as at home as she did in the shadows of the mortal realm. Celeste possessed the means to find her, but the magics were taxing, and there was no point to it. Tissa wasn't an enemy.

Nor was she at all wrong. In fact, Celeste hated how astute the girl was.

She quickened her pace until she approached Tuat and

Li, who'd begun quietly chatting. She couldn't make out the words and didn't wish to, but Tuat's tone was one of familiarity.

Nunut wasn't mentioned in any records. Xal certainly was. Many gods were. So who was she, and how did Tuat recognize her? From whatever had preceded the cycle? Just how far back did that unmapped history go? Ignorance might cost more than her life. It might cost the cycle itself.

How much of this did Zelek know? Or suspect, at least? More than she'd have liked, she wagered.

She needed to get to Mount Shyar as soon as possible and learn more of this anointing. Abandoning Li and Tissa was painful, but both were reincarnations of gods. She needed to remember that. She wasn't an all-powerful sorceress, and they were not students just out of the academy.

They began to climb higher and higher until the path fell away and they walked among the clouds. On and on the path went, giving her time to mull over her path going forward, but eventually it spilled out onto a mountaintop where Tuat waited.

The great wyrm held his blade before him, then abruptly slashed at the sky, which fell away to reveal blue sky and a snow-covered peak...back in the realm of the living.

"Go," he prompted, eyes fixed upon Li. "I do not know your fate. I hope it meets a happier end than your last incarnation. I am sorry for the turmoil before you. Remember, dark times exist so that we will treasure the light."

Li merely nodded, then stepped through without hesitation. Tissa materialized like a second shadow and followed, her scarlet blade drawn and held at the ready.

"Can you tell us if Khonsu is present?" Celeste asked as she ducked through the tear, back into warmth and color.

She gazed over the peaks of Calmora, which stretched before her to the north and west.

"He is not here," rumbled a deep voice from behind Tuat as a pair of slitted eyes appeared, each larger than Tuat. Volos's fangs dripped with saliva...and worse. "The coward hides himself within the dream realm."

"We will continue on and find his scent. Luck to you." Tuat turned from them and the veil snapped shut, leaving the three women alone on the snowcapped peak.

"I suppose this is goodbye?" Li called as she tightened her parka about her, seemingly unaffected by the cold.

"It is." Celeste peered at the sky. "I need to get to Shyar and capitalize on the knowledge Tuat gave us. If I can learn of these trials, then perhaps we can aid Xal in completing them. I fear that is the only chance we have against the forces arrayed against us."

"I see how powerful those two are." Tissa shivered as she stared at the space where the tear had been. "Others are coming. If Xal can stop them with this anointing, then you should aid him."

"Then I shall." Celeste willed herself to become wind, then flowed into the sky and began her journey.

Let the answers she sought be there. If they were not.... No, a possibility best not considered.

Celeste spared a final glance back at the mountaintop, but Li and Tissa had already vanished. Would that she could aid them in a more material way. It would have been fun if nothing else.

She turned east and flew toward the rising sun.

## 12

## PASSAGE NORTH

I writhed uncomfortably as the seed continued to burrow within me. I could feel the tendrils thickening, a sensation I had no wish to repeat, though I wouldn't have called it painful precisely. As the mass grew so too did the connection to the alien consciousness, its influence over my moods more potent by the moment.

If I was not careful, its rage would become my irritation. The emotion could be controlled, but the influence was undeniable, and I already hated it. The insidiousness of it.

Yet the seed carried benefits. I brimmed with physical strength, ready to tear apart an opponent should one present itself. A feral rage drove every action, and it always sought a target. It reminded me a good deal of Nefarius, but a softer version. Easier to manage. I could summon it at will and unleash my full fury upon any fool.

*Worth the discomfort*, Narlifex growled. *It increases our strength in a way I am unfamiliar with. So long as you retain control, this is only a benefit in the days ahead. We will need this power.*

I silently agreed as I exited my quarters and stepped out upon the balcony to find Saghir already waiting. The robed mage hovered in midair, his tail drooping while Ikadra's sapphire blazed.

Our legions were arrayed below, one of them military and the other a sprawling support camp. Every last follower gazed up at us, standing at attention. I staggered under the weight of their devotion, and it wasn't reserved solely for me. Some of it, a goodly portion, was for Saghir.

Something was changing. He was becoming a god in his own right. Or a demigod at the very least.

"Are we prepared, friend Xal? Give the order, and I will begin our march to freedom." Saghir glared at the forest, then back toward the capital. "I would be away from this foul land."

"I never can be." I sighed as I stared into the blood wood, at the tree I could now sense. "I'll carry it with me. It's not all bad though. *Rat & Demon* seems to please it. Or lessen its pain, at least. The more we make, the more it eases. So we can still make a difference here."

"That's something, at least." Ena stepped from the shadows, which caused me to look around for Liloth, but there was no trace of the na'elfen. She'd returned to Olivanticus, and I could see from the lines around Ena's demonic eyes that the pain weighed upon her. "I don't wish them ill, but I'm with Saghir. Let's be away from this place."

I raised my wings high and then my right arm, bringing the arm down in a chopping motion, my wings descending at the same time. "When you are ready, old friend."

Saghir perfectly timed it so the spider mountain lurched into motion at the same time, and every throat echoed the same cheer as our little army lumbered northward, toward new lands.

"Have you considered our path, friend Xal?" Saghir folded his arms and left Ikadra hanging in the air next to him.

"I have. Take us past the mines of Enuria. I'd see them from a closer vantage." I still remembered passing by in *The Fist* as we flew toward the Ashlands. "We won't have time to explore it, but we can get a look as we pass. Then skirt the plains of Arlen. It's faster than clambering over the mountains, but be ready to climb the Khalist peaks if the knights in Arlen take umbrage."

"They likely will, given that you slew their Steward." Saghir gave a grin and pushed his spectacles up his nose. "We will arrive in Lukantria tomorrow, within sight of the mountains where the Arena lies. With our entire army. What a marvel this beast is. I remember wondering why it existed, who would make such a thing, but now I understand how useful it can be. A beast of burden!"

"I'd never have seen it so. My thinking is too limited," I realized aloud. "We've been thinking like mortals. I need to think more like a god. Harnessing tools like this is within our reach, and they had better be if we're going to have a chance against Totarius."

"Do you have any idea what he's up to?" Ena wondered as she joined me at the railing. "I know he's in Valys, but not much else."

"Solidifying worship, I'd wager." I gripped the rail hard. "He's gaining influence in all lands, but his goal is the avatars under the southern ocean. Tissa said he was obsessed with them before she defected to our side. My aunt has control of the ocean of *void* under Hasra. With that power and enough worship, we might be facing two titanic avatars. I haven't seen them, but some of the ones in my vision could pick up this mountain like a lap drake."

"Soo...mountain-sized demon gods?" Ena gave a low whistle. "I had some idea what we expected, but the reality is daunting. What do we do about them? Can we get one of our own?"

"I don't think so." I raised a wing to shelter us from harsh gusts kicked up by the mountain's passage. "Totarius has specific targets. He's taking bodies used in previous godswars and repurposing them, probably with the Forges of Xa. They're named after the soul he carries. It makes sense. If we had the worship and magic, maybe we could get there first, but—"

We trailed off as Vhala jogged up the stairs, the dark-skinned companion's breath misting before her. Her smile surprised me given the separation from Erik. "This reminds me a good deal of home. The snows and the mountains towering above. I came to inform you that my people are now working with Macha to guard the Tree. It is our top priority, myself included. We will see that no harm comes to it." Then her expression tightened. There it was. "Any news from Erik?"

"Not since...news about Jun." I offered a forearm, and she accepted it with a strong grip. "Thank you for the report. If I hear from Erik, I'll missive immediately. I don't want to bother him, given the company he might be keeping."

"I understand." She released me and stepped back, then delivered a nod to Saghir. "Archmage. Your storytomes are spreading through my ranks like consumed past a broken wall. Won't be long until all of them have read it. They are pressuring me to ask when the next volume will be ready... if that's not impertinent."

Saghir gave a chittering laugh, but for me the elation was much more calculated. I could feel the worship growing stronger. Many who'd come for opportunity had found faith in our cause, and it strengthened me daily.

"I have nearly finished." Saghir opened a void pocket and tossed Ikadra unceremoniously inside, then snapped it shut. "I will return to friend Xal's quarters and finish the next volume. Once I have completed it, I will bring it down to you. Our esteemed mount will be walking until the sun sets, so I have plenty of time to be about my work."

"Wonderful." Vhala smiled again, though with less enthusiasm than before. "I shall return to my troops and inform them they will have more story soon." She nodded at me, then turned and left.

Saghir waited for her to depart before finally turning to me. "Why do you not ask her to adhere to the same formalities as the other officers?"

"Her heart belongs to Erik." I smiled wistfully. "To her, we'll always be the bedraggled pair helping to retrieve Brutus's body from that airship. Just a couple urchins. It's refreshing, in a way, to see that not change when so much else has. I like that not everyone reacts to me with overwhelming fear or a desire to be a sycophant."

The spider mountain lumbered north, and the tree line began to thin as we entered the foothills. Large peaks blocked the way before us, but our mount merely scrambled over them, though the quakes did require me to stabilize myself with my wings.

The magnitude of what we were doing—crossing the world with an army—it staggered me. If I could build a real fighting force, I could go around any threat I didn't want to address, while delivering overwhelming force to the areas I did. We could retreat just as quickly, and even airships would be hard-pressed to catch us, especially with the Hasran fleet so severely weakened.

On and on the mountain climbed, and the further we went, the more the snows thickened, and the more a feeling of familiarity grew within me. I'd flown over the Forge of Reevanthara, buried under the remains of Enuria, but now I was passing closer than before. Were I to tunnel through the earth, I could reach it in a bell or two, I imagined.

I couldn't afford that distraction, especially knowing I could simply return whenever I wished. We'd be camped a few hundred leagues north, at most. I could fly back here soon, once I knew we were established and the sapling protected.

Before long, we reached the other side, and the spider mountain clambered down onto the high plains of Arlen, picking up speed as he hurried north. The sun had already begun to set, but even in the short time before it sank entirely, lighting the sky a molten orange-red, the mountain had carried us a dozen leagues.

By the time it set down roots, stabbing its legs into the earth and becoming a simple mountain range, I could make out the glittering lights of Lukantria in the distance. The city lined several mountain slopes, sprawling across two adjacent peaks. Behind them loomed what could only be the largest structure in the world.

The Arena.

Not an arena. Not even the Arena of Gateway, which had been so impressive. This one towered over them all, and every arena I'd ever fought in would have fit neatly inside this one.

"That is where we are heading tomorrow," Saghir chittered as he landed upon my shoulder. "I can scarcely wait. I will have several copies of *Rat & Demon* ready before we leave in the morning. Perhaps we can bring a few to trade within the city when you hire mercenaries."

"Perhaps. I'm looking forward to seeing what this city has in store for us." I couldn't remember the last time I'd actually been excited to go someplace new. Lukantria had retained its freedom for centuries. It was based around war and fighting.

Sounded like home to me.

## 13

## LUKANTRIA

I enjoyed the short flight from the spider mountain to the city of Lukantria, which was lined by high granite spires, many outfitted with docks to serve airships like *The Fist*.

Saghir had made a number of alterations to *The Fist*, including a pair of double doors and a ramp that could be opened with a command word spoken by the declared captain. The interior had been lined with plush pillows and now greatly resembled one of the inns I'd seen in Gateway, complete with an eight-hosed hookah. Several stone partitions had been erected to afford privacy, and I knew Ena had moved into the largest.

I'd hoped to bring her with us, but she'd made a valid point that taking her would weaken the defense around the sapling. Besides, I could summon her at will if I needed her in combat, so she was within reach.

"There we go." Saghir waved a hand and two more story-tomes floated into the new pack he'd constructed from enchanted bone and magical hides. I didn't ask where he'd acquired them. "I thought we might return to the old ways while in this city. I've built a wonderful new battle pack, just like we used in the Arena, but with magical fortifications, void pockets, and several stored summons ready for emergencies."

"Impressive." I approached, knelt, and hefted the pack. "Lightweight too. Perfect for my human form, but if I shift to demon, it looks like I can still use my wings. I assume that was intentional?"

"Good of you to notice." Saghir's grin widened, and he drifted down to the pack. "From the interior, I can release a storm of death and enhance you in a variety of ways. This is the perfect city in which to unveil it, particularly when we have no one we are responsible for protecting but ourselves. I pity the first tough to assail us."

A laugh bubbled out of me, the first since Li and Erik had departed. "Well let's get this cinched so we can go explore the city. Looks like we're landing." I nodded at the earthen map in *The Fist*'s main chamber, which shifted to show Lukantria's spires surrounding the Arena.

"This will be our first official docking." Saghir zoomed over to the double doors he'd created. "I'm quite excited and happy to pay for the privilege. Imagine...our ship being secure and guarded, instead of stashed in the bushes like we are usually forced to do."

The doors rolled open to reveal a howling wind as the ramp oozed out and joined to the tower to provide us with a bridge. I ducked out and onto the path, shocked at the strength of the wind as I ducked inside the tower's relative shelter. A normal ratkin lacking Saghir's magic would be in real danger just exiting the ship.

Nor were there handrails on the way down. A simple stone ramp wound down around the tower until it reached the ground. As our ship was the only one attached to the

tower there, we were the only patrons filing down, and I felt
eyes on us before we reached the ground.

I scanned the boulevard leading deeper into the city and
more importantly, the alleyways across from it. Unsurprisingly, I found the watchers. A half-dozen children, none
older than ten, sat playing some sort of dice game.

I knew immediately it was a cover. Their eyes were too
hard, their motions too practiced. They were acting out a
game children played, but these were no longer children, no
matter their age. They lived on the street. One of them even
resembled a young Nef.

I also knew they could be a problem if not handled
correctly.

"I'm going to get us a little more security." I cinched the
battle pack's straps a bit tighter, the weight strange after so
long not carrying one. I'd adjust quickly.

I approached the mouth of the alley deliberately but at a
slow walk. To my surprise, none of the urchins fled.

"That ship is mine," I called in Hasran, which I assumed
was the common language there. None answered, but I
spied understanding in those gazes. "I want it to still be
mine when I get back. If someone crests that ramp, I need to
know." I reached into my pocket and tossed a violet dragonscale I'd taken from the Mad Imperator's horde. The urchin
caught the fortune I'd given them out of the air, his eyes a
bit wider. "We'll be back in two bells or less."

That got me a nod, still the only response. It was
enough.

I nodded gratefully, then strode off, nonchalantly. It was
important they not see me glance back nor doubt them in
any way.

"Can we truly trust them?" Saghir called softly from one

of the pack's many holes. "We are wealthy, but that was a far larger sum than I'd expect for so simple a task."

"I wasn't paying them," I whispered back. "I was paying whoever they work for. It's a gesture of respect, and it says I know they exist, I respect them, and I will pay whatever fees they might have, without comment or protest."

"Your childhood was vastly different than mine." Saghir gave a chittering laugh. "We were quite...direct in Gateway. In my home, a threat would have been the most common bargain you struck back there."

I scanned the street ahead of me as I ambled away from the dock toward the row of inns and brothels lining the next several streets. That part seemed similar in every city. I spied a large marble edifice and was unsurprised at the statue of Thandres outside. At least some of the Stewards held sway in this city, though I didn't see any temples to justice or magic. There were plenty of kamizas. Dozens. Every few entrances along the boulevard contained another. That told me Zaro held sway there. I wondered if he held a grudge?

I decided to duck inside the next kamiza I passed, under a blue awning, the cries of combatants reminding me of my time in Calmora. I rounded a corner and saw two dozen students artfully pummeling each other in a brutally efficient martial art that focused on grapples and knocking your opponent prone.

As I entered, a bald man composed completely of granite rose and approached. He could have been a statue come to life, though strains of both granite and marble ran through his body.

"Welcome," the strange rock-man rumbled as he offered a shallow bow. "Have you come to test into the kamiza?"

"I...haven't," I admitted, unsure of the proper protocol. I

probably should have researched this in advance. "I've come to the city looking to hire an army. I pay well, and—"

That was as far as I got before the rock-man rose with a huff, spun on his heel, then thudded back over the practice mats. None of the others ever glanced in my direction. We'd been dismissed, it seemed.

"Perhaps he does not like humans?" Saghir's reedy voice emanated from the pack once we'd exited back to the thickening traffic.

"I don't think that was it." I shook my head as I considered what we'd witnessed. "He seemed offended at the idea that I might hire him. We need to find out why. It might be helpful to find some sort of guide, like Jon back in Agora."

I scanned the shops around us and spied a large two-story inn with outdoor seating. The space inside was nearly deserted, which was precisely what I sought. I waited for a drifter's wagon to pass, the elephant taking lumbering steps, then darted across and into the inn I'd spotted.

The swinging sign above the door proclaimed the place *The Whetstone*.

The interior was warmer, almost uncomfortably so, and had a strange musky odor. I glanced around at the patrons, and then at the barkeep, and did a triple take.

The barkeep and two of the other patrons were all dragon hatchlings, about the same size Niu had been when I battled her back in Calmora. I almost drew my sword, half expecting some sort of ambush, but none of the patrons seemed interested in me. Each tended to a mug of a foul-smelling concoction that bubbled and hissed as I passed.

"A human?" boomed the barkeep as he picked between razored teeth with a long claw. "Are you lost? Don't often see your sort in this quarter, much less at an acid bar."

That told me what the hatchlings were drinking.

Imagine enjoying acid. I wondered if it got them drunk? Their body language suggested it did. One stumbled from a bar stool, his wing knocking over a pair of empty cups as he staggered back to his feet.

Yup, definitely drunk.

"I'm mostly after information." I sat at the bar as far from the pair of patrons as I could get, and I dropped my voice. "I'm sure it's obvious I'm new here. I've come to hire mercenaries and was told I could find the very best in Lukantria. Yet thus far, those I've approached haven't even been willing to speak to me. They don't seem interested in gold nor scales."

"They are." The hatchling gave a low chuckle like rocks grinding together. He slapped the bar in front of us, and when his scaly palm rose there was no sign of my coin. "Especially the latter. But most of all, they're interested in fame and glory. Every last one wants to die a champion of the Arena, battling overwhelming odds and winning even as they heave their last breath. They ain't gonna sign on with some random no-name human. You got a name I'd have heard of?"

"I doubt it." I suppressed a sigh. "My name is Xal. I'm a demon prince, and—"

"Yeah, yeah." The dragon cut me off with a hand wave. "And that one is the god of the stone falls. And that one is king of lower skies. And that one is…. I don't think I was even listening when she told me. Everyone is a god here, or at least everyone who matters. Doesn't take much to hit a few Catalysts, impress some peasants, and set yourself up as a little god-king. Doesn't impress anyone here."

"I slew Dalanthar and bested Zaro in the same fight," I offered, hoping that would spend like dragon scales in a city that worshipped war.

"Now that," the dragon muttered with a low whistle, "that will get you some ears if the tale is true. My name is Broff, Xal the demon prince. Unless I miss my guess, there's something living inside that box you wear. There a pet in there?"

"An associate." I said nothing further. Saghir would prefer the anonymity. "So tell me...if I wanted to hire mercenaries, what might be the best way to get them to take me seriously?"

"There's only one quick way." Broff continued to clean his teeth and probably had no idea how intimidating it was. "You need to win in the arena and win big. You came at the right time. Champion bouts begin in a week."

"How does house Enestius recruit then, without such a competiton?" I wondered aloud. "I mean they haven't fought in the arena. I know their family, and they'd...not fare well. I've triumphed in Gateway, and it was well beyond their abilities."

"Reputation." Broff gave a jovial laugh, his ample belly shaking. "Everyone knows who Totarius is. They knew and feared his father. The Enestians are vindictive, have a great deal of gold to spend, and win every engagement. You must remember that mercenaries cannot break a contract once taken. If they do, they never work again. If they take your contract and lose, then it doesn't matter how rich the coin. So they are careful. The truly skilled companies will not take a meeting with anyone they don't know, not even a Steward. Your best bet is to find a veteran of the Arena, make them rich, and ride their coattails to enough glory to purchase what you need. You'd best have deep pockets though, for that plan."

# INTERLUDE VII - ERIK

Erik didn't relax even after the guards closed the doors, leaving themselves outside Darius's chambers and him alone with his friend for the first time since he'd come to Valys. Darius's expression was haggard, eyes bloodshot, and his face a scruffy mess in need of a razor.

The poor man sat at a wide stone table, a mug of spiced wine before him. "Jun is tending to the babe. It's an utter nightmare how often the child needs to be fed. I don't envy either of them. I'm...already growing attached to the little tyrant."

Erik sat across from his oldest friend and set his shield on the floor next to the table.

"Can I get you some?" Darius nodded at the wine.

"No. Thank you." Erik rested his gauntlets on the table. "My needs are different now. Wine is...well, it's not something I generally partake of anymore. My duties require me to be sharp, ideally at all times. Enemies are everywhere."

"What's that like?" Darius rolled his eyes, and then they were both laughing. For just an instant, they were children again, dreaming of the academy. "You don't seem overly concerned that my brother is the Imperator and my father much, much more than he appears. This place cannot be safe for you."

"Safety isn't why I've come," Erik countered. He leaned back in his chair, the only concession to comfort he was going to give until he was safely back in his own quarters. Likely not even then. "I have to oppose Crispus and your father. I have to win people back to the Stewards. The cycle's future depends on it."

"I've never known you to be melodramatic." Darius plucked up his cup and downed the contents, then refilled it by hand from the pitcher next to it. "I care far more about my family. My wife, her child, and our children as yet unborn."

"So you've decided to keep the boy?" Erik tried not to sound overly surprised. "I am certain my brother counted on that fact. That's why I've come. I've had confirmation that Ducius is the guilty party. He admitted as such, in a manner that you can personally scry. Xal has provided me the markers."

Erik removed a parchment from his belt and dropped it on the table. He'd recorded everything Darius would need to perform a simple divination and had no doubt his friend would do so as soon as he departed.

"I see." Darius downed the second cup, then refilled it. He set it down with trembling hands and finally met Erik's gaze. "I am no longer a boy. Neither of us is. I cannot go haring off after your brother no matter how badly I wish it. Besides, it would be far more efficient to hire an assassin."

"You'll find my brother annoyingly difficult to kill." Erik moderated his tone. "I can tell you exactly who can help you do it, though. The same person I think you can trust with

the safety of your family were you to, hypothetically speaking, consider leaving this city and heading to safer climes."

"What would you recommend?"

"Xal informs me the champion bouts are coming up in
Lukantria," Erik pointed out casually while boring into
Darius with an intense stare so his friend caught the signifi-
cance. "Perhaps you and your wife could aid in the games?
The mountain air might do the boy good. Perhaps you could
leave a note informing your brother that you didn't wish to
burden him with your drama any longer. I promise...he will
have plenty to occupy his attention."

Erik gave the same sort of overly confident smile that
had come naturally back at the academy, the one that
Darius had grown up trusting. He couldn't summon that
confidence any longer. All his plans had gone awry, and his
fate was nothing like he had imagined it to be.

"Ah...I take your meaning," Darius was saying. "I'll bring
the notion up to Jun and see how she feels about travel.
Both of our peoples hail from the mountains, so the weather
might remind her of home. I'd like...well, when she's ready,
I'd like to make another baby, and that's a place that might
happen."

His friend's pain broke something in Erik. What Ducius
had robbed him of was far more evil than even he should
have been capable of. Erik's station as Steward demanded
justice. Ducius would need to pay with his life.

"What of my brother's fate?" Erik again tried to
moderate his tone but this time failed. The hatred came
through dark and red.

Darius downed another cup, then refilled it. "I'll have his
heart for dinner. I swear it. I'll eat the entire thing. And
when his soul tries to flee into the boy? I will devise a trap
and fashion it into an iron ball. I'll have that ball dropped in

the legion's latrine, where Ducius's soul will live out the rest of its days."

"That seems...oddly specific, but I can't begrudge you your hate." Erik plucked up his shield and rose from the table. "I'm going to return to my quarters. If I don't see you again...we will bring my brother to justice, with or without you. Tend to your family, my friend, to Jun. I cannot imagine what she is going through."

"I will." Darius rose, leaned across the table, and clasped Erik's forearm. "Good luck, old friend. You're a better man than I hoped for when we were growing up. You're a real leader. Everything my brother is not."

"Time will tell." Erik nodded gratefully, then rapped on the door and stepped through when the guards opened it.

Stewards could die. If Xal could kill one, then Totarius could too. Should he flee? Why was everything within him demanding he stay if it was so dangerous?

It didn't matter. He'd be here until the city no longer belonged to Crispus, and until Ashianna, her father, and Erik's own were free.

Justice *must* be served. Whatever the personal cost.

# 14

# BROTHERS

We left Broff's acid bar and inn with promises to return. Broff stocked human liquors and was more than happy to sell some of it. Saghir and I were happy to have a quiet environment to do our planning. It seemed a good base of operations until we had more of an idea about what came next.

"How do you plan to find a veteran?" Saghir asked, his voice issuing from the hole behind my left ear. "Perhaps there are smaller arenas where we can make a name? Pit fighting?"

"My sentiments, yes," I agreed as I reached for a cloak that no longer existed, then lowered my arm and bore the frigid wind as we strode up the cobblestone road. "There have to be many such places, and if we wander until we find one, I suspect we'll be able to make our own luck."

I prowled slowly up the walk, flaring *fire* to warm myself slightly, something that would have impressed younger me a great deal, now done casually. Then I spent time people-watching. Humans were common, but I'd have wagered they comprised less than half the overall population. Dwarven were common, as were orokh, with dragon hatchlings and elfen sprinkled in.

The traffic thickened as we approached the arena, and I still hadn't seen anything that looked like pit fighting. There were kamizas everywhere, and the sounds of combat rang from within, sometimes steel, sometimes fists, yet there was no other form of combat save the arena itself.

"We are being followed," Saghir breathed through the hole behind my ear. "Five total. Earth hatchling, two humans, two orokh. I have watched them from the rear portholes for several blocks, and every time we turn, they do as well."

"I don't see anything like Knights of the Dawn to settle disputes. Guess that means locals are supposed to look after themselves." My mood rose. The idea of being robbed would have terrified me once, but now? I'd battled Stewards. Having someone to take my aggression out on guilt-free was something to relish, not fear. "This alley looks dangerous. I'm going to walk down it to relieve myself."

I strode down the alley, unlaced my breaches, and added to a small pile of filth. By the time I'd cinched them, Saghir had summoned a ball of water, which I used to bathe my hands. "My thanks. I'd forgotten how useful it was carrying an archmage on my back."

By the time I turned back to the alley's mouth, the hatchling had moved to block it, a battle axe held at waist height in the strangest grip I'd encountered. Behind him loomed the other four, all armed and standing in a way that told me they knew how to fight.

"I can't believe they've limited themselves to attacking one at a time," I murmured to Saghir as I slowly unsheathed Narlifex and advanced back up the alley.

"That's a fancy sword," the hatchling rasped. "How about you just lay it down, and—"

I lunged forward, charged Narlifex with a high-magnitude void bolt, then disintegrated his weapon in a slash, the axe dissolving to particles and leaving him as weaponless as a dragon could be. At least it cut off the flow of words.

I was about to follow up with an attack that would have claimed his life, and probably the lives of his companions, but an unexpected falchion whipped by the mouth of the alley, and one of the humans lost a head. The others turned to face him, and our new friend spoke.

"You are lower than fools. You seek your own deaths," rang a familiar voice, one I couldn't immediately place. It was thick with a Gateway accent, not dissimilar from Saghir's. "Do you know who you have trapped in that alleyway? The almukhtar himself. He who has braved the fires at the very heart of the Blasted Lands and faced the beast within. He has journeyed to the Impossible City. One day he will wed the flame and restore that which was lost to my people. More—he is death incarnate. I should let him eradicate you, but such filth is unworthy of even seeing the first blade."

A tengu glided into view, artfully dancing between the combatants, dropping them one after another. The hatchling flapped powerful wings, began to fly away, and would be quickly out of reach unless I shifted. There was no need to bother.

A thick bolt of void-lightning flashed out from the battle pack and caught the hatchling in midair. There was a moment where I could see his entire skeleton, arched rigid, and then he exploded into dust.

"Hadi?" I blinked at my friend, Caw's son, a half a continent from where I expected to find the Tengu warrior. "What brings you so far from the Blasted Lands?"

I didn't thank him for his aid, as I assumed he'd have found it insulting since he already knew I didn't need help.

"I treasure the sight of you, my brother." Hadi lunged forward and seized me in a fierce hug, which I returned, carefully lest I crack his hollow bones. "I'd never have expected you here either. My tale is a long one and best given with water and shade. Where do you take your ease? Or have you not found a spot?"

"Friend Hadi," Saghir's eager voice came from the box. "What a wonderful sight!"

"Friend Saghir." Hadi's voice carried immense respect, and he bowed to the box.

"We're drinking at an acid bar." I nodded back the way we'd come. "It's close to the dock where we've left our airship."

"You have an airship?" Hadi's black eyes widened, and he gave a little croak. "Much has changed. I've heard many rumors about you. That you devour children. That you killed the Imperator for slighting you back at the academy. That you and friend Saghir keep company with dreadlords. That you have—"

"A moment!" Saghir chittered, then a slot opened on the side of the box, and a pair of storytomes floated out. "We can tell you exactly what happened. In fact, you will be referenced directly in volume five or so."

Hadi accepted the tomes as they floated over and blinked down at the covers. "*Rat & Demon*? I can guess which is which. An amusing title. So this tells your story? Truly?" He opened the cover, and the scene began to play. The tengu's beak fell open and he gawked openly as he slowly turned the pages.

"We've lost him until he finishes the first volume." Saghir gave a tiny laugh. "I believe we have outdone ourselves, friend Xal."

"I can keep these?" Hadi closed the first volume, then after my nod, secreted both away within his voluminous robes, which were colorful, but they'd blend into desert sands.

"More than keep," I explained. "Saghir has made them from the wood of the Tree of Blood. You can reproduce new copies each day, provided you are willing to give it a bit of blood, yours or an animal's."

"Definitely worth the price." Hadi padded the robes where he'd placed the tomes. "I can think of many who would like a copy. Many would pay for the privilege. Why are you giving them away for free? Or is that merely a boon for family?"

"Worship," Saghir answered, his snout poking out from one of the holes. "The more who know the truth, the stronger friend Xal will become."

"I'm curious to hear more about your journey." I started back the way we'd come, retracing our steps more quickly as I now had a destination in mind.

Hadi fell into step behind me, and I noted that people gave us a wide berth as we walked. That berth had nothing to do with me. Their eyes all landed on him, sliding off me as if I did not exist. I even heard a few whispers as we passed.

"Death's shadow?" I asked after I'd heard the same term three times. "Sounds like a name earned directly in the arena."

"Perceptive as always." Hadi croaked a laugh and hooked his thumbs through a wide leather belt. "I have made a name for myself. A small name, at least. I entered the grand melee, a hundred skilled combatants, and I was the last standing. I am a champion of the Arena, due more to luck than skill. There were at least a dozen I could never have bested. There were some you could not have taken, I'd wager. Yet they killed each other, and all I needed to do was pick off weakened prey and avoid the traps created by the Arena."

I spied the acid bar in the distance and led Hadi in that direction while I listened.

"What of you two?" Hadi asked as he ducked into the heated interior, and he began divesting himself of robes to expose shining black feathers. "I get the sense I will need to read many storytomes to catch up to where you are today. Have such been produced?"

"You have all that exist," Saghir called as the top levitated off the pack, and he drifted out to join us. He landed atop the bar next to the stool I'd been making for. "I will have a third soon, but it will take months to catch up. If Xal continues to murder Stewards, it will likely take longer."

Broff ambled over on the other side of the bar, and the mottled hatchling nodded respectfully to Hadi. "You are welcome in my bar, Champion. I am called Broff."

"Do you know who you have been serving?" Hadi nodded in my direction. "You view him and my small companion the way I might a beetle crossing the road."

"No disrespect is intended." Broff raised both scaly hands, and his slitted eyes widened. "I do not understand the ways of humans. I am ignorant.... If they are important, I do not know. You? I was in the stands that day. I watched your shadow fall on victim after victim, heralding their death. It was a thing of beauty. Well fought." Then Broff turned his fanged smile in my direction. "This is precisely what you were seeking. I do not know how you know the

Shadow of Death, but if you can convince him to found a quint, then others will take notice. If you perform well in the arena? You would be able to hire a fair band of mercenaries to aid whatever your quest might be."

"What is it you seek?" Hadi shifted to face me as he rested a wing on the worn stone counter. "If you wish to build an army, there must be a war."

"The war to end all wars," I admitted and caught Broff's skeptical eye roll as the barkeep knelt to fetch pitchers. "The war for the cycle itself. It will likely carry us back to the Blasted Lands on the back of the spider mountain. Saghir has tamed the behemoth."

"Now that is a storytome I wish to read." Hadi thumped the bar, laughing. Broff set a mug of dark red wine before him, the spices familiar and reminding me of Gateway. "Thank you, friend Broff. You know your clientele well." He dipped his beak into the tall slender cup and lapped up some of the scarlet liquid. Then he turned to me and wiped the wine from his beak. "If you need an army, then I will help you obtain it. Let us finish our drinks. There is a match today, and we have the better part of a bell to get there. I can tell you my story and hear yours, while we watch others spill blood and claim glory."

# 15

## THE ARENA

We threaded our way to our seats within the Arena's stadium seating, which was far, far larger than that of the one in Gateway, the size difference apparent once we were inside of it. Guards snapped salutes as Hadi passed, and we were allowed to sit just a few rows from the sands, which overwhelmed me with nostalgia.

There had been a time when I'd lived and died upon those sands daily, when training and a loincloth were all I'd had. It had been even more raw and brutal than my childhood in the dims. There, I'd had friends. Treacherous friends maybe, but still better than being alone. I'd had a family. In Gateway, I'd begun alone.

Which reminded me, as I sat, that now I was not. Hadi sat on my right, and Saghir sat upon my shoulder. The rest of the row was entirely comprised of drifters, all wearing finery in forest colors. Each bore a medallion absent a symbol, which I was sure meant something, but I had no idea what. They seemed unimpressed by our arrival, including Hadi.

Similar groups surrounded us, made of all different races and some cultures I was not familiar with. Many tall humans with thick beards were glaring in my direction, some seated far away from each other. Once I spied the sigil, I realized why. Knights of the Twilight. Guess they were still a little upset about Dalanthar.

I scanned for the pulvinus and found it at one end of the arena, jutting out over the sands, vulnerable. Even sitting there would be a risk, especially given the power level of the combatants who must fight here. Nine nobles in fine clothing and rich jewels, each in a different style, sat in seats arranged in a horseshoe to show that all were equal.

A red-scaled dragon hatchling rose and stepped to the edge of the stone lip over the sands. The other eight rose as one, shifting to face the sands.

"Today begins the first preliminary match," the hatchling boomed, his voice thundering through the stands. "Two quints will face each other in mortal combat. The missio will be neither offered nor accepted. One side triumphs. The other dies."

"On one side, Ukufa, who carries the honor of House Enestius." The hatchling gestured toward the far end of the sands, and I craned to see the combatants as we were closer to the opposite side.

My vision made it easy to take in the quint, who bore familiar purple and black clothing. It was more than that though. The leader was the same tough whose belt I'd cut back when I'd been in school. Apparently, he'd come a long way since then. Nor was he the only one I recognized.

The tall archer in the back was Khwezi, a member of our quint while we had started within Enestius. A man who'd seemed to care a great deal for Ashianna, but who had betrayed us anyway. His shoulders and arms were thick with muscle and sinew, and his beard was thicker now, but he had otherwise changed not at all.

That shouldn't be possible, I realized.

"Friend Xal," Saghir asked suddenly, "is that not Khwezi? From Enestius? I watched him die from poison. From the Hoard of Lakshmi."

"True enough," I agreed. "But there he is. My guess? Someone had him resurrected, either Crispus, or Ukufa, the one leading the quint."

I trailed off as the hatchling opened his mouth to speak once more.

"Standing against them," the hatchling continued, "are the Sky Hunters, local to the mountain peaks surrounding this very Arena. Let the Arena decide their worth." The hatchling lowered his arm, then spun and returned to his seat.

The crowd roared their approval, and I found myself caught up in the energy.

"You wished to know of my journeys," Hadi called as the roar subsided and the match began. "I will tell you as we watch if that is not too much of a distraction."

"I'd love the tale," I called back with enough volume for him to hear me over the hum of the crowd.

"Please!" Saghir echoed.

"After you left," Hadi began, his eyes on the match, flicking from combatant to combatant as he tracked the match, "I was left without purpose. There was no longer a war to fight. I spent time in Gateway and rose to champion, which I enjoyed, but when it was done, I again lacked purpose."

The crowd hushed and Hadi paused as the Arena began to reconfigure itself. Sand bubbled and shimmered with heat until it broke away into a rocky crust over magma, pools of lava already bubbling out from it.

Between those pools rose narrow walkways comprised of the same molten rock, though it was already cooling now that all sides were exposed to the air. If they lacked *fire* protection, they'd definitely take damage.

Neither quint seemed concerned. Enestius treated the walkway as common stone, while the orokh rode cliff drakes, large grey-scaled creatures that I assumed must be local. Those drakes slithered along the stone, dragging their bellies as they enjoyed the heat.

As of yet they were too far away to engage each other. Neither side made any attempt, instead keeping the gap between them and using the time to buff themselves. Chanting and sigils grew around nearly every combatant as both sides powered up.

"I took an airship to Hasra," Hadi finally continued his tale, "but the arena was not a place I wished to be seen. So I took passage in Southshore and sailed across the Endless Lake. What a wonder! I've never seen so much water in one place, more than the Heart of Water perhaps."

"I felt the same," Saghir chittered over the roaring crowd. "Such a vast expanse, and anyone can drink or take their fill."

"I will never be the same." Hadi shook his head, laughing. "The balance of the tale is short. I looked for the next logical challenge and realized I had to come here. I journeyed to Lukantria, and joined a local kamiza, assuming I would be teaching them. They taught me. I grew stronger. If not for their training, I'd have died. I've since become more cautious. A bit more." He trailed off as the two sides finally engaged.

One of the orokh kicked his mount into flight, and the

drake leapt from one raised path to the next. It took three hops to flank the Enestians' position, while his companions began their own assault. I expected the solo orokh to fall back, but instead he charged, his mount leaping at a staff-wielding sorcerer in the Enestian backline.

The sorcerer raised his arm in terror, cowering as the mount came down...and splashed through the illusion into the lava below. The force of the leap carried them deep below the surface, and they did not emerge.

"Kill the dedicate!" Ukufa roared, his voice magically amplified for the crowd.

Khwezi raised his bow and filled the air with arrows, dozens raining down on a club-wielding orokh with more elaborate face paint than the others. Only a third of the arrows were real, but every one thudded home with lethal accuracy, buried in a mount's chest directly over its heart.

"Scree!" the mount cried, tumbling into the lava and leaving its rider to leap for the safety of a nearby bridge.

He'd have made it, but a twenty-cubit-wide snout burst from the lava and snapped him up like a tiny morsel, then fell back into the lava, vanishing without a trace. None of the platforms were safe from that monster, and the crowd knew it. Their roar was truly deafening, and I raised my hands to my ears, wishing I had air to stop them up as Li sometimes did.

"These matches will determine our competition," Hadi called. "It is good we get a chance to see them fight. The Enestians will win. Handily. I doubt they'll take any casualties. The orokh could best many foes easily, but those illusions combined with the terrain are impossible to deal with."

"Especially while taking arrows from Khwezi. He was in our quint back at the academy," I explained as Hadi blinked at me. "The leader is Ukufa, a noble with incredible wealth and a blademaster even back at the academy. I embarrassed him publicly. Let's hope he doesn't remember."

"Would you forget?" Saghir chittered a laugh. "This will be his chance at revenge. Let him try. Their illusions do not impress me. Nor will they impress either of you if we face them upon the sands. The question is...how will we round out our quint? We need two exceptionally skilled combatants. As potent as Ena and Macha are, I'm not sure if I would choose them. You and Hadi will easily manage a front line. We need more magical versatility, a healer ideally, and an archer."

"Perhaps we can recruit Khwezi out from under Ukufa." I wasn't certain if it was possible, but I figured I could at least make the offer. Khwezi had been all about coin the last time we'd met, that and keeping his family safe. I might be able to help with both if he was willing.

"Perhaps." Saghir did not sound optimistic. "That still means we would need to find a fifth. Have you anyone you might consider, friend Hadi?"

We paused as the crowd roared once more, another orokh falling into the lava, this one surviving for several moments before the creature dragged him beneath. Then it was over. Khwezi feathered the last orokh with arrows, not bothering with the mount this time. The rider dropped to the lava, leaving the confused mount to land upon one of the bridges.

It was still scanning the lava when the creature burst out beneath it and devoured the drake. I wondered at how it had selected only one side. Was the Arena saying they'd had the advantage, or was something else at play?

There was no way to know now that the fight was over. The crowd roared their approach, then finally died down.

Our drifter neighbors rose one after another and did not acknowledge our presence as they threaded up the stairs toward the exits.

"I have no one in mind," Hadi admitted, now at a normal volume since the crowd was dispersing. "And I must be honest. I am not nearly so powerful as the crowd believes. I survived mostly through luck, and I know that you are far stronger than I. I can feel it. I assume friend Saghir is similarly empowered. If we are to win, we must attract a pair with strength at your level. Those with such power will not be swayed by my reputation, as they will know the truth. I am powerful, but mostly I am lucky. My bones are hollow, after all."

"Let's head back and get some rest," I decided. "We don't need to solve this tonight. We'll make a list of candidates tomorrow. Somewhere there is a pair we can use. Khwezi or someone else. We'll find them, enter, and win."

"I have missed you, brother." Hadi finally rose, grinning as he ambled over toward the exit. He looked so much like his father in that moment I had trouble telling them apart. Even his voice was similar.

"And I you." I rose and followed, while Saghir slipped off my shoulder and back inside the battle pack.

I genuinely had no idea who we could find to round out our quint. Even if Khwezi agreed, we still needed a fifth. Should I ask Ena? She was strong. Perhaps not so strong as me but powerful enough.

No, she was needed at the Tree.

I would need to trust to prophecy.

If I was wrong, I would have to leave without recruiting the army we desperately needed. All the wealth in the world wasn't getting us any closer to winning this war if we couldn't use it to hire an army.

## INTERLUDE VIII - LI

Li guided herself and Tissa high above mountain passes, the frigid wind kept at bay by a bubble of warm air wrapped in an illusion that made them appear to be nothing more than snow flurries.

As before she kept her wings hidden, though this time less because of hesitation of her own abilities. If word spread that one of the people of the heavens had been sighted, then Khonsu and his children would leave no stone unturned in their search.

She scanned the land below, devoid of all life save a few scraggly trees. Was this the correct place for the rendezvous?

All she had to go on was a short vision from a dream, a place highly suspect when one was at war with the dragon-flight...of dream.

"There," she called softly, just loud enough for Tissa to catch over the wind. "I spy light."

Li descended toward a sheltered cave along a ridge so narrow it was barely worthy of the name. It led to a troll hollow, one of the caves where Bumut's people had dwelt since the dark times, over four thousand years ago.

At least a hundred pairs of eyes gazed up as she entered in a blast of wind, and she decided to make a show of it as she deposited herself and Tissa on the far side of the cavern from where their little camp operated.

"Princess!" Bumut boomed as she shook snow from her cloak.

The great shaggy troll hurried over and seized her in a great hug, and she noted that Tissa's hand went to Nefarius's hilt, though thank all the gods dead and alive, the girl had the sense not to draw. Li had genuinely come to care for Tissa, but she was only one step away from feral.

"I've missed you." Li returned Bumut's hug until he set her down gently back upon the snow. She gazed around the cavern. "You've built an impressive resistance. You don't fear the dragons finding you here?"

"We move every few days." Bumut waved dismissively at the curious onlookers, and when that didn't work, shifted to a fanged growl in their direction. "Get back to work! We need to be packed and ready to leave within the bell." Then he turned back to Li, though he spared a nod to Tissa. "Today is moving day. We have a dozen such sites prepared and are always looking for more. There are also two villages willing to lend aid. It isn't much, but it's allowed all these people to find their way here. They come from all over the nation, not just the Celestial Mountain."

"What news?" Li's heart sped, and she tried not to think about her mother.

"Little." Bumut turned to face south, the direction the mountain lay. "The wyrms have complete control. After the purge, when the dragons devoured all those they thought might resist, the mountain is all but empty most times."

"Like resetting a trap," Tissa murmured, then gave a start when she realized they were looking at her. "I mean...it's obvious. They want us to attack and send whoever we can. They're toying with us like cats did in the dims. You spend all this time gathering your resistance into one place, then attack, and they wipe it out."

"She's right." Li sighed under her breath. "We've been outmaneuvered. The very first thing we'll need to do is recon the mountain and learn what we're dealing with, without springing the trap."

"Getting close is dangerous," Bumut pointed out as he raised a handful of goat fat to slather upon his horns. "They watch and no doubt scry. I will not ask how you intend to do it. The less I know the better. Just in case. A moment.... I need to get my people moving."

Bumut stalked off and left Tissa and Li huddling in the cold, their breath misting.

"You're nothing like Crispus," Tissa said suddenly, shocking Li, who could only blink at the dark-haired assassin. "He never did anything himself. You cast the flying spells. You cast the illusions. You even take your turn cooking. Crispus did nothing but eat, mate, or dream of ruling so he could eat and mate some more."

"Hopefully that makes him easy to beat." Li gave a tentative smile. Were they finally becoming friends? "He wasn't worthy of having your service in any case. A mistake I plan to make fatal for him one day."

Tissa's hand again dropped to Nef's hilt, and a savage smile stole over her features, feral and demonic. "Give the command and his life is yours." It was gone just as quickly, replaced by a more natural half-smile. "Still, you taking care of everything does make it difficult for vassals. You don't leave any tasks for us to care for."

"You keep me alive, and I'll consider your duty well discharged." Li began walking over toward Bumut, who'd finished bellowing orders and gotten the camp moving at an acceptable rate.

"I assume you're departing?" Bumut smiled warmly, exposing his broken tusk. "I wish we had time to reminisce, but everything we might discuss is dire anyway. Thandres watch over you, Princess. Call upon us when the hour comes, and we will come. We will fight."

"I have no doubt." Li harnessed the wind and rose into the air, then lifted Tissa a moment later. "I will be in contact when I am able. When I...know what has befallen mother."

"Of course." Bumut grimaced at the mention but managed a smile afterward.

He maintained it as they ascended, shimmering from view as she added spells, then drifting back into the frigid wind. It amazed her how swiftly they were able to travel the storm. There was no one to observe them, and even if there was, all they'd see is the turbulent wind.

The Celestial Mountain loomed in the distance, far ahead, visible under the ever-present golden radiance of the Halo, where her father and his people cowered away from the world. That angered her, but if she pushed that aside, could she glimpse the reason why? They were protecting themselves in the only way they could.

They had relied on the existence of the lightning people for their defense. Her mother was supposed to wake them to defend the mountain, after all. That was why they had rulers in the first place. Yet that hadn't happened, and now it appeared that Khonsu had left a path open for her to do exactly that.

Was it all merely psychological warfare? Was he convincing them not to use the one weapon that could save them? Or had the wyrm truly corrupted the bells? Would he control the lightning people if they woke?

Already she tired of wondering. Almost she wanted to call his bluff, just to obtain the answer.

"You grew up with Xal," she called over the wind. "What was he like as a child?"

Li couldn't see Tissa's reaction, obviously, so she waited. To her surprise, Nef's insectoid form shimmered into view, alternately vanishing and appearing as it kept pace with them through the storm. "Xal was a coward. He followed Tissa everywhere, and Tissa followed me. Xal was scrawny, but he always had his magic. From right after I met him."

"And you were always jealous," Tissa hissed, finally joining the conversation. "Every six-year-old is a coward. We're supposed to be. And he wasn't following me around. We were friends. We were playing together. I sought him out as often as he came to find us. More."

"Maybe. Water over the edge," the bug-eyed monstrosity replied. "Mark my words, though. Xal will screw it up before the en—"

He vanished. Li didn't need to see Tissa to know the assassin had banished the blade.

"Thank you for that," Li called. "I can't stand your brother."

"It isn't Nef's fault." Tissa's tone was more than a little defensive. "He had to be the parent when he were kids. He kept me alive. Some days he didn't eat so that I could. But... he was also cruel. And angry all the time. Always. Xal was curious. Before...before we left the dims. He was happier if you can believe that. We didn't have much, but it was enough for him. He shared his food with me, almost every day. We'd take turns having breakfast when times were tough."

Inexplicable sadness built in Li as she considered such a childhood, especially when compared to her own. She'd considered it horrible at one point after she'd first seen what life was like in Hasra. They had so many luxuries. Yet not once had she ever known hunger. Never.

They flew the balance of the journey in silence, and Li appreciated that Tissa didn't question her. In her place, Li would have been tempted to ask how they were going to enter the mountain and what their precise destination was.

She led them to a crack near the very peak, close enough to the Halo that she could not ignore it. Almost she considered flying to the golden ring and seeking entrance but knew there was no way they'd allow Tissa, even if they were willing to accept Li.

Li landed next to a trio of rocks in a rough triangle that could very well have been naturally placed...except that they weren't. Lines of power flared between the rocks, and they sank through them, the earth going liquid as it granted them access.

They emerged moments later within the confines of the mountain, hovering over the city she had known all her life. Much of the cavern was empty. Even the noble quarters. Not merely people hiding inside, but the kind of disuse that only accumulated over weeks, then months. Some of the most desirable homes on the mountain were empty, and many of the kamizas were dark and shuttered.

A few remained open, but only a handful. At least light shone from within, and the signs of combat came from one of them...earnest training. It hadn't been abandoned entirely.

She drifted lower and angled her flight to bring them toward the spire of rock containing the throne room and her mother's personal quarters. Those were enemy territory now, but it would be worth seeing who used them now. That person would be her chief enemy, apart from Khonsu himself.

Li landed on the stone, wary that touching it with her booted feet might trigger a ward, and she was relieved when that did not happen. She'd landed directly outside the throne room, within sight of the pillars where she and Xal had battled Niu. The same room where Tissa had later slain the hatchling and pledged her service.

"Should we enter?" Tissa breathed, barely a whisper.

That she'd spoken testified to how nervous she must have been. Li could order her but thought it prudent to ensure she understood the stakes.

"I'm operating mostly off intuition," Li whispered back. "They've left the throne room completely unguarded and seemingly unused. That says there's nothing here they consider valuable. Yet I see the bells. I know ringing them will free the lightning people. So which is it? Are they already bound to Khonsu? Am I only further empowering him? Or are they our only chance at freedom?"

She didn't expect an answer but gained one anyway.

"They're not bound." Tissa's tone was an alloy of certainty. "If they were, then why not wake them? Why not gain the power? Who can ring the bells?"

"I can," Li whispered. "Or my mother. Maybe anyone. I don't really know since no one has ever rung them."

"And your mother was presumably captured?" Tissa's tone went wary, like an oft-beaten dog about to run. Was delivering bad news so dangerous with her previous master?

"All but certainly." Li sighed. She hated that Tissa was right. "If they wanted the bells rung, then in all likelihood, my mother could have done that for them. That suggests that the bells are still our greatest hope, but we need to be cautious."

"I'm always cautious." Tissa rested a hand on Nef's hilt as her gaze roamed the darkness.

"If we enter, any number of wards could go off. Before we do so, I want to understand who's in control here." Li lifted off the ground and seized Tissa round the waist with a tendril of air. "Last I was here, there was a boy who'd remained unbound. Haitao, I believe. I want to locate him and see if he's still free. Perhaps he can tell us more. If we learn nothing, then we'll risk the throne room."

# 16

# THE FIRST TRIAL

After our bout, Hadi led Saghir and me to a large bar just outside the coliseum itself. A stream of impressive-looking gladiators dominated the flow of traffic heading in and out, and I noted that more than one group was turned away by an imposing minotaur with silver-tipped tusks.

By the time we arrived, Ukufa was already holding court near the center of the bar, seated at a large table that barely accommodated his sycophants. Thankfully, his quint had splintered, with different members surrounded by eager fans in each area. I followed Hadi toward the second largest group, which lingered around Khwezi. I recognized the tall archer's laugh immediately, and his darker skin made him a bit more exotic in these lands, which the women seemed to favor.

The outer ring of fans parted as they recognized Hadi. Not a one noticed me, though to be fair, the first armor was not flashy, nor was Narlifex when sheathed. I was just an average human, a bit taller than most, with a bit more muscle.

Only one man took me seriously. One man recognized me.

Khwezi's jaw fell open, and the archer's eyes widened. It was comical really, and everyone around him caught it. They began searching for the source, and of course, most assumed it was awe reserved for Hadi. No one saw us make eye contact, and he dropped it like a scalding coal.

A path opened to allow our passage, and we were ushered in to sit in the same wide booth with Khwezi, just across from him. He had a woman under either arm, and his bow wasn't visible. Void pocket, I assumed, though I didn't rule out an illusion.

Saghir made matters worse by choosing that instant to scurry out of his pack so he could perch on my shoulder. Blood drained from Khwezi's face when he caught sight of the ratkin.

"Congratulations on your victory." Hadi raised a flagon from his side and drank deeply. "I had the privilege of observing from the stands. Fine kills all around, but your performance today was nothing short of spectacular."

"Go away, bird." Khwezi didn't even look at Hadi, a mistake in my estimation. He focused upon me, and the hand around his paramour's hand trembled. He was terrified. Beyond terrified. "I'll hear the demon's threats absent your honeyed words. I dreaded the day you learned I was still alive."

"I don't know why you think I'd threaten you. The past is behind us. You owe me nothing, nor I you. But you're speaking disrespectfully to a man I consider a brother," I cautioned quietly, then leaned forward over the table, eyes locked on his. "I don't take kindly to insults, especially not from a man who betrayed me. I don't know how you survived, but we're not at a university where you can hide behind Totarius or Crispus any longer. So let's choose friendship instead. We'll forget the past, and we start over. I'm putting together a quint for the tournament. One that will include Saghir. One that affords a greater chance of victory than Ukufa can offer."

"My spider mountain will have to wait outside, regrettably." Saghir gave a put-upon sigh. "Fortunately, I possess a number of smaller summons that our enemies should quite enjoy. Oh! I forget myself." Saghir waved a hand and a pair of storytomes levitated out to land upon the table before Khwezi. "A gift. Your death is rendered in a future tome. A fond memory. I promise I will be...accurate. In stunning detail."

"You can guess how I survived." Khwezi smiled weakly and released the women to reach for the tomes. "The truce I will take. I desire no more enemies. Yet I cannot join you. I am bound to Uk—"

"Do not," Ukufa boomed as he strode over to slide into the booth next to me, "presume to use my name without permission, vassal. You serve me for three more years. That was the deal, was it not?"

"It was." Khwezi's eyes narrowed and the color returned. He glared at Ukufa. "I serve you, but that will not still my tongue. You bought my bow, not my soul. Be gentle in how you wield the leash. One day it will be removed. If it chafes, I may be...sore upon its removal."

"I do not like your tone." Ukufa's eyes glittered with a very familiar rage. One that I'd previously seen on Crispus and similarly entitled nobles. He was absolutely infuriated that one of his cogs was not performing precisely as expected.

"I like your belt," I interrupted. I know I shouldn't have.

It called attention to a wound I'd delivered years before. A wound to his pride that had only festered.

"Do not speak to me, offal." Ukufa's eyes slid off me. "You are unblooded. You may have scrounged in lesser arenas, but you have not fought here. You are nothing." He rose from the table and glared at Khwezi once more. "Enjoy the celebration. I apologize for my rudeness. Your services are appreciated, and I do not govern the company you keep, even if I cannot abide the stench."

Ukufa made it a precise three paces before abruptly slipping and tumbling to the sawdust-covered floor. I caught a brief glimpse of the summoned ice that had caused the embarrassment, then it was gone, and only Saghir's mocking laughter remained.

The noble rose, glared at my friend, then turned and left wordlessly.

"You have made a mistake there, I think," Hadi cautioned as he forlornly watched the noble leave. "I do not know your history, but it is unwise to upset someone so thoroughly enmeshed in the Enestian power base here. He will make you pay for it if he can."

"He can't," Saghir quipped, then scampered into the pack. Likely to scry Ukufa if I knew him at all.

"He might," I admitted, then shrugged at Khwezi. "Sometimes you have to tweak their nose anyway, to remind them all their wealth doesn't give them as much power as they think it does."

"Would that I could join you." Khwezi gave a sheepish grin. "I already know you will be a potent threat upon the sands, especially with the shadow of death in your ranks. I would rather not face you, particularly if revenge is still on your mind."

"It isn't," I assured him. "Should we meet upon the

sands, it will be an unbiased match. I crave victory only to recruit an army, not to triumph in the Arena."

"Luck to you." Khwezi rose abruptly. "I will cover the tab for the table. Please, drink or eat whatever you wish. I must return to my quarters and begin preparing for the next match. Today was merely a qualifier. Soon the entries will close, and the fighting will begin in earnest."

"How soon?" I asked.

"Three days." Khwezi gave a shrug. "I can't imagine your quint needs much training, so it should be plenty of time. Who are your fourth and fifth, if you don't mind my asking?"

An awkward silence stretched, then Khwezi laughed. "Of course you would not tell me. I will see you upon the sands!"

He hurried off, a large portion of the bar's patrons following him and leaving us in relative peace. I used the opportunity to pour myself some mead and carve a haunch of meat from the boar upon the center of the table.

I was just settling down to enjoy it when a shadow fell upon me. I glanced up and blinked as Celeste slid into the chair next to me, the beautiful Steward's expression tight and her eyes glittering with purpose. There was no sign of her staff of office, though she'd taken no additional pains to disguise herself.

"I've found you at last." Celeste poured herself a flagon, then nodded to Saghir. "Master mage." She turned back to me. "Tuat inadvertently let something slip, and I've used it to great effect. I've been to Mount Shyar and learned more about the nature of the three trials that will allow you to become anointed. I came immediately, due to the nature of the first."

"Oh?" I downed the goblet and set it on the table, then shifted to face her. I had a feeling I wasn't going to like this.

"The trial of the champion," Celeste explained, "is exactly what it sounds like. Before you can use the crown, you must be anointed by the arena itself."

"I have to win." My heart sank. "There's a quint champion bout coming, but...our quint isn't ready."

"Then it had better get ready." I'd never seen such intensity in her expression. Irritation coupled with fear. It banished the childlike image she cultivated, and I saw the war mage underneath. "Either you triumph here or it will be another year before you can try again."

"At least if it comes to that," Hadi interjected, "it will be the singles year. You won't need a quint, just yourself."

"We don't have a year. We might not have half that." I shivered as I considered all the elder gods in all the realities suddenly returning to ignite the war that had caused them to depart in the first place. Then I focused on Celeste. "We need a fourth and fifth member. You're one of the most powerful archmages in creation. Join us."

"Very well." Celeste sipped her mead. "It's been centuries since I've fought in the arena, but I am a champion. I will join you if you can find us a fifth."

"We must be swift," Hadi cautioned. "Three days is no time at all to prepare to battle the gods and monsters we will face within the Arena."

"Then let's be about that." I downed one more cup of mead, then slid from the table with half a loaf of sweetbread in one hand. "We can head back to *The Fist* and make final plans." I turned to Celeste first as we exited the bar. "Do you know of anyone you could summon who might fill the role?"

"My powers are limited in that regard." She sighed heavily. "Without my staff, I am only a bit more versatile than Master Saghir. I have been to perhaps a dozen more Catalysts than he and have a few more artifacts and a wider pool of spells. There is no vast gulf between us."

"I see." Saghir's flattered voice emerged from the pack. "Still, you will be a great aid to our chances. Especially being a champion."

"There's a story there." Hadi gave a beakish smile. "Perhaps you'll tell it sometime soon?"

Celeste gave a noncommittal shrug, then eyed me hawkishly. "I cannot help you find a fifth. Surely there must be someone upon that mountain you use for a camp."

"I left them behind for a reason," I pointed out as I ducked past a drifter wagon, then down an alley that shortened our route back to *The Fist*. "That sapling is vital to relations with Macha. We need her, and we need the Fomori. More than that, I gave her my word I would see it planted within her grove. If I remove my strongest warrior, then the tree is that much more vulnerable."

"So choose another and lessen our chances upon the sands." She gave another noncommittal shrug. "I will say this. If we fail here...it all fails. You *must* become anointed. Logically, that should include your strongest warrior. Which would that be?"

"Macha, but she would never agree." I started up the open stairs winding around the tower as it climbed to our airship. "Ena would be my second choice. Vhala is strong but relies too much on stealth. Ena can stand toe-to-toe with a strong opponent, and our group will need that. Hadi picks off targets. You and Saghir will likely be summoning or countering their mages. Ena can keep them off you while Hadi and I surgically remove their casters or healers."

"I agree with friend Xal's choice," Saghir chimed in from

inside the pack. "Ena will make us strong indeed and solve the problem we face. That would give us three days to prepare for this tournament. I am sure that will be ample time."

I wasn't, but I was resolved to work with what I had. Everything depended upon it.

# 17

## PRACTICE

Our newly formed quint met aboard *The Fist*, which Saghir had configured into a dueling arena. The walls absorbed magic, which meant that we could let loose without fear of blowing up the ship around us.

What's more, Saghir had worked a void pocket into the ship, and the interior was now several times larger than the corresponding space it represented. We had plenty of room to live, train, and study, all in comfort.

Within the circle, Ena and Hadi glided from stance to stance, darting and lunging as each sought an advantage. Ena abruptly vanished, leaving Hadi standing in the middle of the room, his falchion cradled in both hands and his stance loose as he prepared to react to Ena's ambush.

A demonic tail snaked around Hadi's foot, cinching like a noose even as Ena's clawed foot scythed in toward the bird's face. Hadi ducked under the kick while simultaneously wrenching his blade down and severing Ena's tail to free himself.

The tengu hopped backward, but Ena pursued, tackling

him to the ground. His falchion went spinning away, and the tussle ended with Ena straddling the bird. Her clawed hands were wrapped around his throat, but he'd gotten a dagger loose from somewhere and the blade dug into the hard leathery skin over her heart.

"Break," I called, and the pair obligingly leapt to their feet, then hurried from the arena.

Celeste had been observing the fight with a frown and moved to heal Ena's tail without a word. She wasn't offering feedback, but disappointment rolled off her in waves.

"Our line isn't much of a line." I folded my arms and glared at both Hadi and Ena, in exactly the way I imagined Caw would have. "Neither of you can stand and fight. Hadi, you need room to maneuver. Ena, you rely upon stealth. If you vanish in mid-combat, then our mages are exposed. Both styles are fine, but it makes us predictable. People will very quickly realize I am hanging back to protect the mages. So we're going to need to change things up a bit. Ena, you're going to reactively protect Saghir and Celeste. Hadi, you and I are going to crack their defense and get at the mages."

Celeste knelt and picked up the battle pack, which appeared comically large as she cinched it around her petite frame. Was that what I'd looked like back at the academy and when Saghir and I had first started using the tactic? It might appear comical, but it had been devastatingly effective and would be again.

"Are we assuming combat starts and we have not had time to buff?" Saghir inquired, his voice drifting out of the pack. "If Celeste is watching the battlefield and focused on counterspelling initially, then I could layer protective spells about us."

"I'll act as editor," I announced as I entered the circle and slowly slid Narlifex from my sheath. "We're on equal sands, no aid nor hindrance from the arena. Hadi and I have bypassed your melee line and are assaulting you directly. You've had time to cast, say...three spells? We'll wait."

Power emanated from the pack, but I couldn't see exactly what spells Saghir cast. I expected quint-wide buffs to increase our various attributes and was unsurprised when many duplicate copies of Celeste appeared. What did surprise me was the sheer volume of them. I counted twenty-nine.

I cocked my head and listened. Each image had an independent heartbeat. Each breathed independently. I didn't detect any invisible targets. Every heartbeat belonged to one of the images, so it had to be one of them.

My gaze flicked down and slid from feet to feet. There. Only one set of feet displaced dust from the dueling circle's floor. In the arena, I'd see indentations on the sand, which the other illusions lacked. A subtle difference, but enough.

"Ready yourselves," I called, then leapt into a predictable attack as I descended toward Celeste.

Ena's dark form burst from a cloud of darkness and tackled me to the ground. We rolled, vying for dominance as we clawed at each other.

In the background, I was aware of Hadi making his attempt, but he appeared unable to distinguish the real version from the illusions. He slashed at one of the copies near the real one, as he'd seen me attack there, but the copies moved and shifted, making it impossible to find the real one if you couldn't spot the differences.

A fissure appeared about three cubits above Hadi's head, and five void bolts burst out, one after another. Amazingly, he twisted out of the way of the first, but the others adjusted their aim and slammed into him. He howled in pain, grabbing at his tail feathers as he leapt from the arena.

"Sands, but that stings! I thought we agreed to use low-magnitude attacks?" Hadi glared at the pack as he rubbed at his backside.

"That spell is as diluted as I can manage." Saghir's tone was defensive. I could feel tempers fraying.

"Break!" I released Ena, and a moment later she released me. I'd been getting the better of her, but the fight had been far from decided.

"This was good," I called, my gaze touching each of theirs in turn. "We're starting to identify more strategies."

"But we're out of time," Celeste groused, her tone frayed to match our mood. "Our first match is tomorrow, and none of you seem aware there is a higher level at play. Remember, patrons can influence the match. Every one of our opponents has spent months cultivating influence, and many will have advantages we cannot match. We are still learning basic teamwork that should have been mastered before we arrived in this city. I apologize for being so negative, yet I fear our chances of success are low."

"They'll be higher if we practice." I moderated my tone and shed anything like accusation. "Each of us is powerful in our own right. Together we have incredible versatility and the ability to target and destroy an opponent with lethal intensity. Other quints will underestimate us. We'll be a joke to them, at first."

"He's not wrong," Hadi agreed as he rubbed ointment on his wounds. "A champion who hasn't fought in centuries, and one who triumphed largely through luck. Those with true skill will assume us a lost cause, and we are unlikely to factor into their planning. That might provide a way forward."

"Until the second match," Saghir pointed out, though he was grinning. Wickedly. "After we destroy the first group, they will begin to understand. Full understanding will not come until they read the storytome relating our inevitable triumph."

His confidence meant the world to me, largely because I didn't share it.

"Back to work," I growled, just as Caw would have. "Let's discuss offense. Saghir and Celeste, can you open a match with area-of-effect spells? If you hit the enemy with your strongest magics immediately, then either they die or we learn the nature of their defenses. If any member of their quint is vulnerable, then we'll gain a numeric advantage."

"It's a common enough tactic," Celeste said, tone neutral. She cocked her head to the side, and her eyes were lost to memory. "It can be effective, but opponents will always reserve at least one counterspeller. When they know we have two archmages, or near-archmages, they'll reserve two counterspellers, each assigned to one of us. You can assume that every spell we attempt will be met either with a ward or countered directly. No one makes it this far without answering direct magic. Gateway's historical texts speak of a time when quints comprised of all mages dominated...until a demon prince immune to their magic devoured them all and forced every other quint to adapt."

"An excellent point," Saghir pointed out. "It also means we have no counterspeller of our own, so they may use their own magics with impunity."

"We can vary our assault based on enemy composition," I suggested as I considered the possibilities. "If they are mage heavy, both of you can focus on counterspelling, while Hadi, Ena, and I charge. If they're melee heavy, one of you can focus more on offense, while we fall back and force them to come to us. I can assign roles on the fly, provided you are ready for each."

Words dwindled as we drilled each tactic, switching positions and considering various angles. At some point the complaints and resentment and fear all faded. There was only the activity, our cooperation against the looming darkness.

By the time I called break for the final time, a tiny ember of hope blossomed within me. Could we triumph in the Arena of arenas? I didn't know. I did know this was the strongest quint I'd ever been a part of. That brought me some comfort, but it didn't quiet my doubts.

If I had to pick, Erik would be in Ena's spot. Tissa would be in Hadi's. That quint would savage the arena. Victory would be all but assured.

The one I had?

We had better rise to the occasion, or the cycle would pay the price.

## INTERLUDE IX - ERIK

Erik strode down the main thoroughfare leading through the city of Valys's heart. It began at the very base of Reevanthara's gargantuan Hammer and wound up around the haft, climbing into the sky all the way to the noble district, where he'd dwelt since childhood.

Now Erik was at the very bottom. On the ground, as far from that world as one could get and still be entirely within the shadow it cast. He glanced around him and found a few curious onlookers, but no one seemed overly invested in what he was doing.

He trotted up the narrow steps, which were wide enough for twenty knights on horseback, and approached the imposing edifice before him. It was the single largest structure on the city's ground level, large enough to qualify for a palace and comprised entirely of stone.

Sun symbology dotted the building, along with artfully designed scales to represent justice right at the very pinnacle. This had been the first temple consecrated to Dalanthar when he had first helped the Knights of the Dawn found Valys.

Erik knew that because it had been drilled into him every year for his entire childhood. He'd attended countless services here and had been quite cross at having to fly down out of his lofty palace to do it. What an arrogant little shit he'd been.

Yet those lessons had stuck with him for precisely the reason that had driven him here. Every week he'd been required to tithe a dragon scale. A fortune for the privilege of being lectured by the Steward or one of his equally boring servants.

Erik needed coin. He needed a power base. Could this place provide it?

He gazed up at the temple as he approached the wide double doors. They were granite, as was the rest of the temple, yet when he pushed on one, it opened silently inward. Did that mean that someone was maintaining the place or that it had been so well designed that it didn't require such?

"Out!" rasped a male voice. It came again stronger a moment later. "Out, I say! Your kind are not welcome here. I already told you—"

An old man came around the corner, decrepit and a century if he was a day. The caretaker's skin was worn leather, from long toil in the sun, and his hair had long since lost the war with baldness.

"Apologies, my—I—" He sank to both knees, then prostrated himself. "Be welcome in your temple, Steward of Justice."

"Please rise." Erik offered a hand to the man and aided him to his feet. "I see you recognize me, even if few others do. I did not have an easy time reaching the place. Twice robbers considered me, despite the armor and shield."

"Hard times have befallen us all." The old man bobbed a

bow, then gestured for Erik to follow him. "Come, let's get you off your feet and get some food in your belly. I've kept this place running, more or less. There's even a fresh bed for you if you still need such now that you've been elevated."

"I'm grateful." Erik followed the man, eyes roaming the strange shadows as they passed into the main sanctuary, the same vast hall he'd once worshipped in. It no longer felt right. "Who were you talking to when I entered?"

"Oh, pay that no mind." The priest—still nameless, Erik noted—gave a nervous little laugh. "Just some ruffians as realized this place isn't quite empty yet. They know I've got food and maybe a few trinkets, and they want them all. I keep a crossbow close, and the last group found that out the hard way. They haven't been back since. I thought you was them, if you'll pardon me."

"If they return, I will pass judgment." Erik turned in a slow circle as he surveyed the shuttered sanctuary. "We'll need to remove the covers from the windows if we're going to hold services again." He turned to the priest. "First, I'll have your name. Then a list of things that need doing."

"My lord...." The man's pained expression, the utter torment, touched something within Erik. "We have no one to perform such labors. I would, were I able, but I am too old and too feeble. Time has stolen what strength I possessed."

"You misunderstand." Erik gave the man as friendly a smile as he could manage, a softer version of the one he'd used to woo women at court. "I need a list of labors I can perform. I have no coin. I have no place to stay. I do possess time. If we can restore this place and the flow of faithful, then it will provide worship, which my brethren and I desperately require. It might even provide coin, which will be necessary to keep this temple running. I work with the tools at hand, and right now the only hands are mine and...." He trailed off expectantly.

"Mikel, my lord." He bowed again and reached up to doff a cap he wasn't wearing, then awkwardly recovered. "Forgive me, lord, but I expected to be alone. I never expected prayers to be answered again, much less to have the Steward himself take up residence in my home. If you wish, I will provide a list of maintenance, but it feels wrong to have you the one doing the work."

"Why?" Erik wondered aloud, though for much of his life, he'd have agreed with the sentiment. "I shouldn't ask others to do work I am unwilling to do myself. If I want more faithful, then I need to give the people something to have faith in. Crispus has already done half the work by being so lousy at Imperator. If I can show a better example, then I can mute his influence in these lands. Maybe I can even free Ashianna and her father, who never should have been detained. Be warned...Crispus will likely take action against this place when he learns I am here."

Erik didn't know why he trusted this man with such a plan, save that it no longer felt right to lie or to keep such things to himself. Justice was open. Justice was honest.

"They have already tried." Mikel gave a satisfied smile. "Their magics will not work here, and the doors barred their entry. They could not desecrate the temple. Or at least...they could not at first." Mikel's confidence faded a hair. "Now ruffians seem able to enter. Perhaps whatever protection once existed no longer lingers here."

"We'll restore it." Erik walked over to a pew that had been knocked on its side and hefted it back into place. "I require very little sleep. You give me a few days and I'll be ready to host our first sermon."

A tiny thread of power wove from the man into Erik, a

covenant that Erik accepted and strengthened. It wasn't much worship, but it was something. More than he had. Now all he needed to do was increase that until he could help Xal stand against the darkness.

Darius would be fleeing soon. When he did, Erik needed to be such a thorn in Crispus's backside that the Imperator would be unable to react.

That Erik could do. He'd made tweaking Crispus's nose an art form long before they'd graduated. This would be child's play.

# 18

# ROUND 1

S tepping back onto the sands exhilarated me. I'd never forget my time in Gateway, which had winnowed away my childhood and left a machine of death in its place. That meant there was no fear, even here, though there was more nervousness than expected.

Perhaps because I wasn't responsible for merely my own life, but the entire quint. I was the leader for the first time where it mattered, not a slave forced to fight with other slaves.

The others fanned out behind me, Ena on my right and Hadi on my left, with Celeste in the pocket we created, Saghir and the battle pack affixed to her back.

We had emerged onto a vast expanse of sand in a rectangular arena. We were in one corner, and quints were emerging in the other three corners as well. The distance between each quint was considerable, which meant combat would require revealing our intent long before we reached our opponents.

"Should we linger here?" Hadi croaked. "We could force

the others to slaughter each other. Assuming the arena allows us the choice."

"Hanging back is the goal if we can," I agreed as I slowly strode toward the center of the arena. "But initially, we want to be able to respond to the arena's changes. That means being near the center, like it or not. We have to at least threaten that territory."

A ragged cheer built into a swelling tide and then a deafening roar as the crowd mistook my pragmatism for courage. They were cheering for our quint—I was certain of it.

The cheer died abruptly enough that I knew magic must be involved. I gazed up at the pulvinus, which was larger and grander than even the one in Gateway, especially when viewed from the sands instead of the stands, and saw the same hatchling stride to the edge to address the crowd.

"Today marks the true beginning of the Grand Tourney, held annually for over four thousand years, with no interruptions," the hatchling bellowed, his voice thundering over the packed stands, which sprawled higher than I'd have thought possible. "Our lineage is unbroken. Our traditions sacrosanct. Some promising entrants have already been identified, but others are unknown. Let the Arena itself craft their fate. They will battle it and each other until one quint among them emerges victorious."

The hatchling returned to his seat without fanfare, and a true hush fell over the crowd as they awaited the arena's judgment. The other quints had advanced as well, each close enough to claim the center, but also to fall back as needed. It afforded me my first look at the others, and I cataloged all I could for my quint with my senses.

"The first group are drifters, two mages, two archers, one

heavy," I barked in my best Caw imitation. "Second are elfen, all archers, but blades too. Third are human. Bearded, with axes. At least one dedicate. From Arlen, I would guess. Melee heavy."

Celeste raised a finger and sketched, and a wall of wind sprang up around us, about ten cubits wide. We were at the center of a whirlwind, which would protect us from ranged attacks while still affording visibility of the other quints.

The ground rumbled beneath our feet, and sand began to gather itself then darkened into large brown bricks carpeting the entire arena floor. Some of the bricks began rising into long straight stairways that abruptly ended at a platform high above the sands. A pair of doors appeared blocking the way forward, then more stairs climbed upward until they created another platform.

"It appears we must find a way to open the doors to proceed," Saghir mused, his voice an echo from inside the pack.

"Let's claim the closest platform," I decided, then leaned into a sprint as I shifted into demon form to increase my speed.

There were at least a dozen stairways forming, and none of the other quints had any reason to go for ours. We were able to charge up the stairs, which cracked beneath my clawed feet, and made it to the first platform, which afforded me a moment to survey the rest of the arena.

Those bricks that had not risen into stairs had tumbled into a bottomless abyss to reveal...an eye. Yellow and evil and vast. Well, larger than the arena, but so far into the void beneath that I could see the entire thing watching me and my companions.

I knew with certainty that it would devour my soul and sift through my memories were I to break the plane at the bottom of the arena, which was effectively a giant fissure leading to this nightmarish reality where that tremendous ocular monstrosity held sway.

"Xal," Celeste said as she tapped the bottom of the platform with one foot. "We have a new problem to solve."

I cursed under my breath when I saw what she meant. When one stepped upon the center tile on the first platform, the doors opened. When the foot was removed, the doors closed again.

I was still considering an answer when one of the drifters rose into the sky over their own stairway, either with a flight spell or some sort of artifact or charm. The source didn't matter. The instant his feet left the stones and he ventured out over the abyss, it claimed him.

There was nothing obvious. No spell or tentacle or arrow. The drifter looked down and screamed, and screamed, and screamed. He clawed at his eyes, then curled up into a fetal position and tumbled into that awful abyss, willingly ending his life, it seemed.

More and more stones tumbled away as the other quints made it to their first platform, and each faced the same dilemma we did. We knew the stakes now, and so did the crowd, which held its collective breath.

"What are the odds we can simply weight the stone?" Saghir's tone lay absent hope.

"There was a resonance when I touched it. I suspect it will require someone or something living." Celeste turned a grim expression on our quint. "Someone is going to have to stay behind. I think that's the trap. We can experiment, but—"

"I'll do it." Ena hadn't even really finished speaking before stepping forward to volunteer. "Time is wasting. Let's not agonize over this. Get it done, and get up to the next platform. The cycle is resting on this, remember?"

"Wait!" Saghir chittered as the top of the battle pack burst open. He levitated out, surrounded by storytomes. "The arena has allowed my entire battle pack and all it contains. Perhaps that can be useful. I have many copies within. The tomes are living. Ordinarily, I'd have suggested a simple summon spell, but there is a greater likelihood such a solution will fail."

"Not to mention leaving whatever you summon to face that eye." I shook my head as I imagined him summoning Liloth to stand on the stone while we ascended the stairs. I glanced past the double doors and caught sight of another platform high above. There would be at least one more similar challenge after this one. "Let's give it a try."

Saghir piled books upon the stone until it depressed under its own weight, and to my delight, it stayed depressed as we rushed through and up the stairs, all five of us. I spared a moment as I ascended to survey the other quints, but found none interested in us, thankfully.

The elfen had left one of their number behind, and the remaining four were ascending to the next platform. The drifters were still arguing. The humans appeared to be playing a game of chance to determine who must stay behind.

We weren't the first to make it to the next platform, even if we did retain all our members. I rushed up the stairs, flapping my wings to increase my speed but being careful not to ever expose myself to the eye.

This time there was no doorway, but the elfen were obviously consternated, and none seemed willing to proceed. Another stepped on the center tile, and a ball of negative energy, a rolling disintegration, came down the stairs. There was just enough room on the second platform for three people to step aside, leaving anyone else to stand in the path of the orb.

"Everyone to the side," I ordered and waited as Ena, Hadi, and Celeste all moved to safety, with Saghir still nestled in the pack.

Once they were clear, I stepped onto the stairs and gritted my teeth. I was wearing the first armor and possessed immense *void* resistance. I arrogantly assumed I'd be able to weather the assault, but as the ball rolled into me, I found a ragged scream being ripped from my own throat.

My body began to unravel, and it took all I had to maintain position and not try to flee. I collapsed into a heap and was vaguely aware of Ena scooping me up and carrying me to the next level.

I tried to rise, but it wasn't until Celeste sketched an elaborate healing spell, then pressed the golden energy into me, that I began to recover. I wobbled to my feet and looked around to see what fresh hell we'd found ourselves in.

A box waited at the center. Beyond it lay a door with a keyhole. The implication was clear. The key was in the box.

"I'll take this one," Ena volunteered and took a step toward the box.

"No!" I roared, staggering forward. I pressed my hand to my side and added my own healing, which eased the lingering pain. "Let me. My resistances are higher, and I'm immune to all poisons, venoms, and diseases after the Heart of Water."

Ena stepped uncomfortably back, while Saghir and Celeste began layering me with protective spells. I used the break to scan the other platforms and found that both the elfen and the humans had gained the final platform and now faced the same dilemma we did.

Not only did we need to win, but we needed to win swiftly.

"Stand back." I knelt next to the box, and when my party was clear, I opened it.

A cobra with eight fangs in four mouths, a serpentine hydra, reared up from the box and bit down into me over and over until all sets were embedded in my flesh. Hot venom pumped into me, acidic and burning as it flowed up my veins.

The agony kept me conscious, and the sensation of poison coursing through me made me shake, though I knew I'd survive. I plucked up the key in a trembling hand and tossed it to Hadi. It fell short, but the tengu darted forward to snatch it out of the air.

By the time he'd fit it into the lock, I'd regained my feet and staggered in that direction. Ena took me by the shoulder, and I followed Celeste and Hadi up the final flight of stairs. We arrived at a beacon that lit itself as we approached.

A tremendous roar rolled out of the arena, louder than any I'd heard in Gateway. The crowd exalted us...while all the other platforms fell away. I had one glimpse of the eye, then all three failed quints were gone as if they'd never been, leaving only ours as the survivors.

A reminder of the stakes we were gambling for.

Somehow we'd made it past the first round with all members intact. I knew the next would be thrice as hard.

We'd be facing Ukufa.

# 19

# BLADES

The time between the first match and the next was a blur of logistics reports from the mountain— estimates for how many mercenaries we could support, security breakdowns, and other minutiae. Being a general and the head of a religion was fast becoming more taxing than I'd have assumed it would.

Yet before I knew it, I was able to set that aside. I found myself standing upon the sands once more, with barely any research put into Ukufa's quint or their strengths. There simply hadn't been time.

To my surprise, the crowd gave a rousing cry as our ragged quint took the sands, and I drew Narlifex with a flourish, then saluted the crowd with a grin and bow. Playing to the crowd could provide an extra bit of favor from the arena, and we'd need that favor and more.

The crowd fell to silence as Ukufa took the sands, and a few boos rang out. Then more. I glanced at Celeste, then Hadi, and found both wearing the same puzzled expression. It was Hadi who spoke.

"Ukufa is no favorite," the tengu croaked as he twirled

his falchion. "Yet he is not reviled so far as I know. I don't understand why they'd give him that kind of treatment."

"I have seen it before." Saghir's snout appeared through one of the holes of the battle pack. It was so odd being able to see his eyes when I was used to wearing him on my back. "It most often occurred when a patron awarded someone a boon that they felt was unfair or dishonorable."

"Suggesting Ukufa has given himself an undue advantage." I couldn't help but sigh. "It certainly fits the pattern of our luck."

"Told you so." Celeste rolled her eyes, and there was no smile to soften it. I badly missed the knowledge-girl version of the Steward I'd met in Gateway what felt a lifetime ago. "He's likely spent fortunes and made countless offerings, all to see you humbled for a schoolboy tussle back at the academy that you scarcely remember."

"It's a good thing we brought a Steward then," I quipped, then grinned at Ena, shrugging off the irritation. It was up to me to set the tone, to inspire. "We've been through worse. At least we have proper shoes now."

Ena grinned back, then drew her hand axes and twirled them. I rarely saw them in combat as she preferred demon form in combat, and it harkened back to our time at the academy.

"Friend Xal makes an excellent point," Saghir interjected. "We have been in far worse situations, with far less resources. Our training and abilities layer well upon one another. I, for one, am ready to face our fates."

I shared that emotion for all of about three heartbeats. Then a high-pitched whine began, just beyond the edge of hearing, but strong enough to rattle my teeth in my mouth. I recognized it immediately. "No. Nonononono!"

I struggled but fell to my knees. Everyone did on our

side and in Ukufa's quint opposite us on the far side of the sands. A magical weave covered me, one identical to the collar I'd worn for months. The collar that completely prevented me from accessing my magic.

"What just happened?" Ena frowned down at her suddenly human hand. "I didn't will this."

"A boon." Celeste gave a deeply put-upon sigh. "It would seem that master Ukufa has called in a great many favors and made all the right offerings. The arena has been persuaded to set up a specific match, and it just so happens to be the one that would most severely disadvantage our quint."

"I cannot open void pockets!" Saghir's frantic voice came from within the battle pack. "Nor, ah, can I levitate out. I require aid, please."

"Staying in there is the best protection we can offer." I straightened and focused my attention on the arena and on our opponents, who I expected to all be warmasters or archers. "We have to work with what we were given. Let's see what else the arena does."

Brambles burst from the sands, long and sharp with thorns jutting in all directions, each gleaming with a purplish liquid at the end. We fell back, my quint clustering around me, and I had one final look at Ukufa's quint before the brambles grew higher than we could see.

"They've replaced their mages." I drew Narlifex and began hacking at any bramble that grew in my path. Most did not. They'd left narrow paths leading through the thick undergrowth. "If the arena had left it as sand, they have two archers and a strong frontline that could have made short work of us. I don't like the brambles, but it does somewhat even the playing field."

"Your calm is enviable, my brother." Hadi carried his

falchion close to his chest. "We do not have enough room to swing, much less dance and fight. This is designed for swift, brutal attacks. You and friend Ena will fare well, but my own style is hampered. Celeste wields a staff, which is not possible in these tight confines."

"So it's two versus five." Ena gave a scoff, and to my surprise, I realized the bravado wasn't feigned. "I get that you're new here, but I've been on the receiving end of Xal. No matter what we did, no matter how Crispus cheated or what gear the princeling had, Xal always found a way to win anyway. That was *before* he went to Gateway. Before he learned to fight. I put my faith in him. He will guide us to victory."

No one replied to that, but it seemed to lift spirits.

I had no plan as of yet, so I said nothing but kept hacking and hunting through the brambles, careful to avoid pricking myself. Action almost always beat inaction.

Eventually, I reached a twist where the path widened. Not much, but it was about three people wide.

"Here," I decided, "is where we are going to make our defense. Hack off as many brambles as you can. Ena and I in front. Hadi on rear guard in case they somehow come up behind us."

I made a small pile of larger thorns, then sheathed Narlifex and began burying them in the sand, making a sort of spike trap where the trail widened to where it tapered.

"I begin to see your plan." Celeste's voice held approval for the first time, even if it hadn't reached anything like the playfulness I'd seen back in Gateway. "We wait here and allow them to exhaust themselves hacking through this mess."

"Put thorns along all edges." I drew Narlifex and began hacking loose a fresh pile. "No matter what direction they take, we want to be able to shift to face them and keep Celeste and Saghir in the pocket."

Ena worked tirelessly beside me, and I eyed her side-long. She'd shorn her hair down to the scalp and greased it, something I hadn't realized because I almost never saw her out of demon form. I remembered giving her a miracle to regain her human side but honestly believed she preferred demon now. Liloth certainly did.

Our work slowed, then finally stopped, and we were left panting in the shade the brambles lent. I cocked an ear, and the sounds of hacking were approaching. "They're coming from the northwest. I hear five blades, so they're all working at it."

A final crack sounded about two dozen cubits away, and a gladius emerged, followed by a tall dark-skinned man in mail armor. A bow was strung over his shoulder, and his attire strongly resembled Khwezi's.

Ukufa came next, then another pair of warriors, one woman and one man, each armed with a gladius and buck-ler, perfect for tight quarters. Would that I could have summoned both.

*I will be sufficient,* Narlifex snarled. *You should practice a variety of styles, not always Xakava stance. Always two blades. It makes you predictable. You could will me to be as large as that dull stick the bird carries, and we could practice two-handed style. Grow. Learn.*

*First I have to survive.*

I shuffled into the area we'd prepared, stopping just before the thorny area we'd buried. I didn't leave enough room for Ena, but rather enough for her to stand right behind me, close enough to lunge out with her hand axes whenever an opponent let down their guard.

A pair of familiar twangs preceded a pained squawk

behind me, but I couldn't shift to find out what had happened. I could guess. We'd just found Khwezi, and he'd engaged with our rearguard. I prayed Hadi was up to the challenge and that I could hold my ground long enough for him to settle that fight.

My own problems were fast advancing. The tall man and Ukufa pressed together into the hollow we'd trapped. I forced myself to wait, and when the tall man stumbled and cursed, I dashed forward with an experimental slash.

Ukufa's blade was there, and Narlifex clanged off the scimitar. His other hand came around with a dagger, but I wrenched my scabbard from my belt and used it to parry. I shifted my stance to the sword and shield Caw had taught back in Gateway, a far better defensive strategy when one needed to hold ground. I couldn't be leaping and prancing about, as Hadi had pointed out.

I darted back and the tall man followed, whipping a dagger at me in an underhanded throw from just a few cubits away.

Time slowed. Elongated. Possibilities stretched out around me, and I instinctively chose the best one. My foot came up and caught the dagger along the flat of the blade, then reversed its momentum and whipped it back at the man's throat. He didn't even have time to raise a hand, much less dodge. The dagger slid through the mail and sank in to the hilt, the excessive force knocking his body into the wall of brambles behind him. Poison would finish him, I hoped.

The crowd roared, and its energy rolled over me. Into me. I could feel something shifting, a momentum like a river of power coming from the sands beneath my feet.

I landed and engaged Ukufa but was driven back when the female warrior flanked me. I gave ground until I reached the mouth of our little tunnel and spared a glance at Hadi.

He bled from several wounds and clutched at his shoulder. There was no sign of Khwezi. Somehow the archer had found a way to stay hidden without magic, and Hadi had no answer.

"Ena," I barked, without glancing away from Ukufa and his companion. "Get back there and help Hadi. I'll hold this flank."

Ena turned wordlessly and slipped past Celeste. I knew maneuvering around Hadi would be difficult, but they'd find a way. I had my own problems to deal with.

A dagger flashed from the back ranks at the same time Ukufa went low and his companion went high. They came at me from all angles, and I had two choices. Take a hit, or give ground. I took the dagger to my chest, deflecting it off the first armor with a satisfying clang. I didn't even need Immovable Mountain.

At the same time, I leapt over Ukufa's blade, then swung a leg up to deflect the spear his companion wielded. On and on the dance went, and if not for godsight, I'd have died. The trio worked as one and left me no room for error. I had to cover every flank and only allow attacks to hit Bronya's plates.

That went on for some time, and just when I knew I couldn't sustain it a moment longer, the woman with the spear made a mistake. Her weapon was exposed for a bit too long, and the possibility that appeared filled me with glee.

I grabbed the spear, and she hung on as any warrior would. I used all my strength to fling her into the brambles, the one at neck level specifically. It punctured her throat and emerged from the other side as shock filled the woman's gaze.

Ukufa tried to follow up, but I leapt backward, rolling into Celeste, who caught me and then gently pushed me back to my feet. By the time Ukufa and his last warrior were on me, I'd recovered my footing and parried their storm of blows without any finding flesh.

A tiny knife, not even a dagger really, hummed over my shoulder from behind and thudded into the last warrior's eye. He staggered back, clutching at his face, and I lunged, slashing his throat with Narlifex.

Ukufa made me pay for it and sliced from shoulder to shoulder along my neck, the blade going deep and my neck spurting an alarming amount of blood.

One of Ena's hand axes sprouted from his chest. Then a second. The noble looked down in shock.

So I beheaded him.

The crowd lost their minds, the screams shaking the stands and the sands themselves.

I glanced back to find Hadi with his falchion to Khwezi's throat and the archer giving the missio. I nodded my acceptance.

Power thrummed through the arena once more, and the brambles fell away, as did the barrier between my magic and me.

Blood poured down my chest, but already the magic inherent in my blood began to repair it. Somehow we'd triumphed.

I raised Narlifex skyward and gave myself to the crowd's adulation. I hadn't realized how much I had missed this.

Everything was so much simpler upon the sands.

## INTERLUDE X - TOTARIUS

Totarius wore his finest cloak, with black silks to match and a simple pair of daggers at his belt. Either could become any weapon he envisioned, a dream enchantment, meaning he had all the confidence he needed to stride among his people. He would have been the perfect Hasran noble had he not worn his demon form.

The horns, wings, and tail would have ruined the image, anywhere else at least. Here they were perfect. They denoted his royalty among demonkind. They were a sign that the princes, the true princes, had returned to lead their people.

Tens of thousands of demons thronged the repository below, a vast sea of black blood under a domed cavern lost in shadow above. Of pure magic. They lined its shores, the tunnels leading to them, and the niches and walkways high above. Those who could not be present scryed or found a flame where someone was already doing so.

Everyone, the totality of demons under Hasra, their entire civilization, was focused upon him in this moment. All knew today to be the day proscribed in myth and prophecy. He already had their belief, but today he would have their hearts. He would give them purpose.

"My people," Totarius boomed, wrapping an arm around Lucretia and pulling her close, to many cheers and not a few slanderous comments. "The dreadlord Lucretia has achieved what no other human in the history of this realm has. She has made it possible to free the dark mother once and for all, to right the injustice that created this infernal cycle."

Then he wrapped another arm around Bha, who shrank from his touch. "Soon you will participate in the ritual that will join my sibling Xakava with the avatar under the southern ocean. The black blood? Our magic supply? Once, it coursed through those titanic veins, and it shall again. Once it does, we will be invincible, and at long last we will reclaim the surface world. We will despoil all lands. All works. And then we will destroy the cycle itself, breaking the lock on the titan of void, on the mother of us all. Freeing her to reign, and to build a paradise for her children."

The cheer that followed rumbled the earth so greatly that in Totarius's imagination, it quaked the very palace above them, the nobles wondering at the disturbance and then going back to being oblivious to their coming demise.

"I do not know how you have done this," Lucretia whispered, her voice all but lost, picked out through his divine hearing, a newly acquired gift. The woman clutched her robes closer about her. She was becoming more and more the spinster, aging daily in spirit if not in flesh. "You have pushed all my goals to fruition. The ceremony is ready. The candidate is prepared." With that, Lucretia glanced at the girl and smiled. "You also have eclipsed my every hope and dream, Bha. None of this would be possible without you. You will stride the land

and make it yours, and if any defy you...you will simply destroy them."

Bha shivered and gazed down at the demon hordes. "Not even Xal will be able to hurt me, though with your flame, you'll be able to control us both, regardless of my wishes. This is not the fate I would have chosen."

"Nor I," Lucretia admitted, and the woman either managed a convincing imitation of sadness or actually felt something for the girl. She shrugged off Totarius's hand and gathered the girl into a hug. "You never had time for a real childhood, as I did, and for that I am sorry. For all of it, I'm sorry. You didn't make these choices, and they are not fair. But you carry the wrath of our people, Bha. You will set things right, and when you are reborn in some distant reality, you will finally know peace. There will be no further need for such a war once we have won it. One day the dark mother will take your pain, I promise."

The affection irritated him. They were wasting time. Precious time.

"Await me in the chamber, please." Totarius folded his arms, as the girl clearly did not favor his touch. "I will take you to the site while the hordes begin their chanting. They will not be able to stop until we reach the avatar, so it seems only considerate to be as swift as we can."

"I have saved something special for this." Lucretia produced an orb from her robes and passed it to Totarius, still holding Bha with her other arm. "Crush it when you are ready, and it will create a fissure just outside the Rent. You will be able to re-enter reality, and the demons will recognize your divinity. From there, the southern ocean is a short flight, and you can be there within a bell. Two at most."

"You are ever the faithful servant." Totarius accepted the orb and hid it away. Bha's attitude grew still more frosty, likely due to the treatment of someone she considered family.

"Before you go," Lucretia prompted, "I would ask about Erik. Allowing him to gather support in Valys is worse than foolish. It is dangerous. Those who put aside their faith under threat of punishment may take it up again. Not enough time has passed. Were I you, I would make a very public show of his execution."

"I understand your concerns, and they are valid." Totarius humored her as best he could, though he'd grown tired of her constant caution. "Erik is a threat that must be dealt with. Publicly. By me. Yet for that to have any real impact, he must first build something for me to destroy. If I kill him now, what kind of impact will that have? If, on the other hand, I allow him to build up his temple, and then Bha appears off the coast, while I murder Erik in plain view of his followers...well, that will shatter his faith. I will deal with him when the time comes, I assure you. This will centralize all our enemies in one place, a final resistance if you will. Then we will smash it."

Lucretia nodded along, but her eyes never changed. At least she'd be silent about her opinion on the matter. He valued her counsel more than he'd ever have expected, but had he left her to her own devices, she'd still be skulking behind Desidria, making petty schemes.

Now they were about to awaken a titan.

"What of my brother?" Bha prompted, glaring up at them both. "In all this planning, neither of you has mentioned him, and you know he is out there attempting to stop you."

"He is indeed." Totarius could not help but grin as he considered the plans he'd set in motion. "And I believe your brother fancies himself untouchable. Everything is going his way. My spies tell me he's triumphed in his first arena match, a stratagem he is using to recruit a mercenary army. He has a behemoth under his control. He even has an alliance with the Fomori, which is more dangerous than anyone realizes. They must be separated. And so I will keep them apart. I will give your brother new problems to occupy his attention while we end this war once and for all. Come, are you ready, little one?"

"I wish you wouldn't call me that." Bha's eyes narrowed. "I've adopted the guise of a child, but after my soul merged I am anything but. I am no cog to be inserted in your infernal machine. I do this because it is the best way to win our war and to do what is right. I don't know why Xal can't see that. Why he thinks the imprisonment of the dark mother is acceptable. But we must tear everything down until those bonds are broken. Then and only then can we build something we can all be proud of. I will play my role, and I will do it silently, but never again mistake me for a child."

"Of course." Totarius bowed low. "I forget sometimes that you are my sibling as well, Xakava. From now on, I will use that form of address, one that is proper. You have my sincere apologies for discounting you. I will not make that mistake again."

Ever. Totarius's life and soul depended upon it. He'd made a fatal error, yet Xakava had been kind enough to point it out. What if her conviction wavered, though? What if she decided to join with Xal? It had happened before, he sensed, and he'd paid the price.

Yet the memories were elusive. Outside his reach.

Totarius lifted the orb, then crushed it and stepped back as the fragments scattered to dust. The air split in a familiar way, cracking to show the edges of the lightless abyss where demons dwelled. He leapt through without a thought for his safety, though the environment on the other side would have killed an ordinary human.

Good thing he and Xakava no longer counted as such.

He flapped his wings to sustain elevation as he gazed down at the ground below, where a sprawling bonecrusher army staged an assault upon a crack in the outer shell of the great cycle itself. The shell was an iridescent color, indescribable as it constantly shifted and changed. He cared nothing for it and everything for the crack in that cycle.

Through that rent, he glimpsed a fetid swamp, and in that swamp hardened emplacements where battlemages rained continuous death upon the demonic forces. Celeste's followers, those few who remained. Would that he had time to slaughter them and end her faith forever.

Unfortunately, Bha and the ritual came first. He must see the avatar raised. After that, nothing else in this war would matter.

## INTERLUDE XI - ERIK

Erik strode to the pulpit of his temple, less nervous than he had been the first time. The people had come, and they had listened, commoner and noble both. Now there were more people filling those seats, hundreds whereas last week there had been dozens. Still a tiny fraction of what the incredible building could contain.

He set his burden atop the podium, a stack of Saghir's storytomes, including the third and fourth that the mage had just sent. Erik smiled as he noticed Mikel filing between the pews, handing out additional copies. They'd made enough for people in every row to inspect them, and already families were opening the tomes and blinking down in wonder as the stories unfolded.

A steady stream of new parishioners wandered in, each hesitantly seeking seating. Nearly all found acceptance and were able to join people they knew in the crowd. None came from the truly powerful noble families that Erik had known in his childhood. Not one showed up.

Some were no doubt above it all. Most were afraid.

Those who'd been brave enough to defy the Imperator

had likely been rounded up and either exiled to far posts or killed outright. Crispus and his father had known precisely which were the most devout. If Erik were to succeed, then he would need his own father, a man he despised, but the only one who might match Totarius's political acumen.

"Good morning," Erik called in a loud, clear voice. Many admiring eyes fell upon him, offering the kind of attention he'd so enjoyed back at court. It felt...oily now. "Thank you for braving the Imperator's wrath by being here. He has decreed the Stewards anathema. A failed religion, and one that is not welcome within the lands he deems his."

Angry muttering rose, mostly from older knights. To a man, they had long thick beards, and every one still possessed the build they'd had in youth.

"Crispus pointed out that Dalanthar died. That the Stewards are mortal." Erik gently picked up his shield of office, which had been propped unceremoniously against the podium. "Yet the power of your faith, the power of your belief in the tenet of justice, in what is right and true, is tied not to Dalanthar, nor to me. We are Stewards. The very definition of the word means we act as caretakers for our artifacts. It is that you believe in. The concept, not the man. If I fall, then another will take up this shield, and another, and another. There will always be a Steward of Justice, so long as the cycle itself exists. We are tied to it—that much I have learned, even though I am newly come to my duties."

He paused for a moment, both to let the crowd digest his words and to seek new ones. His true goal today was chaos, and it would succeed, because if it did not, then Darius would never escape the palace. Erik needed Crispus angry, distracted, and ideally kicking in the front door of this temple.

"I've known Crispus for over a decade, and he's always

been a petulant little shit." Now that earned a few scandalized gasps and more than a little laughter. Erik gently set his shield back down, then sat on the top step, his armor creaking as he descended to their level and dropped the volume of his voice to match. Let them crane for his next words. "The Imperator will not take what I say today lightly. He will call it heresy, which puts me in an awkward position. I am to obey the laws of the land, but at the same time, I understand intrinsically what is right and what is wrong. Punishing and imprisoning people who disagree with you is wrong. Usurping a throne after murdering the previous Imperator is wrong, no matter the laws of the land."

A larger collective gasp arose from the crowd at the last revelation, and more than a few curses. After they faded, utter silence reigned. He had every last one of them now, including the spies, who would no doubt be alerting their masters using various eldimagi. The thought of Crispus raging warmed him.

"Dalanthar, my predecessor, said he *must* obey the local laws," he continued in a high clear voice, stepping out into the pews and walking among them. "I suffer no such restrictions. I realized that was a choice he and the other Stewards made to keep the peace. They realized they could gain more followers if they remained neutral. Worship. As currency. That was their motivation."

Erik stopped speaking and returned to the podium, then slowly drew his blade, the blue steel catching the light. He let his gaze sweep them for long moments, as he dragged out the pregnant pause. They hung on his words. "I have a different opinion. I believe that my role is to teach the people the true path of justice. Of honor. Of duty. Not just words, but their meaning. Their practice. I was a boy not so very long ago and had foolish notions of war."

He sheathed his blade and rolled his eyes at himself, at his childhood self.

"Being just means opposing despots." Erik stood a bit taller. He wasn't that boy any longer. He was a man now. "It means doing what is right even when it is hard. It means compassion, yet tempered by wisdom. It means keeping our swords sharp but our hearths open and welcome."

He knew he was rambling, but he needed to draw this out as long as possible. Crispus's response would be swift, but it would take him time to muster a force and descend from on high. How should he use that time?

"I believe examples are the best way to demonstrate my meaning." Erik leaned over the podium and plucked up a copy of the first storytome, then held it up for all to see. "These artifacts are a very special living magic and can replicate themselves. They give the true account of the demon prince Xal and his archmage companion Saghir. I attended the academy with both. How did I treat them? It was awful, to say the least, and you will see for yourselves. Every word of it is true. I did it because my mother bade me. I followed the rules. She literally bound my will to ensure it. That's not honorable. There's no justice there, whatever the law. She tried to kill Xal rather than honor the deal I'd struck with him after he single-handedly broke the Fomori force devouring our armada."

He picked up another copy, then strode out to the audience and handed them out. "Distribute these. Read them. Learn Xal's story. Learn the truth that Crispus and his father don't wish you to know. They tore down temples and salted the earth in Hasra. They fly above you, feasting on fine meats and endless wine while the people starve. They have imprisoned the Praetor and his daughter, whose only crime was standing up for justice. For what was right. For opposing despots. I would oppose them. Who stands with me?"

A blond-bearded man shot to his feet, eyes glittering with passion. "I will stand with you, my Lord. I would renew my covenant. I am willing to stand and die. I am willing to fight for justice. For honor. For Valys."

The doors to the temple crashed open, punctuating his words. That was fast. Crispus had been more prepared than expected. Had he come himself? Everything depended upon it.

"Please remain seated," Erik boomed in a commanding voice. "It sounds like we have some late arrivals to the sermon."

Legionnaires flooded into the room by the dozen, every quint protecting a mage with a staff ready. A full ten quints entered the room, and Erik waited silently while they arrayed themselves for battle.

"There's plenty of seating." He gestured to some empty pews. "Please, take your ease."

"Erik of—" the captain began but trailed off as Crispus strode past.

The Imperator wore full battle regalia, a fortune in eldimagi. No doubt there was a ring on every finger under those gauntlets. He was ready for war and had fifty crack troops to support him.

"You are spewing treason within my realm." Crispus slowly drew his sword. "If you will not enforce our laws, then I will do it myself. You and everyone here have committed treason. The sentence is death, to be administered immediately. You can submit, but I truly hope that you don't."

Erik glanced over Crispus's shoulder at an empty spot along the wall. "Now, Tissa."

Crispus dropped his sword and dove between two pews.

"That's about what I expected." Erik began to laugh, and a few of the bolder knights in the crowd joined in. None of the soldiers took it up. "She's on other business, I think, but who knows when she'll show up in your bed chamber? You used to like that, I hear. Now then...you were posturing and telling me how you were going to slaughter the people under my protection. Was there more to that speech or did I ruin your moment?"

Crispus's face was a mask of rage as he rose to his feet, eyes bulging and a vein throbbing in his temple. He turned to the captain and stabbed a finger at the crowd. "Kill them first. All of them. Only after they are all dead do we send *him* back to the grave where he belongs."

"I don't think so, Imperator." Erik raised his shield and prayed that the wise old man was listening and that his instincts were right. He'd done his reading, the old texts in Mikel's little library, and the reason this place had stood so long, despite orokh invasions and worse, was within his control. "I re-consecrate this temple in the name of justice."

Erik knelt and rapped the shield's base against the floor. It rang like a gong, and golden energy burst out and flowed along the floors, pews, and walls until it coated the entire temple, every stone of it. The energy sank into the stone, then disappeared. Yet it left everything lighter. Stronger. There was an aura about this place. A peace he hadn't realized had been missing.

That peace came from the parishioners, from the worship they had provided. He had merely shaped that force and given it form in the real world. And he could do it again. If he had a huge pool of worship, what more could he accomplish? Even in the face of Crispus's judgment, the prospect excited him.

"You aren't welcome here, Crispus." Erik strode up to the Imperator and looked him right in the eye. To his mild surprise, Crispus held his gaze. "You'll find that no violence is possible. Notice that not one of your guards has followed your orders. If you ask any soldier in particular, they won't be able to tell you why, but I can. It's unjust. And here justice prevails. Unjust acts are no longer allowed. Bye, now. Please drop a scale in the till on the way out if you can spare it. We're quite in need of donations. Justice, watch over you and yours."

*You have done well, Steward.* The old man was more pleased than he'd ever been.

# INTERLUDE XII - DARIUS

Darius could scarcely believe it. Somehow Erik had achieved the impossible.

He plastered himself against the high-backed chair, making himself as small as possible, hunched over his dinner plate, as Crispus rose and spittle flew from his mouth. Their father remained sitting across from the Imperator, calm as never before. In the past, before he had changed, their father would have been just as incensed by the news.

More and more, Darius suspected it wasn't their father at all. Nor was it the man he had become in the wake of whatever dark pact he'd made. The person sitting there was an illusion. Darius was almost certain of it. Somehow their father had found a way to be in two places at once. Who knew where the real one was?

"That smug-faced son of a whore," Crispus roared, slamming his fist into the mahogany as he glared at the mage who had made the report, a frightened woman. All his brother's attendants were like that. "He undermines my throne, in public no less. This demands answer. Father, please attend to the court this morning. I am going to kill a Steward."

Jun shrank down in her seat across from Darius, slowly so the movement did not draw attention. Their meals were often taken this way to avoid the raging and scheming. He'd learned everything he could here, and now it was time to abscond with that knowledge, to take it, and a pair of vital prisoners, to the one faction that might be able to successfully oppose the despot ruling the Imperium.

How had it all fallen apart so swiftly?

"I will handle matters," the illusionary Totarius promised, then rose smoothly. "Tend to business as you see fit, Imperator. I will see that the sycophants are occupied until your return."

That solidified it. The real Totarius would never have allowed Crispus to challenge Erik in his own stronghold unaided. He'd have suggested waiting him out and posting guards outside the temple. He'd have suggested not dealing with it personally. He would absolutely not meekly accept busywork. Ever.

"Well?" Crispus demanded, spearing Darius with an accusing stare. "Are you going to come with me? Defend our house's honor? You remember what that is, right, brother?"

"I have not forgotten," Darius snapped, frayed nerves getting the better of him. He fixed his brother with a disgusted stare. "Do you think I'd participate in the slaughter of my own best friend? If you must do this, then please do not force me to witness it. I've already grieved his death once. I beg of you. Please. I have not asked much. I've left you the glory, the power, and the wealth. I have all I need...my family. Please, brother."

Darius's heart thundered as his brother's face shifted to an unreadable mask. This could end everything. If Crispus forced him to join him, then the entire plan would fall to ruin.

"No intervention, Father?" Crispus spun on Totarius, who'd slowly risen from his chair and was preparing to depart. "You'd let us settle our own squabbles?"

"You are the Imperator." Totarius gave a slow shrug. "I do not question your decisions. Nor does your brother. Your word is law. If you command, then we obey. Our past lives do not matter. So no, no intervention, Your Grace."

"Very well." Crispus turned a suspicious stare back in Darius's direction. "Your words ring true. All that matters to you is the girl and that abomination of a child. Thank you for keeping that mewling thing from my presence. You may retire to your estates. In fact, I do not wish to see you for a few days. I will send for you when I wish it."

"Of course, Brother." Elation soared in Darius, and he struggled desperately to contain it as he all but dragged Jun to her feet beside him. "I will await your word."

Then Crispus swept out, and Totarius left behind him. All that remained were the guards.

"Come." Darius began wrapping a few rolls in a napkin. "Let us gather a small repast and eat alone. I desire solitude. Erik...well, I know he's a traitor, but I cannot erase our childhood. I must grieve his loss. I may require solitude."

Jun nodded in understanding. The vein in her neck throbbed, and her eyes were too wide, like a horse about to flee. He understood the signs but prayed the guards would attribute them to fear of the Imperator. There were even odds that even the real spies were too concerned about their own life to catch such small signs.

He gathered Jun under his arm, and the pair strode from the chamber, then down a short flight of stairs. Down, down, down three levels to his own level. Instead of stopping there, he continued down two more to the private airship dock at the bottom of the manor. It was seldom used, and only two guards were in attendance.

Both were dwarves. Both glared fiercely...past him. Unseeing.

*Did you use an illusion?* Jun signed

*No*, he signed back as he led her past them. *They can see and hear us. Erk and Ferk are loyal to the Praetor. They're choosing to let us pass. They know what we are about.*

*Will they not be harmed?* Jun signed as they continued down the stairs and onto the waiting skiff, which was empty as promised, just a pillar in the center with a tiny matrix to control the thing.

"They may," Darius admitted as he tapped the sigils on all three tiny rotating rings and linked to the vessel. It responded to his will, and they zoomed down and away from the Hammer, curving so that if Crispus happened to glance in that direction, he would not see. "In all likelihood, they will be fine. Crispus doesn't seem to realize they served in the Praetor's household, or if he knows, he doesn't care. Maybe he assumes they are loyal. That is why they remain. If they leave, then the next guard change will know immediately the skiff is missing. By that point, we need to be long gone from the city, and we have dangerous work to be about first."

*I know*, Jun signed back, then moved to lean against the prow, angling a bit to face him. *Do you really think it will be so simple to get them to release such important prisoners?*

"Trickery and charm remove many barriers, but this is possible because so many people still believe in the Praetor." Darius grinned, then laughed suddenly. He whooped into the wind. "We are free, Jun. Just think of it! We'll have a chance to tweak my brother's nose and be away before he can respond. By the time he learns of our escape, we will be landing upon the spider mountain and joining with Xal and Li."

*I do not like sending the baby ahead.* Jun's brows knit together like thunderclouds, and Darius knew he'd overstepped. She craved reassurance, not him being cavalier. Or at least he thought she did.

"I don't like it either, but we can't very well fight and cast with a babe in our arms." Darius restrained his tone. She was right to be afraid. "Besides, you know how my brother feels about the little tyrant. I don't want him anywhere Crispus can reach him, and he's already safely away from this place with the same midwife who birthed me. He will be safe, I assure you. I am more worried about us. Not much, mind you, but a bit. I believe everyone is trustworthy, and my scrying has revealed no undue risk. Let us find out for sure."

He focused on guiding the skiff lower, down toward the blocky fortress along the north side of the caldera, as far from the binders as the knights could build their fabled prison. "Remember, you are a companion who could speak but chooses not to."

They landed in a rush just outside the prison, and Darius touched the broach at his neck, activating a mirror that appeared at face height. He removed several ostentatious pieces of jewelry, which he slid over his fingers and wrists. Then he adopted a contemptuous scowl.

"Come along now," he snapped in a perfect imitation of Crispus's voice. "Your Imperator has no further patience. We must retrieve the prisoners, and be away. I long for my bed."

There were only a handful of people in the realm capable of distinguishing the brothers from each other, being that they were the same height and age. Only their builds and small facial differences separated them. Let it be enough.

Darius strode boldly up to the front of the fortress to a side gate that likely never saw traffic. His heart sped as they approached. What if the guard couldn't—the door swung silently open and a tall woman with a strong jaw nodded at him. Nothing like a smile ever touched her face, which Darius recognized.

Or near enough. The lady looked so much like her daughter Sophia they could have been sisters. And she had not taken her daughter's death lightly.

They ducked inside, then immediately turned to follow the right wall. Darius walked boldly with purpose, ignoring the guards they passed at every intersection. Each set snapped to attention, but he never once acknowledged them. His brother wouldn't have.

Darius wiped sweat from his neck as they reached the top of a stairwell and descended deeper into the fortress. It led down seven levels, below the surface, down below the cellar itself. Jun followed in his wake, and he paused midway down to sign to her. *Stay back a bit. This is the most dangerous part.*

He resumed his passage, winding down the stairs until he spied a thick oaken door and a pair of soldiers. Both hesitated when they saw him, as one might when the Imperator unexpectedly appeared during your watch.

"Stand up straight," he barked, satisfied with the veracity of his disguise. He waved at them. "One of you, open that door. The other, bring your wardkey. We will be removing several prisoners."

"Your eminence," one of the guards began, a man in his later years, likely near the end of a long career. One not eager to jeopardize that career from his tone. "Ah...apologies, but we are not permitted to open this door unless ordered to do so by one possessing the matching wardkey. It's a formality to prevent illusions."

"Don't be a fool," Darius snapped. He raised a hand to wave at the door once more. "This citadel cancels all spells. How could I be an illusion? I tire of your impertinence. Tell me who created this absurd rule, and I will have their family put to death. You may have their lands."

It was exactly what Crispus would have said in that moment. He was always making such moves, punishing one so that he might reward another.

"Apologies, Your Grace, but—"

Darius leaned forward and flung a pair of daggers plucked from his sleeve. One. Two. Each slid through an eye socket, dropping the guards before they could react. They clattered to the ground, and he raised a hand to sketch before remembering his magic did nothing within the prison.

He knelt next to the guard who'd spoken and rifled through his pouches until he found the man's wardkey. It was shaped as a literal key, and he pressed it into the socket on the door. The oak groaned open, but before going through, he darted up the stairs and caught Jun's eye.

She hurried down the stairs and followed him along the row of cells. Darius followed the precise directions he'd been given, finally reaching a block of four cells, each with their own oak doors. He opened the first, then pressed the key into Jun's hand. *Open the other three cells. I will fetch the Praetor.*

He darted in, shocked by the emaciated form within. The Praetor lay naked, save a loincloth, the floor coated in dirt and worse things. There was no furniture and no decor. Only a hole in the floor to defecate.

"Hello, Praetor." Darius did not approach, as he assumed the man's fugue state might be faked. "We've come to free you, your daughter, and Erik's father. Time is precious. We must be swift. Those loyal to our cause have used all our influence to achieve this, but the window is closing."

"Crispus?" The Praetor pried open a bruised eye and raised his cheek from the filth. "Why?"

"It's Darius." Darius scooped him up, straining less than he should have, alarmingly so. The Praetor had lost a full stone. More perhaps. "I've got you. Just relax for now. Stay silent for the time being."

He returned to the hall to find Jun opening the last of the cells. Ashianna had already emerged from hers, wearing nothing but a loincloth and a strip of cloth over her chest, but in far better shape than her father. She'd lost weight, but her arms were still corded with muscle.

A moment later, Jun staggered out of the final cell with a bedraggled Lord Garulan draped over her shoulder, his golden hair soiled straw about his head and shoulders, which reminded Darius of the danger Garulan's son Erik was in. Let him be all right.

Jun was not a strong woman, but there wasn't much left of Garulan. Both legs had been severed at the knee, and one arm was missing.

"Come," Darius called, beckoning to Ashianna as he retraced his steps. "We need to flee. Swiftly. We have less than a bell before the next shift change, and those guards are not favorable to our cause. Tonight took months of preparation."

Ashianna nodded but hurried up to fall in step with Darius. "Give my father here. You can fight. I likely cannot. But I can carry weight to keep your hands free for battle."

Darius gratefully handed the burden over. Without *fire*

magic, it was already becoming unmanageable. He might look like Crispus, but he didn't possess his physical strength.

Their ragged band hurried back through the prison and reached the door where the pair of guards lay in slowly spreading pools of blood. Darius paused and took back the Praetor from Ashianna.

"That one might almost fit you." He nodded at the larger guard.

"What about the other one?" Ashianna knelt and began removing the man's gauntlets.

"Leave him. They'll discover it with the shift change no matter what we do." Darius didn't like how elevated his heartbeat was. It wasn't just the exertion, which was more than he was used to.

Darius forced himself back into the Crispus role and altered his voice to match. "Be swift, offal. And do not speak unless I ask you a question."

A tiny laugh bubbled out of Ashianna, which lightened the mood slightly. "That was a bit too accurate."

Darius let his own smile show for just a moment. "Come now, let's be away from this place. Your family still has support, but we've used up nearly all of it here. Erik and Lady Sophia's mother will pay the price for your freedom."

## INTERLUDE XIII - LI

Li crept along the rocky trail along the mountain's interior, high above the city itself, a place that only rebellious children ventured, as there was nothing of interest to make the climb worthwhile.

For the first time she'd thrown aside her cloak, and exposed her snowy wings for all to see. If people remained here let them know her for what she was. They aided her in balance, and already their use was becoming more natural.

Tissa prowled behind her, and they ghosted through the near-darkness lit only by the scattered wisps within the mountain.

"This is the place." Li raised a hand and tossed her wisp in the air, lighting the little campsite, enough to draw a small gasp when she saw much had been hidden. "There's food and blankets, and a whole lot besides."

"Wait." Tissa rested a hand on Li's shoulder, then slid past her. "It could still be a trap. I do not trust these messages."

The assassin knelt next to the bedroll and prodded it with Nefarius, then crept around the camp, scanning as she picked a purposeful path through the chaos. She paused when she reached the far side, fading into the shadows, save for her eyes and the scarlet of her blade. "I can detect no traps unless they are magical, and that's your area."

"Thank you." Li stepped on the air, a half cubit over the floor, and cautiously moved around the camp, inspecting. "Some of this makes sense. Like the food and blankets, and even a pile of books over here. But these?"

A small rock had been converted into a table, and on it, several dolls had been arranged, each in a combat stance, two with spears. A stuffed dragon with felt teeth opposed them and had a spear sticking out of its stuffing, from a hole that had been torn along the ribs.

"I get bored," came a sudden voice from above them.

Tissa vanished, eyes and blade both, lost to the darkness. It left Li staring upward at a tiny alcove in the stone, a little lip just big enough for a small person. Li might have fit, but it would have been too small for Xal or Erik.

"I'm sorry," the voice spoke again—a boy, Li thought, and a familiar one. "I left clues, but I've had to be very cautious. The dragons have been fleeing ever since the pulse in the sky, but many have remained, and some still hunt. I can't take chances."

"Haitao?" Li blinked up, finally placing the boy from the tourney where they had played each other. "Is that you?"

"It's me." A pair of legs appeared over the lip, then the child wiggled into view. He dropped lightly down, then pushed a pair of spectacles up his nose. "I—it's been lonely. My family didn't look for me when I ran away, and then that pulse happened a few days later."

"How did you hide?" Tissa emerged from the shadows, her blade close enough to gut the boy, though he seemed oblivious.

"It's all right, Tissa." Li waved a wrist, and the sword disappeared into its scabbard. She loved that Tissa was so easy to work with and never demanded the why. "He's not bound. It doesn't appear to be a trap, though I am curious how you've survived for so long on your own. And why here?"

"We're directly under the Halo." Haitao pointed straight up. "These rocks are very close and have been bathed for, well, for a long time. They give off magic. Not much, but…I don't give off much magic either. I've been hiding here hoping no one would scry it. They have no reason to. I don't ever steal from the same place twice or take too much when I do. Especially after the night of scales, I'm careful. It's kept me alive."

Li had no words at first. She gathered the child into a hug, her wings enshrouding them both. At first, the boy stiffened, but then he leaned into her breast and began to sob. She held him and rocked for long moments as sobbing became wailing, and he released the weight no child should ever have to bear.

"You did well," Tissa murmured, and the assassin dropped to a knee next to the child. She rubbed his back through a gap in Li's wings while she comforted him, the sudden compassion shocking to Li. "It's all right now. The dawn has come. The monsters can't get you any longer."

Haitao's sobs grew less frequent, and eventually the boy recovered and straightened himself. "Thank you. I always knew someone would come. I can feel the warmth from above, from the Halo. I know the people of the heavens are up there. I thought you were up there, Princess. I thought you would lead a charge to free us all."

"We have to save ourselves." Li wiped a tear from her cheek, uncertain when it had fallen. Her heart ached for this poor boy. "The people of the heavens will not emerge until the mountain is safe, but that's why Tissa and I have come. To make it safe again."

"How can you do that?" He blinked owlishly up at her, the certainty that she could do what she said absolutely total. The confidence humbled her.

"The lightning people." Li's answer came without hesitation. She noted the widening of Tissa's eyes, then the sudden narrowing. The assassin thought Li had given away something she shouldn't have. She'd understand soon enough. "If I can wake them, then they can slaughter the dragons remaining in the mountain and reclaim it for our people."

"Oh." Haitao blinked a few times, then removed his glasses to wipe them on his tunic. "Where will they all live? There's a lot of them, right?"

"I don't know how many, but sadly, there is a great deal of empty space in the mountain now." Li sighed and glanced over the edge of his little camp, down at the city proper. There was almost no movement. None of the bustle that should have existed. None of the kamizas throwing their doors open. "We will find a way to accommodate them, and if there are too many, we have many settlements throughout the mountains that can take their people in."

Tissa's tension had only grown, and the assassin's eyes were large and pleading.

"Haitao, do you know how many dragons are left?" Li pressed, though she kept her gaze on Tissa, so her vassal could see she'd been acknowledged. "You've been here a while. Have you seen any of their movements?"

"That's all I do." The boy straightened, pride entering his tone and expression. "I watch their comings and goings. Three of them seem to control the throne room, and they guard it in shifts. They've never left the mountain for any reason. Most of the rest have been gathering artifacts. There were big piles in front of every manor for a while. They took everything that had any magic at all, but I don't know where they brought it. Most of the dragons left with the last shipment. I see a few in the mountain still, but it mostly feels empty. Twice I've seen an illusion below, a group of people calling for survivors. They were a trap, I think."

"Your instincts saved your life." Tissa gave a grudging nod of respect and moved to the edge to peer down at the throne room. "Some of the stronger ones are still here, hunting." She turned to Li, then dropped her voice to a whisper. "Why are you being so free with your tongue? Apologies for questioning, but anyone could be scrying."

Li raised a hand and sketched a ward, allowing her expression to widen to surprise, hopefully convincing acting were anyone scrying. Only once the ward was in place did she return her expression to neutral.

"Because were it me," she explained, "I'd have set trigger wards. I'd set them specifically around the bells being rung. I'd watch for groups just like ours. I've given them everything they need to spring the trap, yet they haven't. Why? It's almost like they want us to ring the bells. I don't understand why we're allowed to plot and plan here. Almost I want to make an attempt on the bells."

"Shouldn't we wait for Bumut and the others?" Tissa's expression soured into disapproval. "If we are attacked, we could be quickly overwhelmed. These dragons are old, not like Niu. I don't know what they can do, but if they can use the dream realm the same way we used the spirit realm, then they can come and go as they please. How do we fight them alone?"

"We can speak freely but must be swift." Li's anxiety

grew by the moment. How long could the ward hold if an ancient wyrm sought to break it? "I am trying to ascertain if they wish us to wake the lightning people, but thus far am still unsure. If I am correct, if they really wish it to happen, then we will face no opposition. We could sneak in, right now, tap the bells and end this occupation. But would they gain something unexpected? Would they somehow control the lightning people? If not...why is it so easy? Why can we skulk about without being caught? I can't decide between hubris and cunning."

"I understand, thank you." Tissa bowed her head respectfully in a way Li had not seen her ever do to Crispus. "Do you wish my counsel?"

"Please."

"If we wake the lightning people, they may aid us or harm us." Tissa rested a hand on Nefarius's hilt. "If we rely on our own skills, then we know what will happen. Spring this trap, yes, but do it on your terms. Time is important, yet not vital. It's not as if they will execute someone if we do not attack today. Send a missive to Bumut and have him get into position. We rest here and watch, and see what the dragons do. We test your theory in all ways, save entering the throne room until Bumut arrives."

"Wise counsel." Li returned the same nod Tissa had given. "Counsel I will heed. We'll missive Bumut and speak with Haitao, and learn all we can before touching the bells."

She peered down at the city one more time, but her gaze was pulled upward instead. She couldn't see the Halo, but she could feel it's pull. If Li regained the throne room, her father's people would open the gates once more.

Was that it?

Was that Khonsu's plan? If Li were to wake the lightning people, and Khonsu somehow controlled them, would they take the mountain and then deliver the Halo to their scaly master?

Or was it all an elaborate misdirection?

Either way, if she could retake the mountain without waking the lightning people, then it would prove that the lightning people weren't needed, and this wasn't the prophesied time. She was grateful for Tissa having provided her a way to further test her theories.

Li could not afford a mistake here. If she made one...she would empower a capricious god whose children had devoured her people.

No. Every last one of these wyrms was going to die of flee, and soon. She would do this the right way, and when the time came, would make the right choice regarding the lightning people. Failure was simply not an option she would entertain.

# 20

## MAGIC

You're probably expecting a long retelling of the other battles I faced in the arena. I've certainly done it before, especially back at the academy and in Gateway. I tire of such retellings.

Our quint faced two more matches, but the first was hardly worth mentioning. They lacked Ukufa's influence and backing, and we ended them. Swiftly. And when I say we, I mean mostly Celeste and Saghir, who roasted them alive, froze the ashes, boiled them in acid for good measure, then electrocuted what remained just to be safe.

The other match, however, changed my approach to warfare, and the storytome version will be some of Saghir's best work.

After crushing our previous opponents, we had a week to hone our skills. That allowed us proper practice and time to become more of a unit, while also allowing me to schedule meetings with several large companies. Unfortunately, every mercenary commander gave the same response.

After the Arena had spoken...meaning *if* I were champion. If not, I had the sense some would still take service, but that they would require a higher wage when doing so. Others would only follow the very best, and as those were the ones I most needed, my course was clear.

We found ourselves upon the sands once more a precise week after the last battle and once more awaited the Arena's judgment. This time, the crowd was silent. The winner of today's match would claim the title of champion, and everyone knew that the arena made exceptional final matches.

The sands began to rumble and bounce and then fell away in the center of the arena. A long dark fissure appeared, and then from that fissure blasted a wall of *void*. Pure disintegration. Cross that plane and we would be destroyed.

Then another layer appeared next to it, this one *fire*.

Then one of *dream*.

And *air*.

And *life*.

And *water*.

And *spirit*.

And *earth*.

One after another until the wall of magic completely bisected the arena. There was no way to see our opponents, which rendered all martial attacks useless until we could find a way to reach them.

"We must be swift." I turned to my quint. "Find a solution before they do. Mages, what are we dealing with?"

"It appears," Saghir mused from within the pack, his voice echoing from within, "that this is the precise opposite of our fight with Ukufa's quint. Instead of no magic, this is all magic. I do believe that Celeste and I have been given a chance to restore our lost honor."

"I think you gained that when you disintegrated the last group," Ena pointed out, grinning wickedly in demon form, which the crowd seemed to love. "If you want more revenge, though, don't let me stop you. As long as we win."

"Oh, we shall." Celeste's eyes narrowed, and she glared at the barrier before us. "It appears they've created wards of each aspect. I suspect scrying will be blocked, as will all forms of teleportation."

I nodded along as I agreed with her assessment. "We should try both to be certain. I'll be ready to counterspell, just in case they find a way to breach the wards first. The important thing to me is this is not some boon attempting to limit us. Almost I think the arena is apologizing."

"I doubt that. They have four mages," Celeste explained as she raised both hands and began sketching separate spells, too fast for me to track. "Two are primary, two secondary, like Xal. If neither Ena nor Hadi can counter-spell, we have fewer mages, and I agree our lives depend on reaching them before they reach us."

"I have ruled out scrying," Saghir exclaimed from within the pack. "Nor will a fissure open."

Celeste sketched an *earth* spell of impressive complexity, and the sands began to part near the center of the barrier, being dug away into flanking piles as she tunneled deeper and deeper. No matter how deep she went, they still encountered the barrier.

"What about a mirror?" I pointed skyward. "When we were in the pens and elsewhere in temples, they used mirrors to reflect light where we needed it. It was a wonderful solution for those without magic."

"A fine idea, friend Xal." *Earth* and *void* flashes appeared through the holes of the battle pack as Saghir cast a summoning spell, and then high above us a silver disk appeared, on our side of the barrier, but angled to reveal the other.

My enhanced senses made it easy to see that far, and unsurprisingly, I found a quint of catkin in thick cotton, definitely not from the Blasted Lands, performing a similar series of tests to get around the barrier. Immense power radiated from their mages, one of whom resembled Ephram and I thought might be some sort of shaman or druid.

The other mage wore only a loincloth, and much of her fur had been shorn to reveal glowing tattoos dotting her entire body. She cast spells by tapping tattoos, which flung each sigil up to join the other spells. It was as if she herself were a spell tome.

"You are brilliant, Master Saghir." Celeste's voice held both awe and gratitude. "You've just won us this fight. We can see them, and they cannot see us."

She raised both hands and sketched a spell that dwarfed the complexity of what I could personally cast. There were dozens of sigils of *earth*, *void*, *fire*, *dream*, and *air*. It was more than a greater path, but before I could inspect the spell in detail, it fused, and a ball of power slammed into my chest.

Vertigo knocked me spinning. I had no idea what direction was up, and the situation worsened when blindness extinguished my vision. I couldn't see nor hear nor feel.

And then I could, but my senses were all wrong.

I stood upon the sands behind the cats, or something like me did. A glance down showed that I hadn't been teleported. Some sort of dream-form simulacrum had been formed, a magical version of me, part illusion, but real enough to kill.

And my opponents had no idea I was present.

I held a scimitar in each hand, if held was the right term. There was no place where hand ended and hilt began. All that mattered was that I had blades. I glided forward silently and brought my new weapons forward in a cross to decapitate the shaman.

My enemies were reacting now, and my simulacrum wasn't as fast as I was. I swam through molasses to reach the next mage, rammed a blade into her thigh to pin her in place, then brought the other around to slice through both legs and her tail, spilling her to the sands in a bloody mess.

Sudden agony locked me rigid, and my dream-form unraveled. I caught a glimpse of one of their remaining mages casting a counterspell, then the vertigo returned and ended with me lying on my cheek in the sand, drool leaking out.

I clutched my head with a groan, then glanced up at my quint to learn the situation. Ena was also drooling upon the sands, and as I rose, Celeste completed another spell, and Hadi dropped, presumably adding another simulacrum to the other side.

"Prepare yourself, Xal," the Steward called as she began to sketch again. Sweat beaded the Steward's brow, and several strands of gold had escaped her ponytail. "Finish them off."

"I am watching over your bodies," Saghir's disembodied voice came from above, instead of the pack. "Go swiftly and bring our wrath."

By the time the vertigo released me once more, Ena's simulacrum had already been banished, but Hadi's remained and had added a third body to the pile, this one the warrior who'd been protecting the mages.

Two counterspells slammed into the tengu, and he disappeared. I blurred across the sands and placed a scimitar to each cat's throat. I couldn't speak, it seemed, but the message was clear. I hoped they would take it.

Both slowly raised their paws and delivered the missio.

I lowered my blades, and the crowd went wild. Under ordinary circumstances, the missio seemed to annoy them, but I suspected these were crowd favorites, and this time they seemed to appreciate my honor.

Time ceased to exist. The crowd was locked in place, arms raised and mouths open. In the sky an image appeared, towering to the heavens, as large as any titan avatar. Large enough to wield the Hammer of Reevanthara in Valys and also the being who had created it.

Reeva, larger than life, every curl of that beard large enough to flatten a wagon should it fall to the earth. The deity wore resplendent white robes and a golden diadem across his brow. He looked...regal, in a word. In a way he did not in the other visions I'd seen. This, I sensed, predated those visions.

Even as it swept me up and I took a final glance at my companions, I realized they were experiencing something very different. They were not gazing up at the sky. They were not moving at all. Everyone, save me, appeared frozen.

"And me, lad." Reeva appeared next to me, an unassuming dwarf who barely reached my waist. "I still remember adding this particular flourish to the cycle upon its creation. A sort of welcome speech for new gods, one designed to endure, even should I fall. Back then the possibility of my failure and dissolution still existed, you see. But now? It's merely a quaint reminder of simpler times. Oh... forgive me. The interesting part is coming up."

"—most of you, this is your first trial," the towering version of the titan explained, high up in the sky. "You've proven that you can stand among elder gods and at least hold your own. You may not be the strongest. You may barely possess any divinity at all. Yet you have proven you have the will. Two trials remain. Succeed at both, and you will be elevated to the ruling council, able to influence the future of this realm and all the others it has birthed. Congratulations, Champion."

The vision in the sky ended, and I sensed that time should have resumed its normal flow, yet it did not. Everyone, including Celeste, remained frozen exactly as we'd been at the moment the battle ended.

"What do you want?" I turned to face Reeva, glaring at the dwarf. "What is it you seek? So many things are clear now, but just as many remain a mystery. You tried to goad me into putting on the crown before I was anointed. That would have killed me, wouldn't it? I'd have become like Jhordil, the mad Imperator."

"Perhaps." Reeva gave a guilty smile and made no real attempt to hide it. "The results certainly wouldn't have been good, from your perspective. And it would have all but guaranteed that you fail, which would accelerate my confrontation with Gortha. I stand ready for the final war. The cycle will fail, and I will avenge it."

"You can't avenge something you never defended in the first place." Hatred welled up in me, some of it mine, but the larger portion belonging to past incarnations. "I won't let you destroy the cycle. I will become anointed and use the cycle you created to win this war. I will expel the elder gods, all of them, and I will ensure that the people are strong enough to aid in their own defense. Then, I will march out into the darkness and find a way to end this war once and for all. The cycle will be eternal. I *will* find a way. That possibility exists."

"There's more of you in that noggin than I expected." Reeva cocked his head, scratching at his bulbous nose as he inspected me. "Maybe. Maybe you'll succeed in this incarnation. It's nothing to me either way. If it takes another million years, eventually the cycle will fall, and I will preside over the creation of something far more grand. Wouldn't bet on you, given the odds, though."

The dwarf hooked his thumbs through his belt near the buckle, then grinned maliciously. "Did you know that your eldest brother is about to deposit your little sister into a full avatar? They've got the means, and they've got the magic. Also heard you lost that loathsome cockroach as an ally. His soul will meet an appropriate end one day, I assure you.

"You might be able to recruit some mercenaries here, but how will you found a true religion? That's what you always failed to understand, especially when you were Rei. You did what was just, not what was pragmatic. The hearts of the people are what matter. Their veneration. Their faith. Your brother has it. You do not. He tells them what to believe, and ensures no other voices exist. That route leads to endless power."

Then Reeva was gone, and time resumed its normal flow. The crowd's adulation crashed over me, and everyone around me assumed my stunned expression had to do with the victory. I'd triumphed here, but for what came next I simply couldn't conceive of a path to victory.

How would I stop Totarius if he'd truly raised an avatar like those from my visions?

It just didn't seem possible.

## 21

## SHYAR SPEAKS

The *Fist* docked outside Mount Shyar, the city of the gods that floated high in the sky over the land. It wasn't a mountain as the name suggested, but it was a true wonder, one that filled me with familiarity...and dread.

Saghir drifted over to the Iris, the first staff cradled in his right paw, and a perpetual grin plastered upon his rodent features. He was enjoying this a great deal more than I, though I couldn't place a finger upon the pulse of my concern.

"I can scarcely believe I will be able to see Mount Shyar." He pivoted and focused that grin on Celeste and me. "The Impossible City was a marvel to behold, but this...this is something I have wondered about since my earliest childhood. It is featured so prominently in nearly every scripture, for multiple species, and in multiple epochs."

"It was created with the cycle," Celeste explained as she joined Saghir. I followed behind the pair, listening to the Steward's explanation. "We've puzzled that much out, though little else. If not for Tuat's accidental revelation, I wouldn't even know that much. I have long searched for a control mechanism. I assumed there would be a crystal, or a key, or some means of interface. I didn't understand that the anointing is the key."

A melancholic mood beset me the moment *The Fist*'s iris opened and grew as we stepped inside the golden city. It was far smaller than the Impossible City, more like a station, really. Like a waypoint in the sky for airships or dragons. A meeting place.

"Xal?" Saghir eyed me with concern from behind his spectacles. "Are you all right?"

"Apologies." I came back to myself and entered the station, blinking as I took in the interior and the map at the center. I knew this place. Knew it well. "I—There is something...maddeningly familiar about this place. I have been here. Many times. I don't know if as Xal, or Rei, or some other god that Reevanthara blended in. But I have been here."

"All you need do is speak your wishes," Celeste explained. She raised her golden staff. "In my case, the link to my artifact makes it possible to fully bond. However, simply being anointed by the Arena allows us to converse. To query it for information."

"Shyar," I asked, the word coming instinctively, "Have I been here before?"

Golden energy surged along the floor, a wave aimed in my direction. It swept over me, and I was elsewhere, in the kind of vision I had so often experienced when reaching a Catalyst.

"Welcome to Mount Shyar!" Reevanthara boomed, resplendent in gold and white raiment, almost identical to what Celeste now wore. "The creation has been a success. The cycle stands. Now all that remains is adding our touches. I have offered a land, a canvas on which to paint. Each of you may stake a claim wherever you will. Create a progeny species, or a monument, or anything else you wish. I have only one request. At the end of a season, we, the pantheon that rules this place, will gather and decide upon a wonder we like best. That god or goddess will be gifted a sliver of divinity from all gods, a token to their mastery. We will host this competition annually, all of us becoming greater as we bask in the flow of worship provided by our new children. Who will begin? Who will add their touch to our new cycle?"

I glanced around. Many gods were also. Some I recognized. Many had been depicted in Gateway, though I still didn't know all their names. I did not see Rei, and I sensed that I was not him, not in this vision. Yet I also could not place myself. I had a demonic body. I could see my arms, but not control my field of vision.

"I will populate this new world," rumbled an unfamiliar woman with a disquieting number of eyes. Four pairs of fiery orbs lined the space above her nose, and her skin was dotted with tiny scales. "I birth dragons, to soar the skies as they once did in the first land of Kemet."

There were nods from many gods, who seemed to approve of this. I even recognized a few of them. There was Marid, and Shu, who stood with a fire god, and...they stood before an eye. An eye directly outside the window. An eye attached to a creature of indescribable size, who sat on the ground yet still had his eye to the level of a city clinging to the very highest clouds.

*Trakalon,* Narlifex rumbled in my mind. *The titan of earth before he was split into many pieces. The fire god is Shivan. I do not know how I know him.*

There was a harmony between the gods quite unlike other visions. They seemed to get along, to like each other. There was an enthusiasm to them. They smiled and laughed and joked and wondered. That included my nameless host body, who mingled among the guests, accepted as one of them.

From what I could piece together, this predated Rei's existence. I wished I could know more, but the vision sped along quickly, and Reevanthara spoke once more.

"The Wyrm-mother will add her progeny as our first life, aside from the Great Trees. Most fitting." The dwarf grinned, but he folded his arms and his tone hardened. "It is important we understand the rules before adding more. Your progeny may fight. You may not. Battles between us risks the cycle. To police this, I have preserved the First Catalyst and secreted it into the cycle. I have created a key and currently possess this key. I can call upon the Catalyst, its full powers, which can be used to restrain any god or to eject you from the cycle. I can drop you down into the depths. Into Gortha's realm."

An illusion appeared for all assembled to see—Reeva seated on a familiar throne. On Jhordil's throne, in the heart of the Ashlands. He bore nothing like the Crown of Command, though. The dwarf sat upon the throne and seemed to possess the power of the place. Its lack filled in some likely gaps.

"Each season we will vote upon our new guardian," Reevanthara explained. "Or I can sit out the creation, being that I have an unfair advantage, and be an impartial judge. I will allow the assembled to decide."

"I would hear more of this guardianship. How does one

attain it?" Shu demanded, his hand resting on a scimitar. On...

*On me*, Narlifex inserted. *Or a former version of me.*

"Through an anointing," the dwarf explained as he banished the illusion. "There are three trials. The first uses one of my finest creations...the Arena. A place for our progeny to battle and for us to witness and record their deeds. If one wishes to become guardian, they must triumph in the Arena."

"Meaning even a mortal could do it?" the fiery god called.

"Aye." Reeva grinned at him. "Could be. Not likely, but could be. Course they have to pass the other two trials. Next, they need the blessing of the land. A Great Tree must recognize their deeds and bestow upon them its blessing. If they can get the Trees to accept them, then they must traverse the cycle and understand it fully, passing through the maw unharmed."

"This satisfies me," Marid called. "I would have Reevanthara stand as guardian, for now, but also preserve our right to vote each year, so that we might change our minds one day if we desire."

At some point that guardianship must have passed to Rei, I realized. That was why he had so much power and why he'd created the crown and the other artifacts. Realization stunned me, and I watched numbly as the gods continued their discussion.

Then it all faded, and I was standing the same room, but absent the fabulous gods and the eye outside the window.

"There, just as I promised, Master Saghir," Celeste was saying. "He returns to himself. He experienced the same vision I did, though I do not know through which god's perspective. It has been different for every Steward who tried it. Yet all saw the same."

I shuffled over to the map, the vision still playing through my mind. I focused on the important parts, the second and third trials. I must gain the blessing of a Great Tree, which I now conveniently bore a connection to. Could a corrupted Great Tree still grant me its blessing?

The trial afterward...passing through the maw? It sounded impossible.

"What?" Saghir prompted, drifting closer and poking my cheek with Ikadra. "You have not ever worn this expression before. I do not recognize it. Did you learn the nature of these challenges?"

"I did." I squatted down next to the map of the world. "I have to receive the blessing of the land, from a Great Tree. Then I have to traverse the cycle. I need to pass through the maw and survive."

"What a relief." Saghir's tone bled sarcasm. "And here I was worried it was going to be difficult. Are you telling me that we need to return to the blood wood?"

"Maybe." I looked up from the map. "We have a sapling. I don't know what that means. I bear a seed for the Tree of Blood. I can pursue that route as well. Regardless, we've learned what we can here. It's better than I expected. Less cryptic."

"I'm glad for that." Celeste looked down at the map as well. "I will stay here while the two of you head back to your mountain. I need to think and see if I can commune further with this place. The one vision is useful, but I have to imagine Shyar is capable of so much more."

"We'll take *The Fist* back. Missive if you find anything, please." I shivered and turned from the map. This place made me uncomfortable in ways I couldn't vocalize. I hated it. Hated its existence. Hated the crimes that had happened here. Crimes I couldn't even remember. "I'd just as soon be away from this place. Let's get back to the mountain and hire ourselves an army. Then we can think about the next trial."

# INTERLUDE XIV - TOTARIUS

Totarius glanced skyward and shivered. The day had finally come. He wrapped an arm around Xakava's shoulder, and this time the girl did not shrink away. He'd not addressed her as anything but her princely title since their last encounter, and had been unfailingly respectful. Was it enough? He doubted it. She'd just gotten better at hiding her true feelings, which made her more dangerous.

"I am eternally grateful. We all are." He squeezed her shoulder, then stepped away to rest against the airship's rail. The only one in the world fully crewed by demons, so far as he knew. Stolen from Crispus, though to be fair, the entire Ghost Fleet belonged to Totarius. He had assembled it, after all. "What you do today changes the war forever. You become a titan, able to crush all in battle. You and you alone will end the war."

"How will I compare in size to the spider mountain?" The girl—a mistake to think of her that way—gave a shiver. "I remember hearing the blasts not long after Xal had been marched out of the dims, and I've heard the stories."

"It will stand as a wolf to the warrior," Totarius promised, though he'd done no strict size comparison. "You will be stronger and able to pick it up and throw it if you wish. You will reign supreme. Only another titanic avatar will be able to oppose you, and I promise your brother has no access to such. We are about to lay claim to and combine the only avatars I am aware of, the results of our last clash, many millennia past."

"What about Hasra?" Lucretia finally spoke as the stately woman emerged from the open doorway leading to her cabin, a black woolen shawl draped around her shoulders. "What about the arm itself? Every child in my day knew the spires for fingers. Where is the rest of that body? Could Xal not claim that if he locates it?"

"In short? We don't know." Totarius fixed her with an encouraging smile. "I don't believe that avatar to be in the cycle any longer. All we know is that the arm belongs to my former incarnation, but we've no idea where the rest went. Through the Rent perhaps? Xal will not be able to locate it either. Not in time. By tomorrow, Xakava will menace any nation foolish enough to stand against us. We will find Xal, wherever he goes, and destroy him. If he runs, he will lose whatever support he's managed to cobble together. We've all but won. Yet speed still matters. We should not spend time dickering and worrying. We should act."

"You dismiss him," Lucretia snapped, a frown creasing a face he'd grown quite fond of. How unexpected. "He will make us pay for that if we let him."

"Why would we?" Totarius craned his head back and laughed. "Very well. I will share a secret before I escort my sibling to their destiny. I have arranged a strike at the heart of Xal's stronghold. I will ensure he is never able to put down roots, never able to solidify alliances. One by one, they will melt away, until he stands alone. When that day comes, we will corner and destroy him. Until then, we advance all our plans while harrying him."

"What have you done?" Xakava asked, her petulant frown irritating.

"I dare not reveal the whole of my plans." Totarius rose from the rail, frowning. "He has the rat and the Stewards on his side. He may be scrying. May have a way to hear us. I have already said too much. Suffice it to say...he will pay a bitter price, and soon, and afterward he will be deprived of one of his most important allies, this in the wake of ending his alliance with Ducius. That simple mistake may side the war in our favor. He has no base, and I will see that he never gains one. Be content knowing that. The truth will reach you soon, and when it does, I promise you will approve of my methods. Twin hammer blows will fall, one close and one to a distant but vital target. I will toss obstacles in Xal's path and ensure he cannot aid my true quarry until it is far too late."

He leapt to the rail without awaiting Lucretia's answer, where he balanced with his wings and tail. "Come, sister. The time to fulfill your destiny has come."

He leapt off the side, diving toward the dark waves far below, the heart of the southern ocean, directly above the temple he had recently visited, and the avatars they would soon lay claim to. Somewhere, across a large portion of the world, under Hasra, the demon armies chanted and prayed for the rise of their dark god.

Those prayers were about to be answered.

He was aware of Xakava diving after him, her body smaller and much more human. Yet the lack of fear in her eyes showed that childhood had truly been burned out of her. Her powers had grown considerably, and numerous spells and wards dripped about her like an invisible layer of jewelry.

They hit the water in a cold shock, which was welcome to him now that he could command the waves. Totarius gathered them both and sucked them down toward the pair of intertwined bodies, which were vast and covered in algae and moss, despite him having cleared it away once already. The sea was eager to reclaim what it had lost.

Totarius guided their swell of current down toward the closest titan, the one laying atop the other. He brought Xakava to its open mouth, a yawning cave of darkness. She should have continued to swim forward on her own but did not. No matter.

He willed the current to carry her inside. She struggled briefly, then relaxed and allowed herself to be carried. For a moment, he'd feared she would use her magic to escape. He could not hold her here against her will, nor force her to bond with the avatar. All he could do was make that process as easy as possible.

Xakava disappeared within that awful cavern, and Totarius swam back toward the temple, well away from the avatars. By the time he slowed and turned to watch the avatars, the process had already begun. Across the world, the demons chanted their will, and the magic gathered around the titan.

The moss and algae withered, then fell away in grey tufts, dandruff gathering along the sea floor as the demon's body was exposed. Power rolled through it, tendrils of black power that shot out of the first body and burrowed into the second. The avatars were pulled together, knit into one terrible monstrosity with four arms, four legs, and two heads, the sum of both demonic gods.

Its eyes flared to life, a deep, deep purple, scanning the

ocean depths, first in one head, and then the other. Both twisted mouths angled upward and screamed, the shock wave killing anything that lived in this sector of the ocean. Then the avatar wobbled up from the sea floor, its form obscured as a wall of silt and debris clouded the ocean for miles.

Totarius shot straight upward, his body accelerating until he burst from the ocean and flapped up into the sky. Just in time. The monstrous avatar's arms pierced the water first, then its misshapen heads, and finally its shoulders. The rest lay shrouded in that cloudy water, but the eyes were fixed upon him.

"I live," Xakava boomed, her voice cracking the sky and land, painful even for Totarius. "Command me, brother, and I will carry out your will. Let us end this war. I tire of conflict."

"Go!" Totarius pointed east and north, toward the coast of Olivantia. "Make your way to the coast of Olivantia, then slowly walk north along the shore, for all to see. Let Ducius's people fear you, and let that fear fly ahead to Valys, where they will know you are coming. By the time you arrive, I will have gutted the upstart Steward. You will help me stamp out the embers of his faith. Your existence alone will be enough to do that. I will not require anything but that you plod along the ocean floor for the time being. Rest, sister. In time, your abilities will be needed. War will come, and when that day soon arrives, your opponents will be broken."

The titan strode along the ocean floor, creating tides as it strode toward the continent in the distance. Totarius flapped his way down to sit upon her shoulder. He could take an airship or fly home on his own. It would be faster, certainly. Yet he wanted to enjoy this. Enjoy the terror Xakava inspired. This had been a master stroke.

They had won. Xal was about to lose the very last of his support, all while he celebrated his victory in the arena. It would be a hollow one. Totarius would ensure it.

That would enrage the boy, and auguries suggested Xal would then attack Valys, attempting to free it. All of Totarius's plans had been made to oppose that while keeping his true motive hidden. Let Xal think the true conflict was Valys.

It would cost him yet another ally, one Xal could ill afford to lose.

First the Fomori. Then Gateway. One by one, Totarius would strip away every ally Xal had ever made.

## INTERLUDE XV - MACHA

Macha stirred the cauldron she'd been using for a soup dish, then gulped down the portion that Vhala and her people had brought. The porters, a pair of water mages who used the snow to carry their burden, had already departed and left the dark-skinned companion behind.

"It is good to see you." Vhala gave a tight nod, almost imperceptible. "More and more, I realize how much we have in common, and...well, I consider you a friend. I hope that my presence these nights is not a burden. I have never thought to ask."

Macha set the cauldron down and wiped the back of her palm along her mouth before replying to the comparatively tiny human. "It's not like you to care what anyone thinks. I like that about you. Now you sound like Ephram. Or, goddess forbid, the pompous demon we both serve."

She turned to face the tree, basking in its presence. So young, but so strong. Being near it healed something within her. No...heal was the wrong word. It made her whole. She was meant to serve this tree, to protect it and aid it in its vital mission to preserve them all.

"Do you really dislike him so?" Vhala's tone was playful as the companion settled atop the snow, which did not sink at all under her weight. There would be no trace when she rose. "He has done much to achieve your dreams. Will not the bringing of this tree to your people bring them back together? Are they not scattered after the war with Hasra?"

"A war he helped the Hasrans win," Macha gave back crossly, but there was no heat to it. She turned a smile on the much smaller woman. Had she really been that small so short a time ago? "I am not so bitter anymore, but we have been enemies as often as friends. Still, he did as he said he would do. Few can boast that. That is why I have stayed, because I believe he may actually be able to do what he has claimed. The cycle must survive. He is our best hope. Even I can admit that."

What would Ephram think of the tree? He'd be so excited. Would he leave his little grove and come to the Fomori wood to help tend it? Few druids had his gift. And... she hated to admit it, even to herself, but she was fond of the unassuming druid. He was so genuine, so uncorrupted. It showed her the purity they fought to preserve and gave her hope of a better future.

A longing flowed from the tree into her as she thought of Ephram.

"Is he why?" she wondered aloud, and Vhala gave her a perplexed look. "Apologies. I was thinking of Ephram, that tending this...it could be his purpose. The tree needs him as much as he needs—"

The sky rumbled above them, layered thunder, then bolts of lightning thudded down all over the grove, several striking the sapling itself. It was no ordinary lightning. The strikes were tinged with *fire* and *earth* and *void*.

A hundred or more spells from a hundred or more mages slammed down all around her and it was all Macha could do to snatch up her newly carved shield and interpose it above her head. It warmed immediately as something struck it. Lightning?

Vhala sheltered beneath her, while up the mountain slope, the legion was already responding. Those with magic were erecting wards, and archers were moving to the ready. None were in a position to harm the fleet raining death upon them from the unseen cloud cover above.

Macha screamed in rage, then placed a hand against the sapling and begged it silently for aid. *Help me. Arm me, and I will defend you.*

The trunk cracked, and a sliver of wood wider than her hand extended...a spear dripping red sap. A weapon of extreme power sized just for a giantess such as her. Macha seized it, then darted away from the tree and seized a crackling pine tree whose sap had lit, using it as a torch.

Macha hurled the torch into the sky, high enough to penetrate the clouds. The sudden light exposed the silhouette of several airships, and she hurled her new spear directly at the closest. The sharped log slammed into the bottom of a ship, then punched through the other side.

The wreckage of the airship plummeted to the ground, and screaming mages rained down around it. A few had the presence and the magic to save themselves, but the rest were too stunned or lacked the magic, and so they slammed into the mountainside in a most satisfying way.

A dozen more ships dropped from the clouds, abandoning their stealth. With them came a fresh volley of spells, this one more accurately targeted...at the sapling. At the tree which could not protect itself.

Macha leapt into the sky with a roar and willed the shield to grow larger, as large as needed to cover the tree. It began to expand, but acid, fire, void, lightning, and shards of ice all punched through in near equal measure. Other spells simply went around, reaching areas she could not protect.

The tree shrieked its agony, a note beyond hearing, perhaps one for Macha alone.

"What do I do?!?" she screamed at the sky. "How do I stop you?!?"

She extended her hand and her new spear flew back into it. Macha mechanically cocked her arm and sent another crew full of mages to their deaths. This time they tried to save themselves. Wards and winds sprang up to deflect, but the spear flew fast and true and ended the lot of them.

Ten more ships made the sapling into a torch. Her bark went up, then her needles and the cones still on the branches, popping explosively in rapid succession, like corn over a campfire. She was dying, and there was nothing that Macha could do to save her. The shriek grew weaker.

Once more, the spear returned to her hand, but the ships had already begun gathering the clouds about them, retreating into the sky. For vengeance then. She hurled the spear one more time and caught one of the larger ships. The spear took the mainmast off their deck and left a cavernous hole in every deck but failed to destroy the ship.

She summoned it back, then turned back to witness the death of her people's future. An inferno raged where the sapling had stood, and whatever life had inhabited the tree was gone now, passed into the cycle, or whatever happened to the Great Trees when they died.

"I couldn't save her." Macha collapsed to her knees and wept.

"I am so sorry." Vhala emerged from the shadows and leapt atop a rock to keep herself above the smoldering ground, which was carpeted with the remains of the sapling. "I—there is nothing we could have done. Nothing anyone could have done. This isn't Xal's fault."

"If he'd left Ena—" Macha cut herself off and shook her head bitterly. "If she'd been here, the fate would have been the same. If Xal had known of the assault in advance and had all his allies here, we might have prevailed. But that is impossible. They knew of our weakness, and they exploited it. We are too few and too weak to oppose them."

Macha knelt there until the flow of tears finally ceased, then turned from the tree's charred remains and began striding down the mountainside toward the closest leg.

"Where are you going?" Vhala demanded, anger tightening her voice. "This is a tragedy, but we are fighting the war to end all wars. You cannot simply walk away."

"Can't I?" Macha spat into the fires where the snows had been such a short time ago. "My future is ashes. My people have no tree. No purpose. We are scattered and lost, and now I lack the ability to bring them together. I have no purpose now. I cannot do anything but die. I choose to return to my home, to spend one more season in the wilds before the demons take it all."

"You're not even going to talk to him first?" Vhala's tone held incredulity, but Macha was too weary to care.

"No." She sighed heavily. "He'll try to guilt me into staying. I don't want to deal with it. I just want to sleep in the forest and hear the animals, and wonder at the ones I've never heard before. I want to wander, and then I want to go home."

There was silence for long moments, just the wind.

"Goodbye, my friend." Vhala gave her a Hasran salute. "I am sorry for the times we were enemies. I count you among my sisters. I hope we meet again one day, under better circumstances. I will explain to Xal and tell him not to bother seeking you out. That it will be an insult. We will allow you your solitude, I promise. He will understand."

"Thank you, sister." Macha reached for a pack to shoulder, but it had been destroyed during the attack. She gave a sigh, summoned her spear, and gave herself back to nature.

# 22

# NEW PLANS

The hatchling Broff hummed happily as he deposited a tray of drinks on the acid bar's wide table, rice wine from Li's homeland for me and more exotic brews for many of the captains I was attempting to woo to my cause. A dozen sat around the table, two hatchlings and a smattering of more conventional species. All dripped with enough weaponry to name each a warmaster.

A second stood behind each captain, silent, not drinking, only observing. It seemed to be their custom. The captains were allowed to partake, drink, and dine, but the seconds forever had one hand on a blade and the other ready to sketch a spell.

My second stood behind me as well, Khwezi of all people, as Ena was guarding the mountain and Hadi sat at the table, where the captains would expect to find him. Once, I might have feared having the dark-skinned archer at my back, but with Ukufa out of the way, his loyalty had been secured, at least until he was reunited with Ashianna. After that, I had no idea what he might do.

"Where is your pet Steward?" slurred an orokh with

gold-capped tusks. He paused to finish the last of a very large tankard, then slammed it down and glared at Broff. "Another!"

Broff rushed to refill drinks while I paused until I had everyone's attention once more. I didn't want to deliver the tale more than once.

"Celeste has returned to the Rent." I saw no reason to lie. Our foes could easily scry the truth. "The demonic invasion requires her support, and as I no longer need her in the Arena, that seemed the best place to deploy her."

I let them think the Stewards were mine to send and tried not to eye the copy of *Rat & Demon #6* sitting on the far side of the table under one of the captains' elbows. They were learning our story, and as they learned it, my worship was growing. A paltry thing, perhaps, but present in every land where we'd left copies.

"My war is with Hasra," I boomed, loud enough for it to carry to other tables. "They have earned enemies in every land. They're led by a despot. I'm building the army that's going to dismantle their nation one city-state at a time. I offer a mobile behemoth to carry us into battle and arch-mages to soften your foes. What I need are merchants of death looking to ply their trade."

The hunger lit every gaze, from dragon to human to drifter. Not for gold, as I'd expected. For glory. These people weren't interested in coin. They wanted to lend their names to history, and that was how I would need to sell them on my plan.

"I, for one, would see this war for myself," the orokh boomed back, then reached into his jacket and removed a glittering silver coin. "My challenge marker."

He slid it across the table in what I took for some sort of

formal pledge to my cause, so I accepted it and set it inside an empty pouch.

"And I," a hatchling rumbled.

Murmurs came from all around the table, and I accepted a growing pile of markers, which clinked as I added them to my pocket. Every captain at the table signed, and a goodly number of the others within the bar had an ear turned toward our table.

"Is it true," called a dark-skinned woman who could have been Vhala's stockier aunt, "that you are going to punish Enestius in this war? And is it also true that you have endless coin? If so, then my brethren and I would join you. We are companions, one and all, trained in cruelty and tested by war."

"Both are true." I straightened and met her gaze evenly. "I will see you well paid, and I can grant a chance at revenge. More, I can see that you help bring something even better. Justice."

"My token." She flicked a coin at me, and I caught it. "I will gather my brethren and prepare to march to your mountain. May we approach, or do we need some special spell to avoid the mountain's ire?"

"We'll gather along the eastern edge of town," I explained. "When we are ready to move, then I will have the mountain lower a leg and—"

A missive zoomed up, the fiery phoenix speaking with Vhala's voice. "Urchin, we have trouble of the worst kind. The Ghost Fleet has ambushed us and assaulted the sapling, which did not survive. They have retreated. Their raid was successful. Come as swiftly as you are able."

Everyone froze around the table, and my mind spun as I sought the proper path forward. If I couldn't even protect my own mountain, then why sign on? Yet they'd already given their tokens, even if one or two now eyed me with regret.

"Ah." I brightened and gave a wicked smile I did not feel. "It seems that we'll have a chance sooner than later." I turned to the leader of the companions. "We depart at nightfall. Be ready with your sisters, and I will give you all the vengeance you could wish." Then I rose and bowed several times, once in each direction so no one felt slighted. "If you wish to join our army, then simply be there at nightfall. Spread the word. Any captain who brings another will receive a bounty for the act. Hasra and Enestius are about to go extinct. Anyone who wants a piece of their hoard, be ready for war."

Then I nodded at Hadi and filed out of the inn. Broff gave me a wave as I passed, but the hatchling was busy hurrying out trays of drinks to the many patrons filling the acid bar.

We reached the street and melted into the crowd. I had a few moments to think, then Hadi fell into step next to me, while Saghir's snout appeared from the battle pack.

"What will you do?" Hadi squawked quietly.

"I don't know yet." I frowned as I considered the implications. "For starters, I need to go to Macha and see what can be done there. If she hasn't already left. We can ill afford to lose her and her people, but I won't blame her in the slightest. Her part of our bargain no longer exists. I failed. I wasn't able to plant it in her forest as promised. This also puts us on the defensive. I have no idea what Totarius is planning or doing, and now I have to react instead of act."

It annoyed me how effective the attack had been. A master stroke, one that I couldn't easily answer. I should have anticipated this. I stewed on the matter the whole walk back to *The Fist*, then ducked through the iris and brooded over the map along the floor as Saghir sped us back toward the spider mountain.

Where would Totarius hit? What would be his next goal? He controlled Hasra. He controlled Enestius. Calmora was in the hands of Khonsu. Valys was controlled opposition, in a way. The smaller houses didn't much matter. The Fomori were no threat. Olivantia would be a pain to conquer and held nothing worth the effort.

Gateway might be a tempting target to retake, but Totarius's armies and fleets were a half a continent away, and his newly created avatar was coming this way, suggesting he intended to force a confrontation.

My mind turned back to the sapling as we descended toward the airship dock along the top of the citadel that Saghir and his *earth* mages had constructed. We had a fortress, an airship, a behemoth, and a legion, and none of it had done anything to stop Totarius from doing as he pleased.

Vhala stood waiting upon the battlements, and I strode over in human form, with the battle pack slung over my shoulders and Saghir inside. Hadi trailed after me, silent since we had landed. No one said a word, not even Vhala, leaving me to broach the awful subject.

"Summarize the battle, please." I folded my arms and eyed the distraught companion dispassionately, my best attempt at being a commander.

"The Ghost Fleet launched two volleys of spells. They suffered casualties—easily fifty mages died, and two airships—but the balance of their fleet escaped." Vhala's shoulders slumped and deep sadness chilled her expression. "Macha saw despair. She gave up. She said that she is returning to her people, that she believes the war to be lost. I would not recommend pursuing her. At this point, she'll seek to lash out, and combat would feel good to her."

"She's free to go her own way." I relaxed my posture and rested a hand on Narlifex. "Macha and her people will be missed, but I failed to deliver my end of the bargain. If we find a way to change that, then perhaps we'll be allies again, but I will not pursue her empty-handed and beg her to tie herself to us. We've gathered an army and will be picking it up at nightfall. We have all the force necessary for my answer to Totarius."

"What will that be?" Hadi croaked as the tengu stepped into my field of view.

"Only I will know until the hammer falls." I gazed skyward, at the angle a typical scrying would allow. "Our enemies think they are in control. They think they have maneuvered us where they wish us to be. I will prove that is not the case, that they cannot anticipate, predict, or scry our true path. The war has begun in earnest, and it's a war I intend to win, no matter the cost. Now get the legion to work harvesting the wood. With the sapling dead, we may as well make use of it. That's a whole lot of new storytomes."

It had come at great cost, but we had an army, at last. I already knew precisely where I was going to use it. A place that Totarius would never suspect. One that had no meaning for him and thus would be dismissed by a master tactician, but that would enrage a lesser one like, say, Crispus, to madness.

If that bastard Totarius wanted to destroy things important to me, then I'd damned sure return the favor thrice-fold. I'd provoke his son into coming after me, and then I'd devour his soul.

# 23

## DEMON LORD

A few bells later, our new mercenary host had been situated in the seemingly endless barracks that our *earth* mages had created, a honeycomb of warrens within the mountain, the best defense we could have against any sort of assault.

Why had I not thought to keep the sapling within such confines?

Because it needed the sky, I sensed. The sun. The seed pulsed within my chest, and the awareness of the Tree never really faded. Its pain was ever present but lessened by some of my actions, which made us allies, I sensed. For now, at least.

Like any animal, I also sensed that if I became a threat, the Tree's attitude would return to violent animosity. So long as I soothed it, I remained a friend.

"Xal?" Vhala's voice brought me back to the present as much as the fact that she hadn't called me urchin. "We have another matter that requires your attention. This one may be...less onerous than the bulk of the day."

I glanced up from my writing desk and blinked to see a

couple in the doorway, a young mother with an infant in swaddling and a protective father watching over them both, all dressed for hard winter. Jun, Darius, and their child.

Behind them stood Ashianna, a grin on the warrior's face as she rested her greatsword upon her shoulder.

"How is this possible?" I rushed to Jun and carefully gave her a side hug so as not to disturb the sleeping child.

*Darius impersonated the Imperator,* Jun signed back with a grin that dimpled her cheeks, then she squeezed Darius's arm and smiled. *Erik stayed behind, but it was Darius's plan. We have freed the Praetor. He stays to rally support with Erik. We have come to join your war effort. Where there are wars, there is a need for Aelianna's dedicates.*

"I don't have words." I grinned ear to ear, releasing her then shifting to face Darius. "I am truly impressed. I—"

Darius crushed me into a hug, the kind very few people in my life gave. He was trembling, I realized, and so I returned that hug and held him. "You're safe now. Your father can't reach you here. In fact, we're conspiring ways to kick him right in the gold mines. Hard. If you seek vengeance and want a haven for Jun, then this is the safest I can offer. The true godswar is upon us, and it falls to the people on this mountain to win it, for everyone."

"What of the babe?" Ashianna asked, glaring down at the child. "Can our enemies not use him against us? Who knows what foul sorceries Ducius can work through the boy? I mean him no ill will—none, Jun, don't look at me like that—but we all know Ducius would just love to use our compassion against us."

The top of my battle pack flew open, and Saghir levitated out, lightning crackling around him as his teeth peeled back to reveal tiny rat fangs. "Please allow me to tend to the boy, friend Jun. I will puzzle out the nature of this enchantment, and we will discover a way to turn it back on its master. It is likely tied to souls, and if we can erect a soul trap around the boy, then if Ducius dies, he will never be able to possess the boy. It will not be easy, but I will make it my purpose until the ritual is complete."

*Thank you*, Jun signed to Saghir. *I am grateful to have met you. I could never have guessed who we would become when we marched to fight the Fomori. If you can protect my son, I will do anything in service of this cause.*

"Come. Let us get started." Saghir landed on Jun's shoulder. "I've prepared quarters for you, and we can tour the nursery. If I know friend Xal, then he is ready for war. All who desire rest or succor, come with me. Those who seek vengeance and death? Remain with Xal and see the planning of it made here."

"I'll be along soon." Darius squeezed his wife's hand and smiled down at Jun. "Tend to the boy's needs and your own, and I will find you in bed. We need to earn our place here, and that starts now."

*I love you*, Jun signed, then leaned up to kiss him.

Darius returned it, then mussed the baby's hair with an affectionate smile. "I won't be long, my heart."

Jun departed, leaving Vhala, Darius, and Ashianna. The Praetor's daughter had put on even more muscle since the last time I'd seen her, and her hair had been shorn down to stiff fuzz, but the smile was recognizable.

"My father insisted I come," Ashianna explained as she delivered a friendly nod first to me, then to Vhala. "Both of us staying was too big a risk, especially with Erik tweaking Crispus's nose as he has. The imperator will seek violent reprisal. Is there any chance of bringing the behemoth to liberate Valys? Much of the opposition would melt away as soon as they heard your approach."

"Totarius would certainly expect me to do that." I folded my arms and considered options. "Doing it anyway might still be the best course." It wasn't, and I knew it, but hopefully enemies were scrying and assumed I allowed emotion to guide my course.

A commotion came from the doorway to my quarters, and I blinked up to see an out-of-breath Khwezi muscling his way in. "So it is true...you're free." His gaze locked on Ashianna like a starving lion discovering favored prey.

"So it's true. You're alive." Ashianna's hard exterior softened, for an instant, but then the bulwarks were built high once more, her voice frosty as she replied. "We will speak of personal matters later. Was there another reason you came? The war council perhaps?"

"Yes." Khwezi's shoulders slumped, and he deflated as he turned his attention in my direction. "I received a missive from a friend aboard the Ghost Fleet. He tells me they will soon be deployed to distant shores but does not know the destination. No one seems to care. They are all abuzz about the demon god marching through the ocean, along the Olivantian coast. Its destination seems to be Valys. I have not scryed it to capture its likeness, but if the estimates are accurate, it stands several times taller than the spider mountain."

"Saghir has taught us that size isn't everything," I pointed out, trying to rally hope, but finding precious little in anyone's expression. "We will find a way to deal with the avatar. For now, focus on putting one foot in front of the other, and leave the long-term planning to me. These are my problems to solve, and I will solve them. In the meantime, there are storytomes about if you lack entertainment, and we can see you fed as well."

I knew that where I found the avatar, I would also find Lucretia. My aunt was canny. She knew I'd need to stop it, and if I tried, she could add me to her arsenal. If I sent a lesser in my stead, they'd fail. It was a brilliant plan, but also a transparent one. I could clearly see their motivations. They sought to force me to a predictable course.

They would be sorely disappointed when they learned my true plan. I would show them what I did best. Outnumbered. Facing superior odds. When had it ever been anything else? We'd triumphed over and over.

I would find a way to do it again. Somehow.

"Vhala, I want you to find Ena." I straightened my posture and used the commanding voice I'd been trying to cultivate. "Gather her, Darius, Khwezi, and Ashianna. She is to hunt down Ducius and bring him to us, alive if possible. Jun will decide his fate."

"I will see to it." Vhala snapped the kind of salute she'd have given to Erik, then led Khwezi and Ashianna from the chamber, leaving me alone with Darius.

"I hope coming to you was the proper move," he finally said, breaking the awkward silence. "It's not our intention to be a burden. If bringing Ducius to justice is something you desire, then I promise...we will not fail. He will be very much alive when I deliver him to my wife."

Darius's cruel smile would have terrified even Ducius had he been here to see it. It saddened me to remove it.

*You're not going after Ducius*, I signed, my hand covered by my cloak so that even were we being scryed, it would be hidden from all but Darius. His eyebrows knit together, so I kept signing. *Ducius will never allow himself to be caught or killed. His entire genius is focused around self-preservation, and if you become a direct threat, then he will remove you.*

"It was the proper move," I said out loud, finally responding to his words in a way someone scrying could detect. "Bring him back to me, unharmed, and we will see that he receives justice."

*You will go to Olivantia*, I instructed, *with the sole goal of strengthening Temis, a rival dreadlord, so that the council is united against Ducius. Make trouble for him. Discreetly, so as not to become a direct threat. When the time comes, we need to forge an alliance with the na'elfen, so keep that in mind when dealing with Liloth and her people.*

"Of course," Darius replied, then signed, *I understand.* "I will take my leave then and prepare to carry out your will, my dark prince."

I kind of liked the title.

## INTERLUDE XVI - LI

L i took a deep breath and strode into the darkened throne room, her wings proudly displayed over her shoulders, the feathers visible in the darkness in a way that made her distinctly uncomfortable.

The incursion could have been done at noon, as there were no guards either way, but she wanted to at least pretend she was sneaking in. She had no idea what reaction her presence might evoke. It could cost her life. No matter what, though, she'd find certainty about Khonsu's motives regarding the lightning people.

She padded silently into the room, certain that Tissa was close even if she couldn't see the assassin. Almost, she'd offered Tissa the bow, as she believed her to be the better shot, but she kept the first bow, an arrow knocked.

Shakti belonged to her now.

*We are one,* the bow whispered. *Your enemies will fall before us. If your skill is not yet adequate, then practice it by slaying more foes.*

Li didn't reply. She didn't enjoy conversing with weapons. The bow was alien, and having been reincarnated, she had no idea what it knew and didn't. Yet she couldn't deny how effective a tool of death it was.

Already she'd learned how to deliver a spell through an arrow. Being able to land a disintegrate or an explosion of wind would prove invaluable should the dragons remain behind.

What if they did not?

She paused behind one of the large pillars, which reminded her of the fight with Niu. She and Xal had been all but untrained, but they'd been opposed by a mere hatchling. Had it been one of the creatures Haitao had described, they'd both have died before her mother or father arrived.

A rumbling growl sounded low in the darkness. "I see you've finally come, Princess. We've had a running wager on whether or not you would, and now I can finally collect. Those I feasted upon spoke of your caution and pragmatism."

Lantern eyes lit and a massive wyrm slithered out of the darkness, easily a hundred cubits long. Longer than the throne room, yet somehow its body not only fit but enlarged the area around it. Some sort of *dream* magic.

"There's no point in hiding." The wyrm blinked and when its eyes opened, a woman stood there. A familiar woman. Jun's grandmother. "I know what you seek, and you'll have to get past my sisters and me to reach it. Are you so certain you wish to ring the bells? Certain they will aid you and not us?"

"Why stop me otherwise?" Li strode from the shadows. They likely knew Tissa was out there, but not where. They might also believe she had Bumut with her. No. Better to assume they knew everything. Tissa aimed at the old woman but did not loose. "Why work so hard to prevent us from waking the lightning people? I think all your tricks are nothing but delaying tactics. I think as soon as I touch those bells, your reign here is over. Khonsu has already fled. I traveled with Tuat and Volos. I've seen their true forms. I think your father's days are nearing an end."

"A pity," rumbled a second voice from elsewhere in the throne room, invisible to Li's enhanced senses. A perfect illusion. "That you will never reach those bells."

"Who said I need to reach them?" Li laughed as she leapt backward, her wings carrying her far further than any leap, then loosed her arrow at the bells near the far end of the room. She swiftly added a second, then a third, then a fourth.

A dragon materialized in the path of the arrows, then lowered its wing to intercept the spells. Each contained a disintegrate, and each dissolved a jagged hole in the wing, scales and bone and flesh flowing to dust, then nothing. The beast was too large to be slain by low-magnitude spells, but its entire wing vanished, and it crashed heavily back to the marble in a spray of blood.

"A clever ploy." Jun's grandmother—it occurred to Li she didn't even know the awful woman's proper name—grinned wider than any human could ever manage, fangs shining in the near darkness. "You risked destroying the bells, yet tricked one of us into exposing ourselves. The least of us, anyway. Yet you must know the same trick will not work twice. Go ahead...destroy them if you wish. But if you attempt to approach? Then I will devour you, child."

Tissa's form leapt out of the darkness, and Nefarius's shining scarlet blade punched into the old woman's back. Her elbow came back and shattered Tissa's nose, and the assassin staggered back with her blade, then disappeared into the shadows, her blood staining the stone.

"Your weapons are weak." She rolled her shoulder as if

working out a knot instead of dealing with a puncture from Nefarius. The woman gave a contemptuous laugh, and somewhere beyond hearing a deeper draconic echo sounded. "One day, the first bow could be potent enough to slay me with a single arrow. That scarlet blade could infect me with endless rage, forcing me to turn on my sisters. But that day is centuries off. So what will you do now, Princess? What is your plan? As it stands, it seems you will be devoured, like your mother before you."

The words slid daggers into Li's heart from multiple angles, slashing at her soul. She knew to her core it was true. Mother was truly gone, and this woman, this thing, had taken her. Now she wanted to do the same to Li unless she could find a way to fulfill her purpose and ring the bells.

*We must work together*, Shakti whispered. *I am your hands. Use me to ring these bells. When we are one, I literally cannot miss.*

Li understood. She leapt into the air and kicked off a pillar, then kicked off the air. Once she reached the apex of her jump, she filled the sky with arrows. Hundreds of them. Thousands.

Some were real, a few at the core, but most were illusions. The storm of arrows streaked toward the bells, and Jun's grandmother froze in indecision. None of the dragons were willing to dive in the way, lest they risk some of the arrows containing disintegrates.

Jun's grandmother clapped her hands, and a wave of force, of pure air, rushed through the room. It scattered most of the arrows, but a few had nearly reached their target and still possessed enough momentum to strike. Each impact rang through the room, and as the tones layered atop one another, they grew in strength instead of fading away.

A deep resonance rolled off the bells, and a symphony of

sound rolled out from them, through the mountain, and out into Calmora's valleys and passes. The sound was a living thing, yet she couldn't tell if she had done enough to cause it to crescendo.

Jun's grandmother shrieked in wordless rage and charged. Li slid into a defensive stance, but the moment before the dragon-woman engaged, Tissa appeared and sliced her ankle with Nefarius. Jun's grandmother staggered, and Li flipped away, sending a fresh storm of arrows at the bells.

This time the wounded dragon leapt into the way. Unfortunately for her, many of the arrows contained lightning bolts. Not full-on disintegrates, as her well of power was diminishing. Probably nothing. If simple electricity could have destroyed the bells, Khonsu would have done it long since.

Yet caution guided her. She used lesser spells, yet they were still devastatingly effective. A dozen wasp bites to an already wounded dragon, who crashed to the ground in a smoking heap, unable to control her landing. She wasn't dead, but she didn't seem able to rise.

That left Jun's grandmother and one more dragon who had not acted.

Li filled the air with arrows again, and elation surged when she realized nothing was going to stop her assault. Chimes rang from all three bells, and they reached a powerful crescendo.

Something massive bowled into Li from the side and bore her to the ground. She struggled to get free, but her awkward wings were pinned. She attempted a teleport, but claws tightened around her hand, crushing her fingers, every bone shattering until she screamed the agony of it.

Li couldn't focus. She writhed and struggled, but the

wyrm would not let her rise. A leg snapped. Then several ribs. The dragon was killing her...until it wasn't.

She could suddenly breathe again. The dragon's body slumped to the ground, and she realized Nefarius jutted from the side of the beast's skull, directly over its temple. The assassin had killed the mighty creature in a single blow.

Li sketched a blink and appeared in the shadows behind one of the pyramids. One of her wings hung broken and limp, and she didn't bother counting the abrasions and lacerations all over her body.

She summoned a rejuvenation spell and breathed easier as her wounds began to heal. She couldn't walk, even then, but the agony faded to throbbing pain, enough that she could focus on survival.

Jun's grandmother had disappeared, and Li wondered why...until the flood of lightning exploded outward from all three bells. The living electricity swam through the entire throne room, then out into the larger mountain. Every bit of draconic blood was incinerated, as was the body of the dragon Tissa had killed.

It was too much to expect the sudden electric death to have killed Jun's grandmother, but at least she was no longer attacking. Li rested against the pillar and hoped the lightning would know enough not to kill her or Tissa or Haitao.

Thunder echoed for long moments until her ears rang, but eventually, the noise faded away. Li looked up to find a trio of lightning people, their hair pure electricity around an otherwise human face, bowing before her.

"You have called and we have come," their leader, an older man, wizened and wrinkled, spoke in a tongue she did not know. Had it not been for Celeste's miracle, she'd have had no idea what he was saying. "We will clear Khonsu's get from the mountain. Afterward, we await your orders. Have the demons arrived? How long have we to prepare? Do we still need to gather the citizens into the mountain? I hope there remain many yet to be saved. There are so few survivors. When time permits, I would hear how our people have fallen so low since the godswar."

There were so many questions. *Our people?* They seemed to see no difference between her and them, despite the lack of electric hair. These were lightning primals. Were they all descended from such? In any other time, she'd have been curious.

"How are you called?" Li murmured. It was the only question she could think to ask.

"My name is Indra." The old man bowed low. "I recognize the daughter of the sky, even if you do not yet fully know yourself. How are you called in this life, she who witnesses the end of all things?"

"I am called Li." She squirmed uncomfortably, and not just from her wounds. Everyone seemed to know more about her past than she did. "Once you have secured the mountain, return to me, and we will find my father and the people of the heavens. In the meantime, there are many tribes hiding in the mountains. I am aware of no army of demons, yet. Those that exist are on our side."

"Demons are on no one's side but their own." Indra's eyes narrowed. "That you would name them ally is troubling. Deeply. We will speak of this when I return."

Thunder boomed and the god was gone. Li heaved a deep sigh. She should have realized that waking the lightning people would bring as many problems as it solved.

## 24

## STRATEGEMS

My army arrived in eastern Enestius before dawn, but there was no doubt our opponents knew of our approach. Every step the mountain took quaked the land, and they must have felt the tremors increasing as we grew closer. That was the plan, after all. I had no desire to come upon them unawares.

The sun had begun scraping the eastern horizon in our wake, which sent the mountain's shadow over the city we were about to conquer. Already we saw a steady stream of refugees—elephants, wagons, carts, and other make-shift conveyances were carrying the people away from the town. If they had airships, they had long since departed.

"I'm going to go calm the common people." I flapped my wings, soaring up into the sky away from Saghir, who had only nodded in response. He was focused on guiding the mountain, and I upon my task.

I rose high into the sky and glided over the city, positioning myself so I glittered in the morning sun, visible to all. Divinity amplified my words. "I know what you have heard. I know you believe I am evil, that I will slaughter you. If you are a civilian, then you will not be harmed. We will sack your city, but we will take neither food nor medicine. In fact, we will bring a quantity of each to distribute among those in need. We are here to punish the Umdalas and those who tore down the temples of the Stewards. Watch and judge me by my actions, and if you find them worthy, then consider joining us. We have food, beds, and training for those willing. The time has come for the common people to rise up and let the nobility know that we are not just grains in their bushels. You have until noon to flee, then our assault begins."

Then I winged back to the mountain and landed next to Saghir. He murmured in a soothing voice, and the mountain settled down, digging into the earth with four legs, resting but ready to stand again upon command. A giant pet, basically.

Below us, the city responded like a kicked anthill. About twenty griffins winged away in several different directions, messengers and important personages. I turned toward our fortress and smiled in satisfaction when three dozen of my griffins rose to pursue their messengers. Some would no doubt escape, but that was a good thing. They could carry word of what had happened here today.

The legions began their orderly march down the mountain's limb.

"I cannot believe you made them walk." Saghir gave a chittering laugh. "At least they have boots. They will never quite know what we suffered."

"I'm not trying to build character." I folded my arms as I surveyed the mercenaries and Erik's people, each jockeying to be the first to reach the ground. "It's a show of force. I want Enestius to see exactly what opposes them. We know they don't have enough force to resist, so I'm hoping they'll surrender without combat."

And they did. A steady flow of troops marched from the city. Most didn't even bother with unit cohesion and simply joined the mob. They were no threat, but at the same time, they were escaping with their personal weaponry and wealth.

I had to accept it. I couldn't stop them without punishing the innocent, so I let the guilty flee for now. We'd recover plenty from their city.

"The mountain hungers," Saghir explained apologetically. "I must provide sustenance. Magical sustenance."

"We have just the right snack, I think." I smiled down at the citadel where we'd trained and the many manors, each controlled by a different Umdala. Wheat still grew in patches of snow. Magical wheat. "Tell the mountain it can eat the citadel and all it contains. Surely there must be a great deal of magic within. Materials and artifacts both."

"Truly?" My friend gave a delighted laugh. "It seems wasteful, but the gesture is so...demeaning? It is the perfect insult. Totarius will be furious."

"And we can still loot the rest of the city," I pointed out, now smiling as well. It was nice to win for a change.

A tribe of orokh plainsrunners raced human heavy cavalry, a division that looked to have begun in Valys, and the rivalry was fierce. Both groups jostled, but neither claimed victory. Both reached the city at the same time and spread out across the deserted streets as they began looting every building they discovered, save inns, temples, and granaries.

High overhead, quints of griffin-riders landed at choice locations, rushing to secure their share and meeting no resistance I could see.

"You can sate the mountain's hunger now." I rested a hand on Narlifex and watched the battle—if it could be called that—unfold below me.

"I have been waiting for this. I did not enjoy our time in this city." Saghir raised Ikadra, then gestured toward the citadel and whispered under his breath.

The mountain shuddered, then quaked, then rose and approached. It leaned over the city, almost daintily, the screams of the few remaining citizens growing frantic, and then chomped down and ate the entire citadel as if eating a mouthful of grass.

"Do you think the Hoard was still there?" I wondered aloud, glancing at my friend.

"I do not." Saghir lowered the staff and lent me his full attention. "We know it was moved here. Totarius would not simply abandon it. Likely he brought it with him when he left. Were it me, I would carry it with me but plant rumors that it had never left."

"Agreed." I turned back to the city. "It will probably take three or four bells to loot the place and another three to get it loaded. We won't be on our way to the next target until near dark."

"You seem worried." Saghir cocked his head. "What is it you fear?"

"Totarius's response. He will have no choice but to send the avatar." Uneasiness stole over me. "We need to find a way to stay ahead of it until I can find the right battle-ground, one that advantages us."

"Will you go to Calmora once we are done here?" Saghir's tone neither favored nor disfavored the idea.

"I don't know," I admitted. "My heart wants it, obviously, but my head tells me it is not the right move. Bringing the avatar to Calmora will do Li's people no favors. I need to

fight it where no one is hurt and where we have a chance of
victory. I don't know how fast it can move, but I suspect it
will be upon us before we are fully prepared."

"Then perhaps it is time for me to intervene directly."
Saghir rose up into the air, grinning madly. "I am—if I am
not being too immodest—literally the best spy in creation. I
can find and study this avatar, learn its strengths and weak-
nesses, then return to share them. And I can likely do it in
less than a day."

"Do it," I decided suddenly, glancing at the southern
horizon. "Once we are done here, you can order the mountain to go to the next town, then await your return there. I
glanced back at the battlefield. "It looks like Jun has arrived.
Let's hope it has the effect we wish."

Jun and her fellow dedicates were moving through the
city with care packages, dropping off blankets, food, and
medicine. Each bundle contained a complete set of storytomes through volume six.

"I have to believe that many will take up our cause."
Saghir raised a paw to clean one of his whiskers. "The
common people are ill-used everywhere, and they know
that their leaders lie. We are giving them truth. A simple
struggle that impacts them and their children. The righteous will take up our cause."

"Let it be enough." I nodded gratefully to my friend.
"Without those tomes, we'd have no chance at all. Already
my worship grows." I shook my head slowly. "Still, I'll need
to find a way to outthink Totarius and my aunt. I cannot
confront either directly."

"It feels as if all your training since boyhood was well
selected." Saghir's smile grew until his little cheeks dimpled.
"When have we not been required to outthink greater opponents with superior resources? We have shoes! Magic!

Followers! Every situation we have overcome has been to prepare us for this. To fight the battle of all battles and win."

"Thank you, my friend." I smiled warmly at him. "I suppose you should be away."

"Of course." Saghir zipped up into the sky and then was gone. I had no idea how fast he could travel now but suspected he'd be back well before his estimate elapsed.

That left me to consider his words. I was grateful for everything we had, but I was not foolish enough to think my chances of victory were very high. Totarius had more magic, more worship, and more troops.

What did I have?

Prophecy. A road map telling me what I must do. I'd spent so long rushing around that I'd never slowed down to consider the larger canvas. I had to fulfill two more trials—that much was obvious—but what else was I missing?

The Fomori had a prophecy about a demon prince.

The kodachine had a prophecy. I was to wed the flame, whatever that meant.

The na'elfen had a prophecy. Yeva had hinted as much.

It was time I started fulfilling them, one by one. I needed to study them, learn what I needed to do, and then get out there and claim the legacies that had been left for me. And that was exactly what I was going to do.

First, I'd lead Totarius on a merry chase, and then I'd will the tools I needed into existence. I wasn't alone. I had not just my friends and now worshipers, but also my previous incarnations and the tools and clues they had left.

Victory was within my grasp if I could find a way to claim it.

And claim it I would.

## INTERLUDE XVII - TOTARIUS

Totarius noted the tremor in his hand, the first physical sign of the immense rage, and gently set the spoon down in his soup. He glanced up at the messenger, a terrified girl no more than fifteen, probably a messenger because of a childish love of griffins and now regretting it.

Her wide eyes were affixed to the Imperator at the opposite end of the table. Crispus's lips had peeled back in a bestial snarl, and his eyes promised swift death to any target foolish enough to fall within his gaze. Not an ideal place when you were the messenger who delivered the news.

"OUT." Crispus thrust a finger at the door.

The girl scurried as no one had ever scurried before, impressing Totarius. Perhaps she had more survival instinct than he'd granted her credit for. She must have to have made it this far.

"Everything is falling apart." Crispus shot to his feet and swept the plates and goblets to the floor with a roar, the clatter drawing a wince from Totarius. "You tell me that the dream wyrm no longer responds to your missives. Now these lightning people have woken? Calmora is no longer ours. They have an army of unknown power."

"An army bound to the mountain." Totarius picked up his goblet and swirled the contents as he inhaled the aroma. It calmed him, though not as it would have before bonding with Xa. "These lightning people will not leave it. Calmora is no longer ours, true, but they have not nor will not ally with our enemies either. They hate demons, and I believe he will find an alliance...difficult."

"What of Erik and his treason?" Crispus began to pace before the table like a caged lion. "He's sheltering the Praetor, and likely the Lord Garulan. We all know it, even if we cannot find proof. He has not denied it, and that is proof enough for me."

"True." Totarius paused to drink and assess his son's mood. The boy was growing less and less stable by the day. He'd seen it before. It happened often when one was placed beyond the bounds of their competence.

He had just witnessed it happening to Erik's mother, after all. The stress-induced spiral to full breakdown.

Somehow Lucretia had survived it all, and he glanced at the mysterious woman, seated at the middle of the table, her gown the same shade of ash grey as the cushion behind her, making her blend in. She wasn't invisible, precisely, but he rarely noticed her presence. Enough that he was convinced there was some eldimagus at play. A powerful one. One of the countless toys she had access to, like the flame. Always behind the scenes. Always pulling strings.

"I do not believe Erik to be a true threat." Totarius set his goblet down and fixed Crispus with an exasperated look. "He has less than five hundred followers. If you allow him, he will bring out the vermin and gather them all in one place so you can exterminate them. Should that plan fail, however, and the Praetor somehow seizes control of Valys, even that would also be in your best interests."

That did it. Crispus stopped. His arms fell to his sides and his fists un-balled as curiosity overtook him. "How could it possibly be in my interests to lose a nation?"

"We've already stripped all the material wealth this land has to offer." Totarius moved to the window and nodded out at the caldera. "The Hammer remains, of course, and slaves, *earth* mages, and knights. This is a strong city and a definite asset. Yet it is an asset we know that Ducius covets. The dread council and their endless armies will come for this land, and if you seek to retain it, then it means opposing them. I'm not saying you should or shouldn't, but be aware of the costs of holding this place."

"It's worth it." Crispus balled a fist. "I want to kill Erik and keep this city. And I'll fight to protect it. I will not begin my reign by losing Hasra's strongest province."

"An understandable sentiment, but do not allow it to become the effigy upon your tombstone." Lucretia dabbed at her mouth with a napkin. "This city means nothing in the long term. Our forces have been quietly maneuvered away for weeks. We are nearly ready for a most unexpected strike, one that will secure you a target more lucrative than this dingy mountain."

"What of the avatar?" Totarius demanded of Lucretia. He found the ruse amusing, pretending she controlled the avatar so that Crispus remained unaware of just how powerful Totarius had become. "Can you use your demon to destroy Xal's mountain? That would show the world that there is no war, only a few rebels who have thus far escaped punishment."

Lucretia blinked in surprise but picked up the ruse immediately. "The avatar has not met its equal since the godswar, nor shall it. We took the two avatars who slew each other and have united the power of both. What remains to oppose them? The behemoth cannot cast spells. It cannot think. It is a beast. Xakava is a demon prince of unparalleled strength. Our avatar will destroy their stronghold and send Xal scurrying for the shadows. Their legions will be trampled underfoot."

"What of Ducius?" Crispus ignored Lucretia entirely and focused on his father. A mistake, Totarius realized, possibly a fatal one. She was not a woman to be dismissed and most definitely nursed grudges, as at least two Imperators had learned. "I do not know the worth of an alliance with him. Is he truly worthy? And what will the people think? We have been enemies for centuries. They will not accept dreadlords as friends. And, if they do, would that not mean that everything we have said about Xal is hypocrisy? I have no head for such stratagems. I crave a straightforward battle."

*That you can command from the rear of*, Totarius thought silently, never letting it show upon his face.

"I think you should ponder the matter. You have the luxury of time." Totarius savored a mouthful of soup before continuing. "Let Erik and the former Praetor gather their limited support and then crush it. We will move on our true target soon, and after it is secured, you'll be able to return your focus here if you desire it. After Xal is dealt with. After your finances are secured so that you do not face the same woes that toppled Desidria."

"I do not like it." Crispus seized his goblet and drained the contents. The magical chalice refilled of its own accord, then he drank again before finally resuming his tirade. "If I lose this place, it shows weakness, and I do not believe Gateway—"

"My son," Totarius interrupted smoothly, "apologies, but

you insisted I remind you not to name the city to reduce the chance of being scryed."

Murderous rage flashed in those brown eyes, but it was quickly pushed down, under control. The boy was learning. In time, with guidance, he could be molded into a vicious despot, one the people would revile. Unfortunately, time was short.

"Of course, Father." Crispus set down the chalice. "I will not be a fool, like Desidria, nor complacent, like Erik. We will strike out for our target immediately. What forces have you presently arrayed?"

Totarius sighed, but it was a small sigh, and he kept it mostly to himself. "Five crack legions, Imperator, heavy with mages and in position to strike. In addition, the remaining Ghost Fleet has rendezvoused with them, and their combined might awaits only your arrival. Then you yet again expand the shrinking realm that Erik left you."

Crispus stood straighter. It was easy to see what motivated the boy. Pride. He longed to be a great man but desperately feared he was not. He turned his heated glare upon Lucretia. "You will accompany me, dreadlord."

The woman blinked in surprise, not a common emotion for the crone. "You require my counsel?"

"No, though I will partake it in." Crispus leaned upon the table with both hands, closer to Lucretia. "I want you there because you have survived everything, including a dragon ripping apart the Reactor. You will outlive us all. Thus, I want you as close to me as possible. In my bedchamber if needed. If Tissa comes calling, she hates you too, so you'll do whatever it takes to survive. From this day forward, our survival is linked. If I die, every spy and mercenary I have is instructed to hunt you down. You will never be safe again."

Totarius was actually rather proud of the boy. For the first time, the emotion came both from the demon prince and the man. Such a pity the boy had to be sacrificed. Hopefully, Lucretia was canny enough to avoid the same fate. She'd proven useful.

If not? There were plenty of other useful servants.

# 25

# THE AVATAR OF XAKAVA

I could feel a darkness approaching from the south. Not a visual darkness in the sense that the cloud-strewn sky dimmed. Darkness in the void sense. A reservoir of power, a beacon that would be visible from anywhere within the cycle, blazed its way toward the northern peaks where we'd taken shelter, crossing Enestius in pursuit.

The spider mountain perched atop a range of peaks, further north than I'd ever been, on the edge of the territory controlled by House Enestius. Past this point were trolls, snow, and ice so far as I knew.

"Have you a plan, friend Xal?" Saghir's tail drooped as he zipped down to join me along the battlement. "I have done all I can to prepare the legions. There is no place to debark, and even if there were, the avatar would smash them, then continue pursuing us."

"I'm still thinking." I peered south. Was I imagining the growing black speck? "Xakava was a skilled warrior in some incarnation, or there wouldn't be an aggressive stance named after that prince. My sister, on the other hand, has no martial training. So far as we know, they've taken her and planted her in the avatar, and she was at about the same level as us when we first took the sands. She's never been in the arena nor the academy."

"Perhaps her tombs have gifted her with skills," Saghir mused. "However, absent that knowledge, I would agree with your assessment. I do not know the girl, but I do know what it is like to be smaller and weaker than all around you."

"Given that," I continued, my gaze locked on the rapidly growing speck, "I expect she will rely primarily on magic. She's a battlemage. Eradicators eradicate. She'll be flinging divine disintegrates our way, and unless this beast has some surprises, I don't see how we're going to dodge."

"I have considered this problem." Saghir produced a rough black rod about as tall as he was. "Celeste and I spoke about the ashstaff. She found it hilarious that I possessed it for some reason. She showed me a few more tricks to its use. I can use the ash to screen us. Even a disintegrate will be absorbed if I can interpose enough of the stuff."

I nodded but didn't make an immediate reply. That could give us some basic defense, but it didn't provide a destination or a way to hurt the avatar. Either we needed a way to strike back hard or we needed to run. The trouble was until we saw the avatar and what it could do, we'd have no idea how well-suited we were to battle it.

If we were wrong, then the cycle's hopes would die here. Today.

"Keep pace with her." I raised a wing to block the wind buffeting me. Saghir had no such problems in his bubble of air. "If we're right about being faster, then lead her away from Enestius, toward the Ashlands. North by northeast if you please, Master Dreadlord."

That earned me a little smile and lightened the mood slightly.

The mood soured as the speck grew larger and larger and eventually resolved into a sobering figure. The giant stepped over a mountain peak...a peak nearly as large as the spider mountain. It towered over us, large enough that the behemoth was a scurrying tabby fearing the angry farmer.

Unexpectedly, our eyes met. I didn't think it could happen, not across so vast a distance, but I saw her, and she saw me. We recognized each other in that instant, and her thoughts thundered in my direction.

*This did not have to be*, Xakava roared, with a tiny voice at the center my sister's, but the rest a vast monstrosity too alien for mortal concerns. *This still does not have to be. Surrender. Join us. Submit to the flame and allow us to free the dark mother. We can be a family....*

*Do you even know where Mother is?* I thought back, my eyes narrowing. *What of Panya? Both love you dearly, but I know them. I know Mother and what she believes. If she's hiding from you, there can be only one reason. What do you think it is?*

Rage and guilt and shame bubbled across our tenuous bond, but no words. Not at first.

*She believes as you do*, Bha's agonized voice tore into my mind. *But you are wrong, both of you. All of this is built on a lie. Built on the imprisonment of a titan, unjustly.*

*I know*, I forced love and compassion into my thoughts. I reminded myself who I was speaking to, and the life we'd shared in the hovel. *And I believe there is a way to free her without destroying the cycle. I believe that we can preserve the good things that have been built while righting the ancient wrongs.*

*And if you are mistaken?* she thundered back as the avatar

took a step closer, quaking the land. *Then we lose the war, and Reevanthara is free to do as he wills.*

That told me something. Xakava, or whoever had instructed her, didn't know everything about the titans. They hadn't seen my visions. They had no idea that Reevanthara seemed to want to destroy the cycle to force the creation of something greater.

*I am not mistaken*, I gave back, my mental tone more closed now. *The cycle must be protected at all costs. If we lose it, then what comes in its wake will be slavery for all creatures, forever. A perfect mummer's play directed by the titan of life. Please, Bha. Don't do this. You're right that it isn't too late. Join our side. Help us end this war.*

*Lucretia wouldn't allow it*, she thought back bitterly. *I can no longer hide, even if I wanted to. I am a weapon, and I will end this war. I will do what I must. I'm sorry, Brother.*

The avatar raised a hand that could shelter a city in its palm and aimed at us. *Void* and *fire* gathered around the entire body, thick twisting ropes of swirling sigils. I knew them instantly. How could I not? She was casting the signature spell of every eradicator, just a thousand times larger.

"Saghir?" I called, trying and failing to keep the alarm from my voice.

"I will do all I can." Up came the ashstaff, and all around us, the ash began to quiver around the mountain's peaks and many limbs.

The spell left the avatar's hand, a bolt of disintegration that could have cored Calmora, and it was aimed directly at us. There was no dodging. No fleeing. The spell traveled much too swiftly for that.

A cloud of grey ash rose into the air, darkening the sky as it swirled into a tornado roughly the size of the incoming spell. Each speck of dust tore sigils from the disintegrate, weakening it, but the spell still vaporized the upper third of one of the three peaks forming humps on the spider's back. The resulting explosion sent an avalanche of snow and ash down toward the citadel, and multiple mages among the legions threw up wards, with both *water* and *earth* mages redirecting the flow.

The spider mountain scrambled away, as swiftly as it was able, and I don't think Saghir issued the order. The beast simply whirled and ran, as if sensing a predator, crushing peaks and creating new valleys in its haste to escape.

More sigils gathered around the avatar, but this time they were divided into pools around each titanic fist. Twin spells. My sister held them for long moments as she ran perpendicular to us, trying to line up the shot the same way we would have if throwing stones as children back in the dims. The avatar even moved like she did.

The first spell zipped in, a range-finding device every child uses, and would have slammed into two of the legs had a wall of ash not interposed itself and dispersed the spell. This time the cloud was thicker and directed with more control.

"I am learning." Saghir swirled the cloud around as the second spell approached, but it was greatly diminished.

The second spell slammed into one of the mountain's legs at the base, right where it attached to the thick trunk. The leg shattered, and stone rained down on the mountains below, triggering multiple avalanches. Thank the gods new and old that we'd taken this battle far from cities.

The spider mountain jerked abruptly, skittering to the side as it attempted to right itself with seven legs, and I was forced to seize the rail to prevent myself from being cata pulted off the balcony. The legions below all faced the same challenge, and nearly everyone kept their feet or clung to safety.

A few, however, were caught off guard. Those would have been flung from the mountain to plummet to their deaths...had valiant *air* mages not flown out to rescue them. I didn't know if they caught everyone, but the sight inspired me nonetheless.

Until another disintegrate slammed into the mountainside, and we lost two companies of infantry and a tribe of orokh plainsrunners. Gone.

"Get us out of here!" I roared, stabilizing myself with my tail as the mountain lurched and bucked.

"Easier uttered than accomplished, my friend!" Saghir wailed as he raised the staff and warded off another spell, this one with far more success. "I am getting better at anticipating her spells, but if I continue, I will run out of ash."

"We have no choice but to run." I clung to the rock as my perspective swung round. I could no longer see the avatar, but I knew it was still there. "It appears we're faster. Widen the gap and she'll have to stop throwing spells. These spells have to be costing her divinity."

A disintegrate slammed into a mountain to the south, right next to one of the spider mountain's legs. How many more of those could she manage?

"Friend Xal," Saghir called, a bit calmer now that we were gaining distance. "If she follows us into the Ashlands, what then? I believe we will lose the advantage we now hold. It will be easier for her to catch us in that terrain."

"That's exactly what Totarius is counting on." I cursed under my breath, the words not fit to be repeated. "Who knows what he's doing while we're on the run? Even if we survive, we do no good if all we can do is flee forever."

"At least we are preventing the avatar from being elsewhere." Saghir rose into the air, ash and snow swirling around the protective ward he'd erected. "Yet...*you* do not need to be here for this gambit to succeed. There is little you can add. I cannot deposit the infantry, but you could leave and be about other business. If you must counter Totarius's schemes, then let me lead the avatar on a merry chase."

I peered at the battle damage the spider mountain had already sustained. The disintegrates were fewer now, but if my sister ever cornered them...I'd lose everything. Of course, if I was here, that would happen anyway, but I would die too. What could I do to stop that monstrosity?

Did leaving make sense? Where would I go?

"For the time being, I will stay." I sighed and embraced my fate. "I will be prepared to depart, however. Perhaps it is time you turned over the captaincy of *The Fist*. I will begin gathering a small crew and divining Totarius's whereabouts. It's possible Li or Erik need help. We need to find a way to hit them back. Hard. Swiftly."

# INTERLUDE XVIII- CRISPUS

Crispus stood upon the deck of his flagship, the last surviving Elentian vessel among the Hasran armada. How he had coveted this vessel once, all metal and magic, instead of his own enchanted wood, and envied Erik the possession of it. He'd thought Erik stood higher, because such a vessel could not be purchased, no matter how much coin one's family accrued.

Unless you murdered the former Imperator and took what you wanted. *That* was what the strong did. What Crispus had done. The start of a thousand-year legacy. Longer, perhaps.

"We'll be able to see the city soon, Your Grace, my lady." The captain bobbed a bow first to Crispus, and then to Lucretia who stood behind and to his right in the advisory position.

They crested the peaks at long last, so close the rock nearly scraped the bottom of their vessel, quite exhilarating really, and then he laid eyes upon the oldest city in the west. Possibly in the world. He had no head for such scholarly things and didn't really care. It was the oldest. How old didn't matter.

"Are our legions in place?" Crispus rested a hand upon the hilt of his saber, a newly acquired weapon, one he'd had stripped from its previous master after having the man executed. For the sword, though, he'd invented some charge he couldn't recall.

"They already march. Witness your might, Imperator." Lucretia gestured down at the city, where five separate legions mustered, each choking off one of the exits, all save the tremendous escarpment bordering the city, a thousand-cubit drop down to the desert. His advisor moved to stand next to him, and he did not like the note of flattery in her voice. "I see no resistance. They have been caught completely off guard."

Crispus frowned down at the city. It made no sense to him. They were not defending. They were allowing him to occupy the city seemingly unopposed. There were no airships nor griffins. No kodachine war cries nor explosion of fire spells. The legions marched into the city as if on parade, and the people, what few there were, scurried from their path.

He knew he wasn't the smartest person. He knew that bastard Xal thought quicker and saw more. Yet he wasn't a fool. This was a trap. Someone wanted him to occupy this city, and the only two reasons he could see were they weren't strong enough to hold it and thus had fled, or they were setting an ambush to kill him.

"Tissa left me," Crispus said softly, almost lost to the hot desert wind as they slowly closed with the ancient city. "She loathed me at the end, I think. When I bonded her, I assumed I did not need to feel her emotions to predict them. I thought she adored me. I thought I was her prince, as in a story, rescuing her. Yet she left me and now serves another, I assume."

Lucretia's expression went horrified. For just an instant, he caught a glimpse of the true woman, and in that moment her act failed. She had precisely no idea what to make of what he'd just said, no idea how to respond. The captain's eyes were elsewhere, and he pretended not to hear any of it. A wise man.

"Do you know what that taught me, witch?" Crispus leaned in close, his breath hot on her ear. "I know nothing about snakes because I am not a snake. I am a leopard." He stepped back and peered down at the city, giving her some room. "You have had no choice but to be one. I have seen how you govern, seen how you shred a man with your tongue when they fail. I have also seen you fawn and flatter, and it is...unnatural. I prefer the other. I prefer the disappointed mentor, the way you used to look at Tissa. I remember when Desidria would issue some foolish order, and you would glance at her in contempt because you knew better, yet did nothing to warn her of her folly."

He took her hand gently, and she looked up at him once more. "I am about to issue orders. Before I do so, I need you to tell me. Are they foolish? Do not wait for me to immolate myself, or *you* will die too. I will see to it. If I fall, my last act will be ensuring you fall too."

"I am proud of you." The words flew out of Lucretia's mouth like the damned fleeing a prison. "I never thought to say that. You were a horrible monster as a child, made worse by the potential to be so much more. Your father allowed you to be a bully. Every time a lesser man felt a slight to their pride, they had to carry that wound, and then nurse it until it scarred. Your father allowed you to destroy those who offered such slights. You have never been properly humbled, child. And now such an act will doom far more than you, as you have rightly pointed out. You are cunning enough to see our death waits in that city. They will allow us to grow complacent, while we occupy territory they know, and then they will assassinate us at their leisure if we let them."

"We must show we know this and can still reach them. I will find something they love and crush it." Crispus balled his hands into fists and glared at the city. "That begins by discovering where their forces have fled to. Where are these vaunted kodachine I have heard so much about? Where are their ifrit? Or these marid that dwell under the city? Find them for me, and we will root them out of their strongholds. Did the Elentians not conquer the Heart of Water? Is there a record of that battle and how it was achieved?"

"There is, but the Elentians possessed magic and mages we do not." Lucretia leaned upon the railing, within arm's reach rather than at her previous distance. "You are right to make a show of strength. I would recommend ruling openly from the palace, rather than secluding yourself. Attend the Arena. Treat this as a lark. Show them you are a boy. A fearless one."

"All while being ready for their assassins." Crispus grinned as their shadow fell over a group of tengu children, who scattered like the crows they resembled. His mirth faded as a thought flitted across his mind. "Xal values this place. You are certain that Father has dealt with him?"

"The avatar has been deployed, and I expect your father, or Xakava, to send word of Xal's destruction soon." Lucretia's mouth soured into a frown. "It's troubling we have not heard from Bha since she engaged. My last scrying showed Xal's pet mountain fleeing and wounded if that is any consolation."

"It is." Relief flooded him. "Kodachine I can deal with. We will grind this place under heel." He turned to Lucretia. "You know a great deal you do not share. Have you knowledge of Tissa's whereabouts?"

"Last I knew, she was still in Calmora," Lucretia gave hesitantly as if revealing a secret she was uncertain she should be sharing. "She appears to have taken service with Princess Li. I believe they are occupied with the dragon Khonsu, but I have not scryed recently. You should know she is as a daughter to me, much more so than Bha ever was."

"I will not ask you to betray her. I still love her." Crispus looked away, pretending to survey the city as they drifted toward the palace. He saw none of it. Not really. "I merely need to know if she approaches, because if so, I want to be far from this city until I have word of her apprehension."

"Not execution?" Genuine surprise tinged the crone's voice. "Why would you risk leaving her alive?"

"If she's to die, it will be by my hand." Crispus wrapped his hand around the hilt of his new sword once more. The metal was hot against his skin. Everything was hot here. He already hated it. "There is a possibility we could reconcile. I will not ask her to take service, but perhaps an alliance? I am an Imperator after all. I will grant her anything she wishes if she will return to me."

"You are a fool." Lucretia gave a biting laugh, and it filled Crispus with rage.

Almost he backhanded her with a gauntlet until he realized she'd just done exactly what he'd ordered her to do. She was exposing his foolishness.

"You think there's no chance she will ever come back." He hated saying it out loud but forced himself to meet her gaze and not look away as he continued. "You think I'm a fool opening my heart to the dagger."

"And thus my heart, if your threats are to be believed." Lucretia folded her arms and eyed him like the disapproving mother he imagined most boys had. His mother had rarely raised her gaze from the floor, at least when his father was around. "She hates you. Once a woman reaches that stage, it does not reverse course. Once, she was blind to your flaws. Now they are all she sees. She will come for you and keep coming until she is literally unable to do so. If you wished her at your side, it would take binding spells, renewed daily."

"And I would always run the risk of her breaking free." Crispus gave a tired sigh. His office was incredibly trying. "Very well, I amend my earlier order. Do not attempt to apprehend her. Kill her if she comes. In fact, draft a special group of assassins trained to counter her. I will review them when you feel they are ready."

The airship approached the tower jutting out of the palace, just below them. They had arrived and servants already awaited them. Would it be so simple?

Such a beautiful trap.

Why had his father sent him here? Was Totarius disposing of him? Was that the plan? Take this city, and give the people a target to hate?

Well, if so, they would be sorely disappointed. Crispus would not be discarded. Would not be a puppet. He would show them all.

He was the Imperator. This was *his* realm.

# 26

# PARTINGS

The two most tense days of my life had come to a close. Xakava's titanic form still trailed in our wake, a black speck on a dark horizon, each lumbering step carrying the demonic avatar closer. Thankfully, the mountains had allowed us to open a gap, but that advantage was now at an end.

Before us stretched lower and lower hills until they disappeared into ash dunes. We'd come to the Ashlands at last, which meant our only choices were to enter the ash, go due north into the frozen wastes, or stand and fight.

None were good options.

"Morale is very low," Saghir began, breaking the long silence. "The legions did precious little drinking last night. They are afraid."

"I can feel the loss of faith." I sighed under my breath as I peered down at those camps. "They expected to follow a god to victory after victory, and all I have led them to is flight and possible annihilation. We need a way to turn this situation around, but I don't see how."

"At least we can defend ourselves once more." Saghir

waved his tiny black staff, and clouds of ash rose to gather along each of the spider mountain's legs, replenishing the vast reserves he'd used to defend against Xakava's spells. "I can also achieve things I could not before. If she follows us into the dune sea, I might be able to summon a storm to hinder her."

I folded my wings flat against my back and began to pace as I considered our next move. It did not take long to hatch the beginning of a plan. "We need to force a confrontation now that we have a slight advantage. We'll still lose, but then she'll have incentive to follow us deeper into the Ashlands."

"How do you intend to attack her?" Saghir reached down and clutched his tail, a nervous habit I'd not seen often, but that I remembered from our time among the trash legion.

"It's time I take over *The Fist*." I nodded up at the cave serving as a makeshift dock. "I can dodge her spells easily and harry her, while you use ash to pull her under. We keep her off balance and unable to cast and try to bury her."

"That will only annoy her in the long run. When she rises...." Saghir gave a shudder, then his whiskers twitched as he met my gaze. "I believe this plan could do as you wish and gain her rage, but she is already pursuing us. How will that aid us in the long run?"

"It will allow me to take your advice." I peered west, into the Ashwall, which we were now on the other side of. "I can start to counter Totarius, while you lead the mountain deeper into the Ashlands. Your staff will even the odds, and you should be able to outrun her. You lead her south, to Olivantia, then cross back and make her Ducius's problem."

"This I can do." Saghir's tone did not lend support to those words. "I will get her to pursue me and do all I can to irritate and slow her. I do not know how much time I can grant you, but you will have what I can make."

"Excellent." I glanced back at my sister, now thousands of cubits tall. "First, we have to gain her interest. She could break off and retreat, the last thing we need. I'll go and get the ship ready."

"She can fly now, and Hadi still dwells within, as he has helped maintain the vessel." Saghir raised a paw. "All that you are lacking is the key, which I have configured. It gained existence in the forges when we created the vessel. I have carried it ever since."

A pulse of gold sheathed in black shot out from his tiny paw and into my waiting palm. Frost covered my palm as the frigid magic disappeared into my arm, then it was gone, dormant until needed. "Thank you, my friend."

He managed a smile as I winged into the air and up toward the cave. It took very little time as the wind carried me closer, and before I knew it, I was through the iris and inside the vessel, able to sense *The Fist* in a different way than I had before.

I could feel the vessel, feel its hull and its senses. I could see as it saw. I was an extension of it, and it an extension of me. Fascinating. I could even feel where Hadi was within the ship, training alone in the combat circle.

This was what Saghir felt when we flew into battle.

I guided the ship from the cave, moving it through will, which it channeled through the matrix, manifesting as *void*. Gravity—in this case, ours. Somehow I used it for effortless flight in a way no spell I knew of could duplicate. Not this seamlessly. It was better than any bird could know. I didn't need momentum...I could shift directions suddenly with only wind resistance to deal with.

My moment of exhilaration ended when I became aware

of Xakava through the ship's senses. In addition to the towering avatar my own eyes witnessed, the ship also added several different shades. Thick purple-black clumps lined the avatar's body. Magic, I realized. I could see it flowing through veins and muscles and where the largest concentrations were in the heart and head.

Xakava seemed aware of my approach, and her arm came up, sigils gathering in her palm as she flung the by-now-familiar spell. A divine disintegrate that could have leveled a mountain whipped at me, but it was easy to guide the ship in a tight turn. My maneuverability was unmatched. No griffin or even the Elentian airships I'd seen could do this.

Another spell came, then another, but I lazily dodged them as I approached. *The Fist* was big, but nowhere near as large as the avatar's hands. I was effectively a buzzing insect, a single hornet that could perhaps annoy, but not much else.

Save that the hornet possessed a vast quantity of magic.

*How will you proceed?* Narlifex wondered in my mind.

"This ship works with gravity magic. If it can make us lighter, then the opposite must also be true." I grinned as I guided the ship lower, aiming for the ash as the avatar brought a hand around to swat us, but I easily dodged.

I plunged down toward the ground, then aimed at the back of the avatar's knee. I willed immense magic into the vessel, from my reserves and from the divinity I'd been accumulating. *The Fist* impacted like an arrow with predictable results.

The avatar's knee bent unexpectedly, spilling my sister onto her back in a spray of ash that fountained into the sky and created its own ash storm...one Saghir immediately seized control of.

Ash ropes formed all around the avatar's body, growing larger and more numerous as they struggled to pull the avatar under the ash entirely.

A low subsonic groan burst from its twin mouths, and it heaved itself from the ash, breaking the ropes and regaining its feet. The avatar charged the spider mountain, pouring on speed and quaking the land with every step.

The spider mountain turned and ran, great sprays of ash coming up in its wake and forming drifts in the avatar's path to slow it down. They failed. The avatar burst through them, sprinting across the bottom of the ash sea, narrowing the gap with the spider mountain.

"She's begun thinking like a warrior." I cursed under my breath as I considered what to do next. "She's not wasting time with spells anymore. She's closing to melee."

I simply couldn't let that happen, or my followers would be knocked into the ash sea, those who survived the initial attack.

I whipped *The Fist* around and flew away from Xakava, then came back in a straight line, pouring on more and more speed as I approached her back like a hurled spear tip. I increased the ship's mass once more, making it far heavier, large enough to seriously impact even the avatar itself, larger than I had with the knee.

Xakava was running full tilt, and my attack caught her completely off guard. The attack knocked her face-first into the ash, and she slid through it, accumulating a larger and larger wall as she slowed, and the spider mountain accelerated away.

I pulled up and away, zooming around at an angle as I flew off toward the west, the Ashwall looming in the distance. *The Fist*'s senses were omnidirectional, which meant I could focus on her rising even as I flew away from her.

The titan crawled back to its feet and began lumbering after the spider mountain once more. If she was aware of me or cared, she did not turn. A large gap had opened between her and the mountain. Would Saghir be safe? He had infinite ash to work with here.

I had to trust him, hard as it was to not stay and try to protect my people. He had his orders. I needed to discover how I might start turning this war in our favor.

Xakava lumbered after the mountain, and I ignored her as I sped back toward the west and my friends. Once the ship was at maximum speed and high enough that I didn't need to worry about slamming into a mountain, I suppressed my connection to the ship and began missiving people I cared for.

I began with Li, then Erik, then Ena, and gave each a brief report of what had happened here and a request for an update on their situation. I did not mention that I was leaving the Ashlands nor that I could help them.

If one needed me, then I'd be there before Totarius could even react to my presence. He'd find that without his avatar, it would be a very different battle.

## 27

## RENUNIONS

Hadi had finished his training and retired for the night by the time answers to my missives began to trickle into *The Fist*'s darkened interior, about two bells after I'd passed the Ashwall, somewhere over the highlands of Arlen.

The first was from Li, her tone full of tension, though the news she delivered all seemed good. The dragons had been driven from the mountain, and the lightning people freed, yet her father and his people had not yet returned. Why the apprehension? I had the sense she couldn't or wouldn't share.

Nothing about us, but I supposed we'd reached a point where we did not need to include sonnets or prose to prove our feelings every time we talked. I was happy she was safe and made a note to contact Celeste to see if she could provide clarity about these lightning people.

The second response was from Ena, only saying they had arrived and made contact with their new benefactor, Temis. About a bell after that, around what I guessed was dawn in Valys, a missive arrived from Erik. That one caught the most attention, as it delivered dire news.

"I'm glad you missived," the phoenix began, Erik's voice older somehow. More mature. "I've come by hard news, news that has little to do with me directly. Crispus threatened my temple but then withdrew. I expected a strong response, but nothing. Now I know why. The whole of Hasran strength fell upon Gateway. The city has been occupied, its rulers fled or dead. There are proclamations plastered all over Valys which promise new prosperity taken from the Blasted Lands. I'm sorry. I know you value that city, though I have never been. I will missive again when I have news. Totarius has returned to Valys, and I expect he'll come for me soon enough. I've certainly rendered enough causes."

And there it was, my course of action. I'd been wondering where I could be of use, what I could do to counter Totarius and his plans. With the avatar out of the way, it was time I struck back. The fewer people worshiping Hasra, the more were free to worship the Stewards or me.

Gateway could not be allowed to remain in Hasran hands. So I would ensure that it did not.

I reached through my senses to the ship and adjusted my heading and speed. I gained altitude, a tiny speck in the sky if any chanced to look up through the spotty cloud cover. The Endless Lake rolled by beneath me, and in the distance, the Halo's glow told me where to find the Celestial Mountain.

I spent quite some time comprising my missive, then cast it once I had it right in my head. "Frit, this is the almukhtar, and it is in that role I speak. I am coming to the Blasted Lands. I am told there is a need for someone who can slaughter Hasran invaders. My brother Hadi and I will arrive with the sun."

Then I flew in silence for a long time. The ground vanished beneath me as the ship sped through the skies, the entire west there and gone in the space of a single day. It was humbling really, thinking about how many months it would take a single person to cross that same span. Even another airship would have lengthened the voyage to a week.

A missive flitted through the deck on fiery wings, the style very different from what I was used to. The bird had a desert feel to it, right down to the curling flames on the wings. "Almukhtar, I hear your words and will meet with you and your brother in person, as due your station. The kodachine stand ready for war. All we await is your arrival."

One more problem dealt with.

I passed over the mountains, a good hundred leagues north of the city of Gateway, which put me above the verdant triangle. I did not spy any sign of its druid guardian, though I knew Loxclyn would be aware of my passage. She had a thousand eyes, from lizards to eagles, all watching, standing sentinel for her domain.

Then I was out into the deeper desert, which rolled out endlessly before me for nearly a full bell before I spied the white necromancer's sprawling black pyramid. That brought me back to traveling with Brim and Gronde and Isharah and the others, and I missed them. They were too canny to have fallen to the Hasrans, but I didn't know where they all were. What of Mina? Isharah would be with her.

"Good morning, Brother." Hadi rose with a throaty croak, then scratched at his feathers as he began adjusting his turban. "I slept as the dead." He peered over at Saghir's map sprawled across the floor and gave a beaky smile. "It appears we are nearly home. You have bypassed Gateway for the deep desert. We meet with the kodachine?"

"Within a bell." I smiled down at the map. We were

nearly there. "I have need for neither food nor sleep, it seems, but thanks to Saghir, we are well provisioned. He's enchanted a stone to stay permanently cold, so there is chilled water as well to quench your thirst."

Hadi helped himself to the water while the sun rose higher and higher over the horizon. The bird ate swiftly as our destination grew larger before us, and in that moment, I missed my mortality. I no longer craved food, and that simple fact separated my old life from the new.

*The Fist* began to descend, and I guided her in for a landing outside the cleft leading down into the oasis where I knew that the kodachine had gathered.

I was mildly surprised when a delegation emerged to greet us, including several familiar figures. Gronde and Brim towered over everyone else, the orokh brothers each carrying their respective first weapons, Narlifex's axe and hammer cousins.

Behind them stood Frit, the flaming kodachine much shorter but every bit as intimidating. Her magma skin and flaming hair were exquisite, so like a human's save for the exotic material. She nodded when she caught me staring, and I nodded back.

"Hasran!" Brim boomed. "You've returned. I like this vessel you have arrived in. All you need now is some massive weapon for it to wield, and you can slay gods."

Narlifex thrummed at that in something like recognition. Anticipation?

"It is good to see you, Brother of the sands." Gronde stepped forward and offered his forearm, which I accepted. I was able to meet his grip, which surprised him. "I see you've continued your training. You are stronger, but you look older as well. I am sorry for whatever tragedies have befallen you since our last meeting."

"Where is the mead?" Hadi croaked from behind as he emerged and joined us. "I would have shade and water and laughter!"

There were rousing greetings all around and smiles as I'd not enjoyed in some time. It was a welcome respite from the death and battle and setbacks of the past few months, and I allowed myself to be led down into the cleft to a well-stocked pavilion, where I slid down onto comfortable cushions.

Wine and mead and ale and smoke flowed through the room, and I gave myself in to the pleasure of it, allowing my guard down briefly, as much as I ever could anymore. Narlifex didn't chide me, so I couldn't have slid too far.

Eventually, the evening wound down, and Hadi drifted off to an axe-throwing contest with the brothers, leaving Frit and me to converse in peace for the first time since my arrival. At first, the fiery woman looked around as if hunting for an excuse to leave but then seemed to find her courage.

"We have not spoken of wedding the flame." She wouldn't meet my gaze, and her tone had an uncharacteristic hesitation. "I still do not know what the prophecy entails, but nothing has changed for me. I have no desire to wed at all, much less a man."

"My heart belongs to another, but there is some hope for us." I raised my flagon in salute. "Prophecy has proven a tricky thing so far, all allegory and metaphor. They very rarely seem to speak plainly, so I'd wager wed the flame means something else entirely." I paused to drink, then wiped my mouth before speaking again. "There is something you and I are meant to do together. Given the forces arrayed against us, neither of us is likely to live long enough to find marital bliss with anyone, much less each other."

I hated saying it aloud, but after all this time with

Narlifex, I was beginning to understand all his cryptic mutterings. I would never know peace, save for brief intervals. Li and I were together, but we would never remain so in the way I truly wished. The universe would endlessly keep us apart.

"Let us hope you are correct." Frit picked up a flagon of something like lamp oil that burst into flame as she drank it down. She wiped her mouth when she'd finished. "I am more than happy to ride into battle alongside you. I've resented you ever since I learned of the prophecy. I hope your version is the truth, and I will pretend it so until I cannot any longer."

Our conversation died down as Hadi and the orokh brothers came over to our pillows once more, laughter booming as they approached. It appeared Gronde had won their contest, though they were already discussing other topics.

I seized the conversation as they approached, both to avoid any awkwardness with Frit and because I needed the information.

"Come," I boomed, drawing their attention as I motioned at the nearest pillows. "Sit and join us. The time has come to make something like a plan. You know why I've come, yes?"

"As soon as I heard Hasrans were in Gateway," Brim confirmed with a laugh, "I knew you'd be back to send them packing. You helped free this place of your wretched countrymen. I can't see you letting that work be undone."

"What can you tell us of this Imperator?" Gronde's eyes glittered with intelligence, despite the quantity of mead he'd consumed. "We're told he keeps a sorceress close at hand, an eradicator of incredible strength, they say. He also has a number of elite warriors as bodyguards, and they say that you must have at least ten Catalyzations to even join. Are these truths or exaggerations?"

"They're likely downplaying his true strength." I set my flagon down, my thirst gone. "Crispus is a puppet, one any of our quint can deal with. His bodyguards will be the best mercenaries money can secure. Worse, the rumors of the sorceress are true. She is my aunt and is incredibly powerful. One of her artifacts can control demons. She can issue orders, and I must obey them, so long as she has a tongue to speak."

"Ahhh." Gronde leaned back against his cushions, some idea coming to him. "I understand at last. This is why the hand of fate was gathered. This is the role we play. You say this woman can control you, yes? Well, she cannot control me nor my brother, nor the rest of the hand. Let us return to Gateway and meet with Isharah and Gak. We will gather our companions and slay this new Imperator and his pet binder. Shall I order our legions to break camp?"

"No." I gave a truly wicked smile. "If you can deal with my aunt? We won't need to risk the kodachine or alert our enemies to our approach. I can deal with those legions. Personally. Publicly. I've come a long way since Magnus."

# INTERLUDE XIX - ERIK

Erik heaved the second to last pew against the wall, shouldering the polished oak, then lifting it so as not to scratch the marble floor with each long bench. He set it down and was about to push the final one aside, but something stopped him. A darkness approached, one so powerful he could sense it through his shield.

He scanned the temple, which now stood largely empty. His efforts had provided a wide area where two combatants could circle without destroying furniture that had no doubt taken thousands of hours to produce. Hopefully this place would survive the coming confrontation.

Erik strode to the front door and waited. The darkness grew closer and closer, and his heart thudded in his chest. He expected the door to be flung open, but instead it opened quietly to admit a single cloaked figure, then closed.

The purple cloak fell to the stone and revealed Totarius in supple black armor, some sort of leather, armed for war. Daggers were attached to well-muscled forearms in cunning sheathes, and he held a pair that had somehow appeared after he'd closed the door. The armor glittered with illusion magic, and Erik did not want to guess where the leather had come from.

"Hello, Steward." Totarius gazed around and noted the empty space where the pews should have been. "Doing a bit of cleaning before your next service? I'd have thought you had worshippers to perform such menial labor. There was a time you'd have been ashamed to be caught doing such."

"Only because I was but a boy." Erik shrugged and made no attempt to deny the charge. "As for why I cleared it? Because I suspected that our discussion might grow... heated. I would like to spare my temple damage while we work out our differences."

"So you know why I've come then?" Totarius raised a thick eyebrow, then shrugged. "I suppose it was easy enough to predict. You understand my motivations, and you know that I've removed your demon prince from the board. You stand alone, boy. And now I will claim that shield, as my little brother claimed it before me. I too will slay a Steward of Justice and rob him of your support, while also gutting whatever power your brethren still hold. No one will follow you after what I do today."

New boots rang on the stone as Erik's companion strode out of the shadows. If there were any person he'd rather have than Vhala, then this man was it. Praetor Etrian Valys in gleaming plate unsheathed his ancient sword, then rapped the eldimagus against his shield.

"He does not stand alone," the Praetor corrected. "I am here to defend my faith and my Steward. You have always feared me, Totarius. Do you still?"

Totarius rolled his head back and laughed. It went on for long moments, not a cutting laughter, but a good-natured, friendly expression. Finally it subsided and he smiled at the Praetor. "I am Totarius no longer, not the man you knew.

That man? Yes, he feared you, Praetor. Because you were greater than he. But me? I am not just a demon prince, but the eldest of princes. The one who birthed the others. I will slay you, and then I will kill your Steward within his own temple."

"Bold of you to come alone." Erik eased his weapon from its sheath, then hefted his shield of office. Faith flowed around him, an ever-growing pool of power provided by his temple and increasingly by the pockets of Olivantia. "You really think you can best the both of us at the same time?"

"I'd have expected more to be honest." Totarius stifled an exaggerated yawn. "The Lady Shulk and her lapdog husband should be here, yet I don't know if they are even in the city. If they were, then you might have had a small chance against me. Yet they are not, so you have no chance at all."

His hands blurred and a hundred—no, a thousand—glittering daggers whirled outward from him, a storm of weapons that enveloped the both of them, peppering Erik with lethal shards. He got his shield up and deflected the flow, but by the time he'd lowered it, there was no sign of Totarius.

Erik chanced a look at the Praetor, but other than a single line of blood across his cheek, Etrian appeared unharmed.

A shadow crossed the room in the blink of an eye, and before Erik could move, a dagger emerged from the Praetor's shoulder, directly between the metal plates. It had been rammed in from behind and was left there as Totarius melted back into the shadows.

Etrian gave an expert slash, high with his blade, then low with his shield, but Totarius easily evaded both. The shadow was simply too fast. And Erik knew that while he was skilled, Etrian was more so. If Etrian couldn't hit Totarius, what chance did he have?

"My son has taken Gateway, you know." The smug voice rang from the shadows, but it was impossible to locate the source. "Every land belongs to Hasra once more, and Hasra is your enemy. You face a united empire, one that fuels my every spell and strike. The power in that faith...I cannot describe it, Steward, save to say you will never taste its like."

Another storm of blades came out, and they bypassed Erik's armor completely, slicing into his thigh and the ankle on his other leg. He dropped low using the shield to cover his entire body and weathered the rest of the assault. Could Totarius really infuse every spell like this? If so, then how could he and Etrian beat him?

Erik leaned into a sprint and poured on his speed, all while blazing more and more light from his shield. It was reflected in the mirrors and pools throughout the temple, amplified to impossible brilliance, which did not harm Erik's gaze in the slightest.

In fact...it made it easy to see Totarius. There were no longer any shadows to hide in.

Erik angled his sprint toward the demon, then shoulder-checked him into the wall with his shield. The artifact met resistance, and they thudded into the wall together, but Totarius laughed as he flung Erik back, then spat tendrils of darkness that wrapped around Erik's arms, then his legs.

"Yaaaaah!" Etrian brought his weapon down and severed the shadow tendrils, then kicked Totarius in the chest hard enough to fling him back into a pillar, which cracked under the impact but held. He turned to Erik. "Can you continue?"

"I'm fine." Erik rose and shook off the chill the tendrils had brought. Whatever it was faded swiftly, and warmth returned. "Take cover!"

He was forced to dive into a roll and take cover under his shield as an ocean of dark liquid flooded the temple. It did not touch him, the shield kept it at bay, but everything else was coated with the stuff. The level continuously rose, and it wouldn't be long until he was completely entombed.

Erik thought furiously. How could he solve this? How could he strip Totarius of his power or counterspell these divine attacks? He reached deep within the reservoir of divinity that had gathered around both him and the shield and willed the liquid to be gone.

And it was.

Yet the act took a frightful amount of the divinity he'd stored. He could do it again, perhaps as many as a half-dozen times, but then he'd have no more worship. How much could Totarius field? He'd already used several spells and hadn't slowed down his usage.

Erik clapped his sword on shield, then circled over to join the Praetor so they could stand shoulder to shoulder. Totarius kept his distance, merely watching, lazily like a lion who is unsure if it wants to engage the prey before it.

"What do we do?" Erik whispered to the man he'd idolized growing up. "How can we best him? I can stop a few of his abilities, but we haven't come close to harming him yet."

Totarius vanished, then appeared behind them. He rammed a dagger into each of their backs, sinking the weapons in to the hilts. "Nor shall you."

Then he blazed away, well out of reach before Erik's blade came around. And here he'd thought he was fast. His best attacks were like swimming through murky water. There was no way his abilities would allow him to win this fight.

It was a unique experience. Was this how Xal had felt all those times in the beginning? Outclassed and with few resources, he'd always found a way. How? Erik needed that same ingenuity, and he needed it right now or the Stewards were going to need another replacement.

"I am a full god, boy." Totarius boomed out another laugh as he leaned casually against a pillar, unlaced his breeches, and relieved himself upon the floor. "Ahhh. This is what I think of your faith, what I do in the heart of your holy places. First, I will desecrate it, and then I will desecrate you."

Erik knew despair but refused to show it. If he were to die, then he would face death on his feet, fighting for what he believed in, just like that damned urchin had always done.

## 28

## THE HAND OF FATE

I greatly enjoyed showing Gronde, Brim, and Frit the luxuries Saghir had added to *The Fist*. It had become a proper airship, not quite up to Elentian standards, but a good degree more comfortable than the first day we'd created her in the Forges of Xa.

We sat in comfortable chairs around the map, watching the desert scroll by as we approached the city of Gateway. I flew at an angle well away from it, keeping north towards the verdant triangle where I knew Loxclyn would be waiting.

"I wonder how the druid will greet us," Gronde rumbled as he rested on the haft of his axe, its head placed firmly against the deck. "We parted on good terms, and she has no love for the Hasrans. Perhaps she will even render us aid."

"Perhaps." Brim gave a tusky grin. "I suspect she will seek out my company, and I'd welcome it. But what do I know about the mind of such a woman?"

We descended to the sands just outside an explosion of life signifying the edge of the oasis, and the iris opened to admit a hot desert wind, which was more humid this close to the triangle.

I saw no sign of the druid as we exited nor anything beyond the usual wildlife. A hawk screamed its ire above us, and a coyote stood at the top of a ridge, just outside a cave that likely served as a den. The land knew we were here, and thus Loxclyn knew, but perhaps she saw no need to make her presence known any further.

"We retrace our steps." I led the way across the sands, moving at a comfortable run, which Gronde, Brim, Hadi, and Frit all matched.

We operated in a comfortable silence, the kind that had been built across countless training matches. I'd fought on the sands with these men and knew them as they knew me. We were a force of nature. Five minds functioning as one deadly assault. Frit might be a new addition, but she was just as skilled, if not more so.

It took several bells to descend into the bowels of the earth, yet I never slowed, nor did my companions. Not once did anyone ask for a break, though I could tell Hadi flagged near the end.

I drew up short unexpectedly when I approached the water's edge, not because the water was there, but because we were no longer alone. Two lone figures awaited us. Familiar figures. Gakk's tiny body and giant head stood grinning at us, next to Isharah, her fur a lush scarlet tinged with white.

"Welcome." The kitsune's face split in a wide grin. "We knew you would arrive today, but not the time. We have been here since dawn."

"Gakk hungry!" Gakk picked up a rock and tossed it into his mouth, then chewed with that ocean of fangs. "Sharis say we kill Perator. Gakk get to eat?"

"Maybe," I allowed. I squatted down next to the goblin. "There's a woman who looks a lot like me, and she'll have a black flame in one hand. I need you to eat her. She's the biggest threat. She can use the flame to control me and make me attack you."

"I see," Isharah interrupted, while Gakk just nodded enthusiastically. "There's even odds the goblin has no idea what you're talking about, but I certainly do. It sounds as if this eradicator is the real threat. Does she have additional defenses we should know of? Is the plan to attack her, then have your tribes invade the city?"

"No tribes." Gronde gave a shrug, then nodded in my direction. "The Hasran claims he can clear out the defenders all by himself."

"And I stand by that." I stood a little taller. The dew of divinity gathered thickly about me, more so every hour. "The people know I am here. They know the almukhtar has come in their hour of need. Their worship flows. They need a miracle, and their strength will allow me to provide one."

"Very well." Isharah shrugged and accepted it. "I will focus on countering this eradicator then. Her defenses?"

"They're likely to be considerable." I sighed under my breath as I thought of all the decades she'd had to prepare. "She'll have a number of powerful defensive artifacts and wards and the ability to escape via teleport. She'll be tough to deal with unless it is with overwhelming and immediate force."

"Our specialty." Brim boomed a laugh. "Between my hammer and Gronde's axe, I assure you she will find no respite. We will deliver little Mina back her palace and return home."

"Odds are good they will see the assault coming." I began wading into the water, then turned to Isharah. "If you'd handle the magic, I'd appreciate it. I know you can speed our passage and allow Hadi to breathe."

"I'd forgotten you received a different gift." Isharah gave a vulpine smile and flicked her tail behind her as she too waded into the water. "I can handle our transport. The marid have a device that will send us directly into the palace, very near to our goal. However, it only allows a handful of people at once, and we may not all fit."

"We'll decide on a strike team when we see the size," I decided, realizing I'd seized control but noticing that no one else seemed interested in the role. It was my mission, I supposed. "All we need do is hold the room. Gronde and Brim can handle that, and if there's room, Hadi and I will go too."

The lot of us waded deeper until Isharah raised a silver staff and directed the water around us, a sudden current sweeping me deeper, then depositing me into a bubble of air just as Saghir would have used.

We zipped along, retracing steps back to the Heart of Water, which shone before me, illuminating an entire underwater vista complete with hundreds of blue-skinned marid swimming between the structures built into the coral around the Heart.

I had until we arrived to consider mistakes in my plan. If there were any, and if my aunt anticipated them, then I could be the reason this all failed. Should I stay behind entirely?

No, that was the worst part of it. I had to go. I had to be bait. If I wasn't there to control, the spider would never leave the shadows. I had to risk it all and hope for the best.

# INTERLUDE XX - SAGHIR

Saghir hadn't ever felt so alone or so powerless, and the irony was not lost upon him. He controlled a living mountain and the ashstaff and was very nearly a god in his own right. More and more worship flowed in daily, as the *Rat & Demon* storytomes spread.

Yet, again, he had never been so powerless.

They fled through the ash, which he whipped into storms that barely reached the avatar's waist. It simply wasn't deep enough, and if he approached areas where it was, the spider mountain would flounder. The best he'd managed was keeping the avatar from closing the gap and diffusing its enraged spellcasting when it occurred.

It scarcely met the bounds of reason that the giant pursuing them was the little waif of a girl Saghir had once met in friend Xal's hovel, back when neither of them had known the wider world they were stepping into.

"Lord Saghir?" An orokh barked as the mercenary stepped into Saghir's field of view. "I've been waiting for some time. You.... Are you fighting the avatar? You've been staring off into space for half a bell."

"The battle ebbs." Saghir adjusted his spectacles and floated over to the orokh's chieftain, the ashstaff clutched in his free paw. He missed Ikadra there, but the ashstaff was more useful. "You have my full attention. Magorkokian, was it not?" He was proud he'd remembered the warrior's name. It had taken three times, though, which was a testament to his level of distraction.

"Thank you, lord." The orokh bowed again, deep like an Enestian would. "We.... Here are the problems, lord. People came to follow the demon lord, and he is no longer among us. All know, though we also know that is not common knowledge and we do not whisper it, even to each other. Now our magic falters. We can no longer summon water nor feel wind or sun. Our stores dwindle, and we are afraid. Many speak of deserting, were there any way to flee this madness. Yet there is not. Can you at least tell me there will be an end to it?"

Saghir took great care in composing his reply and smiled warmly when he gave it. Xal had insisted that was very important when speaking with subordinates. "I must beg your indulgence, master orokh. Further, I must ask you to convince the others to be patient. I have learned to battle this nemesis, and we have not lost a single life in two days. Give me but one more and we will be over the Ashwall and back into Olivantia. We've already paved a path there. All we need do is follow the same scar we already created. The avatar becomes the dread council's problem, a fitting gift for Ducius, and we continue on to rejoin your demon lord. It is frightening and requires bravery from those who have sworn to our cause. That is all I can offer, I am afraid."

He knew it wasn't much, but what else could he say? He could not change what was, and reality was determined to see them destroyed. He could delay, but for how long?

"I will do all I can, my lord." Magorkokian half-turned, then ventured a hesitant question. "It would help a great deal if I could tell them when the next storytome would be available. We do not wish to pressure you, of course, but the last one ended on such a precipice...."

"I will have it to you on the morrow, I promise." Saghir bowed in midair. "Sleep well, Chieftain."

Saghir knew that he himself would not. He would need to spend all night penning the tome, as he had not even started the next one. Thankfully, Xal had provided reams of story, so he never needed to pause for motivation, just animate a story already told well. That he could do.

How could he harness the gathering divinity? Xal didn't need to sleep, and that would be a distinct advantage now. Saghir decided that after he finished the tome, he knew what his next task would be.

It was time for him to become a true god, just as Xal had.

All he needed to do was survive long enough.

He whispered to the mountain, guiding it toward the same path it had taken before, exactly the same path. That made it easy. Hopefully, the forest would not further impede their way. Hopefully, it had not reclaimed the area they had demolished, for if it had, then they would need to assault it again, and that was the last thing he wanted.

The goal was fewer enemies, not more.

Time ached by, moment by moment, with Saghir constantly watching the avatar to see if she was making another push. If she tried to run, then he could trip her again with ash. If she began to cast, he would be able to counter it.

Yet the Ashwall loomed in the distance. They were nearly there. Once beyond it, he could no longer replenish their reserves. His only chance would be outpacing the avatar, by leading it to other enemies...like Ducius.

Not a friendly thing to do to Temis, a man Saghir respected, but there was little choice in the matter. He must keep his people alive. He could apologize for his actions later.

The mountain finally began scrabbling up over the mountainous Ashwall, one of very few ranges taller than the behemoth, and Saghir's stomach lurched as they awkwardly climbed across to the other side. The trek was more challenging now that the behemoth had fewer legs.

The turmoil ended a half-bell later as they reached the forest floor, and thank the demon and the rat, the trail was preserved. The forest had made no attempt to recover any area covered by ash, and the scar stretched before them, a flat plain perfect for the mountain to run at full speed.

They accelerated away from the mountains, and by the time the avatar's head and shoulders appeared, Saghir dared to hope that they might actually escape.

# 29

# DEATH BY OROKH

I was the last member of the first wave into the palace and emerged in a spray of water from the very same chute where I'd seen Li gain her *water* Catalyzation so that we could resurrect Erik. Gronde and Brim had already waded into the room and were ending guards in glittering plate, some sort of new royal guard that hadn't existed when I'd last been in Hasra.

They were not very effective.

Not a one lived long enough for me to reach them, which allowed me to inspect the room around me, or rather its magical signature. This would be the center point of Crispus's defenses, and were it me, my response would be both overwhelming and magical. I didn't know if it would be a ward, but there would be....

Tremendous magical power blazed from a quartet of blue metallic golems flanking the set of double doors leading into the next room. They held no weapons, but their fists were menacing enough. They were forged from the same metal Erik's sword had been, Enurian steel, which was virtually indestructible.

Four sets of eyes flared open as Gronde approached the doors, then each statue cracked and took a slow step. They accelerated the longer they were active as if the magic were still waxing somehow. Just how strong were these things going to get? For now, they were like slow shamblers, too slow to even touch us, much less harm us.

One of them blurred suddenly and punched Brim in the gut with its oversized fist. The blow caught the orokh and flung him back into the wall, where he crumpled with a groan. There wasn't even a quip, and Brim always had something to say.

Gronde brought the first axe down on the golem's leg with a defiant roar, but all he received for his trouble were sparks as the weapon refused to find purchase.

I filled my weapon with *fire*, *void*, and *earth*, then punched Narlifex into the golem's throat. Magic exploded outward, but my weapon clanged off, and other than discoloring metal, I accomplished nothing.

The other golems were getting faster, and two had settled on me. I found myself focused on dodging and rolling. It was still easy to evade them, but they were getting faster and better. "Isharah, Gak, can you find a way through those doors? If we drag these things into Crispus's throne room, he'll have to worry about stray punches too, and we can use them for cover against other spells."

I hopped backward as a metallic foot crushed the stone where I'd been standing, cracks radiating outward from the impact point through the dense stone. That got me thinking.

I rolled around the golem, allowing it to line up shots, and tried to make them land near the damaged portion of the floor. The dense marble cracked and cracked again. I didn't know what the level below us contained, but I did know that if I kept this up, eventually the floor would give.

"Focus their blows!" I called, dodging again. "If you have space to cast, cast at the floor. Make their weight a disadvantage. I doubt they can fly."

I rolled away, and the golem followed, every movement a bit faster than the last, but just as predictable. I grabbed Narlifex with both hands, filled the sword with *void*, then slammed him into the marble and discharged the spell...at the precise instant the golem's foot slammed down a meter away.

The marble had been raised by literal gods, but even it had limits. The floor crumbled, then broke into a shower of rubble raining down on the thankfully empty dining hall directly below us. The golem and I suddenly found ourselves weightless.

I had wings. It did not.

The shiny blue golem tumbled end over end and utterly pulverized the remains of the table dominating the room. The blue construct quickly rose to its feet, then spun around as it sought a way out of its predicament.

Gronde seized another golem by its leg and whirled it like a discus, hurling the thing directly at the hole. His aim was just a bit off, and the golem's hand shot out to seize the edge of the hole. Isharah swept her leg down, and the fragment it clung to broke, snapping off and sending the golem tumbling after the first.

One of the remaining golems charged me, proving their lack of intelligence. I still hovered over the hole, and when it approached, I simply darted out of the way, well out of its reach. The golem stepped right into the hole and tumbled through.

Only one remained, and I spun to see how it was being

handled. These things were predictable, but a single mistake could mean death, and the best we could manage was temporarily getting them away from us. How long would it take them to find a way back up?

"Yaaaaaah!" Brim charged the last remaining golem and slammed the first hammer directly into its back. Metal rang on metal like the world's largest temple bell, then the golem was launched through the marble wall, out into the sky, then crashed down out of sight.

A tremendous boom echoed a few moments later, proving that the golem had landed somewhere well away from us.

"When the rat pens this tome," Brim boomed, a tusky grin in place, "I would have it be a bit more interesting than we knocked them through the same hole in the floor."

There were a few chuckles, but we were already moving. Isharah raised her paw, then flung counterspell after counterspell at the door as she peeled the wards back like the layers of an onion. I considered helping her but would probably just have gotten in the way. She seemed to have the task well in hand.

Within moments the layers shrank and shrank, and then finally...the door stood unprotected. The raw metal was barred on the other side by a single crossbeam.

"Gronde, would you announce us?" I nodded at his axe, which seemed the most applicable weapon to the task.

"Of course, Hasran." Gronde flicked his axe out almost casually, and it sliced through the door, through the crossbar on the other side, and then through the marble floor as it slammed into the ground. The orokh used the weapon to vault into a kick and flung the doors wide, exposing the throne room before us.

Crispus stood behind a makeshift throne, a blade in one

hand and a shield in the other. His body dripped with magical protections, and his armor was forged from the same blue metal as the golems.

Between the Imperator and my quint stood dozens of disparate warriors and mages. I recognized a few from Lukantria. Some had turned down my offer of contract, and now I knew why. Every last one was a highly sought master, as good or better than those who'd joined my forces.

"Crispus of House Enestius," I boomed as I stepped into the room to join Gronde and Brim in a line. "Your unlawful occupation of this city is at an end. I hereby sentence you to death by orokh."

There was no sign of my aunt, but I knew she must be near. Near enough to see me. Near enough to whisper a command, should I let her. I stepped back into the shadows and vanished, then as an additional precaution, summoned *void* around each of my ears. The pockets devoured all light...and all sound. Every signal or thing touching it. It stung my ears, but the pain focused me, while the sudden deafness reminded me that I had no margin for error.

I leaned back against the wall and waited. My part in this was over until I knew for certain that Lucretia had been dealt with. I had to trust in my companions. This was why prophecy had welded us together, this and all the battles that followed. I wasn't in this alone, and that thought, that fact, robbed my aunt of any of the terror she'd previously inspired.

We were going to win this, and she was going to pay for her many, many lies.

# INTERLUDE XXI - ERIK

Erik landed in a heap on the temple floor, and his sword clattered away from his numb hands. He'd thrown every attack he knew and had nearly exhausted his dwindling supply of divinity. There was perhaps enough for one more counter or miracle, not that he knew one that might aid them.

He rolled to his feet in time to block a trio of shadow daggers from Totarius, each making a hiss like butter on a hot pan as it impacted with his shield. Erik rolled over to seize his weapon, and Totarius made no move to stop him.

By the time Erik regained his feet, he saw why. The Praetor and Totarius were circling each other. Blood leaked from Etrian's lip, and one eye had darkened into a black eye. His helm was missing and there were gaps in his plate where the armor appeared to have melted away. The worst wounds were likely hidden from sight, but he could see them in the set of the man's jaw.

"The end nears, Etrian." Totarius gave a ghastly grin to the Praetor. "Your legacy dies. Your son is corrupted. Your daughter exiled and, as I understand it, sheltering with a demon prince. Not a safe place to be at the moment, I assure you. My avatar will catch and slay them all. You stand alone, and after you fall, everything left that you honored or loved will be tinder around a bonfire I light."

"So many promises," Erik roared as he sprinted toward Totarius from the side, his shield and blade at the ready. "Let's see you keep them, monster."

Erik kept his shield high as he circled and noted the Praetor's breathing slowing, returning to normal. If he could buy a bit more time, they would have a better chance, though still just a sliver of one. There must be a way. Must be something he was missing.

*You think as a warrior because that is all you have ever been,* the kindly old man thrummed in his mind. *Today you must be more. In the beginning, the boy you call Xal was a mage but had to learn to think like a warrior. You are a warrior who must think like a mage. You cannot triumph with martial ability. Not against this foe. He is beyond you. But you are not powerless in such a situation. You stand upon holy ground, consecrated by a power greater than his.*

Erik realized the voice was right.

Totarius's eyes blazed with glee, and his smile had never slipped. He had them outmatched, knew it, and was merely toying with them. Erik needed to change the game, but how? How did one use holy ground against an enemy? He understood that it imposed a weakness upon demons, but even with that weight, Totarius seemed unimpressed.

What was he missing?

The demon blurred forward and Erik raised his shield, but Totarius swept out his leg in a low kick and knocked Erik from his feet. Somehow Erik flipped his legs around and landed on his feet, just in time to take a dagger to the eye.

An explosion of pain ricocheted through his skull, and his sight was reduced by half. He had been partially blinded, which he knew would cut his peripheral vision. If he'd had any chance of winning in a fight, that was gone now.

Either he used holy ground in an inventive way, or he would die.

Erik placed both hands against the ground and prayed. He prayed to justice. He prayed to the gods who had made the cycle. He prayed to Rei, whom Xal had told him a bit about. He even prayed to the urchin. "The powers who watch over us all, over the cycle, and over this place. Those who enforce oaths and bindings and ancient covenants, I beseech you." Gods liked that sort of thing, being beseeched. "Expel the demon that defiles this place. Render his powers nothing against the sanctity of your holy temple. Keep him at bay."

Biting laughter rang out from the demon lord, who twirled a dagger in each hand as he watched and waited. When nothing happened, he spoke. "It seems your gods are dead or gone. Whatever power your station grants—"

Light blazed from Erik's shield, a beam of pure brilliance, and surged into Totarius's chest. The demon stepped back with a grunt, blinking in surprise. Another bolt struck him, this one coming from the temple wall. More blasts came, from the ceiling and floor.

Totarius dodged as many golden bolts as hit him, but he grunted each time one did. The demon finally sucked in a breath and expelled it, drawing a wince from Erik.

Nothing happened.

Had the temple nullified his powers? How long could it do that? How could he capitalize on that?

"Flee, demon," Erik boomed as he strode forward and launched another beam from his shield.

This one the demon dodged, then ducked behind a pillar...where another beam hit him, fired by the ceiling directly above where he sheltered.

"There is no safety. No refuge. Not here." Erik kept the pillar between them. The voice had only been half right. Thinking like a mage was smart, but thinking like he was in the arena was smarter. If he kept Totarius at bay, he could pepper him with bolts until the demon died. "Do they hurt? These are the prayers of the faithful, demon. Literally. You are feeling the wrath of the righteous, of those who will ensure you and your son never succeed. Flee now, or die here. The choice is yours."

There was no more biting laughter. No more insults. Not even an enraged scream. Totarius reached into his jacket, and a shimmering portal appeared next to him. Erik blinked as he recognized the entrance to the Hoard of Lakshmi. Then just as swiftly as he'd seen it, Totarius disappeared inside, and the portal began to close.

Then came the insult. The taunt. "You must leave this place someday, little princeling. When you do, I will be waiting." The boast was punctuated by mocking laughter, and then it was gone.

Erik sat shakily on the steps near the altar. He slowly sheathed his sword, and then lay back against the stones, exhausted.

"I don't know how you did that," Etrian began with a groan, then sat next to Erik. "But I am grateful, lord. You are truly a Steward. I suspect he will return and that given enough time and attention, he could level this place. If his avatar comes to Valys, we would make a light snack, divine protection or no. What will you do next?"

"I don't know." Erik stifled a yawn and fought the sudden exhaustion. "I do know that we need a plan, but for now? I'm just reveling in being alive. People need hope. Now they have it. Totarius and Crispus and Ducius cannot simply do as they will. We will oppose them, and the people see that we can do so successfully. All that remains is to show them we can triumph. Then this war is ours."

# INTERLUDE XXII - LUCRETIA

Lucretia's heart thundered in her breast, and her pulse quickened to an erratic level. She had no control over her body. Conscious emotions, yes, but the insidiousness of panic? At a biological level? She could not control that. Not without becoming a goddess, which in hindsight should have been her goal from the start.

Too late now.

She had backed Totarius, unleashing both Xa and Xakava upon the cycle. Now that choice might mean her life if she erred even a little. Yet it could also be a chance for her to seize ultimate control. If she could capture Xal's will with the flame and then apply layers of obedience, she would have all three demon princes. They would stand unopposed.

She could end the war today. Right now. The cycle could be dust in a matter of weeks or months. Had she the courage? Despite all the boy-king's threats, Crispus could do nothing to her. Lucretia could literally hide outside the cycle itself. She could not be reached and could return long after he was dead. At worst, she might have to deal with the occasional assassin dispatched by the soon-to-be-dead ruler.

Yet...if she stayed, if she triumphed, then the fear was over. The constant wondering when Xal or one of his allies would catch up with her. They were growing stronger, the lot of them. The ratling especially, but the presence of the Steward of Magic troubled her greatly as well.

Yet...neither were there. There was no rat. No Stewards. He was with his slave companions from the arena. Powerful, yet martial. A force of nature that could be predicted. Handled. All she need do was wait.

She braced herself as the door crashed open and the brutes invaded the room. A forest of spears and swords awaited them as the best warmasters in the realm interposed themselves between the hand of fate and the Imperator. Let them focus upon him...yet she knew they would not. Xal would not, at least.

There he was. The boy stepped out, boy no longer, and gave a brief verbal threat. Had she the courage, she could have acted in that moment, yet she did not, and then the opportunity was lost. Xal disappeared into the shadows, just as she had, both now hunting the other, waiting for the other to make a mistake first.

Whoever did was doomed.

She watched the battle play out before her, the warmasters meeting the legendary orokh brothers and their first weapons. The kitsune's feet and fists were everywhere at once, and the goblin devoured limbs, weapons, and even a spiked shield. A storm of chaos ruled, the din of overlapping combat making it difficult to think.

And then the moment came.

Xal stepped from the shadows and began to kill. His barbed black tail took a man through the throat, while each midnight wing scooped up a warrior, then dashed them together with a crunch of bone. Narlifex carved the next trio, their wards crumbling as their lifeblood fountained.

In a few heartbeats, he'd cleared a quarter of the room and allowed the orokh brothers to surge forward, nearly reaching the throne where Crispus sheltered with the last of his guards.

Lucretia stepped from the shadows and whispered into Xal's ear the words that would damn him and bind him forever. "By the flame, I—"

A furry foot took her in the midsection, and she doubled over...into a furry fist. The kitsune beat her mercilessly, and Lucretia struggled and failed to shield herself from the blows. She yanked a dagger from her belt and called upon its terrible magic. "Flee!"

The fox's expression melted into horror, and the beast fell back in revulsion but did not run. That did not bode well. The spell had only been partially successful. Lucretia scanned for Xal, locating him behind the kitsune as he watched her warily.

She raised the flame into Xal's field of view. He stared at it...mesmerized. She had him. "You thought the flame so simple an artifact? That I need to issue orders for it to impact you? Now then—"

The little goblin leapt upon her back, then opened its enormous mouth wider than seemed possible and bit down on her shoulder. The creature ripped the limb free, shoulder, arm, and flame all...and then devoured the lot of them in three swift bites...including the flame. Her greatest weapon gone, vanished into the belly of this *thing*.

Xal's greatest inhibitions remained in place, thankfully. He could not kill her directly, but as she clutched her chest with her good arm, she realized he would not have to. His allies could. She twisted her ring on her remaining hand and teleported away, landing in a pool of clear blue water, which immediately eased her pains and began to heal her.

She expected the arm to regrow, and swiftly, yet as the wounds scabbed over, she realized it was not to be. The creature had both taken her greatest weapon and maimed her permanently at the same time. Not even the Tears of Marid could heal her.

Lucretia began to weep, hot tears running down wrinkled cheeks. She had lost. Her body was broken. Her power doubly so. Crispus would soon be ashes, as would the legions with him. She didn't know Xal's plan for dealing with them, but the odds of a single legionnaire making it across the mountains was...slim.

If they did not, then Hasra's empire was at an end. They had no more coin. Whoever became the next Imperator would be responsible for the debts, and no one with the strength would allow themselves to be shackled so.

Gateway had been a last gambit, and now the empire was broken.

If there was a consolation, and there always was, she lived. So long as she lived, she could scheme. Hasra had never been all that important in the first place, had it? Merely a means to an end. Now they were free to pursue that end.

Totarius had spoken of a tide of demons sweeping humans from the city. By the dark mother, let that day come soon. There were few ways she could hurt Xal. That was one such.

Vengeance would keep her warm.

# 30

## GODS & MORTALS

I couldn't process what had just happened, it all occurred so swiftly. I stepped from the shadows and ended a dozen combatants, knowing that I was revealing my location. I did it after Gronde and Brim had established a line, which I knew would allow Isharah and Gakk the space to react to Lucretia.

My aunt emerged, and a moment stretched to eternity as the Flame of Obeisance lulled me to complacency. There was no struggle, no chance to fight back. I simply stood there and waited, a calf led to slaughter.

Until Gakk bit off Lucretia's wrinkled arm and swallowed the flame, and I was free. Not in time to stop her. Of course, she escaped, dropping backward through a fissure, which snapped shut in her wake. She abandoned Crispus, as I'd known she would.

I no longer cared. Her tool of control was now resting in the belly of a goblin.

Gakk rolled on the ground, groaning and holding his middle. He gave an abrupt belch, and black flame spouted from his mouth. When it faded, smoke began to rise, and his eyes glazed over as a beatific smile overtook him.

Then Gakk lay down and went to sleep...in the middle of a battle.

I returned to my surroundings and waded into combat, but found most of the hard work had already been done. Gronde and Brim had collapsed Crispus's guard down to a dozen hardened warmasters flanking the throne to create a safe pocket behind it where the Imperator stood.

I hadn't used any resources the entire fight. I still had all my magic and divinity. I decided to do something flashy and flung a mass disintegrate, one bolt targeting each of the warmasters, a display of magical strength only one of divine magnitude could manage.

As expected, the warmasters flipped and dodged and rolled, each performing a different maneuver to carry them out of the way. Over half would have lived, but in my free hand I whipped Narlifex around and willed his upper quarter to burst into razored fragments, each coated in *void*, *air*, *fire*, and *earth*.

The shards swam through the warmasters still hanging in midair, ripping through their bodies, shredding muscle, bone, and sinew. By the time they hit the ground, Narlifex was whole once more, and Crispus stood alone, his back to the wall.

"Hello, Imperator." I stepped forward, joining Gronde and Brim in a line. "Your advisor has abandoned you. Your guards are dead. Do you have any other tricks you wish to employ?"

Crispus licked his lips, then slowly sheathed his blade. He lowered his shield and stood at ease. "I can't win. You've bested me. Imprison me, then. My father will pay whatever ransom you ask, and I know you're trying, and failing, to build an army."

I wish I could explain the maelstrom of emotions that overtook me. Inexplicable rage overpowered everything else. This man had kidnapped Jun and sent her to die with the trash legion, inadvertently saving my life. He'd wounded Tissa over and over to the point where I doubted my friend, my heart sister, would ever seek love again. Or anything for herself.

He'd ruined my nation. He'd imprisoned the previous Imperator, a man I idolized. He'd cheated repeatedly at school and lived a life of privilege and wealth and security. In short, this man had never known fear. He still thought he was in control.

"Look into my eyes, Crispus. What do you see there?" I stared wide into his eyes and let him perceive the depths of the void in mine.

Crispus paled but said nothing. He licked his lips again as if applying some sort of balm that would summon the words that save him. "Nothing."

"That's right." I leaned closer, almost nose to nose. "I am a demon, Crispus. Not just any demon, but a demon prince. One of the first. A shard of a titan. And I am hungry, Crispus. Do you know what I eat?"

The Imperator's eyes widened, and then they narrowed, infused with supreme confidence that he was still in charge of the situation. "You wouldn't dare. I don't fear your threats. I know I am too valuable as a hostage, and you wouldn't kill an..." He trailed off of his own accord, eyes widening.

My jaw distended, and *void* flared all around me. "I am a demon, Crispus. I eat souls. Your crimes are numerous, but I'm not passing judgment. This isn't about justice. This is about revenge. This is for what you did to Tissa."

I lunged out like some great serpent, and I ate him whole, armor and all, in one bite. It shouldn't have been possible, the physics of it, a detached part of my mind realized. But I also realized that physics were simply the will of titans imposed on reality, and I could make of those laws whatever I wished.

Power flooded through me, along with memory and something else. All that Crispus was diffused into me. His soul was mine. Dark power, perhaps, but power nonetheless. It oozed out of every part of me, so thickly I could scarcely contain it.

"That was horrifying." Isharah shuddered and took a step back from me. "I know you are a good person and a strong ally, but that...was difficult to watch."

"I'm sorry." I shifted back to human form in an attempt to be less menacing. "He's harmed so many people. It was wrong, and I know it, but...I don't regret it. He met precisely the end he deserved, and now he will never again reincarnate to trouble another lifetime. I have removed him."

Isharah nodded sadly. "Your words make sense, but I cannot condone your actions, even if they were necessary. I am sorry."

"I can." Brim clapped me on the back hard enough that it knocked me a step forward now that I was in human form. "I do not know his crimes, but he seemed a slimy little beetle. If I could have the look he held at the end on every one of the legions' faces, I could die a happy orokh."

"I can arrange that." I moved back into the ruined room with the golems, who were still in the pit and still trying unsuccessfully to climb the walls back to our position. They were simply too heavy.

I continued to the hole in the wall Brim had made but did not see the golem that he'd used to make it. What I did see was the position of multiple Hasran legions. At least three. That meant there were two more I'd have to locate, but it gave me a starting point.

I turned back to the others and gave a low, confident smile. "I am the god of the sands. The almukhtar. It is time I proved it. Let this act show all who witness it that I am the god who cast down the Hasrans."

"Leave some for us...." Gronde's voice trailed off as I leapt from the window.

I shifted into demon form again in midair, then pulled at the divinity around me. I knew I could fashion miracles. I knew that being faster than everyone else meant winning every fight. Speed was the most important thing.

Divinity pooled in my hand, and I used my will to fashion it into what I needed. I created a miracle that would convert magic or divinity directly into action. The more power I poured in, the greater the speed it yielded. I knew as I did this that the ability wasn't new. I was remembering, not discovering.

All of my available divinity went into the fashioning, everything I had, to make it as strong as I possibly could. When my miracle was finished, I invoked it upon myself, and the universe answered.

Time appeared to freeze. Nothing moved below. Ugly vultures with their scarlet necks froze in the sky. Merchants hawked their wares, mouths frozen open. Legionnaires diced, the dice still hanging in the air, mid-cast.

Despite being in the air for a dozen flaps of my wings, time had not yet advanced.

I flew down to the closest legion.

*Devour them all,* Narlifex hissed. *Let us grow in strength while giving the world proof of our power. Show them a dark miracle.*

"That's not the sort of miracle they need," I countered, blurring toward the closest legion. I wasn't merely Xal. I was also Rei. I didn't have to destroy. I could create. And creation was far more useful to my cause in the long term.

I blazed by dozens of quints, not touching a one...until I found their commander.

Every centurion or above died. I devoured them whole, and I can't lie...I enjoyed it. Every time I took one, I gained a little rush of dark power and a few flashes of memory. That eased my conscience a bit. These men were exactly what I'd have expected of those who stuck with a leader like Crispus. The best of them were weak and deeply flawed. The worst made Crispus appear chaste.

I don't know how long I kept time frozen like that, but I do know that I was able to kill every officer within three full legions, spread across a third of the city. I spied the other two in the distance and also realized why I hadn't located them before. The troops had left the city and made for the pass, marching like ants.

I flapped into the sky to pursue them, but sudden weariness overtook me, so I descended to the balcony below, landing in a barely controlled crash not far from where I'd taken wing. I collapsed against the hot stone and lay there as time resumed its flow and the city's noise crashed over me once more.

"I thought you were going to deal with the legions." Brim prodded me with a foot. "You're just lying there, like a Hasran. Next, you'll be asking me to bring you grapes."

I swayed back up to my feet, the exhaustion as bad as it had ever been. It was as if every night of sleep I'd forgone had all come back to haunt me all at once. I knew I needed to get back to *The Fist*, and soon, and that I wouldn't likely emerge for many hours.

"Three legions have been dealt with." I used my tail to stabilize myself and keep from toppling. "I killed every one of their officers. That means only men fighting for bread or fear of punishment remain. We'll disarm them and keep their weaponry. Many of these people were conscripted. We'll see if we can convert those to our cause. I'll leave that to you and Brim."

"Perhaps a diplomat should be involved." Isharah stepped out to join us, her scarlet fur ruffled by the hot wind. "I will endeavor to get them to lay down arms. They have no allies and no leaders, and their Imperator was devoured by a demon prince. If I do so, I need someone to tend to Gak. He is sleeping comfortably and appears fine, but I do not know if he will need healing."

"I will tend to him." I stifled a yawn, then leaned against the wall as I approached the gap leading inside. "I'll take him back to the ship with me, and we'll sleep it off."

That was the last I remember before darkness took me.

# INTERLUDE XXIII - LI

Li sat numbly on the central throne, her mother's throne, and wondered how it had happened. How had she lost control of the situation so fully?

She shifted uncomfortably. Wings did not make sitting easy, forcing her to stiffen her posture in a way she did not enjoy.

Before her stood Indra, once again, the lightning god beseeching her to contact the people of the heavens.

"—long past time." The god blazed as he ranted, his hand upon the hilt of a human spine that had been fashioned into a sword. The weapon did the opposite of inspiring trust in her. "The ancient ways were clear and effective. The sky binds the heaven and the storm together. You are the central bond that unites the three peoples."

Li closed her eyes briefly. He'd been on about this for days. Relentless that they must fulfill the prophecy, and swiftly. And what he asked was...well, it wasn't something she could accept. Not just because of Xal, but because the arrangement described was not marriage as she knew it.

"And yet by your own words," Li snapped, allowing her

own lightning to flare in her eyes, matching his fury, "such a union would require the people of the heavens. My father's people, who have chosen not to reveal themselves. I wonder why that might be?" Li leaned forward on her throne, and unfolded her wings, one to either side of the throne, which relieved the pressure on her back, while also reminding Indra of her parentage. "They have not emerged, because they fear you, Indra. Fear your intentions. Your people dramatically outnumber both ours and clearly crave power."

"No." Indra blinked suddenly, the handsome god deflating like an emptying wineskin. "I—that is a deeply troubling revelation yet one I cannot easily refute. Apologies, Princess, but I am eager to complete the ritual because I do not know how much time remains before demons sweep the world. Vajra is mighty, but our enemies are numberless." He patted the hilt of his disquieting sword again, and Li sensed recognition from Shakti. "I will account for my share, but we need the people of the heavens to heal and protect us from the darkness our enemies will summon. I—I do not understand how the world has changed. But I do know prophecy. I know that war comes again and again. The cycle never ceases, even if I have been beyond its turning for a lifetime of lifetimes."

Li took it all in, so much in that speech. The important part was that he seemed willing to listen.

"There is a chance," she began again, moderating her tone and her expression, "that you have been corrupted by Khonsu in some way. Until we have proved that you are no threat to the mountain, I do not think we will see my father's people."

"Are we such a threat? Can you not trust us?" Indra pled, his eyes searching. "I realize I am...intense. I also realize our system of government may seem different, but it works as it does for a reason. It welds together three disparate peoples who all need each other to survive. Your people are our conscience and our mediators. My people are our warriors. Your father's people are our healers and sages. I am too aggressive. They are too passive. It falls to you to lead us to a moderate course, which is what the three thrones represent and why yours is the largest."

"Your words make sense." She couldn't argue with any specific part of it and wanted to find common ground. "I know of no tide of demons. We are at war with them, yes, and a titanic avatar walks the land. Yet their forces are limited and confined to the caves under Hasra, so far as I know. I am more concerned about Khonsu, who everyone seems to have just forgotten. We cannot assume Tuat and Volos will simply slay him and solve our problem, or that if they do, Khonsu's children will not return to wreak havoc and take revenge."

"The tide will come, and once it begins, it is too late." Indra's azure shoulders slumped. "We must be ready, and yet I can see no way to achieve that. No way to build cooperation in the time allotted. I will leave you to your prayers, Princess, but I will return again with the same question. We must find a way to convince your father's people to return. We must find out why they stay away, or all of us may be doomed. It is not accidental you rang the bells when you did. Now was the prophesied time. If we are here, then the demons are too."

Indra turned on his heel and strode from the chamber, leaving Li in peace. There were no guards, though Bumut had tried to insist. Not enough Calmorans were left alive to set such a guard without relying further upon Indra and the people of the lightning. She would rather have Tissa as a second shadow and her only support than have Indra's people here watching her all the time.

Li raised a hand and sketched a simple missive, reveling in the *fire* magic, in the mastery of every sigil, its form and function united. She whispered her message, then fused the final sigil together. The phoenix flitted skyward, up to her father.

Would he answer? How long would it be? Days? Never? The people of the heavens could live up there literally forever and never need sustenance beyond what the Halo provided.

A beam of light shot down into the room from above, directly over her. Li knew enough to know what was happening now and did not resist as the light pulled her aloft and up to the Halo and her father's people.

Their radiant tribe stood in a horseshoe, all watching her expectantly as she appeared, their wings high above them, as if standing at attention. All Li could do was stand there and stare back...expectantly. What did they want from her?

"We have been watching, Granddaughter," her grandmother began, folding her arms and pursing her lips in a way the girls back at the academy would have envied. "You have wondered why we will not emerge, while also stating the very reasons that motivate us. Indra is a bully, to put it mildly. We have observed his treatment of your authority. He flaunts his own, circumventing you whenever he wishes."

"He claims he's doing it because a tide of demons will sweep the world." Li folded her arms to match her grandmother, then pursed her lips to match. She kept her own wings raised, though she couldn't have said why she was making it a contest. "If he's right, then we do need to consider fulfilling this prophecy."

Thinking about it made her sick. If she married not just one, but two men, then there would be no space for Xal, whatever they both wished. Love was not enough to sustain a relationship under the demands of such a political union, and she knew it. Yet she also saw the reason for its existence, and if there really was a tide of demons....

"We are unaware of any such," her father broke into the conversation, the first friendly face, though his smile was wistful. "But we are not seers. The demon horde could be upon us soon, but if they are currently outside the cycle, we'd have no way of knowing. If Indra is right, then the union would be important, but until we have evidence, I do not believe it worth risking our safety. This could be a way to lure us down from the Halo, and if we go, the people of lightning control everything. We could be driven from this sacred place if the warriors deem it so. There are fifty of them to every one of us, and it seems your people are not much more numerous."

"Our people have many mountain villages," Li countered. "They can help us keep our culture alive. Yet I have no counter for your fear of being driven from this place. I know with certainty that Indra will do anything to fulfill his purpose and does not care who gets hurt in the process. I will return, then, and tell him we do nothing until we have proof that an army of demons is upon us."

"Very well." Li's grandmother gave a stern nod, then clapped her hands. "Now leave us. All of you. We have work to be about, and my granddaughter will wish to speak with her father in confidence."

Her grandmother turned and hurried off with the others, leaving Li standing with her father. He smiled at her but waited just a hair too long to embrace her, and it was awkward in a way it had never been before, and not just because they both possessed wings now.

"I...have another reason for my stance." Her father looked over his shoulder to be certain they were alone. "Li, I have argued against us returning because as soon as we do, your wedding takes place. I do not know which of our people will be your betrothed, and I fear it may be someone who does not suit your temperament. Your mother and I were extremely fortunate that we were willing to grow together. We found love. We did not have a third person in our marriage. What you are being asked to do...you can see why I delay. If demons come, then we will do as we must, but Li...enjoy your youth as long as you can. Once you make this pact, you will never be able to be with your demon prince again."

Li burst into tears. She couldn't stop herself. It was all so much, not just Xal or the wedding, or the prospect of a coming war. It felt like everything she loved was ending and that soon she would be alone, save perhaps for Tissa and Bumut.

Her father held her, but it wasn't the same as it once was. She gently disengaged and smiled at him. The appearance of strength was the best she could manage. "I will return and speak with Indra. Thank you, Father."

# 31

## WEARY

I awoke to find myself inside *The Fist's* cool interior, though I had no knowledge of how I came to be there. Hadi and Gakk were my only companions in the vessel, and the goblin was still asleep. I rose with a yawn, then sat heavily in one of Saghir's chairs as I struggled to shake off the lethargy. I hadn't been this bad off since my first semester as a student, before both that training and the slave pens in Gateway.

"How long have I been out?" I slurred to Hadi, who eyed me with beaky amusement.

"Two bells." He cocked his head and eyed me critically with one of those dark eyes. "Enough time for the remaining Hasran legions to almost reach the pass. The ones in the city have lain down arms and have been collected into the slave pens to deal with later. What will you do about the remaining ones?"

I leaned back into my chair and lent my senses to the ship. We were parked on a rise beside the palace, so I launched *The Fist* up into the sky and surveyed the pass to see what had become of the enemy. There they were, marching in file, the head of their column already out of sight.

"Wait, something is happening," I murmured, then returned a part of my consciousness to the room with Hadi. "They're falling down. The pass is quaking. There's magic at work. Powerful magic." I began to smile as I saw insects boil from the ground, scorpions, beetles, and things I did not know all burrowing into the flesh of sunburned soldiers. "It looks like we might have to content ourselves with those troops who we've already taken. I do believe that Loxclyn is making her presence felt. I suspect not a man of that force will survive to reach the other side."

I willed *The Fist* to hover in the air and smiled down at Gateway. We'd done it. The Hasran force had been shockingly easy to overcome. This was what happened when gods fought mortals. Mortals lost. Every time.

New worship already flowed in, some from the legions, but most from the citizens of Gateway itself. People who had not believed before, but now did. The god of the sands had delivered his promise, delivered them from the Hasrans a second time, and word would spread.

My forces finally had a base of operations, a city where the populace wasn't conditioned to be hostile to our existence.

*That is a product of your decisions*, Narlifex hissed quietly. *You chose to make alliances here and to spare the Hasran soldiers. Now I see why. You are different. You are Xal but not Xal. The changes are...deep. But they may serve us well. They have certainly aided us this day.*

I stood speechless for several moments. How could I not? It was the most philosophical the blade had ever been. Narlifex had always adopted the role of an older sibling, one used to being right.

"Xal?" Hadi repeated, and I realized I'd missed something he'd said. "I asked how you felt about your aunt escaping and about the goblin? Did he not swallow this insidious flame? That is what I understand. I have been watching him in case...well, I'm willing to sort the mess if there is one. That is the love I have for you, Brother."

That wasn't a pleasant thought, but it was a necessary one. I sighed as I gazed down at the goblin's tiny sleeping body. Gakk's distended body had already gone back to normal size. There was no sign he'd devoured the flame. Nothing visible, at least. And there had been nothing visible after I'd eaten Crispus.... I'd digested indestructible plate armor as a source of magic. I was a god...and so was Gak.

So what had become of the flame? Could I extract it? How? I'd likely need Isharah.

"I'm not best pleased that Lucretia escaped." I sighed a second time and looked my tengu brother in the eye. "She will be a powerful ally for Totarius and will find ways to make our lives awful. But she no longer has the leverage she once did. My mother will need to know. If I know her, she's been building a resistance, and they're just waiting to act. I hope so anyway. As for the flame, I—"

I paused. The ship had detected something. Another airship rose, an Elentian vessel, likely Crispus's flagship. "A moment, Brother. Brace yourself against something."

*The Fist* accelerated as I drew at the newly refilled pool of divinity. There wasn't much, but I didn't need much. I used speed on my ship, the same miracle I'd used to slay the legions, but at a lower magnitude.

Time did not stop, but it did slow, enough that *The Fist* casually zoomed around a trio of disintegrates. Several lightning bolts did impact, moving far too fast to dodge, but they grounded into the hull, and we felt nothing inside, insulated by whatever divine material we'd usurped when I'd created the vessel.

I wrapped *The Fist*'s fingers around the enemy vessel's silver midsection, and the ancient ship exploded. Remnants rained down over the desert just outside the city, and the few scavengers desperately screamed as they dodged falling wreckage.

"The great Elentian fleet is no more. Saghir will be disappointed." I reversed our course and headed back to the palace where I hoped I'd find the rest of the hand waiting. "We've ended an empire today. Hasra will never again be what it was."

The words should have cheered me, but I knew only numbness. Somewhere out there, Saghir was desperately trying to evade a titan. That was the true threat and one that would need to be addressed.

We landed swiftly, docking next to the ruined balcony, and to my relief, there stood Isharah and Gronde. There was no sign of Brim. I willed the iris to open, then nodded at Hadi who fell into step behind me. The hot wind was still a shock after the cool interior.

"I am impressed," Gronde called and offered his forearm as I approached, his own strength still greater than mine when I accepted. "What you did to that ship...it will live in song in these lands for generations. A fitting end to their reign here." He nodded down at my arms. "What of the goblin? He lives?"

"Yes." I set Gakk down before Isharah. "I don't know what the artifact has done to him. I can use *life* magic to aid him, but there's nothing to heal that I can see. I thought you would know more and wanted your advice before we attempt anything."

Isharah gently toed Gakk in the stomach, and he swatted

her hand away. She probed a few different locations, and he began to giggle, then sat up with a terrifying grin that was worse than any dragon's.

"Gakk's tummy hurt." The goblin stood up and stretched. "Usually Gakk fix by eating more stuff. What Gakk eat?"

"Gak?" I squatted down next to him. "I need to test something. Can you give me an order? Make me do something."

"Sure!" Gakk's smile widened and he began to hop back and forth from foot to foot. "Hasran get Gakk something yummy. Now!"

Nothing. There was no compulsion. No trace of the flame's power. Was it really gone? Could it be that simple?

"Isharah? Hadi?" I turned to the pair of them. "I have the worst sort of favor. I need to return to Saghir and my forces in Olivantia. I cannot stay. Yet if that flame still exists? It could well decide the godswar. It is that powerful. I need someone to watch Gakk until we know for sure what has befallen it."

"A duty I shall accept gladly." Hadi perked up. "I enjoyed Lukantria, but I have yearned for home. Now that I am here, the desert blossoms call me, and I am not speaking of flowers. I have no wish to leave any time soon. I will watch over this goblin and see to his needs."

"I must return to Mina." The kitsune offered me an apologetic look. "It seems the goblin is in good hands. I suspect that the war will only grow more intense from here. You have the look of a man bracing for a mountain upon your shoulders. I will prepare this city as best I can, and see that Gronde and Brim do the same in the desert. We will be ready when the darkness comes."

"I understand." I drew her into a hug, then gave one to

Gronde and then Hadi. "I must be away. I don't know what the future holds, but today has given many people hope. Here at least. I can feel their prayers."

"Be well, Brother." Hadi saluted me.

Gronde merely nodded, but the orokh smiled as if this were his idea of the best time he could possibly have. I don't think he cared about a coming apocalypse. No, that wasn't right. It wasn't that he didn't care. He welcomed the prospect. It was eagerness.

I hurried off with a wave, *The Fist* rising into the air before the iris was even fully closed. My work here was done, but I was no longer a conventional hero in a tale. I'd become a god. A god did not get to sleep. A god flitted from errand to errand, as I already was. No thought for our own comfort.

Selfishly my mind strayed to Li. On a whim, I sketched a missive. *Can you escape for an evening? I am flying by to meet Saghir and aid him. Gateway is free once more.*

Then I flew over the mountains and into Calmora. It wasn't long before I received a reply, and I perked up immediately, as soon as I heard her voice. She was so beautiful. I didn't even need to see her to remember that. Just hearing her brought her scent back to me

*I'm sorry, my love. It canot be. Now is not a good time. My home is free, but politics are...complicated. Having a demon show up would throw lamp oil upon the hearth. It cannot be. Contact me when you and Saghir are safe.*

...And that was it. I don't know why the missive made me so melancholic or filled me with regret. I don't know why I felt a growing distance between us.

*You do,* Narlifex crooned, *but you will not admit it. Your happiness, your peace, is never to be.*

"Gods forge their own reality," I snarled back, with more

heat than I'd expected. I refused to accept never having the life I wanted. This war, however terrible, was temporary. Some day, or in some lifetime, I would be free of it.

I focused on flying the ship and on dealing with the avatar when I arrived. Unless we recovered the flame, I had no real plan to stop the monstrosity.

All we could do was run.

# INTERLUDE XXIV - ERIK

Erik strode from his temple for the first time in weeks, emerging into the late morning sun upon the temple's wide marble steps. A sea of people waited, far more than he ever could have expected or dreamt into existence. Men and women and dwarves and orokh thronged the courtyard, stretching up the road as it wound around the Hammer's haft up toward the noble district.

There was no sign of the Imperial guard nor Crispus. No sign of Totarius. No lingering airships in the sky. He scanned the crowd, which was silent as they watched him expectantly and waited for him to speak. Before he did so, he wanted to understand what he was walking into.

A sudden cheer erupted from the people as they spied the second figure, rippling outward, swelling to a crashing wave as Praetor Etrian Valys stepped from the temple doors, his armor repaired and gleaming. There was nothing to suggest the storied leader had nearly died two days prior. The power of magic.

"Citizens of Valys," Erik boomed, his voice carrying

through the entire city, yet not too loud to those in the front ranks, aided by the temple. "I present your former leader, stripped of power by the usurper Crispus, the same man who had me murdered so he could steal the title of Imperator. Both of us would be dead were it not for the demon prince Xal. The man whom they have fought so hard to demonize. Even the word should make you think. Demons are what we consider to be the very worst thing, the thing all other bad things are compared to.

"Yet Xal brought me back," Erik roared. He raised his shield and let it shine in the morning sun. "He gave me this. He elevated me to the rank of Steward and ensured that I can now stand for justice in a way I never could before. I have returned from death to replace Dalanthar, a man who lost his way. A man, not a god. He gave in to grief and despair. That is why my office is controlled by the shield. Do not worship me. Worship justice. Worship the Stewards and the ideals they embody. I am but a vessel, and one day I will fall. I will be replaced. Perhaps by the very least of you standing here today, whoever you might be."

He paused then, caught up in the passion of his own words. And they listened. They drank his words like the parched discovering water.

"Together we can take back this city and eventually the entire west. We can restore sanity and compassion," Erik roared, raising his free hand in a balled fist. "Together we can prevail, and I ask you to help me do that. Restore this man to his station, to his palace. Throw down Crispus. Put off the shackles of Hasra. What was once my nation is no longer. I stand above, with no loyalty to any land. And as an unaligned Steward, I believe that VALYS SHOULD BE FREE!"

The cheer was deafening, and it went on for long

moments. One by one, row by row, they sank to their knees and offered prayer. A rush of worship flowed into him, raw divine power, and in quantity. Erik did not think they'd have any problem retaking the city. Etrian would be able to stroll right back up to his palace, but the question was why?

"I don't understand," Erik called out of the corner of his mouth, speaking to Etrian. "Why did Totarius abandon the city? It makes no sense. We didn't win. We survived. And now we have a base of power. It's not like him to make a tactical error, but I can't find the reason in it."

Etrian smiled at Erik then, a fatherly smile, the opposite of what his own usually offered. His father who had gone into hiding after being recovered alongside Etrian and had made no effort to contact Erik. Though to be fair, Erik had made no effort to missive Lord Garulan either.

"It's good to know I can still instruct you," Etrian called back in a low voice, which was almost swallowed by the crowd. "At least in one area. Totarius's motives are clear. He left because we aren't a threat. Punishing us was a treat, not a necessity. I'd wager that now that we are no longer useful, we'll receive a visit from the avatar we saw marching north. If that thing returns...this city is doomed. It could pick up the Hammer and wield it. Who's to say it won't? Our days are numbered, and that number is short unless we can find a solution."

Erik waved to the crowd with a smile he did not feel. He needed to inspire worship and morale, even if he personally knew they were all likely to be dead soon. The end didn't matter. The struggle did. The example did. It was fine if he couldn't find hope, so long as he projected the illusion of it.

So long as they believed.

Hope must survive.

# INTERLUDE XXV - DARIUS

D arius wasn't quite certain how he'd found himself in charge of their endeavor, but somewhere along the way, that was precisely what had occurred. He'd have expected Ashianna to take the lead. The towering noble had the experience, the demeanor, and the respect of both Vhala and Ena, while both bristled at any suggestion Darius made.

Lingering memories of their time at the academy and to whom Darius was related. Khwezi's presence had only made it worse, a constant reminder of Darius's family, and their many abuses of power.

Yet the more they'd traveled and planned, the more he'd found himself directing, guiding, and suggesting. At some point, they had just started coming to him for instruction. There was no more cajoling.

A sharp rap sounded at the door to his quarters, which the dreadlord Temis had graciously provided. A most curious host indeed. Glowballs lit the room, a type of wisp common during the Elentian Empire, each orb constrained within a wrought iron cage. The ironwork was everywhere, and every bit of it exuded dread. Magical dread. This place had been built from the bones of something powerful.

The spacious apartment was very nearly the equal to what he'd occupy in Hasra or his homeland, which surprised him. The dreadlords had lived well with many comforts, it seemed, before they had been overthrown and this haunted place became a last vestige of their rule.

"Come," Darius called, and the door opened to admit Ena in human form, followed by her ever-present shadow Vhala. Both had their weapons close at hand.

Ashianna lingered outside, but then the taller woman stepped in, eyes roaming ceaselessly. Her cheeks were still too gaunt, though she had once more donned her plate armor and carried a new two-handed blade strapped across her back. Khwezi lurked behind her of course.

"Temis has summoned us," Vhala said, usually the spokesperson for the trio, though sometimes Ena took the role. "Dinner is served. He wishes to make it an informal council, to discuss our looming problem."

"Is that what we're calling it?" Darius raised an eyebrow, but he set down his stylus and rose to his feet. "I could use a meal, and we'll see if any of us have an idea to help Saghir that doesn't involve running swiftly in whatever direction it is not going."

No one laughed. Jun would have. Politely, but she would have. Stewards, but he missed her and the boy. Yet not having knowledge of her whereabouts meant that knowledge couldn't be stripped should Ducius discover him. Still, it meant that Jun would have to care for herself and the boy, and Darius did not enjoy that prospect. It was hard enough with two people.

They marched downstairs toward the dining hall, the entire house devoid of life, save that one room. Temis did not seem to favor guards the way other dreadlords did. He served his own table, though Darius had no doubt the binder could summon any number of dark allies to his aid should he be threatened. It seemed a solitary existence, one alleviated by house guests, Darius hoped. Temis seemed a kind soul despite his nature.

"A most heavenly aroma," Darius called as they sat around a table cut from the trunk of a giant redwood. It was the largest slab he'd ever seen. "I'm told you wanted to discuss tactics over dinner?"

"I do." Temis smiled as he sat, his fangs briefly visible. "Please, everything is ready. Help yourself. Let's get something into our bellies if we're going to be talking about how bleak the immediate future looks."

Darius removed the lid to a platter to find steamed potatoes and helped himself, then passed the dish. He added a steaming hunk of bread and a meat slathered in rich dark sauce. Temis did not speak again until all of them were contentedly munching.

"I have had word from friends in the Ashlands." Temis set his fork down, and the dreadlord gave them a worried look. "The spider mountain is passing through the blood wood as we speak. Saghir is leading the avatar here. I would wager he seeks to aim it at Ducius, but whatever the reason, we now have something of a more pressing concern than the wretched soulless bastard we seek to oppose."

"Are you suggesting we evacuate?" Vhala asked. The dark-skinned companion did not seem overly concerned and was currently adding another hunk of bread to her plate. The first had already vanished. "We are well outside

the path the avatar is to take if it follows the spider mountain, assuming Saghir uses the same path he took last time."

"That appears to be the case," Temis allowed. "Yet it may
force Ducius to desperation. He needs the final artifacts of
Olivanticus to truly reclaim his full power, and he can never
have those without the one I possess and the one Saghir
possesses. Both of us are in his nation at the same time. Both
of us are distracted with concern for the avatar. If ever we
are likely to make a mistake, it is now, and I know he will be
waiting to capitalize on it. That's how he thinks. He pressures an enemy, patiently, while exposing no weakness until
they reveal one of their own."

"That is why we're here," Darius countered. He nodded
at Ashianna. "She is here to teach your armies to fight
dreadlords, to arm you against Ducius." He shifted the nod
to Ena, then Vhala. "They are here to ensure you live long
enough to oppose him. I am here to advise you tactically. My
advice? Stand your ground. Let this threat pass by. Ask
Saghir, as soon as he arrives, to consider giving you the Ring
of Olivanticus. That makes you Ducius's equal, and then it
becomes a race. We find the other artifact, or artifacts, first,
and when you have three, you are greater than him."

Temis nodded along, his perfect face showing no
emotion as he considered Darius's proposals. That was the
dreadlord's way. They never knew how he felt until he
spoke.

"I think we are doomed to failure." Temis picked up his
fork and speared a piece of meat. "For my part? I am willing
to try. I will be a rallying point. I will oppose Ducius publicly
and attempt to win the council to our side. I expect all of us
to die for this, but better die free than a lackey to a
madman."

"Precisely how I feel about my brother." Darius smiled

broadly. "Now let us discuss these other artifacts. I may not be much of a warrior, but tracking magical devices? Solving mysteries and riddles? I am precisely the man to help you beat Ducius. Together, we *will* get revenge for my wife and all the others he has wronged."

# EPILOGUE

Totarius landed upon a swampy hillock in his magnificent demon form, alone and unaided. That was the best way to accomplish such vital work. To generate a dark miracle, one that caused demons everywhere to worship him. If he did not provide such, he risked being eclipsed by Xakava, for all demons would worship the avatar, or Xal, who had already layered storied deeds atop one another.

...Besides, this would be fun.

"Pitiful followers of Celeste, HEAR ME!" Totarius lent divinity to his voice and his demeanor. "Death has come for you. Your long struggle against the darkness is over. I am here to usher you into the cycle and claim this fetid place for my people."

It echoed through the swamps, through the twin camps flanking the rip in the sky. The Rent. The only hole in the cycle, so far as he knew. A way that demonic armies could flood through, or that he could use to escape.

If he was right, if he truly thought the way his previous incarnations had thought, then one of his tombs would be directly on the other side, kept in a holy place by the demonic hordes.

They would know to expect the arrival of their prince, and if he could get out there and claim his legacy, then he would have a separate army, one not connected to Lucretia, Kazon, or Xal. One that would see Xakava as his loyal hound.

An army loyal to him, and to him alone.

Totarius accelerated, leaping to the first group of defenders, a quartet of battlemages, two on duty and two off. The white-robed mages were far from the front, in an area ringed by spikes and protected by multiple layers of wards. He crashed through those wards in an explosion of magical force, then cut down all four mages...casually. Not a one was able to ready a defense.

They were simply too slow.

He'd arrived at the rear of their ranks, which were beginning to shift in his direction, but it did not save them. Totarius blazed across three more hills, slaughtering as he went, then devouring souls to enhance his own strength.

By the time he reached the fifth mound, they'd erected a dome of scintillating wards far more complex than any of the others, and of the type that would make destroying it very, very time-consuming.

Totarius ignored it and went to the next unprotected hill and the next. He focused solely on mages, but removed every last eradicator from the fight, devouring them all, not a one able to resist. Where were their gods? The Stewards should have been here. Celeste should have....

Then it occurred to him precisely who had erected the ward he'd avoided. She likely was there but unable to oppose him directly. Totarius renewed his assault, blazing through the enemy ranks and leaving nothing but empty camps in his wake.

At first, it had little effect on the eternally raging battle at the Rent itself. The knights in the breach stood fast against the demons, each blazing with radiant golden light, each a beacon against the tide of darkness.

Yet without their support, the tide of demons emerging from the darkness thickened. And thickened. More and more emerged, and the knights were being forced back. Not enough to break them—there was no rout here—but pressure all across the line. Endless pressure.

Totarius finally landed at the back of the knight's line, behind a dozen or more of their strongest heroes locked into a shield wall, with a row of healers behind them, the dedicates of Aelianna. Would that he had time to devour them all, but here he might be vulnerable and thus needed to move swiftly.

He extended a hand, and a thousand tendrils of darkness exploded outward, wrapping around limbs, weapons, and necks and then snapping them. Men and women were choked, smothered, or simply had their spines broken. It all happened in a few seconds, and once he had created a hole in their line, Totarius leapt into the sky, his wings flaring before him.

"Hear me, brothers, your prince has come at long last!" he called in demonic, one of the oldest tongues. "Their lines are broken, their mages dead. The time has come to claim this place and make it our own. No longer will this be a battleground. We will make it a fortress. Go! Slaughter the humans. The time has come to take the cycle. Your demon prince has been delivered by prophecy, at long last. It is time to triumph over them all! Xa has come to deliver you."

A bestial roar sounded below him, and bonecrushers

charged the weakened line, which held briefly, then shattered. Now there was a rout. Demons ran down those who attempted to flood, more of them exploding through the Rent by the moment, fliers zipping out like bats, while bonecrushers and worse things sprinted along the ground.

There was no end to the tide, not that he could see. Satisfied that this place would fall and that Celeste would be forced to flee, he turned to the Rent itself. It was time to claim his destiny. He flapped his wings and slid through the fissure, out into the void itself.

The chill and the lack of oxygen would have killed a human instantly, but of course, neither troubled the endless tide of demons before him. They'd arrayed themselves across a dozen floating rocks roped together like a series of islands, each serving as a staging ground for arriving demons.

In the distance floated larger planetoids, and those too brimmed with demonic life, visible to his eyes even within the perpetual darkness. Perhaps strengthened because of it.

Totarius stared at the infinite vista around him and realized in that moment he was truly a god. This place, the vast darkness, was home to him, a home he'd left to enter the cycle and only now realized what he had missed.

There in the distance glittered something. A gemstone, utterly massive, shaped so that together the facets formed a huge temple with a glittering archway. The stone was black. Ebony? Jet? Some other magical substance? He didn't know. Whatever the material, the construction was magnificent and the purpose beyond clear.

That must be his tomb, what he had sensed must lay out here. This is the repository he had left himself so that he might triumph over his wayward sibling and at last free the dark mother.

What awaited him within those fabulous halls? Memories? Power? More?

Totarius flapped, and though his wings should have done nothing without the wind to kiss them, they propelled him through the darkness, closer to the temple, which grew larger and larger in his vision. Every bit of every surface had been carved with magical sigils, which together appeared to create some sort of spell.

Not a traditional spell, he realized, but...a word? The word of a god? Of an elder titan? He sensed that was right, though this primitive mortal shell could not yet comprehend the vastness that was such a word.

Totarius flew into the temple entryway, floating through the magnificent arches, and into a room with a single sarcophagus in an otherwise empty room. He knew it as he knew his own bedchamber, knew he had spoken this place into existence and left his earthly remains within.

He leaned against the lid and heaved, flinging the impossibly heavy gemstone away from the sarcophagus to expose the contents.

Within lay nothing identifiable as a human body, only a pulsing cloud of darkness. Purple-black divinity, crammed in to fill every bit of the interior. Raw power, and so much more.

Totarius distended his jaw and ate the sarcophagus and its contents, devouring them all and allowing the power to wash through him. Memory flooded him, beyond potent, so powerful it scoured away his conscious mind and dropped him into itself, a cork floating down a river, with no more control.

He was no longer Totarius nor Xa, though at the same time, he was both.

Instead, he was so much more. So much greater.

Totarius became Gortha, the titan of the void herself, across the near-infinite gulf of time from the present moment, all the way back to the beginning of the first universe, the First Moment of Creation.

*Gortha was. She existed.*

*It was a new thing, this awakening, this thing called consciousness. She was separate from the universe, from the endless darkness all around her, in the most unnatural way. Once, she sensed, she had been that darkness, until something had awakened her. What a curious thing.*

*Who or what could awaken darkness?*

*She peered around the empty vastness of space, which was infinite, yet also knowable, as she could perceive everywhere the darkness existed. And the darkness existed everywhere.*

*Seven other curious beings existed in the void. Each was markedly different from the darkness, making them easy to locate. And, in fact, she realized she also differed. She was now other than the void, no longer a seamless part of it. Her formless body was a cloud of undulating purple-black, similar to the other beings, save for its color.*

*None of the other beings approached each other, for such a concept had not been birthed. Nor was there any need. They could converse without movement, and their thoughts were known to each other, broadcast to all the others without effort, a property of this new existence they shared.*

I am FIRE, *thought the brightest of their number, a raging nuclear inferno.* I burn.

I am VOID, *Gortha found herself thinking, excited to be able to converse with this entity.* I devour.

I am EARTH, *added another titan that was their kind, she sensed.* I endure.

I am SPIRIT, *chimed their next member.* I bind.

I am WATER, *echoed the next.* I nourish.

I am LIFE, *came the next.* I create.

I am AIR, *sang another titan.* I change.

I am DREAM, *came the last of their number.* I envision.

*They sat in silence for an eternity, and Gortha waited expectantly. Existence was so interesting! She had no idea what change was. Or creation. Or vision. They sounded fascinating!*

I have an idea, *sang DREAM.* I propose we create something other than ourselves. FIRE. You burn. Can you remove a tiny piece of yourself and place it somewhere in the void, wherever you will?

*FIRE answered with action, and a tiny slice of flame drifted off, pulsing in the void, brilliant, just as the titan who spawned it.*

Light, *SPIRIT spoke suddenly, and power thrummed from the word.* That is what I name you, the shining brightness that comes from LIFE and from FIRE. And this new thing that FIRE has created shall be called the star. These names do I bind.

*Gortha watched in awe. She longed to contribute to what she saw going on before her but had no means of doing so. Her ability did not seem useful unless they wished to extinguish this light.*

I have another idea, *DREAM spoke again, excitedly.* We should make many things. Each thing we make will need a name. Then there will be many things!

*Everyone agreed that was a fabulous idea, and it filled them all with curiosity, itself a new thing that had not existed before. What would they make next? What could they make?*

The things we make, *Gortha began,* they must be pieces of ourselves, yes? There are no other things from which they can be made.

*EARTH answered by hewing off many small chunks of himself. The jagged rocks floated in space, and while there were many, which was interesting, they didn't do anything. They merely sat there, tiny pieces of the whole.*

*That certainly wasn't very interesting.*

I have an idea, *Gortha spoke, surprising them, perhaps because only DREAM had had ideas thus far.* I think these objects should interact with each other. I will create a force, throughout the void, that causes the things we create to be attracted to each other. That way they will be able to find each other and form an equilibrium.

*She willed the new force to be, and it was. The little flecks of rocks slowly swam toward the star and began to circle it, exactly as she had envisioned, almost worshiping the tiny flame, because it was larger than them.*

*Gortha addressed SPIRIT.* What shall this new force be called?

We shall name this thing gravity, *SPIRIT proclaimed.* Now the rocks, and the star, know these names. They will obey gravity.

I shall add bits of myself, as FIRE and EARTH have done, *WATER decided, her mind clouded with a new emotion. One that would need a name. A desire to eclipse the others.* I will use this new gravity. I will place my bits to honor EARTH, as he preceded me.

*Droplets flung away from WATER and landed upon many of the orbs of rock orbiting the star. The water clung to them, but the droplets were ugly things, frozen and crusted across the surface.*

I will add bits of myself as well and see what they make, *AIR decided, flinging himself toward the orbs. Now they had clouds above the water, and something blew across its surface.*

I am last, *LIFE proclaimed sadly.* I have added nothing. I can make something bright, but no more bright than the star. How am I to aid?

I have another idea, *DREAM offered, as she filled with a*

*new emotion, a desire for LIFE to not be sad.* You can create. You can make things that have never existed. Make something that will dwell upon the orbs we have created.

*LIFE was quiet, thinking many thoughts, then finally took a bit of itself and set it upon a rock.* I bring life, where the water will nourish it and help it thrive and grow.

*LIFE's progeny fell to the waters, which would need a name, and began to swim, changing as they moved. They took a hundred different forms, each suited to the part of the world where the new little life dwelt. It was all so fascinating.*

*The orbs closest to the star warmed, and the water became different. A new form that needed a new word. Liquid. Life emerged from the waters and assumed all manner of unpredictable forms. The creatures had physical bodies and used them to move about the orbs, which they seemed confined to by the new force of gravity.*

*Life bloomed and bloomed, and bloomed...until the planets were choked with it. It became an ugly thing and the life turned on itself, changing. Many new words came into existence then.*

*Violence.*

*Death.*

*War.*

*It was fascinating, but eventually, the world's evolution collapsed and their game expired. Gortha knew then that it was time for her to understand her purpose. She devoured. What did that mean?*

SPIRIT, *she asked,* I need to take part of myself and make it a new thing, but a thing that can think and act, as I do. I will make this like the life on the world below, but springing from me. To do this...I will need names.

Hmm, *SPIRIT thought, pulsing for many revolutions of the orbs around the star.* I believe I can do as you ask. First, you will need a name. I bind you as Gortha, titan of VOID. Now that you have a name, we can create your progeny.

I see. *Excitement thrummed through her as Gortha understood what she must do.* I hew this piece of myself, the end of my name, Xa, and create a lesser titan in my own image.

*A piece of darkness boiled away from her cloud and coalesced into a creature. It had wings, a tail, and scales, like many of LIFE's creatures, but also their fangs and claws. And it was much, much larger than the others.*

What is my purpose, Mother? *the new titan asked, unable to sense her will or that of the others, it seemed.*

To devour, *she explained patiently, with love for her offspring.* Go to those orbs and remove the life so that we may begin anew....

And then Totarius was himself once more, gasping in lungfuls of...nothing? There was no air here. That was merely a reaction of a mortal body. A habit. He was mortal no longer.

This place may not have contained useful memories, but it had contained power. Vast power. It had made him strong. He was ready to ride back through the Rent and slaughter anyone that his brethren had not already devoured.

That was their purpose after all.

They devoured.

# NOTE TO THE READER

Whew! What a ride.

Yes, I know that *Rat & Demon* was shorter than previous books.

I apologize for that, but I made a creative decision to focus on the story. Like you I'm a reader of fantasy. I grew up on Robert Jordan and Robin Hobb and Tad Williams and George R.R. Martin and countless other series. *Battletech, Shadowrun, Forgotten Realms*, and most especially...*Dragonlance*, which did something new and unique.

The *Wheel of Time* threw a whole bunch of unnecessary chapters at you. Sure, the books were long, but by book 7 they were also pretty bad. Most of my friends bailed out. By book 10 only I soldiered on to the end. Length became a curse.

Meanwhile *Dragonlance* had a main story broken into several trilogies. You could read these and get a complete amazing story. However, if you loved the universe you could also read novels about *Huma*, or the founding of *Qualinesti*.

Readers were not kept hostage by narratives they were not interested in. That stuck with me.

I could have included chapters about Khonsu, and what happened to him. I could have added fluff from Morog building armies on the plains. I considered both. I rejected both, because neither is a part of Xal's story. Morog's story will be told elsewhere. Khonsu's will be left a mystery.

If I were reading this tale for the first time I'd want to read the main tale, the MSQ or main story quest for you video game fans. Even doing just that the series is already *over a million words*. There are still two books remaining, and both are likely to be far longer than this one.

The thing is...they'll be organic about it. The next book needs its length, because there is a great deal going down in the blasted lands, and in Olivantia. The war is in full swing.

Anyway, I hope you stick around for the finale. The penultimate book will need a year to write properly, and the final book a year as well. That means from the release of book 1 to the finale will take 4 years. Not too shabby in my opinion, but still no fun as a reader.

By way of apology I've reduced the price of the preorder of this book. It's shorter. It should cost less.

I'm about to dive into my next novel...the *Earthfather*. It's time to give Magitech Legacy a proper ending! After that I have a couple new story ideas germinating.

I've been playing a lot of Dungeons & Dragons using *Shattered Gods* as a setting >=D.

-Chris

Made in the USA
Las Vegas, NV
21 November 2024

12302966R00236